NOT BUILT WITH HANDS

✦ CLUNY CLASSICS ✦

RICCARDO BACCHELLI
The Mill on the Po (THREE VOLUMES)

ROBERT HUGH BENSON
Come Rack, Come Rope
Dawn of All
Lord of the World

GEORGES BERNANOS
Joy
Under the Sun of Satan

WILLA CATHER
Death Comes for the Archbishop
My Ántonia

G. K. CHESTERTON
Wanderings over the World

MYLES CONNOLLY
Dan England and the Noonday Devil
Mr. Blue

F. MARION CRAWFORD
The Saracinesca Tetralogy

ALICE CURTAYNE
House of Cards

GERTRUD VON LE FORT
The Pope from the Ghetto
The Veil of Veronica

MARIELLA GABLE, O.S.B. (EDITOR)
Many-Colored Fleece (*Short Stories*)
Our Father's House (*Short Stories*)

JOSÉ MARÍA GIRONELLA
The Cypresses Believe in God (TWO VOLUMES)

RUMER GODDEN
Five for Sorrow, Ten for Joy
In This House of Brede

CAROLINE GORDON & ALLEN TATE (EDITORS)
The House of Fiction (*Short Stories*)

CAROLINE GORDON
The Malefactors
The Strange Children

PAUL HORGAN
Humble Powers
Things As They Are

CARYLL HOUSELANDER
The Dry Wood

ELISABETH LANGGÄSSER
The Quest

GABRIEL MARCEL
Thirst: A Play

BRUCE MARSHALL
Father Malachy's Miracle
A Thread of Scarlet

FRANÇOIS MAURIAC
A Kiss for the Leper
Vipers' Tangle

EDWIN O'CONNOR
All in the Family

BEN J. REINHARD (TRANSLATOR)
Beowulf

IGNAZIO SILONE
Fontamara
Bread and Wine
The Seed Beneath the Snow

SIGRID UNDSET
The Burning Bush
The Wild Orchid
The Faithful Wife

LEO L. WARD
Men in the Field: Eighteen Short Stories

HELEN C. WHITE
A Watch in the Night

NOT BUILT WITH HANDS

A Novel

Helen C. White

CLUNY
Providence, Rhode Island

CLUNY MEDIA EDITION, 2023

This Cluny edition is an unabridged republication of the
1935 The Macmillan Company edition of *Not Built with Hands*.

For information regarding this title
or any other Cluny Media publication,
please write to info@clunymedia.com, or to
Cluny Media, P.O. Box 1664, Providence, RI 02901

✳ VISIT US ONLINE AT WWW.CLUNYMEDIA.COM ✳

ISBN: 978-1685952303

Cover design by Clarke & Clarke
Cover image: Hans Memling, *The Chalice of Saint John the Evangelist,*
between c. 1470 and c. 1475, oil on panel
Courtesy of Wikimedia Commons

CONTENTS

To My Mother

* * *

❋ BOOK I ❋

ROME

CHAPTER I

"It is like a ship in a great sea," said Matilda softly, reining in her horse from the brink of the cliff and looking out across the miles of blue air to where Rome lifted her towers and walls white above the plain. At first there was nothing to be seen but a translucent space of sapphire floating above the gray-green earth in the broad basin of the hills, with a miraculous craft of snowy marble, half rising out of the low-lying earth, half floating in the liquid radiance of the afternoon. But once her eyes had become accustomed to the medium of this sudden vision, she saw that it was a stormy sea that lay at her feet, with sudden troughs of darkness in the streaks of forest, and threatening waves in the bare heaving of the waste lands, and here and there foam in the shimmer of stream and pool. For the plain of the Campagna was as illusory as the floor of the ocean, taking much of its peace from the leveling of distance and the even wash of the soft spring air.

It seemed at first a perfect desolation with only the many-peaked mound of the city to break the sovereignty of earth and sky. But as she gazed, fascinated by the spacious integrity of the scene before her, the level monotony began to yield unsuspected intrusions. The long line of arches, striding the plain like treasure bearers, seemed to carry the web of the heavens above their stately heads. Here and there the ribbon of a road threaded marsh and hill and grove with inexorable majesty, and, as the eye grew subtler in its discrimination of shades of blue gray from deep purple to gleaming white, the piles of fortresses on crag and hill deepened into view. So Matilda saw that what had seemed at first a vast monotony of blue and green and white mist was in truth a great field of roads and hills and marshes and castles and aqueducts, with all the majesty and wonder of Rome lying at her feet as if sunk at the bottom of a blue sea of air.

The triumph of the field of Aquino was still warm in her heart. The greatest pride of all her twenty-one years still beat within her veins, the pride of the lordship which with her sword she had made her own at the brook of Aquino. True, she had been lord of Tuscany ever since her brother died in the Emperor's prison at Mantua. But that was simply because she was Boniface's heir. Now she had taken the sword, and she had defended her lands and her allies, and she had put the invader to rout. As she thought of these things, she drew her tall, strongly built body to its full height. But the mad delight of battle had faded in the last week's riding, and now in a moment the pride of victory had come face to face with a pride more ancient. It was as if a shadow from the passing clouds had suddenly fallen across the sunlit heights on which she stood.

So seen, the prospect frightened her, and for sheer relief she looked at the firm ground at her feet, at the coarse shafts of hill grass, the clumps of asphodels like day stars new-fallen on the green lances of their leaves, the blue vervain, and the cyclamens with their purple flame. Then she looked at the faces of her companions, all wrapped up in silence now with awe of the scene before them. The plump, middle-aged gentlewoman's face of Ermengarde seemed for a moment to be carried out of its usual smug inertia into a curious and uneasy watchfulness. The warm, honey-brown features of Alberic, that she had known all the days of her life since he had first come like a woodland sprite into the gray hall at Canossa on some forgotten feast day, looked now remote and estranged. Even Godfrey, whom she knew better than anybody in the world except her mother and loved perhaps even more tenderly for all he was but her stepfather, seemed anxious and wary, as if his grave strength and quiet, rock-like assurance were at last confused and perplexed. Looking at them, she suddenly felt very empty and very lonely, and she laid her hand on the companionably warm neck of her horse and rubbed the damp flesh slowly.

She started when at last one of her companions broke the unaccustomed silence. "At any rate, our friends the Normans will not see Rome this year." The men laughed, but Matilda to her surprise suddenly discovered that she could find no mirth in the thought of the Normans' discomfiture.

"Not for 1067 anyhow," said the man at her side, the tired face breaking into a smile and then sobering as quickly. "But for 1077, who can tell what ten years may bring in days like these?"

Matilda felt the hot blood in her cheeks leap to her stepfather's challenge, "Nay, Father Godfrey. We've stopped them this year at Aquino. What is to prevent our driving them back to Sicily next year, and then the next perhaps, into the sea, back to their savage north?"

She turned to the other side to see Alberic lifting his eyebrows in mock awe, with a quirk of mischief in the corners of his mouth. "Your horse is ready for the attempt even if my lord your stepfather is not, Matilda."

But before she could reply, Godfrey had laid a restraining hand on the neck of the horse. "Not today, I think." And then he looked at her—"Thanks to you, Matilda, we did turn those barbarians back from Rome. But don't be too sure. Until you rushed in, we were beaten. They thought the battle was over, and they were resting there by the brook. If you hadn't dashed in then—" he paused— "what was there between them and Rome?"

It was strange to hear Godfrey of all men talk so cautiously. For an instant Matilda wondered if he were getting old. Ever since she could remember, she had heard that there was no bolder soldier in all the world than Godfrey of Lorraine. And though every year he had been growing gentler—or so it seemed to her now, as for the first time she looked back—yet she could not remember that he had ever hesitated when there was any chance of fighting.

"If we hadn't stopped them at Aquino, we could have held them back here," she said, thinking aloud.

"Don't forget," said Godfrey patiently, "that it was only one half of their army that we had to fight at a time. The rest did not know what was going on, and when they found out, it was too late to do anything. It would be a very different thing to face them all at once."

There was no answering what Godfrey said. It was Ermengarde who came unconsciously to Matilda's rescue. "I don't see why those Normans want to take Rome and make all that trouble anyway, the horrid barbarians!"

Even Matilda laughed. What magnificent-looking bronze giants they were with the water glistening on their great shoulders!

Again the shrill, complaining voice of Ermengarde broke in upon her thoughts, "War is so tedious. Those loafers have been gone a good hour, and they have not found the road yet." The rosy face of the speaker swelled red with indignation in the bowl of her blue veil.

But Alberic laughed at her. "Ermengarde, did you ever try to find a road in the Campagna?"

Ermengarde bridled with offended dignity. "Master Alberic, I am the gentlewoman of the Countess Beatrice. This going to war—"

Again the young man interrupted her, raising his hands with a wide gesture, "I know, Ermengarde, and you would not be here for a moment if the Countess Beatrice had not insisted that you come with the Countess Matilda to keep her out of mischief, and the tales you will tell when you get back to Rome, and—" The merry, mocking voice of Alberic, as sparkling as his face, paused for breath.

"I must say, Alberic," protested Ermengarde, with a certain smothered explosiveness that contrasted oddly with the small, officious movements with which she tried to soothe her horse.

"Don't," he laughed saucily, and then as she pouted a little, he took one stride to her horse, and tilting his head, he held up a hand to her. In spite of herself Matilda smiled at the little flourish of plump coquetry with which Ermengarde took it and slid to the ground.

How like her to be fussing about the lost road with all the pageant of Rome at their feet! But Ermengarde had turned her back upon the view and was placidly shaking out the folds of her petticoats.

"I never did approve of this business of women going to war!" she began again, and now there was a certain complacency in her indignation as she smoothed down the front of her green dress.

With a comic gesture of despair, Matilda surrendered. "Ermengarde is of the ancient pattern. She thinks a lady should stay in her bower and spin wool in the primitive Roman fashion."

But Ermengarde shook her head indignantly. "I hold with no heathen, but with Our Blessed Lady and the Saints. A lady should not be gadding about the land."

"What? No pilgrimages allowed? Nor leave to consult mine uncle the Canon and my cousin the Bishop on the state of one's soul?" jeered Alberic, and the whole company joined in the laughter.

"A lady is a Christian like anybody else, with a soul to save," protested Ermengarde, her cloak billowing over her squared elbows.

"Take care, Ermengarde. You're getting into theology. Like those Patarine heretics of Milan," added Alberic, warningly.

"My lord, I appeal to you," protested Ermengarde, turning to Godfrey who seemed to be enjoying a moment's respite from his own preoccupations. "Will you let him call me a heretic and a market woman?"

For the first time Godfrey smiled with open-hearted amusement. "I'll let you take up the heresy with your uncle the Canon. That is not my field, exactly. But I shall charge him not to call a gentlewoman a market woman, for that is against knighthood."

"You have only to command, my lord," said Alberic.

"Better not finish that sentence," warned Matilda. "Too much humility would awaken the suspicions even of Father Godfrey." Again the whole company laughed.

But Alberic was now contemplating Ermengarde with rare seriousness. "Why do men fight anyway, Ermengarde?"

The gentlewoman was not to be surprised, however. She shut her plump lips with a firmness that narrowed them almost to a line. Amused and a little penitent for her contempt of a few minutes back, Matilda intervened, "Don't be foolish, Alberic. You know the answer—wealth and power, but the best of men fight for glory."

"Glory," echoed Alberic sardonically. Startled at his tone, Matilda followed his glance. But he seemed absorbed in looking away to the plain below. Puzzled, she was about to ask him what he meant, when the beauty of the scene again took possession of her. The afternoon was passing even as they stood here waiting, and the fluid light below them was changing its color with every moment. Where before it was blue, it had taken on a tinge of purple. Not the heavy, umbrageous tone of the hills, but a purple shot through with opalescent gleams of rose and sapphire and tawny gold, quick and translucent, so that all the air seemed to be made of distilled light. Yet the effect was not so much brilliant as tender. For the folds of the plain and the castled crags and the marching aqueducts were seen as in a dream, with the city in the midst riding high like that city of vision which came down from the heavens once to an old man on Patmos.

"It is Rome," she said softly. And all the irritation of the last minutes went out of her. She thought of the Normans in their horned helmets with their long golden hair and their red beards, riding over the plain with shining round shields and long bronze-tipped spears of ash. She had never believed, she was sure, that the Normans would ultimately subdue all Italy. What she had thought, she would find it hard to say now, gazing out over the scene that had suddenly dwarfed all the rest of her experience.

She could recall how bitterly disappointed she had been when, after weeks of riding here and there, Godfrey had at last decided that there was no use in their trying to meet the invaders openly. Even then she had realized that he was afraid of losing control of their discouraged and frightened men if he should try to drive them into battle with the dreaded northerners.

It seemed very remote, now, the anguish of that moment when she realized that the very first army she had ever been allowed to lead, would have to go home beaten. Nor was her disappointment due just to her own pride. After all, she had been representing her mother, and the fame of Beatrice of Tuscany was not to be lightly tarnished with defeat. How she had dreaded telling her mother that she had failed in her name!

That shame was what she had been thinking of, when, straining to outflank the Normans and reach Rome before them, they had decided to ride through the night. The Normans had not been more surprised than she was when, spurring ahead in the cool of the late afternoon to find some relief for her anger and grief in the sheer driving of her muscles, she had come upon them there at the ford, bathing. It was then that the sight of their carelessness with all it implied of contempt for their foes had wakened in her a madness—even now her blood tingled at the thought of it.

"It is Rome," she repeated to herself. But something purer than the pride and the triumph of her first victory came into her heart as she looked out upon the scene before her. She thought of Virgil and the dream which the old pagan gods had brought to pass. This city had veritably ridden high over the sea of the world, and all the world's ships had come home to her. And all the nations of the earth had trembled at her name, and she had ruled them, and giving laws to savage peoples, she had been the heart of the world's civilization.

All this was in the very earth at her feet. In other lands men suffered the bounds and restrictions of the world they had been given. And where the water sprang from the earth, there it burgeoned, and men slaked their thirst and sated their hunger. And where the water failed, the earth shriveled, and men moved away for want. In other lands men rode with ease where the earth was smooth, and they stumbled in the rough places, and presently they gave up riding beyond the confines of their necessities. But here in the world at her feet, men had brought the waters of the hills across the arid miles into the dwelling place of their choice, and at their will they had made the dry places to bloom, and they had drunk where they wished to be. And they had made the wilderness as smooth to their feet as the pavements of their houses.

Then the barbarians had come. The roads had been choked with weeds, and some of the great arches had been broken. And if one were in Rome, on every hand, the destruction which they had wrought was still to be seen. There was almost nothing of the splendor of Rome that did not bear the scars of its history upon its face where the fire had passed through the marble, and the axes of the barbarians had shattered the delicate craftsmanship, and the penury of these later ages had plundered the vast quarries of ancient abundance. Yet there at her feet, Rome outrode all the hazards of fortune, a wonder and a mystery to this world of darkness and poverty and confusion. The heart of Matilda leaped when she thought that in her hour she had taken her sword for this at her feet, for this glory that had outridden the storms of the ages.

Suddenly a voice broke in upon her thoughts, seeming to come from far away. Slowly and reluctantly, she drew her consciousness back over the brink of the cliff on which she stood.

It was the voice of Alberic, and he was laughing at her, as he so often did, especially these late years.

"I was thinking," she said, shamefaced, with a vague gesture of her free hand over the plain.

Alberic's face sobered. "It is something to think of."

For all its quietness, his voice struck her as a challenge, a challenge she was not in the mood to suffer passively. "I was thinking of the glory of Rome," she said.

He nodded. "So was I." He looked serious, but there was also something, a little cynical, she fancied, in the shadows of his mobile face.

"It is there still," she said defiantly.

Again he nodded, but this time he said nothing, and she wondered. She was about to demand an explanation when she saw that the men whom they had sent to find the road had returned. Ermengarde was looking from them to Godfrey in high disgust. "Devil take that sidetrack!" Matilda heard him grumbling.

Then aloud, "The men found the road on the other side of that pool two miles back. As if I had not been on the Appian Way often enough to know it when I saw it!"

"But that was obviously the end of nowhere," protested Ermengarde, pulling her cloak about her plump figure and straightening the loose folds of the veil about her throat.

It was with a new sense of excitement that Matilda felt her horse set his feet on the strength of stone, and a moment later the covering mud and weeds of the edge of the bog had worn thin, and unmistakable through the dust stretched the close-fitted, square lava slabs of the Roman road. Involuntarily, she clutched tighter the sword at her knee, and she thought of the look on the face of its Norman owner when he saw that he had yielded his sword to a girl.

"It is the old Roman road," said Alberic, not looking at her, "down which so many conquerors have ridden to glory—" Though Matilda waited, he said no more, but rode with eyes fixed on the great blocks of gray stone.

CHAPTER II

RIDING along in the early morning of the next day, Matilda tried to recapture the wonder of that half hour on the heights. It had seemed one of those rare moments when time itself stands still, and by the very fullness of its perfection, the present takes on the serene lastingness of eternity. And then in a twinkling, with almost grotesque suddenness, that perfection had vanished.

They had simply ridden down from the crag, perhaps a hundred feet to the road below, and the great view had vanished as completely as if there were nothing in the world but this thin fringe of alders and beeches on either side of the patched stretch of stone and dust. Sometimes the ground along the way rose lazily out of the morass to give foothold to cypresses and umbrella pines. Sometimes the trees failed altogether, and there was nothing to be seen but the golden-flowering broom and the wild rose and the thorn, clinging precariously to the slopes and gullies of the red-brown earth. But even then, the restlessness of the Campagna, forever tossing up to the soft blue sky, made it impossible to see more than a few rods away from the unending road. For now the vast plain of the Latin races had swallowed them up, and only the steady marching of the great square blocks of stone up hill and across marsh and down into the

low-rimmed valleys gave any hope of a world beyond the narrow cage of the
minute.

Matilda tried to conjure up before her mind's eye that sweep of plain, that
vast yet warm freedom of the air. She could not. Even as she seemed about
to seize on it, the picture faded like a dream that one tries to remember on
waking. And like one who has just swum up the warm waves of sleep into an
alien world, she found herself suddenly chill and desolate, there in the warm
May sunshine.

There was no reason why she should feel this way, and she knew it. She
still rode lord of Tuscany, and the sword of the Norman knight whom she had
fought to his knees rubbed the wool of her garments into her flesh, irritating
but reassuring in its tangible reminder of her victory. She was a little tired,
perhaps, after this week of steady riding, and the shirt of mail she wore over
her scarlet tunic was growing heavy, but she rode easily with a certain content
in the response of the muscles of her body to the steady rhythms of the horse's
movement. The wind lifted her loose veil, and a heavy braid of hair fell over
her shoulder. For a moment she gazed down its dark length while the wind
whipped the thin wool from her forehead, and the cool air sucked about her
face.

With a sudden flash of that insight that comes in moments when the restless heart tutors itself, she thought how much more exciting it was to be riding
with the free throat and temples of the maiden than close-scarfed with the de-
corum of a wife. She was a fool to miss any of the heady freedom of this spring
day when the days of fast riding with free hair floating in the wind might so soon
be over. Gently, she pressed her knees into her horse's sides and let the rein slip
on his neck. For a moment it seemed as if the great creature held its breath, and
then he shot forward with a leap that sent all the warm blood hurrying through
her veins. And the dull mediocrity of the moment suddenly quivered into life.
The brown-red earth and the green grass and the purple-gray road lay about her
still, inert in the flat brightness of the morning sun, but the wind was in her hair
and in the large movements of her body and in the washing of her garments
against the warm tingling of her flesh and in the speed-born harmony between
her horse and herself.

Then she became aware that somebody was riding up to her side. She had
been so absorbed in her own thoughts that she had completely forgotten her

companions. But now—she did not need to turn her head to know who it was who had caught up with her, was keeping pace with her, even watching her. It would always be—

So surprised was she at the idea that had just come to her that she turned her head without thinking. And the amused eyes of Alberic met hers, with that curious suggestion in their dark brown depths of curtains that were never drawn. Suddenly, she wondered if her eyes, too, seemed veiled and reserved to him. But she could not imagine how eyes like hers, clear gray-green like the placid color of the ancient verd-antique columns in the basilica of Saint John Lateran, could ever look mysterious. At any rate, Alberic did not seem in the least puzzled, only amused, with perhaps a faint tinge of mockery in the glint of his eyes.

Involuntarily, she reined in her horse and looked away. She could feel the blood rush into her face and her breath come quickly.

She heard Alberic chuckle. "I wonder—" he began and paused, as if not sure after all whether he would say it.

"What?" she asked shortly.

"I wonder," he repeated after a short pause as if deliberating, "what you will do when your husband comes."

She stared at him. No, he could not have guessed what was in her mind as she turned a moment ago.

"When my husband comes," she said half to herself, looking away. She felt a pang of shame that even Alberic should have looked in on her thoughts. No, again she was sure he could not guess. A quick, passionate instinct of loyalty made her turn defiantly upon her old friend. His eyes fell.

No, she never forgot that she was affianced to Godfrey the Hunchback. When her mother had married Godfrey of Lorraine, it had seemed perfectly natural that she should marry his son. She was only seven at the time, and her mother had explained to her that it would be many years before her Godfrey would come to stay with her, but that when she was old enough, he would be her husband and her lord. She still kept that childish memory of her Godfrey, a great hulking fellow, very strong and powerful-looking with his thickened shoulders and his bright chestnut hair and steady blue eyes that seemed to her rather cold like the water in the lakes at Mantua in November. But she had given him a ring and promised to love and obey him, and he had put on her hand the ring she still wore. And ever since, she had known that he was her lord and husband. And she had prayed for him night and morning, and from time to time she had sent him tokens and gifts into his land of Lorraine.

She would have gone into Lorraine, and it would have been her land just as her mother had come down from Germany and made this her land, but she was the only heir of Boniface of Tuscany, and she was lord of Tuscany. So her mother had decided that she must stay here to carry on the work of her dead father and to sustain the glory of the house of Canossa until the son whom Godfrey the Hunchback was to give her should be old enough to relieve her of the power and the labor. For two years now Godfrey had been going to come down into Italy to consummate their marriage, but always it was the same story—the young Emperor could not spare him from his service. She had been proud to hear that he was the bravest and the ablest of the young Emperor's generals, but now she remembered with sudden shame that she had not grieved at the postponement of his coming. It was not, she told herself, that she was not ready to take a woman's part in the world and do her duty, but that there were so many other things to fill her days and her thoughts. There was all the excitement of the traveling with Godfrey, and the books she read with the young priest, Donizo, and the people who came to Canossa, and the friends she and her mother visited in Rome, and the learning to use arms, and now that she was a woman, there was this wonderful new excitement of battle.

"When my husband comes—" she repeated less certainly.

Alberic laughed. "You have said that before."

She looked at him without speaking, and the laughter faded from the bright face before her. The wind had died down, and her veil lay awkwardly against her face. She straightened it.

"Why do you ask that?" She looked at him full and directly.

But before he could answer, another rider came up at her side, and Matilda turned almost with relief to look into the face of her stepfather. It was a gray face that seemed as if it had been cut from granite until he smiled, and then all the hard lines softened.

Impulsively, she put out her hand and laid it affectionately upon his horse's neck, as the creature nosed close to hers. But the smile had faded, and the look of care on the face of Godfrey had deepened. She saw Alberic look quickly at his lord, and then as the latter nodded to him absentmindedly, drop slowly back.

She laughed a little awkwardly. "I think Alberic has been trying to hint that Godfrey might not altogether approve of my behavior."

To her surprise he looked up at her sharply, peering through his shaggy eyebrows as he always did when surprised in thought.

"I have been thinking of young Godfrey, too," he half muttered.

"You, too, Father Godfrey?" She tried to control the spasm of fear that made a sudden empty place deep within.

He saw her concern, and he hastened to reassure her. "It isn't anything you have done."

She only stared at him. And presently, he raised his head and saw her looking at him. "I am not sure," he said gently, "that I have not hurt you."

"Hurt? You?" She was so startled that she could say nothing more.

He shook his head. And then as she stared at him, he tried to explain, "I am afraid I have not been fair to you."

"Fair!" Again, she could only echo his word in astonishment. For she could find no clue to these riddling words of his.

Then as he did not answer, she put out her hand to him, "Why, Father Godfrey, who could have done more for me than you? The way you have always taken me with you when Mother was away! The way you bothered with me when I was only a child—"

He smiled a little as if at some sudden absurdity. "You know that you have always been a comfort to me, that it was a joy to have you. And after the Emperor seized your mother and the boy—the damned scoundrel, pretending that he could not have so important a vassal married to his enemy—there was nothing else to do."

"And later, when Mother had to be away in Mantua or in Rome, it was such fun riding everywhere with you," she encouraged him.

"No," he said in a low voice as if trying to reassure himself, "there was nothing else to do. Then when your brother died there in prison, we were afraid that the Emperor would try to seize you, too. No, there was nothing else to do but take you along."

"Of course not," she agreed heartily, her own anxiety scenting his uncertainty, his readiness to be convinced. "Why, Father Godfrey, how I should have teased you, if you had left me cooped up in that dark prison of ours with the whole beautiful world outside to wander about in! And think how dull I should have been with nothing but prayers and poetry and old wives' tales to rattle around my empty brain."

For a moment it seemed as if the jesting had succeeded, for Godfrey laughed his low, throaty laugh. "We'll tell Donizo how seriously you take all these poets he reads to you and all this learning of yours. Shame on you, Matilda! You're no learned lady at all, but a vagabond and a gadabout like these tumblers we see at the fairs."

She laughed with relief. "Books are but mirrors, Father Godfrey. Good enough when the door is shut, but not to compare with the road and the city."

Then as she heard him sigh again, she said very quietly, "Tell me, my lord, what did you mean?"

Godfrey looked at her for a minute. "It's hard to put into words, but I'll try. At Aquino you were quite the best of us, Matilda. No," as she tried to protest, "I mean it. You went ahead when the rest of us were ready to run. You put us to shame."

Matilda considered. "No," she said at last, resolved to face the facts, "it was simply that I am a woman, and men—"

But here there was no doubt in Godfrey's voice as he interrupted her. "No, it's not just a woman's putting us to shame. You saw the moment to take a chance. That is half of generalship, and the whole of the young knight's half."

Matilda laughed. "You know me too well, Father Godfrey, to look for any generalship in rashness of mine."

She was relieved to catch the low chuckle of amusement as he answered, "It wasn't just rashness. The way you rode, the way you held that lance, the way you bore down on that old savage—Arduino is not claiming too much for his pupil, Matilda, when he says you're a real soldier. And yet," and again his face softened, "there were tears in Arduino's eyes when I found him after the battle."

"I know," she agreed briefly. And then recognizing that the time had come for complete candor, she added, "A woman's spring is so terribly short. I have heard all the women—"

But Godfrey broke in quickly as if he recognized the fear never till now credited, and even now held at arm's length, "No, it isn't just that a woman can be a soldier only for a few years. It is—" he hesitated, and after groping for a moment seemed to decide to take what lay at hand, "well, a woman is a woman and not a man."

Godfrey seemed again to flounder, but Matilda was suddenly relieved, for this was ground on which she had stood before. "Father Godfrey, you yourself have said that most of what people say about men and women is nonsense. A woman has a soul like a man, and she loves and hates and dreams and prays just like a man. And like a man she thirsts to drink all the joy and the pain of this wayfaring world, and like a man she aches to tear aside the veil of this mystery and with her own naked spirit come face to face with God."

Godfrey brought his horse closer to hers as if he would shield her from his own fears. "That is true, my child, but the paths that open out before us in this world were marked out long ago, and even to the same end they are not the same for man and woman. God knows why, but He has traced them for us, and if we try to break out of them, it is—it is—" He paused, the firm voice shaking like a child's.

Again Matilda reached out her hand until it touched his. "Father Godfrey, the fault is not yours, if fault it be," she consoled him, choking a little as she spoke. "It was not you who decided how I should be brought up."

"Ultimately, it is mine," he corrected her patiently. "After all, I am responsible for what my wife does."

But here Matilda had a sudden vision of her mother's calm face, and at that picture she laughed almost hysterically. "Oh, Father Godfrey, you know that nobody in the world would hold you to blame for what Beatrice of Tuscany did."

"She is a great woman," he said.

"I know," said Matilda proudly. "And for this anxiety of yours, this problem of—" She looked at him uncertainly.

"Problem of order, shall we say?" suggested Godfrey, striving to lighten his somber voice.

"This problem of order," she agreed, "we shall not be called upon to solve it today, shall we?" She was getting tired of the long ride, she told herself, not just frightened at the thought of facing problems she had hoped to avoid.

Godfrey was instantly penitent, and she suspected, relieved, too. "God forbid me for spoiling this day with my worries."

"But I am not afraid, Father Godfrey. In fact," she laughed, a little unsteadily even to her own ear, "it's rather thrilling for a woman to have a chance to fight, isn't it?"

He did not answer but stared straight ahead. Following his gaze, she saw that at a sudden turn in the road, they had come out into full view of Rome. Not the magnificent view from the crag on the edge of the Campagna, but a homely glimpse of a corner, a gate and a wall with a pile of marble behind it, and the fern-like tops of trees looking over the buildings.

"It is thrilling, isn't it, Father Godfrey?" Helpless, she heard her voice run up the scales of panic. For answer, Godfrey leaned over and took her hand for a moment in his firm grasp. Then their companions rode up about them, and they went through the Appian Gate into Rome.

It must have rained that morning, for even now with the sunlight mellowing in the cooler air of afternoon, the stone blocks of the roadway sparkled with countless runnels and rivulets, and the beeches tinkling softly on the May breeze shone with a yellowish-green light. The rain had washed the marbles clean and brought out the soft veinings of color in lintel and doorpost and porch in the houses they passed. It had washed too those little nosegays of fern and flower that burgeoned wherever the gnawing of time had left a little of the tufa bare beneath the marble and caught the passing dust for the momentary seed.

With a flourish of trumpets they rode into the city. From ahead, trumpets answered, and presently a crowd had tumbled out of the shops and the palaces and the hovels, strange spawn of the squalor and the splendor of Rome. As the mob rushed upon the newcomers, Alberic and Godfrey pressed close to Matilda, but the shouts that greeted her appearance on every hand soon made it clear that the story of Aquino had reached Rome. Sometimes cheers for the Countess Beatrice mingled with the huzzas for Matilda. Sometimes the cries rose simply for "the Beautiful Countess," as boys with shining teeth ran along the gutters trying to catch at the hem of her mantle. Women with naked babies wrapped in an end of the shawls that veiled their heads held up their children to see, and old men, lifting dim eyes and toothless jaws to the passing rout, blessed the great lady who had saved the Holy City.

At first Matilda was astonished, and a little frightened at the press. Then honesty brought the blood to her cheeks, for after all it was not much of a fight, that skirmish by the brook at Aquino. And though, when the rest of the company turned back, she had charged and rallied the fleeing, yet she could not believe those blue-eyed northern giants would long remain quiet for the memory of a girl. But the shouting and the shining of eyes and the blessings and the gathering of all this enthusiasm from every hole and cranny of the narrow streets fired her own enthusiasm so that by the time the captain of the Papal Guard with a great flourish of trumpets rode splendidly around a palace corner to greet them, Matilda had yielded herself to the emotion of the occasion. As she thought of her tutor Donizo for a moment, she made one last effort to keep her head. Frantically below her smiling she clutched at a tag-end of his admonitions, "Vanity of Vanities"—she tried to remember that this world is a vale of tears, and its brightest hope the anticipation of our release. The very effort was the sheerest hypocrisy. Never had the wind of life blown so sweetly in her face. She threw away all the grave cautions of philosophy and drank the sweetness of the moment as if it were a spring that would never go dry.

It was by a street fountain that the papal captain dismounted and kneeling down on the muddy pavement took her hand to his lips, while the thronged piazza roared its homage and the sunlit walls tossed the echoes from amber to coral surfaces. And then the alert consciousness relaxed its vigilance. Automatically, Matilda smiled and murmured some word of grateful acknowledgment, which she heard as if from a great distance. For in her immediate consciousness was but one thing, the soft pattling of the water on the worn marble, and the flat tinkle of its slipping through the little ground ivies that streaked the base of the fountain. Whenever she thought of that moment for many a day to come, she was to hear the sound of the water and the moist brush of the ivies that strained its sparkling way. Before that sound so cool, so impersonal, so irrelevant, the cheers and the trumpets and the stamping of horses and the ringing of spears and shields faded into a dim roar like the sound of the sea on the shore at Pisa or the thunder rolling away across the bare Tuscan hills.

It was not until a couple of hours later when she found herself looking up into the quiet gray eyes of the Pope that this veil of remoteness was torn. The cool pressure of the great amethyst ring she had kissed was still on her lips, and the thin hand, the thinner seeming for the heavy ring, was still cutting the twilight in the movements of the blessing.

"Were you not frightened, my child?" came the still voice, effortless and steady as the gray eyes.

"There was no time to be frightened," she answered, trying to recall.

"You are right," said Pope Alexander. "There is no time for that."

The light was fading in the room, and for the first time, Matilda became aware that the tall, austere figure before her, with the craglike head and the proud mouth held so firmly and the still eyes, was yet that of an old man. She did not feel ashamed of her strength and her stature and the fresh warmth of the fire that burned within her veins as sometimes she did with Arduino, whose body though strong was yet small and ugly, like a vise on the proud spirit within. But suddenly she felt like a child, and she looked up at the Pope from the stool on which she was sitting, and without saying anything she waited.

"Even a summer day is short," said the old man, smiling a little as if he had read the feeling she could not put into words. "We are not leaving you quite so bad a world as we received. It is wild enough and dark enough and lawless enough, God knows, but at least there are men to try to bring some order into it. When I was a young man, it seemed as if there were none, as if Christ Himself were asleep in the tabernacle of the Church, and outside there were not enough light for people even to remember that He was there. But now if you teach your son to love God and to keep His law, he in his day will find at least a few to help him, I think."

Matilda thought of the water flowing in the sunlit fountain but a couple of hours ago.

"Am I to leave it to him, Holy Father?" she asked timidly, yet resolutely, for it had suddenly occurred to her that she was not likely to meet again soon one in whose authority she could have so much confidence. Half-absurdly, she thought of Jacob wrestling with the angel, and she knew that she must not let this moment go.

For answer the Pope looked at her keenly, and she was afraid that perhaps the challenge in her question was more apparent than the homage that had inspired it. But as the Pope smiled, she knew that the impertinences of the world had long since ceased to vex that pastoral preoccupation.

"You may plead the frailty of your sex," he said whimsically. And then as Matilda leaned forward, clasping her hands tightly until the tendons burned, he added more tenderly: "You need not be troubled about not doing enough, my child. You will be asked to give all you have and more."

"But I would not have life easy," said Matilda proudly.

"You will not," and the Pope rose. Matilda looked sharply into his face as he lifted his hand to bless her, but there was nothing of pity or of condescension in it.

Again, she heard the cool splashing of the water in the fountain. It was the most exciting day she had ever known.

CHAPTER III

NOR had this sense of excitement faded when Matilda came that night with her mother into the vast banqueting hall of the Lateran Palace. Often as a child, on her not infrequent visits to Rome, she had looked around the great pillars that separated the hall from the gallery without and gazed curiously upon the huge blocks of darkly rich pattern that covered the floor with their reds and dull saffron yellows and hard cool greens like the rinds of melons. Tonight she remembered with sudden amusement how try as she would to keep her eyes on the wonderful pavement, they would always rise at last to the remote splendor of the walls, where the definitely blocked and paneled and lozenged colors of the marbles faded into the remoter darkness of the great spaces above. There the little glazed windows looked through the mirk like the ghosts of winter moons, and the great timbers of the roof leaped out of the shadows in breathtaking fantasies of moving darkness. Try as she would to hold those great arms and tentacles in their gross patterns far above her head, they would always sooner or later swoop down upon her, and she would shrink back to the sunlit safety of the gallery.

Tonight as she stood on the threshold of the great room that terror seemed suddenly incredible and, like all vanished fears, strangely dear. And then she forgot everything but the splendor of the scene before her. Among the rafters it was still dark, but just below, the windows were arched oblongs of dusky blue, and lower still on invisible chains swung softly luminous balls of red and amber light. It was their radiance that melted the heavy mid-air in the great room, but it was the tapers of alabaster wax in the hands of the servants, in bronze and silver sconces on the tables, in great holders of carved marble standing against the walls, that struck the eyes of the women to light and the jewels in their dress to fire.

All over the room they were standing, in little knots and groups, half hidden in the shadows, touched with light here and there where the windblown flames moved softly over the pearl-sewn collar of a brocaded dalmatic or the gold-embroidered end of a girdle. Then the rose and the green and the blue of the silks and brocades flushed with light and an intenser fire of color. There was an added sweetness in the flame-starred air, something richer and heavier threading the smell of the pine knots crackling in their bronze cradle in the middle of the room. For the first time, Matilda noted two boys swinging small gilded censers in the hollow square of the long white tables. Yet it was not the incense that she smelled, but something sharper and sweeter, as if the very draught of the common air had become a more splendid thing for these beautiful creatures before her.

"Yes, it is amusing." The voice of Beatrice, so fresh, so cool in its sweetness, broke in upon her wonder, and Matilda looked up to catch the mocking good humor in her mother's clear blue eyes.

For a moment, as always when her enthusiasm was brought face to face with the imperturbable matter-of-factness of her mother, Matilda felt a little foolish. But Beatrice looked away as if she were no longer interested in her oddly impressionable daughter, and seemed to devote all her attention to pushing a stray lock of bright brown hair beneath the purple-blue silk of her veil, with a large, slow-moving hand that seemed the index of her unpretentiously majestic presence.

Again Matilda turned to the scene and yielded herself without resistance to its spell. Astonishingly beautiful as it was, she yet had a sense that she had beheld it before, a teasing sense of familiarity, of something seen for a moment and now across much time recognized. But it was not until the Empress Agnes made her entrance that she grasped the teasing strands and pulled them together into one coherent recollection. For a moment the Empress stood shyly on the step above the pavement of the hall, and her ladies pressed close behind her, the stiff silks of the mantles rustling together like dry reeds in the wind. Of many colors, of amber and green and blue and red, their dresses were yet all of one fashion, of the straight dalmatic pattern which the imperial ladies of Constantinople had made the whole world's fashion. Stiff about the long straight robes beneath, the brilliant hues of the mantles sloped back upon each other like some great wave of color slowly breaking into its component stripes. And then Matilda remembered where she had seen it all before. It was in the great mosaic of San Vitale in Ravenna where the Empress Theodora with her ladies about her stands on the threshold of Paradise, high above the craned necks of earthbound worship.

Only the contrast between that imperial Theodora, tall and proud with a great stateliness in her long, slender face and in her almond-shaped eyes, and the dainty Agnes, little and wistful, with worried eyes in the prettily flushed face under her crown, brought Matilda sharply out of the spell of the scene. The world is as beautiful as the artist's dream when you take it, running, in the total effect, at the first glance, but when the eye lingers on it, there is always something wanting, some lapse from the arrogant perfection of the imagination. And Matilda remembered with a sudden unreasonable spasm of disappointment that the widow of the great third Henry had not been able to face the perplexities of her wardship of the boy King and had taken refuge in Rome. Matilda had heard Godfrey curse her weakness, and Anselm, the bishop of Lucca, praise her piety, and Beatrice herself pity her misfortunes.

As if to read her thoughts, the light voice of Alberic broke in upon her regret. "Your mother might be the empress."

The ranks of color behind the actual Empress had broken as she came down the steps, and accidentally they seemed to have formed behind Beatrice as she took Agnes' hand in greeting. Tall and majestic in her assurance and her repose, Beatrice might well have fronted the great Byzantine empress herself, but whether it was the austere chestnut of her hair or the warmer, fairer skin of the northern blood in her veins that made the difference, there was nothing in her of that almost stern grandeur that gave its character to the swarthy face of the Greek woman. Or was it perhaps the artist who made that splendor? Ever since Matilda had first seen the mosaic years before, as a child, it had seemed to her the ideal expression of the splendor and power of this world.

But aloud she only said to Alberic, "Yes, I suppose so."

The whole company had thronged about the Empress, who with nervous coquetry was holding out her hand for them to kiss. For a moment at a loss, Matilda looked to her mother. Beatrice smiled and motioned to her to come forward.

As Matilda rose from a shy curtsey, the Empress came up to her and took her hand.

"You are grown a fine woman, Matilda," she said a little breathlessly. "You are as tall and nearly as big as your mother even if you have your father's dark hair and complexion." She looked up at Beatrice with touching admiration in her rather faded eyes. Beside her friend, the Empress looked, indeed, small and frail. Matilda remembered one childish glimpse of her in the hall at Canossa, an exquisitely lovely vision. She was still pretty, this woman who had found the burdens of power so heavy, but there was something faded about her prettiness, like the yellowing of old linen, and something helpless about it. Time had brought out strength even in the coarsening of the lines in the face of Beatrice, had given substance and volume to her warm color and the calm light on eyes and mouth, but it had only brought something vague and confused into the worried prettiness of Agnes' face.

The Empress turned to her friend with a sigh, and Matilda dropped back into the crowd, beside the waiting Alberic.

"The Pope will not come?" she whispered.

"No, he is very old, as you saw today. But there is his captain now," and Alberic pointed to a magnificent figure with a shirt of mail just showing under his brilliant mantle. "And there is His Eminence of Conti."

Matilda had no difficulty picking out the Cardinal Conti in his scarlet robes. It was a noble head, white and proudly graceful above the cardinal's robes, with an arresting face, a little too full in the lower lids of the eyes, and in the under chin, but sensitive and highly bred in every cool line.

"He is a great gentleman," said Matilda at last.

Alberic laughed. "Ho, that is not the beginning of it. He is what all the rest of us hope some day to be. He is that most indestructible of all the Almighty's creations—a Roman nobleman. Empires may rise and fall; they will only bear him on their crest, and when the inevitable decline sets in, lo, he will be swimming up the new wave. We boast of a century or two and look down our short noses at other squabs, but he has struck that easy balance between pride and grace for a thousand years."

"I can't see," interrupted Matilda, laughing, "that that in the least awes his huge friend with the cross." For a moment, the two companions said nothing as they gazed upon the bronze-cheeked, golden-haired giant sweeping with great strides in the wake of the Italian. His purple robes were quite as magnificent as his colleague's, but there was something in the stride and something in the firm clutch of a strong hand on the emerald-studded cross on his bosom that suggested the fighting man rather than the priest.

"It is Thor himself," said Alberic.

"Thor?"

"Adelbert, Bishop of Bremen, if you prefer. God, he does not know anything about it at all," said Alberic enviously. "So far as he is concerned, it does not exist."

"But from what they say, he is ambitious, this Adelbert of Bremen."

Alberic smiled. "Spoken like an Italian. There are other worlds to conquer besides Rome. Adelbert thinks he has one up in those snow fields of his."

Matilda looked at Alberic thoughtfully. "Why not let him have it? Who else would want it anyway?"

Alberic laughed gayly. "Quite like a woman. Now and then you comfort me, Matilda. I begin to think there is some hope for that husband of yours—I'm sorry," impulsively as Matilda's face darkened. For a moment, neither spoke.

Then Matilda asked, "But why not let Adelbert have his world in Bremen?"

Alberic sighed. "Well, there is one answer to your question there in the man who has just come in, the Archdeacon."

"Who?" asked Matilda, scanning the brilliant company on the short flight of marble steps at the entrance to the hall.

"You must have heard of him—Hildebrand of Soana. He is Pope Alexander's first lieutenant."

"Father Godfrey was talking about him." Matilda looked questioningly at her companion.

He laughed. "All Rome is."

"Which is he?"

"He is kissing the Empress' hand, and she is fluttering more than usual. She admires him volubly, but I think she is a little scared of him."

"Not that dark little man!"

Alberic laughed again. "You are positively feminine tonight, my dear Matilda. That dark little man is the most important man in Rome."

"You are the most rude, I think." Matilda shook her head with mock severity, and Alberic looked at her for a moment before he laughed again. Then curiosity overcame her indignation. "I have heard Mother speak of him, I think, but I had no idea. He looks rather like one of those awful parish priests who's been scrubbed up and put into a cast-off monsignor's violet robe."

Alberic shook his head with graver amusement. "If I were to gamble on it, I should put my money on him for the next Pope."

"Him? Pope?" Matilda looked at her friend to see if he were joking. Reassured, she went on sagely, "There are a lot of these lower-class men thrusting themselves forward, nowadays."

"There is no lot about Hildebrand," said Alberic shaking his head. "Even his enemies admit that."

"You know him then?" But at that moment, a trio of young cavaliers with richly hiked swords gleaming in the folds of their long gowns came up and stood bowing before Matilda. Alberic spread out his hands with a comic gesture and a whispered, "If you need me, just look at me," and slipped off with dramatically emphasized despair. From nowhere Beatrice was suddenly at her daughter's back, and the three cavaliers, bowing as if their long curls would sweep the pavement, were kissing her hand. It was the tallest and the most richly dressed who took the tips of Matilda's fingers in his and escorted her to her place at the table.

Again Matilda felt her heart swell with pride when she saw her mother sit down at the left of the Cardinal Conti opposite the Empress, with the great blond giant of the north in his magnificent episcopal robes on the other side. For a moment Beatrice had stood in her deep blue robes with the green borders and girdle against that purple, and it seemed as if for once her stately presence had found its fitting counterpart in the splendid magnitude of the Archbishop of Bremen.

"These, too, are men," said a low voice at her side. Alberic had slipped in at the table next to her. Even as he spoke, there flashed on her eye the memory of some of the wretched serfs they had passed on the Campagna that morning, foul bundles of filth and whining with nothing but their misery to lay claim to human fellowship. And here for a moment as these two stood together, even the memory of the Empress Theodora at Ravenna seemed a faint and far-away thing.

As the Countess Beatrice took her seat, and the Archbishop Adelbert leaning over to speak to her shut her from view, Matilda looked beyond down the table. First, there was the Empress Agnes curiously young and petite-looking beyond the exquisite age of the Cardinal Conti; then another Roman, of middle years, looking for a moment upon the company with sly indifference like a hawk with film-sheathed eyes, and clasping and unclasping the ivory-clawed arms of his chair with long fingers; then a matron with the heavy repose of the patrician matriarch in the spacious brow beneath the folds of her purple veil, and last of all, looking straight into Matilda's wandering eyes, a dark, haggard face with piercing glance from under heavy brows, a face raked to the bone with thought and will. Matilda's eyes fell. When she looked again, the dark face had turned from her, but even in the soft candlelight the high brow and the lean cheek seemed bitten out of the shadows behind it.

"You may be right," she said to Alberic. "I suppose the Archangel Michael looked like that when he had beaten Lucifer."

"It is a good figure, though there are some in Rome would change the part."

"He's a dreadful man, that Archdeacon," said the Roman gallant, playing with the jeweled hilt of his sword. For the first time Matilda looked at the man beside her, measuring the low voice, and the white, scented hands, and the cameo-like profile with the long curls soft on the alabaster skin. "They should not let him in to a feast to scare the ladies." And one of the ivory hands rested on Matilda's, making it look coarsely brown. Gently she slipped her hand free, and hid it in the long sleeve of her gown. Then repentant of the moment's rudeness, she looked shyly at him. His long lashes fell and the corners of the full-curved mouth lifted luxuriously.

"Madonna Matilda, I knew your father," interrupted an older man beyond, leaning across the perfumed splendor of her escort.

Several voices around broke out in admiration: "Ah, that Boniface. There was a man for you!"

"He was the bravest fighter I ever knew," pursued the older man across the exclamations of the younger knights, his thin, dry face glowing duskily with the memory. "When everybody else gave up, he seemed to begin again. And how he would lash the laggards with that deep, scornful voice of his! One felt ashamed of being alive then, and one fought if only for a claim to hell. That was a leader for a man to follow!"

"That is what Arduino della Palude says of you, my lady Matilda."

"Oh, no," protested her companion, "the Countess Matilda is a queen of beauty. She needs no harsh words to rule her subjects."

There was a chorus of laughter: "Beware of him, my lady Matilda. He is the worst deceiver in Rome."

"There never was such a knight," persisted the older warrior. "Alone, with his axe in his hands, he beat off six men from his chamber in the priory of San Martino when they ambushed him in the night."

"And at the ford of Santa Lucia, with his horse drowning under him, he swam to the shore, and he sent his spear through the heart of the Lord of Montemagno, even as he sat on his horse above him," said another.

"There never was such a man for standing by his own," added still a third. "Do you remember when that wretched little village—it was some paltry business over a girl—stoned Sasso, his man, and he burned it down? And those Burgundians who took some of his men for ransom—he hanged every one of them but one, and him he sent back to the King of Burgundy to tell the tale. That was a lord for you!"

The enthusiasm rose warm and glowing about the table, but Matilda, whose cheeks had been burning with pleasure, suddenly became aware of the tapping of Alberic's fingers on the back of her chair. It was the smoothly rhythmic tapping of the absentminded, but it sent a shiver down her spine. For a moment she looked at Alberic, but he seemed completely oblivious of her regard.

"Do you remember when the Emperor sent for him?" The older knight's voice fell, and the younger men leaned over each other. "He had meant to slay him that night, but Boniface took a band of his tallest warriors, and with their swords by their sides, they went into the Emperor's presence, and they knelt down before him, and Boniface told him that he had brought his best warriors with him to pay homage to his lord. I shall never forget the look on the Emperor's face!"

The laughter of the young men rose over the older man's discretion, and the Cardinal Conti looked around from his absorbed conversation with the Empress and Beatrice to raise questioning eyebrows. The younger men sobered, but still another veteran, sun-bronzed and wind-bitten, with scarred cheek above his festal robes, rose from his place and came and stood by Matilda.

"He was the ideal knight, my lady Matilda. Always he fought for honor as a knight should, and never for wealth as these parvenus do nowadays. I remember once when he was very angry with the people of Miroalto. They had taken the horses of some of his troops on the plea that they were damaging the harvest in their fields. When Boniface heard of it, he flung his forces against their lord's castle. The owner of the castle refused to obey his summons to surrender. Instead he made a sortie, and failed. So Boniface took all the men of the castle and gave orders that their noses and ears should be cut off."

There was a roar of laughter from the young men, and even some of the women smiled.

"There were three shields full of the cut noses, and they blackened in the sun until they looked like ripe mulberries crushed on the stones by a roadside."

Again there was a roar of mirth, and again Matilda was conscious of the tapping of the fingers on the back of her chair. The story-teller, flushed with wine and with his success in capturing the interest of his audience, sobered with difficulty and went on.

"There was a very rich lady of noble and ancient family, and her son was waiting his turn to be cut. She gathered up all her silver and her jewels, and she brought the treasure to the Lord Boniface, and she laid it at his feet, begging him to take it and spare her son."

For a moment the tapping on the back of Matilda's chair ceased, and it seemed as if for that moment her nerves had respite. The company leaned toward the speaker in silent expectation.

"But he flung it to the ground, and in a great rage he cried, 'God forbid that what was won with steel should be bought with silver.' And he bade the soldiers go on, and the young lord's nose went with the others into the shield. For he was a great lover of honor, this Boniface."

There was a burst of hearty applause, and all the young men gazed with admiration upon the daughter of their hero. But the fingers on the back of her chair had resumed their tapping, and the chill spread through all Matilda's body, and she sickened.

The talk rose around her, but it seemed now too loud to be heard. And Alberic went on tapping his fingers.

"For God's sake, stop that, Alberic," she whispered passionately. And then as his arm fell, and the cool night air rushed between them, she was sorry.

"He was a great man, my father, was he not, Alberic?" she cried, searching his face for comfort she knew she could not find.

"Yes, my lady, a great man!"

"And so pitiless a thing it is to be a great man?"

Alberic shrugged his shoulders. Then as she suddenly stifled for air, she felt his hand upon hers.

"Now you know why I am going to do what I have decided to do." He paused. "Matilda, I am going to take the cowl."

For a moment she did not understand. Then—"You, Alberic, a monk!"

For the first time she realized how she had counted on Alberic's always being at her side—even when the young Godfrey should come. Ever since her brother died, she had looked to him as a brother. And now—she stared at him incredulously. A monk—he who enjoyed the world so much!

"A monk!" she repeated. Alberic smiled mirthlessly.

"Yes. It may not be the road to heaven, but the other is—what you see." He spread out his hands with affected lightness.

"But what will I do without my old neighbor?" she asked, striving to master her astonishment.

Alberic smiled, it seemed to her, with a twinge of bitterness she had never caught before in his light-hearted mockery.

"You will be a great man, Matilda."

"A great man? My God!"

CHAPTER IV

"ON the morrow you will not care so much," she told herself that night as she strove in vain to go to sleep. But she knew, too, that she would not care so much about anything else.

"You will be a great man," she said to herself the next morning when the breeze before dawn blew white the dim walls of her room, and she fell asleep, restless and troubled.

And she repeated the words to herself when some hours later, after Mass, she joined the company in the small audience chamber off the disheveled banqueting room of the night before. Most of the younger people had ridden out for a morning's hawking beyond the city wall, but though Alberic had raised his brows quizzically when she refused to join them, he had wisely asked no questions, and, made silent by his unexpected tact, she had volunteered no explanation. After all, why should she so suddenly turn delicate at the expectation of a handful of bloody feathers or a torn wing? She had eaten her meat for breakfast, and she would certainly not fast for dinner.

It was half with surprise, half with gallantry, that the little company in the guard room rose to its feet when she came in. She curtseyed to the spontaneous homage, and gazed placatingly at the suppressed impatience of some of the older men, particularly the ecclesiastics in red and violet caps and straight traveling dresses. Her mother seated amply in a Roman chair with her strong hands resting firmly on the ivory-clawed arms, gestured with level eyes to the cushion at her feet, but pretending not to see, Matilda rose from the deep curtsey and with a hiss of her stiff morning dress on the marble floor, slipped to the low, arched window behind the company. Here in its deep embrasure with her feet barely touching the floor, and her head leaning against the carved gray stone, still cool in the morning sun, she took refuge. For a moment the silence seemed to be waiting for her, and she felt shy, and a little apprehensive of her mother's inevitable rebuke. There was something soothing in the coolness of the stone and the breeze in the spring air, and something tangibly comforting in the way the warmth of the sun lay softly about her. The voices rose again, but she felt a little sleepy, too sleepy to be interested, too indolent for even the night's pain to be more than a lingering aftertaste of a bitter draught.

Some of the company went out. She felt her mother's eyes rest questioningly upon her, but there was nothing to say. Again, she felt rather than saw her mother's eyes leave her with the same calm indifference with which Beatrice of Tuscany faced most of the world's rebuffs. Later, perhaps, but now it did not seem worth the effort to conciliate that quite unoffended majesty.

Then the voices went on unbroken. One of them was slightly guttural with a curious catch in the throat now and then, and yet strong and resonant. It reminded her of her father's voice. And the thought came to her of the time when a choleric huntsman had whipped her pony because it had held the whole chase at the brook and the boar had escaped. She had explained that it was not her pony's fault, that the water was running high. The chief huntsman, a great fellow with fierce eyes had cut at the pony savagely, and she had leaped from its quivering back and torn at the assailant's leather knees like something possessed.

A strong arm had seized her, had held her seven-years old fury at cool arm's length, and that same guttural voice had spoken: "Now Matilda?"

She felt her throat burn at the memory of how, choking, she had answered him, "He beat my pony, and I told him it was not the pony's fault, the beast!"

She saw the bully's sneering face blanch to a dirty ashen. And then he crumpled up absurdly as her father's gauntleted fist came down upon the tawdry cloth hood. There was an angry coldness in her father's blue eyes that suddenly relaxed her contorted throat. And all the anger went out of her in a clean wind of triumph and vindication as her father said in that heavy voice of his, "Now get back on your pony, Matilda." God must have looked that way when he smote Pharaoh, and so must he have spoken to Moses.

She had thought of that moment a thousand times in the years since, with pride and wistfulness. And thinking of it, she had been envious of a certainty that had faded somewhat in the vicissitudes since. She remembered how later when the Emperor had been so angry with her mother because of her marriage and had held her prisoner for months and months, and alone at Canossa, she had gone to sleep night after night sick with terror, she had prayed to her dead father to smite the Emperor flat like the bully, like Pharaoh. Even the thought of her father standing there behind the brutally quiet evening sky as he had stood above the huntsman had comforted her, had filled her with a resolute defiance that was more nourishing to the spirit than comfort. She had thought of him so night after night, month after month until even now when she prayed for her dead at night, he still came to her memory in the same posture. But in all those years, never once had she seen the fallen man after she had turned from his sudden crumpling to the glorious vindication of her father's contempt. Never once had she wondered if he had come to himself again, if painfully with his comrades not daring to help him, he had struggled out of the mud into which he had fallen. Now for the first time she thought of him and wondered. And for the first time as that glorious surety of her father rose in her memory, she found herself wondering—She was startled even at the mere thought of a doubt.

In that surprise, for the first time she listened to the voices, especially to the voice that had brought her father back before her. Positive and deep, it spread out and laid hold upon her where she sat in the solitude of the window.

"You can't change human nature. Men fight, they have always fought, they always will fight." Something crisp came into the low grumble of the voice, and the silence closed in upon the knife thrust of the last word.

"My lord Bishop, you and I are sworn to try to change human nature. We know we can't—as men, but every time we invoke the Grace of God in curse or in blessing, we are assuming that human nature can be changed by the Grace of God." It was a lighter, quieter voice that so answered, but one no less positive.

"The Grace of God has nothing to do with the present case. Hildebrand of Soana, it is like you Romans to be always bringing in things that have nothing to do with the immediate matter in hand as if you were to hold a council every time a man opened a window to take a smell of his diocese. We don't have such nonsense up in the north. We've too much to do fighting and building up there. The very cold drives such vapors out of a man's head. He is willing to fall asleep by the fire and leave the Grace of God to the monks." It was Alberic's great blond Thor who was speaking, and it was impossible not to sympathize with his contempt as he gazed down upon the slender, taut, mean little figure of the Italian who had gainsaid him.

"My lord Bishop, the Abbot of Cluny here will tell you that there is nothing monkish in setting up the Peace of God. These last two years, ever since the meeting at Poitiers, he has hardly known what it is to have a chance to doze by the fire you speak of. And the Prior of Vézelay here, who told the Count of Nevers that he was excommunicate for attacking his vassal's castle on a Friday, still bears on his cheek the cut of a ring on the hand with which that irate lord struck him to the floor." She could see that the little man had his own pride in the hollow gray cheeks, in the level lower lip held so firmly beneath the upper, in the deep-set eyes under the heavy brows.

A less sure note of exasperation crept into Adelbert of Bremen's growl: "Mad, mad. Knights and earls are not nuns. Men, men, I tell you, Hildebrand of Rome. They will fight, and they will gather gold, and they will burn and kill, and they will whore, and they will get children for all your celibacy, too, you monks of Rome." Thor paused for breath.

There was something a little tighter about the corners of Hildebrand's mouth, but his voice did not rise as he answered coolly enough, "It isn't a question this time" (Matilda thought she detected a slight emphasis on the demonstrative) "of celibacy but of murder, and every form of violence and disorder. How do you think, my lord of Bremen, you and I are going to get men to listen to any serious thought of the love of God and the brotherhood of men with the clash of arms drowning out our voices in the very church itself?"

His old confidence blossomed again in the voice of the Bishop of Bremen as he took up this challenge. "But they don't brawl when I am preaching. I post guards if there's any trouble. By heaven, I have struck a man to the pavement for breaking into my preaching and wiped his blood from my hand."

"That is it," said Hildebrand, as if they had reached a turn in the road for which he had been watching all along. "The very hands that offer the bloodless sacrifice of the Mass are stained with the blood of their brethren and their children, and blasphemy completes what anarchy began."

It must have been the despair in his voice that made the Abbot of Cluny break in with his quick, sympathetic reassurance. "Nay, but, Hildebrand, we are

making some progress. Remember what I told you. All the knighthood and nobility of Champagne swore on a piece of the True Cross that for the duration
of Lent they would take their sword against no man unless in dire peril of their
lives or their vassals'. And all the men of Burgundy have promised that they will
not take their sword against priest or serf. And last Christmas all the bishops of
France but that hireling of Bayeux swore that they would not draw sword in the
service of any prince or knight but such as had sworn to observe the truce for
cleric and peasant."

"A pretty pair, the priest and the peasant together," snorted Adelbert. "Who
is confounding the order of society now?"

"Not on the same ground," replied the Abbot of Cluny with a still gravity
that brought back to Matilda's mind the peace of the great bare pillars in the
choir and cloister of Cluny.

"What I say," said the Bishop of Bremen, "is that the priest should stick
to his job. Of course, the Church should insist that her servants be immune to
any violence, at least as long as they mind their business, but the peasants are a
different matter."

"Where then is the Church's commission as the protector of the helpless
and the oppressed?" asked Hildebrand quietly.

The sheer absurdity of the idea seemed to restore the natural good humor
of Adelbert. He roared with laughter. "Do you seriously think that the Church
is some ubiquitous Saint George going about the world smoking out all lurking
dragons and slaying them on each dung heap in every foul little kitchen midden
of a village in Christendom?"

"I seriously think," said Hildebrand, "that the Church has a duty to the oppressed and the helpless." There was no tightening of the stripped muscles in his
lean face; neither was there any sign of weakening.

"But not to destroy society? To free one class of men from the rule to which
God has given them?"

"To insist that God has given the great the obligation of rule along with its
power is not to destroy the order of society."

Adelbert of Bremen threw up his hands, "More of these Roman hairsplit-
tings! Hildebrand, my friend, it's all right here," and the Archbishop of Bremen
threw out his arms with a gesture that made the audience chamber suddenly
seem a little place with all the sunbeams focusing in the glints of his bronze

beard, "it's all right here in this world of gardens and lazy old cities with all the elegances of civilization about you to be sentimental, but up where I come from, it's a very different story. What I must cope with is not a peasant or two being knocked on the head for refusing soldiers the cows they need or some reed-stockaded little village being burned down of a windy night. It's earls spattering their mother's slippers with brother earl's brains. It's kings burning down abbeys because they do not give up their treasure for some raid on a rich vassal. It's bands of pagans battering down your cathedral church because they know the white Christ is drawing in upon their oak groves year by year. We're struggling with real problems in the north, not this cabinet splitting of hairs that flourishes in your gardens here."

The dark face of Hildebrand had grayed during this tirade until it looked to Matilda as if it might have been carved out of the gray volcanic tufa itself, with the bitterness and the fire of the original molten lava still frozen within it.

"My lord," he said quietly, "God knows that what you call these pleasant gardens have run with blood enough these last years. And your northern barbarians—"

The Archbishop of Bremen leaped from his chair and letting his purple sleeves fall back to the elbow, he brandished his brown, knotted arms until the black veins swelled in the bursting muscles. For a moment it looked as if he would throttle the little southerner. But Hildebrand did not move. Indeed, it was as if the sight of the other man's wrath had released some unexpected calm within him, for he looked steadily up at the giant glaring above him, only the level corners of his mouth tightening a little. The Abbot of Cluny laid a cool hand on the arm of Adelbert.

"Adelbert, we all know that the battle of Christianity in this dark world is not to be won in any one way. We know that none of us is enough, and there are many ways." The thin, fair face of Hugh of Cluny softened into a smile, the tenderer for the austerity from which it broke.

The huge bulk of Adelbert shook as he strove to control himself, and slowly, as if against his will, his arms fell to his sides.

But the Archdeacon did not move. Then as Adelbert stepped slowly back, Hildebrand put out his hand to Hugh: "Nay, Hugh! I am to blame."

Then he turned to Adelbert: "My brother, I am sorry."

The two men looked at each other, the dark face of Hildebrand expressionless, the face of Adelbert from which the color was even now fading, cold with suspicion and uncertainty.

Hildebrand took a step toward the giant, and something softer, more personal came into his voice: "I'm sorry I spoke with such passion, Adelbert." There was very little change in the tense face; but something in the vibrancy of the voice, something suddenly warm and pleading, something in the look of the eyes must have gone to the heart of Adelbert, for suddenly flinging his arms wide with enthusiasm, he rushed upon Hildebrand with such violence as nearly to knock him from his feet. "By God and Our Lady, man, that is handsomely said. I lost hold of myself, too."

Matilda saw Hildebrand wince; then his face lighted at the magic warmth of Adelbert, and he caught the proffered hand in his without saying anything.

"We've had enough talk for this morning," interposed Hugh. "It is too beautiful a day for us to spend it entirely behind walls."

Adelbert dropped the Archdeacon's hand and stood looking down upon him as if until now he had never seen him.

"Hugh, why don't you show my lord of Bremen the new stables that the Pope has built at the end of the fields?" said Hildebrand.

"I have it," cried Adelbert with fresh delight. "Do you come, Hildebrand, and I will let you pick out the finest horse in my train, and you shall have it for a pledge of friendship between us."

Hildebrand shook his head, but seeing the wide blue eyes of Adelbert darken, he hastened to say, "I should prefer your judgment of these northern horses to mine. Do you pick for me, and that we will put in the Pope's stables as a pledge of loyalty from us both."

Adelbert frowned. "There you Romans are again, always bringing in—"

But before he could finish the puzzled grumble, Hugh of Cluny slipped his hand through Adelbert's arm and gently drew him toward the door. For a moment the northern giant looked at the tall slender monk in surprise, but though no shadow flickered on the open face of the Abbot of Cluny, there must have been some pressure in that thin hand on the purple sleeve of Adelbert, for presently he had gone out the door.

Then Matilda realized that she had been eavesdropping. Noiselessly, she slipped to the floor. She should perhaps speak to the Archdeacon before she went out, but at the thought of that look of concentration in the lean, gray face, she felt suddenly that to speak would be an impertinence. With a hand still resting on the stone frame of the window, she looked around. And then she saw Hildebrand, standing in front of her, with his dark eyes waiting for hers. He stood very still, his eyes meeting hers patiently. "Like a spring all coiled up and ready," thought Matilda, but she said nothing. Only the hand resting on the window frame fell to her side.

"That was a brave thing you did at Aquino," he said quietly.

"I?"

And then she remembered, and she felt the blood in her cheeks from pleasure and confusion. But he seemed to be waiting, quite oblivious of her embarrassment.

Still more confused, she reached for the first thing she could think of.

"That peace you are speaking of makes all the fighting seem a little thing."

His eyes fell. "I am glad to hear you say that."

Some impulse of honesty made her add, a little frightened of her own pleasure in his approval, "Not but that I enjoy the fighting like another."

He nodded absently.

"Only," she went on, "there is the other side to it."

He was a little man, standing there rather stiffly in his straight, plainly neat, dark robe. Yet every muscle in the firm body, every thread in the somewhat worn dress seemed to be held tight in the grip of an extraordinary resolution. In the very austerity itself, Matilda fancied that she beheld some unusual authority.

"Then you did not hear what they were saying last night?"

He looked at her uncertainly.

"About my father?" Even now she shuddered.

Noiselessly, Hildebrand's firm lips rounded. She covered her face with her hands, and as they trembled, the light of the morning flickered between them.

Then she found herself sitting in the chair from which her mother had risen, with the Archdeacon standing before her with the same intent look on his face, waiting.

"They're used to it by now," he said gently. "And your father knows, too."

Puzzled, she searched his face.

He drew up a stool and sat down almost at her knee.

"Power and strength," he raised one hand, with the fingers open, "are like that. Blind and brutal."

"But he was a great man," she interceded.

He nodded. "A great many of them are, but to what ends?"

As to an equal, he looked across to her. She smoothed the heavy folds of her dress before she replied.

"Rule? Glory?"

"Whose rule? Whose glory?" His eyes held hers, and suddenly she was no longer shy.

"But, father, God has given the lord the rule, and the brave man the glory."

"To what end? For whose sake?"

"But God surely meant that the great should be great—" she faltered.

"And those on whose backs they climb to that greatness?"

"But God made some men great, and some—" again she suddenly found herself less certain than when she had begun the sentence.

"My lady Matilda, was it of God this mutilation?"

She winced, but his eyes held hers.

She tried to speak, and she could not.

"Is it of God all this war we see? All this burning and killing and pillaging?" He had risen to his feet, and he flung his arms wide as he spoke. "He is greatest who burns and kills the most. He is mightiest who tramples down the weak most ruthlessly. He who knows no conscience and no pity, he is the most glorious. They blow bravely in the wind these lords' standards, but they are dyed in blood and made fast in tears. They walk proudly, these lords, but their robes are stiff with the mud into which they have ground their betters."

Every muscle frozen in horror, Matilda watched the little man stride back and forth, his dark face blazing with indignation.

"And then they say God has given this. Nay, it is the Devil himself has given his charter to the princes of this world, and it is they who do his work. Work," his voice rose, "that the fiends in hell for very pity would refuse to touch. Power and glory! I think, Matilda, that God Himself on His throne in heaven must shudder to hear those words!"

And then something snapped within Matilda's breast, and she was shaking in great, fierce sobs.

When the first storm was a little spent, she dried her eyes and looked up to find Hildebrand gazing down upon her, all the wrath gone from his face, and all its fierce darkness lightened by a look of wonder.

"Do you understand this?" he asked incredulously.

And then he took hold of her arm and looked into her face.

"Perhaps it is because you are a woman and not a man," he said thoughtfully.

But Matilda only gazed into that face, so appallingly burned-out after the outburst of its passion. For answer, she shyly put her hand into his, and for a moment he held it wondering.

Then he sat down again on the little stool.

"Listen, Matilda. Do you remember how the Gospel of John opens?"

"In the beginning was the Word," she began obediently.

"Yes, but you remember what comes a little after? 'And the light shineth in darkness and the darkness did not comprehend it.'" He looked at her as if he expected her to see it all now. But she was puzzled.

"It is dark," he said. "Never since the world began, I think, was it darker, so far as this world is concerned. But there is this light, this light of the Word of God, shining in the darkness."

She nodded. "You mean this peace that the abbot was speaking of?"

For the first time in the last half hour, he smiled.

"That is one thing, but there are others." He stretched out his hand to her.

"There is all the law of God. If we could make men hearken to that law, if we could bring them to see it only, then verily I think the light would shine in the darkness, and every man be lightened."

"But how shall we see this light?" she asked, carried along but not quite entirely possessed by his enthusiasm.

"It is the Church," he answered. "That is the lantern which holds this light and lifts it up so that men may see."

"The Church!" she repeated thoughtfully to herself.

"To bring order into chaos, to make light shine in the darkness."

"And the prince?" she challenged him.

"He is a Christian, too. His power is of God—not to satisfy his own whim, his own greed, his own vanity, but to keep the law of God and to defend it."

"Ideally," she agreed, "but in this world?"

"Even in this world, Matilda. If only I could make you see. One just prince!"

"I am only one, and a woman." The self-mockery fell bitterly on her ear, and she was ashamed even as she spoke.

He rose. For a moment he stood there with his hands folded against his black dress. Then he bowed to her, and before she could say anything, he had left her. She heard the door close, and then she laid her head in her arms and wept without any restraint of pride or conscience.

CHAPTER V

IT was late afternoon, and Matilda and her mother had just ridden out of a pass in the hills above the Baths of Lucca. It was at that point where the Lima hurled its stormy waters into the slow-flowing Serraglio, and the restless energy of the mountain stream was turned to quiet in the sunlit shallows of the plain. Here and there a fleck of foam, borne on that smiling surface like a fallen oleander blossom, still rode the placid dimpling of the shadows, but for the most part the full and spacious river seemed as quiet a thing as the folding of the hills above.

Moreover, it was the hour when the weary day at last relaxes its clutch on the bald surfaces of the world. The colors were as bright as ever—the dappled greens of the vine-shot terraces, the aquamarine of the lightly-moving river, the luminous turquoise of the distant mountain, stopping the angle of the river banks with its warm arc against the flushed sky. Indeed, the radiance of the close of the day seemed to have evoked some hidden magic in the familiar colors of the landscape, bringing out unsuspected light and vivacity. But the sharp angles of the terraced hills rising steeply from the river bed had yielded in some mysterious way to the tacit importunities of sky and flanking mountain and the melting plane of the river. It was as if some larger rhythm had swept up their wonted dissonances and composed them in a new harmony.

"Yes, the world is as beautiful here as you would like to have it," said Beatrice, smilingly surprising her daughter's thoughts.

Matilda drew her breath slowly and raised her eyes to her mother's for answer.

For some minutes she said nothing but sat there with her mother, watching the soft colors move over the still sunlit world. Then she said more to herself than to her companion, "Rome might never have been, so far as one could tell from this spot."

Beatrice laughed with that fresh rill of merriment in her voice that now made Matilda remember with a start that her mother, too, had once been young.

Then Beatrice pointed down the river bank.

"You cannot forget Rome so easily as that. See that pile of stone down there? When we come a little closer, you'll see that it runs its tentacles out all over the ground, under the ivies and the lichens, back into the hill and out into the water."

Matilda followed the pointing hand. "It was a fortress then?"

Her mother laughed; and then she sobered, and as she answered, the amusement in her voice yielded to bitterness.

"A fortress? Like that tower of ours at home? No, my child, the Romans had done with fortresses."

Matilda looked around her. "There is no town in sight. How did they hold it then?"

Beatrice's horse whinnied restlessly, but with a firm hand she held it in.

"Who would take it from them?"

Matilda considered. "Was it a church then?"

Again, Beatrice smiled. "No, their temples were smaller than that. These were their baths."

"Baths?" asked Matilda incredulously.

"Baths. Great marble buildings, vast as the whole enclosure of the Lateran, like a great monastery of gleaming marble."

"Baths of marble?" Then as Matilda thought of the bare sandstone walls of the little chamber in which the lords of Canossa bathed now and then in a wooden tub with the maids bringing copper jars of tepid water from the kitchen below, she laughed.

"These were public baths," said Beatrice. "Great crowds of men and women came from all over the land to visit them."

"It must have been a very great lord who held them then."

"No, Matilda, there was peace in the land. And these great buildings lay open to any one who wished to visit them."

"Peace," Matilda repeated softly, and the breeze waking in the tops of the poplars above their heads seemed to take up the word. A great hawk came down the left river bank, gray and sinister on level wings. Suddenly, it swerved and swept majestically into the middle air between the steep banks, flat against the western sky. And there before Matilda's eyes, the shadowed gray of the fierce wings beat white, and the bird of prey flew from their sight, shining like any dove.

Something wistful came into the full, sure voice of Beatrice as she answered, "It didn't seem so impossible then. Did I ever tell you that when your father first brought me down from the north to Rome, we passed through here?"

Matilda shook her head.

"He had promised me that he would make me queen of a land of sunshine and beauty. He would conquer all the land of Italy, and he would beat the swords and the spears not into pruning hooks but into bells to make sweet the summer air and into cymbals and all manner of music." Beatrice laughed a short, half-wistful, half-mocking laugh, and then she sighed.

"We rested at a little house of monks just above the bend of the river—where we're going tonight. And that night—it was later in the summer then—Boniface's boast seemed possible, entirely possible."

"He did conquer a large part of Italy," said Matilda, proudly defending her father from the implication of failure. "And what he did not live to overcome, perhaps I—" she added to herself.

Her mother seemed not to notice the interruption. "The next day we explored the ruins on foot, from the edge of the river to halfway up the hill slope. Great blocks of marble, and columns with flutings and rich capitals, and carved seats, and benches—all broken and half-buried in the damp earth and the thicket of green, and soiled with mold. I was young then, and I cried for all the wreck and the destruction of it. But Boniface laughed and swore that he would pull the pieces of it all out of the earth and build it fresh and leave it white and shining to the ages to come for a memory of his bridal."

"That was a beautiful thing " said Matilda. "It was like him—" She paused. Perhaps it was the reddening of some lichens on a stone at their feet, perhaps it was the dry husk of a bird that had died in the winter snows and been washed clean in the spring rains, and now lay black at her horses' feet, that stayed her, but she did not finish the sentence. Rather, she paused to gather up all her defenses against something just around the corner of her consciousness, something she wished to forget, a picture she was afraid to look on.

Her horse started, and surprised into relief, her hand relaxed. Beatrice followed her.

"There is a bridge here," said Beatrice presently, reining in her horse before a low hummock of green earth, tapestried with water and weeds and floating rushes. "See, under the water there."

For a moment, all Matilda could see was the restless dappling of light and shadow as the ripples of the water sucked at the slimy edges of the stone. Then as her eye became used to the uncertain opacity of the moving water, she caught, like the ghosts of shadows beneath its gray surface, the juttings of piers of marble. Great blocks of marble catching the opalescent lights of the water—she gazed as if fascinated.

"I told your father," broke in her mother's voice presently, mingling coolly with the falling of the water over the stones, "that I would not hold him to the porches and the chambers of the baths, but that I did want the bridge. It would be a proud vaunt in its slender spring against the background of the mountain there, and men could save themselves weary miles crossing the river on its sure strength."

"A bridge is a beautiful thing," said Matilda, hardly taking her eyes from the hypnotic restlessness of the water slipping over the broad stillness of the stones.

"It is a useful thing," said Beatrice firmly. And then more gently as if an afterthought, "and a beautiful."

The breeze of the poplar tips suddenly swooped to the earth and blew the quiet water in a whitening gust of raindrops on the gray surface.

"But Boniface never was able to finish the fighting," said Beatrice. "I suppose one never is."

"It would take a great many men to build that bridge again," Matilda went on, "but it would be a proud thing to leave for memory of one's passing."

"Of course," said Beatrice, "your father did a great deal of building at Canossa. You remember when he built the outer curtain around the towers. You were little then, and you said the yellow stone was pretty, and everybody laughed at you."

Something in the rare tenderness of Beatrice's voice drew Matilda's eyes to her, and she looked up to find her mother regarding her with a wistfulness that went to her heart. For a moment she felt as she had felt that night when she had found her mother weeping over the bier of her dead father. So the two women looked at each other in a silence of perfect understanding. Then it broke.

"Of course," said Beatrice, seeming to draw the mantle of her habitual imperturbability up around her again, "I have been able to build a little here and there, a piece of a city, a church, a fountain, a manor house, but nothing like those great things of the Romans."

"They must have been giants, mother."

"I suppose even if we had the opportunity to build, we would find we had forgotten how."

Matilda turned from the water and faced her mother. "Mother, I shall build that bridge, and I shall have your name carved on it for a memory of you. Oh, mother, when my Godfrey comes, we will build."

Beatrice shook her head. "When Godfrey comes, you will finish the circle of forts to guard you from all sides. A husband will bring you fresh forces, but he will also bring you new enemies, and you must be prepared."

"Forts—great ugly, bare towers of gray stone to gash the bright fields with their terrible shadows. Oh, mother, I want to build things of white marble to catch the sunshine and the shadows of the ivies and to make this Italy beautiful again. And I want to hear those bells of Father's filling the bright air with music."

But Matilda saw that her mother was not listening to her. She was gazing up the valley into the sunset.

"The world should be beautiful," said Matilda doggedly. But even as she spoke, she realized that the light was fading from the valley, that something darker, more austere was coming into the lineaments of the very earth, and all the crystalline rose colors were hardening into the colder blues. Even the breeze over the water was freshening.

"It was meant to be beautiful," she repeated her defiance in the teeth of the coming night.

Her mother had recovered her normal mood, "We must not forget that it is this world and not the next. We were never promised what we should desire here."

"But a little of it, surely—"

"That is what we are all busy about, young lady. If you had not been mooning about in Rome, you would have seen a good deal going forward."

It was the face of the Archdeacon Hildebrand that seemed to look out of her mother's words. And for a moment Matilda gazed at her in astonishment. Then Matilda seemed to hear those words again, "Law—order—God."

"But that was all of rule and law," she said aloud.

"Rule and law, that is the business now. The rest is dreams. I should have known better than to be sentimentalizing over a wedding journey." Something grimly efficient had come into her mother's voice.

"I shall never forget the bridge," said Matilda.

"You'll be busy enough when your husband comes. The years go quickly. With what we shall leave you, you may see your son build yet." Again Matilda felt a spasm of anger at the implied cowardice.

There was a shout from a clump of willows ahead of them, and Godfrey, followed by a crowd of noisy shadows, rode out into the open space by the river.

"It is a lonely place for you to linger, Beatrice," he pleaded with affectionate reproach.

"We knew we should catch up with you," answered Beatrice lightly as if to mock his anxiety. And suddenly, as the company rode up around them, Matilda felt a warm sense of companionship flow into the deepening chill of the sunset. It would be a pleasant evening in the little monastery around the bend in the river. And she was tired. She would be glad of the sweet-smelling hempen sheets in the great whitewashed guest house.

But she lay awake a long time that night, with strange fantasies of white marble rising before her wavering consciousness, and gleaming bridges shooting across the blue rivers and mountains. One vision lingered longer than the rest, a slender white bridge framing a trinity of hills, gleaming an incredible blue against a bluer sky. She could not decide which was the lovelier, the view or the bridge, when suddenly a dark cloud rose and the whole brittle beauty snapped. Then the cloud took form and sharpened into the face of Hildebrand, a little shadowy as seen through tears.

"Order, order," he was saying, and his eyes held hers until she stopped weeping. She tried to look past him, but there was only darkness now where the bridge and the beautiful landscape of the day had been.

✳ BOOK II ✳

THE FULLNESS OF THE YEAR

CHAPTER I

"It is going on six years," said Alberic, bowing again to the Countess Beatrice. Even the simple gesture seemed a little solemn to Matilda, watching her old friend with astonished curiosity after their long separation. For a moment, it seemed to her as if there must be a line of monks behind him bowing, too, for there was some suggestion of corporate rhythm even in the isolated movement.

"How quickly it has all gone since that day at Aquino!" said Matilda, lightly, to tear her mind away from too obvious regard of Alberic's black serge habit and cowl.

It was the old Alberic who looked out between tonsure and cowl as he raised his brows with a swift sidewise look at her: "That hardly sounds like the bride of the Canticle—such patient waiting for the coming of the bridegroom."

"There is another lady who, I should think, would more fitly come to a monk's thoughts."

Again, it was a flash of the Alberic she remembered that touched head and throat with long, swiftly mocking fingers. "Lady, you may hood your falcon, and you may put out its eyes, but slip the silken cord for a moment, and it will take the whole air for its range."

"I never thought you should be a monk," said Matilda in a sudden impulse of pity.

But something new and gentle came into the familiar mockery of Alberic's smile. "That is a different matter, Matilda. I am a monk. The livery I wear I chose freely, and I wear it gladly."

"They always say that," said Beatrice, turning her eyes at last from her absorption in the road. "It is amazing how the religious life lays hold upon a man of the world."

The old quizzical look flashed again into the eyes of Alberic. "Yes, I suppose it is rather astonishing to see us come jingling our chains so gayly into our old haunts."

"It is a great calling," said Beatrice judiciously.

"Thank you, my lady Countess," replied Alberic, bowing again. "It is a great freedom."

"Freedom?" The word slipped from Matilda's lips before she realized it. For this was not the Alberic she knew, like a leaf fluttering in the wind. Even there, alone with them on the parapet, this man still seemed held in another context, as if he were moving to a music invisible to his momentary companions.

"From myself, Matilda. It is the only freedom that matters, you know. But come, what is this text you would commend to my monkish heart?"

Matilda gazed at him in astonishment, and then she remembered. "It is the valiant woman of the Book of Wisdom, who rose in the night and gave her household food and wove garments for them, and stretched out her hands to the poor."

"'Strength and beauty are her clothing'? Be sure you remember that, Matilda, when it is winter, and the midnight rising grows tedious. And do not forget a little sheepskin in your night shoes. It is very comforting in the hours before dawn, when not even poetry will keep the feet warm on a stone floor."

It was the old Alberic. Matilda felt the blood rise in her warm cheeks. Was it vanity and self-dramatization after all, this new dream of her old self? The passion of self-justification which Alberic had so often roused in times past woke again.

"Alberic, it is not what you think. I do want you to understand."

He smiled.

"If it is a sudden passion for the domestic life, it would be hardly becoming to my habit, I suppose, to say that I understand. If it is a feminine desire to be subject to a husband, it would certainly not be professionally becoming for me to do anything but approve, however I might wonder."

"But I do want you to understand. You have been my friend since we were children" (No, Alberic did not wince. For the first time, Matilda realized what his habit implied) "and now that I have changed my ways, I want you to know. I have been visiting my mother's cousin, Caterina. You remember her at Mantua, the pretty girl with the fair hair, the dainty one, who giggled so, and was so gay?"

"What nonsense, Matilda!" interrupted Beatrice. "Caterina is a sober married woman with children, and you remember such trifles!"

"I'm not talking about her now, Mother, but about her as she was then when we were all children."

"You and Alberic always did talk about such absurd things. Anyway, I must see if that cellarer has drawn enough wine for the garrison. He has grown stingy ever since Godfrey left us." And the Countess Beatrice rose from where she had been sitting on the edge of the parapet, looking very stately in her black widow's dress and veil.

"Countess, I said Mass for a month for the repose of the Lord Godfrey's soul, when the news came to Cluny."

"That was good of you, Alberic," said Beatrice gently. "He thought very well of you, and he was very glad when he heard that you had put on the cowl."

"There was no limit to the Lord Godfrey's charity, m'lady. I am proud that it covered me so generously."

"You will pray for us both, won't you?" asked Beatrice. "For I shall soon be lying by his side."

"That God forbid!" said Alberic courteously.

"No, the measure of my time is filled up, and when I have seen Matilda safely in her husband's hands, I shall go gladly from where I am no longer needed."

Matilda turned upon her mother sharply. "You must not say that, Mother, for the young Godfrey and I will need you now as much as ever, and I shall need you more than ever."

"No," said Beatrice slowly, "the generations have each their day, and when they have finished it, they should make way for their successors. Even as the year draws to its close before our eyes."

Matilda followed her eyes out to the scene spread below them. The afternoon was wearing on, and a faint mist in the autumn air was softening the rich colors of the world. Below the castle, the fields in the valley were a warm gold, only less rich than the slowly reddening leaves of the oaks and beeches on the hill above. How softly the white stems of the birches gleamed like veinings in marble through the serried colors of the foliage! Beyond, came the hills, in ranks of purple, fold on fold like some great wave undulating from the edge of the world and threatening at any minute to wash the tranquil fields with night. Yet rich as was this varied magnificence of nature, there was a certain calm in its opulence as if the earth in its fullness were resting on the soft October haze.

It seemed to Matilda that something of its peace came into the hearts of those who looked down upon it from the ramparts of the castle. The wistfulness faded from Beatrice's face, and even its habitual expression of pride and resolution softened as she turned to her daughter and the monk and made her excuses.

"She has taken Godfrey's death harder than I should have thought," said Alberic when she had disappeared into the capped tower in the corner of the battlements. Then as he saw Matilda hesitate, he hastened to add, "Not, you know, that I ever doubted her love for Godfrey. But—after all, he died in his bed with the Sacraments, not cut off suddenly like your father."

Matilda was grateful to Alberic, but she only replied as if thinking aloud to herself: "I have often thought of it. I have heard old friends and relatives like the Empress Agnes say that after my father's death, my mother grew hard. She must have been frightened. I was only five, you know. It seemed to me then as if she drew away from me so that it was harder for me to reach her with anything I said. But this is different. She did not weep for Godfrey's death as she did for my father's. But she has been very gentle. I heard Arduino telling Ermengarde the other day that he wished she would scold him the way she used to. He would feel better, he said."

"Of course, she is older, nearly six years older now than when I last saw her."

"No, it is not age; not that. It is like a fire dying down a little in the ashes. It is there still, but it does not burn so bright."

"We must all come to it in our day," he said, somewhat abstractedly.

"I have been thinking of that, too. And if it were just oneself, however great one had been, it would not seem much to look over the autumn fields and not know whether or not anything of one should see the spring."

"Did Caterina suggest that?"

Matilda smiled, "Not exactly. And yet—she has five children, Alberic. You should have seen them kneeling about her in the chapel at Mass, with her pretty fair hair. She looked like an angel with little angels about her."

The familiar teasing came into Alberic's eyes. "I don't think even five little angels would make you look like an angel, Matilda. No—I'm not being rude. Judith, perhaps, or Saint Catherine of Alexandria with her wheel—"

"At least, you will admit me into the circle of good Christians. Still it was Judith with the head of Holofernes that came first to your mind. I don't suppose that I shall ever be able to convince you, Alberic, that I am changed."

Something gentler came into the monk's face. "I don't know that I want you changed. Why should you be different?"

For a moment Matilda looked into his face uncertainly, as if trying to read it. The look of amusement about the corners of the lips, slightly pursing the thin folds of the mouth, was familiar. But there was something behind the smiling eyes, something steady and still, that puzzled her. It was not merely that the costume, the look of the man, was changed. That would have been easy to understand. It was something under the surface that had been altered, something within the man that had been laid hold on. It eluded her; yet she knew that it was this change in him that made her so anxious now that he should not misunderstand her.

"Perhaps, the word change is not quite the word for it," she tried. "It is not that the old thing is bad, but that it simply is not enough."

"You are too young, Matilda, to be weary of the world, and not of the temper, I think, to be disenchanted with it."

"I'm twenty-six, Alberic."

The monk laughed. "It is against our rule to flatter ladies. So I shall not make the proper answer to that. But even at Cluny word of you has come. The Beautiful Young Countess they used to call you, but this last year or two, it is another name that they have given you. The Great Countess, it is now."

Matilda felt her face flame suddenly. "It makes me ashamed. At least half of me!"

Alberic considered judiciously. "What I heard was nothing to be ashamed of. The friend and defender of the Pope, the friend and intercessor with the Emperor, the peacemaker and the valiant soldier, the mother of her people, the protector of her cities—"

"Don't. It sounds as if I were dead." She was laughing now.

"It is nothing to scoff at, what I have heard. Men are turning to you. They are putting something rarer than their trust in you; they are putting their hope in you. That's a great thing, Matilda."

She had sobered. "I'm afraid, Alberic. You know how you feel in a fight, when suddenly you find you are all alone by yourself in the field. You can hear your companions shouting as they come toward you, but you could be dead before they reached you."

"And so you will hide behind a husband's name?"

"No, I was not entirely fair to myself. It is only partly that. I am not afraid of death, I think. What I am afraid of is something different. I am afraid of being wrong, you know. When I come up to give an account of my stewardship, I am afraid I will be accounted the unfaithful servant."

As she talked, Alberic had sobered, too. Now there came a certain tenderness of pity into his voice as he asked wonderingly, "But what are you not doing that you should be doing? Certainly no one could accuse you of idleness or timidity."

"It isn't the not doing," she thought aloud, struggling to lay hold upon her ideas. "It's the doing the wrong thing, the being on the wrong path altogether."

"But surely you do not expect a churchman to condemn what you have been doing to serve God and the Church? At Cluny we thought of you as the proper pattern of a prince. We wished we could make the princes of France over on this Italian model."

"Don't you remember how Godfrey wondered whether he had dealt justly with me?"

"Yes, you did tell me about that afterward. But you reassured him as I remember. Didn't you mean what you said?"

"At the time. But after, especially when he lay sick, he used often to speak of it. Just before he died, he talked to Mother about it, too. He told her that only in the common ways of humanity was there any health or safety for anybody. He thought it was a mistake for me who am a woman to try to live like a man, that there was no happiness in it for me."

Again the light of amusement came into the grave face. "What did the Countess Beatrice say to that?"

"At first, she was so wrapped up in her anxiety about him that she did not hear him, but presently when he seemed to get a little better, she began to talk it over with him, and she agreed."

"The Lady Beatrice? She must be growing old, indeed."

"It was no laughing matter, Alberic. She sat there holding Godfrey's hand, and she spoke very low so that he never took his eyes from her face as she talked. It was not much that she said, but one day I heard her tell Godfrey how sorry she was. It was not two people that made a marriage but one, and alone each was less than a whole person. And two separate were less than two as one person. She wept as she said it, and you know that you do not often see my mother crying."

But Alberic's mind seemed fixed on another point. "What did Godfrey say to that?"

"He said nothing, but he just held her hand in his very tightly, and when she cried, he rubbed it gently as if his thoughts were far away, as one sometimes does with a child."

"Was it that made you send for young Godfrey?"

Matilda knew she blushed. "Partly. And partly what happened that night Godfrey died. It was getting toward morning. Once I climbed up and went out on the balcony. The stars were growing white, and it was lightening over the rim of the mountains. We had been kneeling by Godfrey's bed, with candles on either side of his pillows. He was just breathing, and that monk from Reggio who is so skilled in sickness had told us that he might go on thus for hours; so we had sent everybody away but Donizo. He was sitting at the foot with his breviary resting on the edge of the bed and a taper at his elbow."

For a moment Matilda paused. How strangely irrelevant it all seemed now even as she talked, but Alberic did not take his eyes from her face.

"When she realized he had died—it was just a light sigh, you know, Alberic—she did not say anything to either of us, but she put her head down on his hand, and she kept sobbing over and over again, 'Godfrey, please, Godfrey,' like a child crying to her father to take notice of her."

Alberic nodded. "It was then you asked young Godfrey to come down and take you?"

"Yes. I gave the messengers a letter when they started north at dawn."

"And you signed it, 'Your obedient wife'?"

"Yes, but how should you know?"

Alberic smiled. "I never knew you to do things by halves, Matilda."

She considered. "No," she said presently, "not when I knew."

For some minutes they gazed out over the fields to the mountains. The deep quiet of the half hour just before twilight had settled down about them. It seemed to Matilda then as if the whole world were too still a place to disturb with words. Only the voice of a dove in the eaves of a grange a little way below the castle broke the silence about them.

"You will put your hands in his, and you will promise in all things to obey him as your liege lord?"

She nodded.

"I hope you will be very happy, Matilda."

She smiled her thanks for his understanding. "I was visiting Caterina this last month, over at her castle at Parma. With her children and her household and her lord, she was busy from dawn to dusk, and yet she seemed always so calm and happy and even undisturbed with all the people coming and going about her as she sat in the hall there. She used to seem a silly girl, you remember, Alberic?"

"Yes, I remember. She tried to kiss me once when we were all playing at bowls."

Matilda laughed. "You got so red, Alberic. We all roared, and then you were angry. You wouldn't know her now. All her curls are hidden behind her veil, and she sits proudly in her chair by the hearth, and she orders all the affairs of the castle like a queen. You should have seen her with her little son on her knee. She was holding his grandfather's great sword in the other hand, and she was telling him how the Emperor gave it to him for holding the way open so that he could come down to Rome and take his crown at Saint Peter's."

Again Alberic smiled, and he sat down on the edge of the parapet nearer to her, with his sandaled feet thrust straight before him.

"But it was at our cousin Piero's wedding feast at Mantua that I liked her best of all. The way she looked at her husband as they sat down at table, the way she listened to him when he spoke, the way she looked up at him, when he looked at her as others were talking. It said so plainly that they were one—together before the whole world, as if they would front eternity together, like that."

Again Alberic smiled a little wryly. "Do you think that is any way to talk to a monk, Matilda?"

And the quick pity came to her heart to reproach her with her stupidity. "Oh, Alberic, I am so sorry."

"I was only teasing you. You do not think, Matilda, that I gave all these things up without thinking what they were, do you?"

But the pity deepened with her self-reproach. "It is cruel of me to remind you—"

"Of what I know I can do without? You mustn't pity me too much, Matilda. For I am not alone. There is the rule of life I have chosen, and the fellowship of my brethren. They encompass me round, even when I am here, away from them."

A literal simplicity had come into the usually debonair voice of Alberic, and something of awe to warm it.

"I know," she said gently. And then before he could answer, there came from the deepening blue before them the faint, far note of a horn, borne like the silk of the milkweed pod on the evening air. Nearer to them came an answering note, rising sweet and triumphant in its greeting.

Matilda slid down from her seat on the parapet. "It is Godfrey."

Even as she spoke, the horns rose again in a flourish.

"Let us go down to meet them." She gathered her mantle about her, and as she tried to clasp it again at the throat, her hands trembled so that she gave up the effort and wrapped the heavy folds tightly about her.

"God bless you both," said Alberic, offering her his hand to go down the stairs.

"Thank you." As she took Alberic's hand, she was astonished to find it so warm.

CHAPTER II

MATILDA laid her head comfortably against the edge of the marble rail before her and drew her furred mantle a little closer about her neck. And then the warm content that had come so often these last weeks rose gently about her. She tried to collect her thoughts, to offer her thanks for the Communion she had just received, for the pleasant comfort of these winter months now nearly past, for the strange new hope of these last weeks, for the peace and amity of her world—but her mind seemed too lazy. It reached for all these ideas in a casual fashion like the water of a brook reaching for twigs on the shallows at its edge, lapping at them aimlessly without force enough to sweep them into its quiet current. There was thankfulness in her heart beyond all question, but it was a diffused warmth of content rather than any liveliness of affection or gratitude. Her conscience reproached her faintly, and she tried to force her thoughts into the well-worn channels of an old prayer of thanksgiving, but even the familiar words seemed to slip aimlessly from her grasp.

And yet underneath this lethargy of the busy mind something was awake in her consciousness, deep below all the groping of her will. She heard the soft sliding of the sandaled feet of the monks over the stone pavement as they moved in procession from the altar rail to their stalls on either side of the choir. For a moment abandoning the effort at concentration, she opened her eyes. And though she did not raise her head, she saw the light from the chapel windows break and whiten again at rhythmic intervals, as the slowly moving line of dark figures passed between her and the wall. Some compulsion in that rhythm laid hold upon her and seized her fugitive attention in its own firm pattern. It swept her out from her comfortable lassitude, and yet it seemed, in another way, merely the projection of her own repose. With a sense of deeper implication she yielded to its power, and it seemed as if the dimly groped-for prayer had at last found its utterance.

From outside the stone walls came the roaring of the wind, made gentle by the muffling of their strength. It was cold in the chapel, and Matilda pulled the fur-lined mantle closer, but neither the chill bleakness of the wind nor the surrounding cold of the early morning air could reach that warm comfort deep within her own spirit. It seemed to her that all the days of her life lay before her in a spacious certitude, and her heart rejoiced in them. Last night she had lain awake in the darkness in the guest chamber of the abbey, listening to the even breathing of her husband asleep at her side. Outside, the winter wind rose in a great roar and rattled at the shutters above her head in the darkness, and the night cold lay heavy on her face, but she lay content and wondered how she had ever feared the dark and the night. For the warmth of Godfrey's body held her close, and the sense of his strength wrapped her about in an almost physical security. Gently, so as not to disturb him, she laid her hand on his body and mused how the slightest pressure would wake that companioning consciousness to fence her from the terror of the night. Luxuriously, she had lain there thinking of all the terrors she had ever known as a child, of all the anxieties she had ever watched with as a woman, and found them ever more incredible in this perfection of security.

The soft sound of the passing feet had ceased, and the pale light of the chapel lay about her, unbroken. The regular breathing of Godfrey roused her, and she lifted her head and almost mechanically crossed herself. Then she turned to Godfrey. He had fallen asleep. For a moment she waited; then seeing that a couple of the men of their household had come up to where they knelt in the middle of the chancel and stood now respectfully waiting for their master to rise, she touched his shoulder gently.

The sleeper stirred and shook off her light touch.

Then he raised his head. "What the devil?" he began. Matilda's hand fell.

She smiled. For a moment he gazed blankly at her. Then he shut his mouth and nodded with that brisk efficiency characteristic of him. Gathering his heavy green cloak about him, he stumbled to his feet, and without stopping to kneel before the altar, he stalked quickly to the door of the chapel. Matilda strode after him.

At the door Alberic was waiting for them. He had taken off his vestments, and he had pulled his cowl over his head.

"The Abbot awaits you at breakfast, my lord," he said with a bow.

Godfrey nodded, and then as an afterthought he added, "We shall ride right after breakfast. Have the horses ready."

Without more ado he strode down the arcaded walk to the Abbot's house. Matilda stood for a moment looking after him, watching, fascinated, how the long legs carried the hunched body over the flags and the slight hitching of one shoulder as he walked punctuated the almost arrogant confidence of his gait. So seen, like some gigantic spider threading the long passage of the arcade, he looked for once as strong and as proud of his strength as Matilda knew him to be. Something of his pride infected her, too, as she turned to Alberic, standing before her with his hands folded in the deep sleeves of his habit.

"Thank you, Alberic," she said gently.

There was nothing meek in the flash of the eye he raised to hers.

"I thought you were going to stay the day with us—with the Abbot," he corrected.

Matilda's lips relaxed at the correction, but she hastened to answer in all simplicity, "My lord has changed his mind."

Alberic caught his breath. "How long is this farce going to go on, Matilda?" The steadiness of the voice, the sharp insistence of the inflection belied the excitement of his breathing. Matilda gazed at him for a minute without saying anything, looking at him, she knew, and yet not entirely seeing him.

"What do you—" she began, and then she broke off. "Alberic! You forget your habit and my—" A flash of delicacy made her pause.

Alberic laughed unpleasantly, but there was no trace of bitterness in his voice as he protested, "Don't misunderstand me for God's sake, Matilda. It is of you and Godfrey that I am thinking, and for the present of you alone."

Matilda started and instinctively let her mantle, tight clutched in her excitement, fall more lightly from her body. But Alberic seemed unaware of the gesture as he drove on: "It is 'my lord this' and 'my lord that,' and 'Yes, my lord,' and 'My lord, as you will.' It is the meek and obedient wife of a Lenten preacher's homily."

Matilda laughed with sheer relief. "Are you quarreling with the preacher or the exemplar? It is always safer in things ecclesiastical to do the latter, I fancy. Far be it from me, however, to admonish Cluny."

But she saw that he was not to be drawn from his purpose, whatever it might be.

"Matilda, do you really think that all your life you are going to think just what Godfrey thinks, want just what he wants, do just what he does?"

She sobered. "I think that I am going in all things to be a true and obedient wife, as I promised when I took Godfrey for my husband; at least I am going to try to," she added a bit lamely under some inexplicable impulse of honesty that made her cheeks burn with mortification as soon as she had said the words.

There was a certain relief in Alberic's voice as he spoke again, but a certain indignation, too. "Do you think it fair to Godfrey?"

"Fair?" Matilda repeated the word in unfeigned astonishment. "What do you mean?"

"This." Alberic planted his feet firmly apart, stretching his frock as he did so. "You have given Godfrey to think in these months that he is the master, that all he has to do is to say what he wants, and so far as you are concerned, it will be done."

"What else would you have me do? Surely you would not give over the first year of marriage to the disagreements and the quarrels which are vulgarly supposed to chart its latter end?" A note of passion came into her voice, "I could not respect myself, I could not bear it."

"I am not talking about quarrels or disagreements, Matilda, or the vulgar jests on marriage or anything else. What I am talking about is this: you are a human being, with your own mind and your own judgment and your own standards and your own decisions, more than most women, more even, I think, than most men. Every human being has certain responsibilities. You have been trained to take those responsibilities seriously. You can't abdicate suddenly like this."

Matilda shivered. It was cold here in the porch of the abbey church.

"I have sworn to obey my husband," she answered doggedly. "Why, Alberic, should you bring up my old willful self?"

Something gentler and tenderer came into his voice as if in answer to her appeal. "Matilda, willfulness is one thing; integrity is another. The first you should give up. But the second? Matilda, you know you couldn't if you wanted to. That is why I think you are being unfair to Godfrey. You are making him sure of something he should not be sure of—your continued submissiveness. There is no use in your pretending that you will always want to do his will. You know you won't."

Perhaps it was the cold, perhaps it was the lassitude that so often came upon her these days, but Matilda suddenly felt very tired. "Do you think I am likely to do so badly as all that, Alberic?"

But he was not to be cajoled. "That isn't what I am talking about. It is simply facing the facts and giving Godfrey a chance to face the facts. This way, you are lulling him asleep in a fool's paradise, and you are giving pledges that you should know you will never be able to redeem."

"Perhaps, then, if the future is to be so stormy, he will be grateful to remember this year of peace and amity." There was mockery in her voice, she knew. Impulsively, she put her hand out to him.

But somebody had come up behind her, with the heavy fall of metal on the stone flagging startling her into attention.

"My lady"—it was Arduino della Palude—"my lord begs you to attend him in the Abbot's chamber. He waits breakfast for you." Arduino spoke quickly, somewhat explosively. He is growing short of breath, thought Matilda, but that is not the whole reason for this confusion. She looked sharply at him, and as she looked, the terracotta red of his face deepened.

"Thank you, Alberic," she began as coldly as she could.

Arduino took her sleeve. "I'm sorry, Matilda, but Godfrey the Young will not be kept waiting."

Again the color seemed to deepen. "What did he say—what were his words?" she asked on a sudden impulse.

Arduino shook his head. "It was no way to speak; I'd be ashamed. Don't ask me to, Matilda."

In a swift glance Matilda saw Alberic's lips purse as if he would whistle, but no sound came. Gathering up her mantle on one arm, she gave her free hand to Arduino and without looking again at her old friend, she almost ran down the passage to the Abbot's house.

Alberic was in the crowd of monks who stood in the arched gateway of the Abbot's house to see them take their leave. But he did not look up once, even when Matilda raised her voice in farewell. She longed to speak to him, to call his name at least, before she left the courtyard, but she felt her husband's eyes upon her, restless and impatient as if he suddenly found himself obliged to pay attention to something he would have preferred to disregard. The Abbot raised his hand in blessing, and she murmured something conventional about the hospitality the house had shown them. The other monks smiled, but Alberic never took his eyes from the cobblestones.

Godfrey had ridden ahead, and now Matilda lightly touched the rowels of her spurs to the sides of her horse. With the sudden motion her veil flew out, and the wind smote her face and throat. Struggling to gather her veil about her head, she did not notice that her husband had stopped his horse and was waiting for her by the side of the road.

"It is no weather for a woman to be out in," he grumbled, holding her horse until she had caught her veil firmly about her face with a silver brooch.

"Oh, I like it," she said gently, smiling down at him, yet with a little upward toss of the head as if after all she were looking up at him. "If I had one of those hoods I used to ride in when I was a girl, I should not mind even this wind. But a veil is not so easy to manage."

"A married woman should be decently at home," he went on, disregarding the smile.

"Home is where my lord is," she retorted gayly.

"Poetry!" He was indignant now.

"My lord!" She knew, even as she spoke, that shock had crept into the surprise of her cry. And she knew at once that it was a mistake. Godfrey's face flushed. He was ashamed, and he would in very self-respect seek to justify himself.

"Moreover," he went on, viciously jabbing his spurs into his horse, yet holding it in with a tight rein, "I won't have those lily-livered, skulking monks setting my wife to wheedle favors from me that they haven't courage to come and ask for like men."

"Favors?" There was no need of her feigning the surprise of that exclamation.

"What else was the fellow holding you for after Mass and keeping me waiting with that silly la-de-da of Arduino and those other old flunkies of yours?"

He knows he is being rude, thought Matilda, and to justify himself he will be even ruder.

"He was not asking me for anything, Godfrey, believe me, please. He would know better than to try to influence you that way."

The flattery told, and, given as it was without love but to make peace, it sickened her. Nor could she bear to have him see her shame. As her head dropped, her veil fell about her face. She made no effort to lift it.

"Matilda, my love, do not cry. It is all right." There was real concern in his voice, and for a moment affection strove with pride. She thought of what Caterina, her cousin, had said when once in their girlhood, Matilda had rebuked her for her cowardly yielding to tears. "Don't be silly, Matilda. Crying saves a girl a lot of trouble."

Godfrey leaned over and put his arm about her tenderly, and without thinking she yielded to its pressure.

"There, my dear. Now there is some business I must talk to Arduino about. I will ride ahead, but you take your time. Here, you," to one of the men-at-arms, riding a little behind them at a respectful distance, "keep close to your lady and see that her horse behaves."

As Godfrey rode on, the soldier came up at arm's length behind her and waited for her to start. She looked him over quickly. A dull, impassive country lout—there was no need for her to say anything to cover up her embarrassment.

So struggling to recover her composure, she looked about her. There was not much sign of spring in the red-brown earth of the plowed fields, or in the thin, dirty straw fringing the narrow strip between the fields and the road. Here and there the swelling hills were still veined with streaks of ice. The buds on the trees were a little larger where they netted the cool blue of the sky, but there was no trace as yet of the red of spring in their close-fisted blackness. Only the rooks were calling in the gray tops of the trees.

It was a strangely eloquent country for all its winter bareness, with an inescapable vivacity in the rolling of the plow-ribbed hills and in the wind-tossing of the treetops in the thickets that filled the gullies between. In the distance the sharp sides of the mountains were still washed with snow, contrasting oddly with the deep color of the bare earth and the faint, thin blue of the sky.

"It is a good color, the color of the earth," she said aloud. The man-at-arms was staring with open mouth when she looked behind to see if he had heard.

But to herself she said, "This is really what the earth is like—this dull red-brown against a thin sky in the flat light of mid-day. No matter how exquisite it is in spring nor how magnificent in autumn, this is really what it is like, naked and unadorned." For a moment, it seemed to her that she had been asleep and had just awakened. And all that her eyes looked upon seemed as cold and cheerless as the world of the dawn always seems after the warm, vague intimacy of the world of sleep. Already her mind was blinking. It was mid-Lent, three weeks still to Easter. There was no reason why it should not still look like winter.

"For God so loved the world"—from nowhere came the lines of Saint John into her mind as if a voice from without had spoken them in their complete irrelevance—"as to give His only begotten Son."

Over and over again the line repeated itself in her consciousness, driving all other thoughts before it, focusing her sense of awareness until presently she knew herself the cool, steady woman she had been struggling to recover this last half hour.

"There is no reason why we should hurry so," she said to the man-at-arms spurring his horse behind her. And to herself she said, "After all there is something to this raw, insistent earth of March. It will bring forth in its due season, and it will bear patiently till then."

CHAPTER III

As they rode out of the pass through the hills below Bianello on the third day, it seemed to Matilda that she was looking upon her home as she never had before in all these years she had known it. Not that there was anything new or startling in its aspect. She had known its fierceness since those first childish days when she and her dead brother had coaxed to be allowed to ride with the men on hunting expeditions. There was one time in particular that came to her mind now with the tricksy irrelevance of all associations. It was late in the afternoon, and she and her brother on their small mountain ponies were lagging a little behind the others. As they rode out of the hills at much the same point where she now paused, they suddenly saw the height of Canossa silhouetted against the southwestern sky—its steep crags, its sudden clumps of trees and shrubs clinging perilously to the bare shale, its gaunt, turreted fortress at the top, all black and fiercely solid against the boiling gold and flame of the clouds.

"Look, it is a magician's castle!" she had cried to her brother.

They had stopped there and gazed upon it in awe. Then something had stirred in her mind, and she had clutched her brother by the sleeve.

"There is a terrible ogre lives there, and he is waiting to devour us," she whispered. As they looked, the first of the riders in the hunting company came out on the edge of the path against the sky, men and horses sharply marked out in ebony against the brilliant color. For a moment the little black wooden figures moved perceptibly on their high perch; then they suddenly disappeared, swallowed up in the gulf of blackness around a crag.

"Look," she shouted, in her excitement disregarding the whimpering of the little boy, "the ogre has opened his mouth, and he is swallowing them up. No," as the rising wind blew the clouds into deep swirls of flame, "it is hell mouth, and the devils are sucking in—" But her little brother was howling now, and Ermengarde, her face flushed with indignation, was alternately coaxing the little boy out of his terror and predicting an appalling future for girls who frightened their brothers with such lies.

There had been an investigation that night in her mother's chamber.

"But I saw it," Matilda had insisted.

"But you found all the men at supper, didn't you? The same ones that you thought had ridden down into hell mouth?" Matilda considered. The tone of reasonableness in her mother's voice was unanswerable. And her clear blue eyes had held her daughter's uncomfortably long.

"Yes," Matilda had admitted. And then as if a fresh access of stubbornness had laid hold upon her, she added, "but I saw the other too."

She was in disgrace that next day. Her brother had teased and teased to have her let out into the courtyard to play, but her mother had been unmoved by all entreaties. And then as the sun went down on that miserable day, the first report reached the castle of the tragedy that had befallen. As the whispers ran through the great hall, all work stopped, and men and maids clung together over a table, in a corner of the dais, in the doorways, gabbling over and over the few details that had drifted in from the forest. One Matilda was never to forget. Indeed, few of any of the things she had actually seen happen in her life had ever been half as vivid. It was the singing of the nameless arrow as it sped through the air, straight to its mark in her father's breast. Even the bringing-in of her father's body on a bier of pine boughs with the sun-distilled fragrance of the needles about it, and the terribly limp falling-down of one arm as the bearers stumbled at the threshold, was less vivid in her memory than that sound of death singing blithely through the unsuspecting quietness of the forest.

Even now she found herself wondering afresh, "These things I have seen, and these others, too?"

A loud, harsh voice at her side broke into her thoughts: "Here, fool, take the bridle of your lady's horse. I told you to look after her, and here I find her freezing on the drawbridge of her own castle. By heaven, if I find you loafing again, I'll have you whipped out the castle gate."

"But, Godfrey, it is not the man's fault; I myself—"

"His fault! He ought to know you were tired out with the ride from that damned monastery."

Before she could control her indignation, Matilda had protested, "Godfrey, I have ridden the whole length and breadth of these Tuscan lands. Do you think I'd be tired from a two or three days' ride?"

"I don't care what you have done in the past. You are not going to carry my son the whole length and breadth of Italy—"

Godfrey stopped. For a moment Matilda was too angry to notice that the harsh voice had ceased. Then her eyes followed her husband's. Behind them rose a squall of yells and jeers and screams. It looked as if half their retinue were piled on top of one another in a heap, struggling for some invisible prize at the bottom of the pile.

"A mob of apprentices in a village square. Here, you rogues!" Putting spur to his horse, Godfrey galloped forward. For a moment the heap staggered in kicking legs and thrashing arms. Then it seemed to explode.

A ragged creature was running toward Godfrey, beating the air with out-stretched arms, and half-sobbing, half-shrieking, "For the love of God, gracious lord!"

Several of the men-at-arms had started toward him, but seeing Godfrey in the path, they paused, swaying unsteadily on their buskined feet. The stranger seized the foreleg of Godfrey's horse grotesquely by the hock, and the astonished animal plunged, nearly throwing the rider to the ground. The men-at-arms roared with laughter but sobered almost immediately at the white fury on their lord's face.

"He is only a peddler," said Matilda, putting her hand on the neck of the frightened horse and rubbing it softly. The animal steadied, and the color oozed back into the rider's face.

"Lady, mercy!" cried the man on the ground, groveling from Godfrey's horse to Matilda's.

"Where do you come from?" she asked, hearing with one ear the loud voice of Godfrey cursing his followers to the castle path.

"I am a Greek from Constantinople, my lady," answered the man, scrambling with agility to his feet and bowing low.

"That is a long way to come to these barren hills," said Matilda.

The white teeth of the man gleamed in his dark face, and he raised his voice more confidently. "Ah, madonna, but I heard there was a great lord here at Canossa, with gold to buy spices and knives and things that a lord needs."

Godfrey seemed not to have heard, but Matilda noticed that his harsh voice was quite steady now. When all his company were in the path, he turned to his wife and nodded to her.

Then as if from an afterthought, he spoke to the man waiting behind her. "Help this fellow with his horse."

"To the castle, my lord?"

Godfrey raised his riding whip, but the man had ducked, and now he rode after the peddler racing up the hill slope.

"It will be entertainment for you women at any rate," grumbled Godfrey as he carefully guided his wife's horse into the path.

"The poor man was so frightened it was funny to see the way he clung to your horse," said Matilda, forcing a little laugh.

She felt Godfrey's suspicious look on her face for a moment, and then he spoke quite easily for all his grumbling, "Those ruffians will never keep any order if your eyes aren't on them every minute."

"From Constantinople!" said Matilda, as the horses slackened their pace for the climb to the castle. "That will mean spices and silks and steel. There is really no other place in the land for him to come, Godfrey, but to us."

Her husband made no answer, but as they clattered over the drawbridge into the castle yard, he called at the top of his voice, "Here, you women! Look to your mistress. She is tired." Matilda made no protest when he caught her in his arms as she slipped from her horse. Looking up into his face, she saw the hard lines of his mouth soften a little.

Something of the morning's content came back to her when she found herself in the great chair by the fire, with one of her maids chafing her feet and another kneeling before the huge logs, with wine in a copper cup.

For Godfrey had risen from the table where he was drinking red Rhenish wine with some of his men and come over to her with a little silver flask in his hand. "It is Chablis from the wine the Abbot of Cluny sent down last Michaelmas. It will warm you faster than these thin Italian wines." And he had stood at her side while she sipped the flinty, straw-colored wine, and when she coughed a little, he had patted her shoulder. Then he went back to the opposite side of the hearth and gave himself up in earnest to his drinking.

After the rush of their arrival, the great hall seemed quiet now with the smoke from the fire in the center coiling lazily in the thin light from the louver far above the rafters. Behind her some of the house serfs were laying planks on trestles, now and then striking a ring from the armor on the walls as they miscalculated the distance.

The girl at her feet rose and stood waiting.

"Thank you, Maria. I am quite warm now." The girl's eyes flashed with pleasure, and she lingered, holding her mistress' heavy riding shoes stiffly thrust out before her. Again, Matilda felt the drowsiness that had overcome her at Mass rise about her. She would like to sleep, but the girl seemed to be waiting for a chance to talk.

"Yes, Maria."

"The Greek would like to show you his wares."

"But there is nothing I want, I am sure. Let the maids take him into the kitchen and pick out ribbons. And if any of the men needs a knife, let him have it."

The girl smiled. "But your ladyship forgets. There will be spices needed for the christening feast, and perhaps a little silk for a cap."

Even as Matilda nodded, the Greek was opening a canvas pack on the floor at her feet.

"These are things for a lady," he bustled importantly. "The ribbons and knives we'll keep for the kitchen. Here we are in the very heart of the pack, the heart of the treasure. Ginger fit for a queen. Take a piece of that, my lady, and it will warm your stomach more than all the wines of Sicily. Cinnamon. Sugar." He rose and opened carefully a small latten box. "Put this into your warm wine, and you will feel like our mother Eve before she ate the apple." He held a couple of the gray-brown grains on his forefinger, and all the women laughed with anticipation and envy.

"Nard, ginger, cloves, cumin, mace," the steward checked over the little packets of roots and herbs tied up in squares of linen and laid them in the spice chest.

"So far as looks go, you might gather up the like of that box in any corner of the castle yard on an autumn day," laughed one of the men from the table where Godfrey was still sitting, drinking from a huge silver-gilt cup.

The girl Maria sniffed delightedly at the chest as she held it up to her mistress for her inspection. "And yet it costs so much gold that only a great lord could pay for it," her voice rose proudly.

"Here," called Godfrey, loosening the string of his purse and handing a gold coin to the waiting steward.

"It is too much," said the steward, bowing gravely.

"It is my magnanimity and not your baseness that pays," retorted Godfrey.

The silence that followed roused Matilda from her lethargy. All around in the crowded hall men and women seemed to be waiting. The lean face of the steward showed no sign of emotion but a tightening of the lips as he passed the coin to the Greek. There was a glint of mockery in the latter's eyes as he took it with a respectful enough obeisance.

"Antonio," said Matilda quietly, feeling the eyes of the household drawing to her. "Here is the key of the spice chest. You take charge of it."

The old steward, who had been the servant of her father, said nothing as he came and took the homely pledge of her trust, but she noticed that his hand shook a little as he fastened it to the chain about his neck. A low hum of comment rose about the group.

"Are spices the only wares you have, peddler?" asked Godfrey, calling loudly from his side of the fire.

"No, my lord. I have cloths of Damascus and silks from the Copts of Tinnis and embroideries and cloth of gold from Constantinople. Here," said the Greek, undoing a linen bundle, "is a piece of the cloth of gold which the Empress herself chose for a robe when her last son was born."

With the quick flourish of the born actor and showman, the Greek opened the packet of soiled linen and flung into the arms of Maria and another maid what at first seemed like a shower of gold. There was a loud outcry of wonder from all the women, and even the men on the opposite side of the open hearth looked up from their cups. It was a long tissue of gold, with an intricate pattern of arabesque woven in the very fabric like a brocade. In the half light of the hall the glittering web caught the diluted sunlight from the slender, deeply recessed windows high in the sandstone walls and the thin flames of the firelight and tossed their radiance in its shimmering folds. It seemed to Matilda as if for a moment a river of exquisite light had been caught in the arms of her maidens. She put out her hand for it, and the Greek laid the end of it across her knees.

"The Empress had a robe made of it for the christening of her son. I saw her stand in it in the baptistery of Santa Sophia," said the Greek, with the facility of his profession.

"A dress of this?" asked Matilda incredulously, lifting the material to her arm so that it fell along her dark traveling robe in a cascade of light.

Maria clapped her hands in delight. "Would not our lady look beautiful in this gold?"

The Greek agreed enthusiastically. "Not even the Empress would look half so splendid."

As she looked about her, enchanted with the strange beauty of the gold brocade and pleased with the enthusiasm of her household, Matilda's eyes for a moment rose to the wall before her, naked stone, dark with the soot of countless fires on the great open hearth, its only ornament the heavy swords and axes and shields and helmets of her ancestors, rusting a little now in their iron holders. Then they fell to the pavement at her feet, gray stone, dirty with the passing of many feet and white wood ashes from the hearth and straw from the stables and the yard. The wooden trestles, the heavy oak stools and settles, the great chests by the walls, the roughly wrought iron sconces and firedogs, the men's riding cloaks, worn and mud-stained, heaped in a pile on the benches, the pikes and swords stacked against the walls, the knives gleaming on the rough table, the pewter cups, the leathern flagons of Rhenish wine—in this milieu the thought of the golden dress of the Empress made Matilda laugh at the sheer absurdity of the idea.

"No, that is not for a Tuscan lady here in our hills. For the ladies of Constantinople in marble halls and rose gardens, perhaps." Matilda shook her head wistfully. Through some chance trick of the imagination the ruins of Lucca came to her mind. Perhaps such fabrics had moved among those marbles when they stood in their gleaming place along the river bank. Again there came to her the overpowering ache of the vanished beauty of the world.

And then the truculent voice of Godfrey from the other side of the fire broke into her reverie, "The wife of the lord of Lorraine and Tuscany can have such stuff as well as the Greeks in Constantinople. Here, peddler."

The gold coin rang softly on the pavement, and the Greek knelt down with an obeisance to the giver. There was a fresh exclamation of wonder from all the women pressed about their mistress.

"Do you not wish you were a lady?" whispered the light-tongued Maria, audibly.

"Hush, that is sinful," said an older woman. The other women began to talk quickly, praising the munificence of the Lord Godfrey. But Matilda had risen, pushing the golden fabric from her into the hands of her maids.

"Thank you, my lord, but it would be wicked for me to wear so beautiful a thing and soil it with common use. I will give it for a gift to the altar, for a gift from us both."

The altar!" Godfrey banged his cup upon the table. "I bought that for my wife to wear, not for some damned monks to boast about and show off."

Matilda felt the blood rise in her face, but she said nothing, looking steadily at her husband. Then she noticed how tightly his fingers were gripping the ivory foot of his cup, the knuckles white as the freshly carved bone.

That night after supper, when Matilda was laying the gold cloth away in the chest that held the richest robes of her mother and herself, Godfrey chanced to be near.

"I gave it to you. Do as you like with it," he said, shame softening the surliness of his voice.

For a moment Matilda thought. Then she took his hand. "It really would be sin for me to wear so rich a thing for a woman's vanity. I will tell you, my lord, what I will do. I will give it to the Florentines for the feast of their San Giovanni. They can lay it on the new altar they have built, for a gift from us both." Her voice rose coaxingly.

"As you like," he said. "You women are always thinking of the Church."

"It will be to your honor and the glory of God," she added. With a good-humored laugh he pulled his hand away and went over to the fire to take another cup of wine from the table before it.

CHAPTER IV

"YOU have not sat down once since early dawn," scolded Ermengarde. "It is a sin for a woman with child to spend herself so."

Matilda laughed. "But I haven't been tired. And nobody knows when this fine weather will end. Ermengarde, tell the men to take that foul straw from the hall and burn it out by the cow sheds where the wind will bear the stench away. We have smelled it long enough."

The girl Maria whispered to her mistress, "That is why Ermengarde wants you to rest, I think. So long as you work so, everybody else must hustle."

"But there is so much to do, Maria. Everything is so dirty after the winter you would think you were in a stable rather than a castle. Oh, those skins on the chests. Tell the men when they've got that heap of straw out of the doorway to take the skins and spread them on the south wall in the sun. That white bearskin the Emperor gave my father has fleas in it."

Then Matilda caught sight of her mother sitting in the middle of the courtyard in a low chair by the well, sitting very tall and straight with the sun bright on her white veil and black mantle. She held a distaff in her hand with some very fine thread between her fingers, but at the moment she was doing nothing, only watching the maids tussling with dripping copper pails at the wellhead, and the men carrying out the heavy winter gear of blankets and feather beds and skins to bake in the warm April sunshine. A look of amusement came into her fresh, clear face as her eyes met her daughter's.

"Ermengarde is a little noisy, as usual, but, as usual, she has some reason.

Come over here and rest with me for a moment. When your hours grow fewer, you learn to treat them better."

She pulled a stool beside her out from the folds of her dress so that there would be room for the ample sweep of her daughter's gown. Half to humor her mother, Matilda sat down and for the first time that day took stock of the busy scene. It was the same old courtyard in which they had walked all winter, but the wet cobblestones glistened in the sunlight, and there was a tender down of new green on the yellowish-gray stones of the surrounding walls. There was something winelike in the air, still fresh with the snow of the distant hills, yet warm and glowing after the chill dankness of the hall. The smell of the newly plowed earth came up to them from the fields below, and the sharp, acrid tang of the burning straw from the stable end of the castle.

"I was looking at your herb garden this morning," said Beatrice. "You had better put a couple of the men to work in it these next days. The earth still looks pretty dry. And the quinces on the south wall need pruning."

"Why do you say my garden? Even if you did insist on spending the winter in Mantua, this is still your home, Mother."

Beatrice patted her shoulder. "You can't have two masters at once, still less two mistresses, child. You're enjoying your housekeeping, aren't you?"

Matilda considered before answering. "Yes; it is strange after what I used to think of women's fussing, but I do. It is fun to provide for one's household, to see that things are kept in order, that all the work is done in its due season, that every man is provided for according to his need."

"Yes," said Beatrice. "There is more to it than men think."

"Sometimes," said Matilda, "I think there is more to be done with this than with men's things. Here at least when the day is over, the castle will be cleaner. And when I tend my herbs, I know that I will have them when I need them for the sick. And for these people of my household and of the village below, I can actually do something—food and clothing and comfort and teaching. But with battles and missions and counsels, it is more than one's own reach that is involved. Whether or not you can do anything depends on other people."

Beatrice shook her head. "Even this depends on whether you have peace, and whether your lord will let your order stand."

"Well, we have peace now," said Matilda, "and my lord is impatient with all this housekeeping, and has bidden me do as I like, and gone off hunting."

"God knows quiet days are to be thanked for," Beatrice agreed. "There was much talk in Mantua of trouble in Germany. Henry is impatient as usual, and willful. He will not give those proud Saxons time to get used to paying their taxes and to obeying the new laws he has given them. And he will not settle down with Bertha, his own wife, as a decent man should."

At that moment Matilda caught sight of one of her women coming from the inner courtyard. "Richilda, tell the steward not to forget the extra measure of beer for the men from Baise. It is so hot down there where they are working that those who are plowing have taken off everything but their drawers. And send them extra bread, for their ribs look thin and white after this hard winter."

"Madonna, the steward says that he is short of men. My lord took almost all the men with him this morning for the hunting."

"But I told him—" began Matilda; then quickly remembering: "Never mind. Send some of the older women to help."

Beatrice smiled. "You are fast becoming a housekeeper, for as I talk to you of great things, you sit there and think of little. And presently when your child is born, you will be able to think of a dozen things at once, and quite forget that you ever sat the whole day long with Donizo in the garden reading poetry. Such is the life of women."

"No," protested Matilda, spreading out the red folds of her gown over her sandals and folding her hands quietly in her lap. I shall never forget those days nor the poets either, for it is they who tell us what is the meaning of our lives. But it is a long way from Germany to here," and she swept the courtyard with one hand. "Even Rome seems a long way off," she added. "I was actually glad when Godfrey decided that he did not want to bother with going to Rome to Pope Alexander's Lenten meeting this year."

"Hildebrand was disappointed," said Beatrice. "He rather counted on Godfrey, you know, now that he is in Italy, to take his father's place."

"But, Mother, you know that everybody counted on you more than they did on Father Godfrey in such things."

With a pang Matilda saw that her mother winced a little, and she thought wistfully of that time when nothing that anybody could say would ruffle the composure of Beatrice of Tuscany. Nor did it seem quite fair that the wall that she had so often beaten her head against should now crumble, and pity fill the breach of broken power. But aloud she hastened to add, "For your counsel was the best in all the land." And striving to lighten her tone, she went on: "As indeed, it is now. So Godfrey and I said that Hildebrand had the best of the family for his council and should be content."

"Nonsense," said Beatrice, but there was more of her old confidence in her voice and more of her inalienable authority.

"What did they talk about?" asked Matilda, following out of the corner of her eye two of the women of the household passing through the outer gate with copper jars of beer balanced on their kerchiefed heads.

"You ask that as if it were a matter of what the gossips said at a christening feast," chided Beatrice, beginning to pluck at the twisted flax in her hand with her long fingers.

"Is there so much to choose then, woman to woman?"

"One of these days the crisis will come, Hildebrand says. Things are not as bad as they were, but men will not be forever patient with the Church."

"But I thought he said it was not the Church's fault. The last time I was in Rome he talked of the way the nobles had taken possession of the Church."

"Yes," said Beatrice wearily. "It is for what they have made of the Church that they blame her. That is why he says the Church must get free."

For months Matilda had hardly thought of Hildebrand, but now his face came before her with its old hard-bitten power, the pained lips held so firmly, the dark eyes burning so brightly out of the haggard face. It was not a beautiful face that so came to her, but now even in the busy satisfaction of the spring cleaning she found herself held by it.

"There will be some snowdrops down by the brook," she said inconsequentially, "that I will have the maids gather and put on the altar in the chapel."

"Hildebrand is not sure that Godfrey understands what it is all about," said Beatrice, as if hanging on to a point achieved only with difficulty. And then as Matilda did not answer, she went on, "Of course, he realizes that Godfrey has been busy enough with his affairs in Lorraine and in Germany. I am afraid that perhaps I kept his father so busy here in Italy that his son has to make up for it there. But it seemed the best thing to do then," she added, as if she were defending herself against her daughter's criticism.

"I am sure it was," said Matilda.

Her mother said nothing, and Matilda slipped her hand into hers.

"Do you think any husband was ever entirely satisfactory?" she asked suddenly, astonished herself at the question when the words had left her lips. She did not raise her eyes to her mother's, but she felt a slight start in the hand in her own.

"That," said her mother at last, speaking very slowly, "is a question no wise woman asks."

Matilda shook her head soberly. What a mad thing to have come into her head, and still more to have found utterance! But she only sat still. She could hear the maids splashing water on the stone floor of the hall. She could see out of the corner of an eye, around the edge of her veil, two men staggering through the gateway under great faggots of willow wands, clean and white, with the sharp freshness of newly cut wood about them. Some pigeons were picking at the thin wisps of grass in the mold between the cobblestones. A half-crushed earthworm wriggled in hideous pink nakedness at her feet. But she said nothing, though she could feel her mother's glance upon her.

There was a sharp blast on the trumpet from the tower to the right of the gateway. The maids rushed out of the hall, the faggot-bearers dropped their burden where they stood.

"No," Matilda answered the inquiry in her mother's face. "Godfrey said he would be gone the whole day." She turned to one of the faggot-bearers. "Go up to the watch and find out."

The man was soon back, stumbling down the circular staircase in the corner of the wall.

"It is Guido," he said.

"Guido?" asked Matilda.

"Guido the Bailiff, Madonna," answered the man stupidly.

"He should not return for another week," Matilda explained to her mother. "I hope nothing is wrong. They have had a hard winter up at Castellara like everybody else, and there have been rumors of trouble among the serfs. But I should have thought nothing serious."

"Hard," said Beatrice, "but nothing like sixty-two when men really hungered. They found strange flesh hidden in a wall of the grange up at Marda, and the wolves came into the street at Rubiera."

"My lady," spoke up one of the men who had come from the inner courtyard, Piero the Steward, "two weeks ago, when my lord was hunting up at Castellara, some of the serfs in the fields held up their plows as he passed."

"He said nothing to me about it," Matilda replied before she thought. And then hastily, "Did my lord listen to them, Antonio?"

"No, my lady, but he told the steward of that farm when he came out to meet him, that the ground was still hard for ploughing and to spare them for another week."

"I wish he had listened," said Matilda half to herself.

The grave professional manner of Antonio softened a little. "There is no need for worry, my lady. You know how serfs are. They are always finding fault."

"Aye, my lady," interposed one of the now numerous crowd of bystanders, pulling a dirty canvas apron down over his paunch as he spoke, "I remember in your father's day how he was passing a fellow in the road by one of his farms once. And he asked him what sort of lord he had, and the fellow said, 'Oh, an old fool in his dotage, too feeble to make his hand felt any more.' And my lord Boniface, my lady, he jumped from his horse and gave him a blow that laid him flat in the dust. With his bare fist, my lady, and he says, 'Give thanks that I am not in my prime, then, you rascal.'"

There was a roar of laughter from the company about the well, but Beatrice's face was veiled in its old look of haughty imperturbability. And Matilda wondered afresh how little pleasure she had come to take in these stories of her father's prowess. The old steward seemed to catch the mood of his mistresses, for he turned to the company and with a wave of his hand bade them return to their work. There was a scuffle and much backward-looking, for already horses' hoofs could be heard from the other side of the lowered drawbridge.

At first, Guido was loath to trouble his mistress, loath too, Matilda presently suspected, to reveal some unwisdom on the part of his lord. But the authority of Beatrice overcame his scruples.

"I had heard from the other farms and villages that there was trouble. Nothing very definite. The bailiffs would not say anything about one of their own position, and the serfs were frightened. I told my lord, you remember, that it was not wise to put a stranger as bailiff up at Castellara."

"But last year," said Matilda, "the returns from Castellara were better than from any other of the farms. My lord said that it proved what he had always said, that Lorrainers could get more out of these farms than Tuscans."

"I know," said Guido, "but these are hill farms, these valleys up among the mountains. You must not expect so much from them. I told my lord." There was,

Matilda noted, nothing of complaint or of criticism in the dry tones of Guido, only regret expressed with perfect deference.

"But what happened?"

"Well, my lady, it really goes back to what happened last fall. You see, Dietrich the Lorrainer, took from the serfs some of what they had been accustomed to consider their share of the crops. Especially, did he take wheat and hay."

"I remember," said Matilda, "I wondered that there should be so much hay as Arduino reported when he was up there hunting, but I thought no more about it."

"They were very angry," said Guido. "They might have laid in a larger store of leaves even then, but they would not. And when some of the cattle began to die this winter before there was any grass, Dietrich blamed them. He flogged some of the young men whose duty it was to look after the cattle. He threatened to kill anyone who should let any more cattle die. They were very short of bread then, but he would not let them have any of the cattle that were dead, for meat. There were other things, but that was the main."

"It was a bad year to begin with," said Beatrice. "Nowhere were the crops anything like normal."

"The priest at Rubiera reported that the serfs believed that Dietrich had taken the oil and the wine that should have been theirs and sold it to some merchants for silver to hoard for himself. But the wine of Castellara has always been pretty coarse; so I cannot imagine merchants paying silver for it. On the other hand, he may have threatened them with the power of his lord, and having been in more disturbed parts of the world, they may have believed him."

"That would be a scandal for us," said Beatrice gravely.

"But what happened?" asked Matilda.

For a moment Guido hesitated. "Somebody," he said with emphasis, "set fire to Dietrich's hut back of the farm house, and the next morning he was found burned beyond recognition in the ashes."

"It may have been an accident," suggested Matilda hopelessly.

"You know the sort of hut, my lady—wattles and thatch. Nobody would take any chance. And it would be perfectly simple to get out if a man were alive. Then, too, they did not send to Paverna for the priest, as they might well have, to give him Christian burial. They simply buried him in the softened earth beneath the house. They said they were frightened."

"What do the serfs at Paverna say happened?" asked Beatrice.

For the first time the grave face of the steward relaxed. "They say nothing to their priest or to the bailiff or to me, but I met a peddler on the road, and he said that the men who buried the steward first took a blackened knife from his back, and that night two of them took it up to the tarn in the hills above and threw it in there. Nobody knows the bottom of that pool, you remember."

"Did the peddler say which ones they were?" asked Beatrice.

Guido shrugged his shoulders. "He crossed himself and said he slept too often alone on the road to take any chance of being wakened by the ghosts of men he had helped to hang. There is nothing to be found out that way. Somebody might tell if they became too desperate for hunger, but they all know that whoever did such a thing would have too many friends alive. And who would fuss about a serf found with a knife in his back?"

"It is a terrible thing to kill one's lord's agent," added Guido piously.

Matilda thought of the little village with the clay and wattle huts and the women who had lain down on the straw at sunset all through that winter with the cold, and the hunger, and the long dark to lie awake and wonder and fear. Some of them, too, would be carrying children.

"They must be very short of food now," she said.

"They are starving," responded Guido briefly.

"I will not say that our people have always been treated as I would wish," said Beatrice. "God knows, there are very few women who would be able to say that in this hard world. But nobody has ever starved on our lands that I have known of."

"They deserve to starve, these parricides and traitors," said Guido with an eye on his mistress.

Matilda rose. "Come, Guido. We can at least send a man to tell the men at Paverna to send bread over to Castellara."

Guido looked at Beatrice and then at Matilda. He cleared his throat.

"Perhaps, my lady, we should wait till my lord comes home tonight?"

"But of course, he will want to—" she began indignantly. Then she stopped, and a sick feeling of helplessness came over her, and she sat down. "We will wait till he comes. Go in and get some food and some wine yourself, Guido." For a moment the man stood and looked at her. Then he went through the inner gateway very slowly, and as he went, Matilda heard the pattering of footsteps and the whispering of voices round the corner of the hall.

"But Godfrey will want to send them food," she protested to the air.

It was the cool voice of Beatrice that came to her rescue. "The sun is not so hot now. Why don't you take a couple of your maids and go down for those flowers you spoke of? The ride will do you good."

Matilda had just finished arranging the brook flowers in two little clay bowls on the altar in the chapel when the horn sounded again from the gateway. Then she knew that for a few minutes she had forgotten. Perhaps it was that respite that made her fear of the afternoon seem preposterous. Leaning her forehead on the cool edge of the stone altar, she prayed. Then she hurried to the courtyard.

Guido was telling his tale at terrific speed, and Godfrey was standing there, still holding his riding whip, apparently frozen in horror and indignation. Behind him stood the hunting party, two men still holding on to a stag trussed up to a sapling, the whole company in various stages of horror, indignation, and amazement. Guido was quite obviously enjoying the sensation he was creating, but at sight of his mistress he stopped. Something in the shamefaced deflation of his manner stirred her anger and her contempt, and she forgot her anxiety.

"My lord, he says those poor wretches of Castellara are starving," she plunged in without greeting.

"Starving!" Godfrey exploded. "They have murdered my agent. Murdered in cold blood, in defiance of every law of God and man—the fools have murdered *my* man."

Her anger died, and the fear of the afternoon came back, making her voice very gentle and patient. "I know, my lord, it was a terrible thing."

"A terrible thing!" he roared. "I will burn their wretched village and hang the murderous traitors higher than the church tower."

Her fear made her wise. Not until the next morning did she bring the subject up again. They had just heard Mass, and they were coming out of the chapel hand in hand.

"My dear lord," she said, speaking low that no one might hear. "I do beseech you for the love of Christ, let me send word to Paverna to send bread to Castellara for the women and the children who are innocent of this crime."

She had spoken very low, but anger filled his voice so that everybody around them stood and listened.

"Bread to parricides and murderers! If you have no sense of the duty of your station to maintain order and justice, I have. As soon as I have breakfasted, I am riding to Castellara to inquire into this. When I have hanged the guilty, then perhaps we will hear of food. But till then—" He flung the hand she had laid on his arm from him and strode muttering to his place by the fire. For a moment she stood trembling by the wall which she had clutched to save herself from falling. The world was still swimming before her eyes when she felt an arm about her.

"The filthy German brute! If his father—" It was Ermengarde.

"Silence! Help me to my chamber and say nothing."

Lying on her bed, she sobbed over and over again, "He is my lord, he is my lord, he is my lord," until from sheer exhaustion her agony was somewhat spent.

Then she became aware of a rustling outside her door. "My dear lady," whispered a voice, choked with weeping. But her pride made her rise, and look about her for some escape from the sympathy that filled her with shame.

Hardly knowing what she did, she opened a little door in the corner of the room and groped her way up the stairs that rose before her in the darkness. As the light glimmered at the top, she remembered where she was. It was a little oratory in the tower above her chamber. Once as a child she had gone up there, and her mother had forbidden her ever to go up there again.

It was a bare chamber, lighted by a single slot window in a wall so thick that the sunlight came through in what seemed like a single, dazzling beam. There was nothing in the room but a solitary statue, covered with dust, on a little pedestal of carved stone. With her veil she cleaned it off until the bright colors stood out in the sunlight. It was an image of the Madonna, a straight, stiff wooden figure in a red robe with a gold border and a blue mantle. There was a grotesquely large crown on the veiled head, but for all its stiffness there was something at once sad and compassionate in the roughly painted face that spoke straight to Matilda's need. Putting her head against the feet of the Madonna, she wept with complete abandon, with nothing of anger or pride or even grief in that complete release. And looking up into the face of the little Madonna, when the storm of her weeping had abated, she could believe that the Mother in heaven was looking even with such compassion upon her child on earth.

Without any word of prayer or thanksgiving or supplication, Matilda kissed the hem of the gilded robe, pushed back the locks that in her anguish had slipped from under her veil, put straight the veil, and started down the stairs. Just before she reached the bottom, she stood listening for any sound from her chamber. There was none.

She closed the door behind her and looked up to find her mother standing by her bed, looking at her. She was wearing a traveling mantle and in her right hand she held leather gloves.

For a moment neither woman spoke. Then in her most matter-of-fact manner Beatrice broke the silence, "I used to go up there often in Boniface's day when you were children."

It was the first time in years that Matilda had heard her mother make any allusion to the brother and sister who were dead.

It was the thought of that going-back across the years that broke Matilda's newly won control.

"You are not leaving me?" she cried, throwing herself upon her mother.

"I am going to see what I can do to help you."

"Help me?"

"Listen, Matilda. Godfrey will make his inquiry and do whatever he is going to do. That is his right. We cannot stop him. He is a just man. He won't do anything atrocious."

"Mother, are all men brutes?"

A grim smile came to the lips of Beatrice.

"You're old enough to know the answer to that question. Most of them are. There are some exceptions, not many. It's our job to make the best of them, not complain about them."

"But those poor people!"

"There are a lot of people in this world who are in just as hard a plight. No, no," as Matilda drew back. "Don't be silly, Matilda. I'm going over to Reggio. One of the monks there will go up to the house near Baise. They'll have some grain. Nobody will question the charity of monks, and when they have exhausted their store, they can come into the house at Reggio."

"Oh, Mother." Again, Matilda burned to cross that barrier.

"There isn't much one can do in this world," said the older woman pulling on her gloves, "but that one can do."

So matter-of-fact was her voice that Matilda was astonished, when she kissed her, to feel a cold tear on her cheek.

CHAPTER V

"I am grateful to you for your escort, Godfrey," said Beatrice, as Godfrey helped her from her horse in the square before the Lateran Basilica. Not for many months had Matilda seen her mother so much her old self. Indeed, ever since that day, now six weeks past, when she had ridden up to Canossa with the new Pope's messenger and invited her son and daughter to make ready to accompany her to Rome, there had been a vigor and light in her face and her manner that as of old had carried all before her.

That was the first time she had been at Canossa since she had ridden off to Reggio to get help for the villagers of Castellara. Matilda remembered now with some amusement as she watched her husband bow low to his mother-in-law, how very stiff he had been, when she first arrived a month ago. But Beatrice had seemed entirely unaware of any cause for embarrassment as she greeted her children, and when Godfrey had somewhat sulkily objected that his affairs would soon be calling them to Lorraine, she had been very coolly explicit.

"Any pope would expect the Countess of Tuscany and her husband to support his coronation," she had said; "our position in the land puts that beyond any question. We must not forget, either, that in Pope Stephen of blessed memory Godfrey's family has given the Church a Pope. But especially an old friend like Hildebrand—June thirty of 1073 be a date that men will not soon forget."

"Has the King approved of Hildebrand's election? You must not forget that the Dukes of Lorraine are his liege men," Godfrey had objected, Matilda noticed, a little less stubbornly.

"So are we all," said Beatrice placidly. "Peter the Deacon told me that at the same time he left Rome other messengers started north to inform the King."

Godfrey had gone hunting, as usual, leaving the preparations for the journey to Matilda, but when the time had come for them to start for Rome, he had set out, if not enthusiastically, at least tolerantly.

But now, as Matilda observed with amusement, Godfrey took the hand of the Countess with great pride and led her into the basilica at the head of all their company. Indeed, he had cause for pride, Matilda reflected, as she looked about her before dismounting. The whole place in front of the basilica for the length of the great wall of the palace was thronged with their own company and the host of retainers and vassals and friends who at various points on the way had joined them. It was a following that any man would be proud to have at his back on the threshold of Rome.

As she knelt before the altar of the Madonna to give thanks for their safe arrival, an old delight which she had forgotten came back to Matilda. She remembered how as a child she had been awed by the great sunlit stillness of the ancient Roman basilicas. No matter how large the always restless crowd that thronged the marble pavements, the bright stillness of the upper air dominated the noisy scene and kept it in its rightful place among the lower shadows. But as she grew older, she had discovered something else about these great structures. In all the mystery and magnificence of Rome they seemed somehow a clear and simple and even homely thing. And now after months of dark little country churches and cramped castle and manor chapels, the great nave of Saint John Lateran came to her with fresh astonishment. Above the thronged five aisles of the lower church the arched windows of the triforium filled that quiet upper air with a serene luminousness that more than any of the gilded figures of the wall frescoes seemed to express the peace of faith itself.

For the first time, she wondered if perhaps she had not been in truth rusticating in a ragged eyrie of the country. There was nothing disturbing in the thought. It was rather with surprise and the exhilaration of a fresh adventure that she suddenly found her beloved Tuscan hills a remote thing.

It was a pleasure, too, to see her mother assuming her old state as if she had never abandoned it. All that afternoon she received visitors in their lodgings in the house opposite the basilica where the new Pope had lodged his most distinguished guests. And Godfrey by a great oak table in the loggia dispensed to knights and bishops and princes from Lorraine and the German countries some of the excellent Moselle wine which one of the many monasteries of Beatrice's benefaction had sent down to Rome for the occasion.

In the garden where Beatrice was receiving her friends, the air was sweet with the scent of lemon trees, and pale pink camellias, and oleanders, and heavy, fire-red pomegranate flowers. In the lengthening shadows of the marble arches of the loggia the dresses of the company seemed hardly less flowerlike in their colors—richly embroidered borders of gold and silver and precious stones edging the straight, softly falling robes of men and women alike. But festive as was the appearance of the company, the perfumed air was heavy with talk of politics and all the accidents of power. Nor were they all of one opinion by any means, as Matilda soon found.

For the German princes and bishops were much divided over the question of the King's part or lack of part in the recent papal election.

"The King should have been consulted first," said one of the bishops, a tall man with a great silver cross which he seized now and then as he talked, with a firm gesture as if he were taking a sword by the hilt.

"But you notice," said one of the abbots in the plain dark dress of the Cluniac reform, "that the Pope waited for his coronation until the King should have a chance to give his approbation."

"Nonsense," interrupted a Roman ecclesiastic, with the sharp, hawk-like face of the Crescentii above his violet robes, "the people and the clergy of Rome had acclaimed the Archdeacon Hildebrand at the funeral of Pope Alexander. What more was needed?"

There was a dry chuckle at Matilda's elbow. Another of the same darkly suave type in a Benedictine abbot's dress, whom Matilda at once recognized as the most austere and learned representative of the present generation of the same family, was following the conversation with obvious amusement.

"But that is true, isn't it?" she asked.

"True? Oh, yes, most things you hear in Rome are true, if it comes to that. But truth has many shades in this Roman air that I fancy it does not have in that clearer air of your Tuscany."

Then, as Matilda continued to look at him in perplexity, the old man sobered. "If you knew Rome as well as I do, my dear young lady, you would not look so charmingly puzzled. Rome has changed a good deal since my unlamented grand aunt, Marozia, made and unmade popes at her wicked will, but the Roman noble is too old a leopard to change his spots. Look about you here and think of the people you know in Rome. I don't mean my cloth, though there are cynics enough who would waive that exception, but the people who count, the ancient families. Do you think a peasant's son from Soana is their idea of Pope? To say nothing, you notice, of what this particular peasant's son is like."

"But after all," objected Matilda, shocked to hear what she knew perfectly well put into words, "the first Pope was—"

"The proper Christian answer," smiled the old Roman, "but allow me to remind the Countess of Tuscany that it was not in Rome that that fisherman received his election."

The old man raised his hands lightly for a moment. Then the mocking smile fading from the finely cut lips, he went on: "Countess, it was not I who raised the cry 'Hildebrand, bishop' at the funeral of Pope Alexander, nor did I make one of the light-headed mob that milled around Hugh Candidus when he urged his fellow clerics to choose the Archdeacon. But if you asked me to name the strongest man in Rome, the man most likely to put through anywhere, any time, what he thinks should be done, Hildebrand of Soana would be the name I would give you. You have the reputation of being a clever woman, Matilda, daughter of Beatrice; so I need not tell you what a turbulent, proud aristocracy like this of Rome is likely to think of such a choice."

"But so far as I have seen today, they seem pleased."

"For the present and in the full tide of the coronation pomp, yes. They can say the Romans have chosen their pope again without the interference of the Emperor as they used to do in the bad old days. That is true, but wait until they see what kind of pope they have, and they will sing another tune."

But now the voices beside them had risen again.

"The King sent his chancellor with his congratulations. What could be a clearer sign of approval than that?"

"Have you forgotten that only this year the Lenten Synod excommunicated his favorite advisers, and threatened to do the same for the King himself, if he were known to consort with them?"

"But that was the Synod," interposed the abbot.

"The Synod?" The bishop clutched his cross, and then he broke into a hearty roar of laughter. "I knew you Cluniacs starved your bodies. Do you starve your brains as well? The Synod? The Pope, the College of Cardinals, the Curia, the Synod—you know that it is all Archdeacon Hildebrand—"

For a moment the scornful voice rang in the sudden silence; then it fell sharply. Matilda turned to see the cause of the falling-back, the sudden attention on all sides. A soft, caressing voice was speaking her name, and she looked up into a finely carved face, supple like the faces of the Roman nobility about him, but for their brown a fine gray, a majestic presence in the flame brocade of a cardinal.

"You will not remember me, my lady Matilda, but I knew your stepfather's brother when he was the Cardinal Frederick. I rested once at your mother's house at Mantua when you were a child."

"My lady Matilda, I will resign you to the care of Cardinal Hugh Candidus," said her Roman friend with a smile. "He will be a much more potent guide to Rome than I. All doors open to him now." The emphasis on the last word was so slight that Matilda was not sure that she had not imagined it, but the slight flush in the cheek of the cardinal confirmed her impression.

She had no time to think more of it, for Hugh Candidus had turned all his attention to her, delivering with great solemnity the Pope's invitation for a visit after Vespers. And then he swept her along in his train to find the Countess Beatrice, asking news of her lands, comparing her reports of the winter in Lombardy and Tuscany with what he had seen of the winter in France, giving her the latest news which Hugh of Die had brought to Rome from the French king's court, and describing appreciatively the splendor of the embassy which William of Burgundy had sent to congratulate the new pope. He discussed each topic vividly and urbanely within the compass of the five minutes it took them to reach the chair in which the Countess Beatrice sat enthroned on the other side of the garden.

And the impression he had made in those minutes was confirmed by her mother's greeting. A spark of coquetry gave vivacity to the stately graciousness with which Beatrice greeted her old friend, but it sheathed a little, too, her daughter noticed, the usual candor of her manner.

She thought of that reserve again when after Vespers she and her mother, escorted by the debonair Cardinal, went to the Lateran Palace. From the inner room to which the Cardinal had gone to announce the arrival of the Tuscan countesses, his soft voice sounded in the evening stillness.

"That Eppo of Zeitz was babbling in his seditious way at the Countess Beatrice's levee this afternoon."

"Never mind, Cardinal Hugh, we must trust men all we can," answered a very weary voice.

The lofty-ceilinged room on the threshold of which they stood was so dark with the twilight that tapers had already been lighted, and in their glow the face of the Pope looked drawn and stern.

But at sight of the two women, he rose from the table and came toward them, the fierce tension of his face breaking in a smile so charming and unaffected that the whole aspect of the man was changed.

Even as he completed the sign of the cross over their bowed heads, he exclaimed, "I knew that I could count on you, my daughters. With you here I shall not dread even the day after tomorrow."

"My lord," said Beatrice gently, "why should you dread the day after tomorrow?"

"Can you ask that, who know so much more than do most men what the work is that I must do?" Motioning to his two guests to be seated on stools at his side, he sat down in a low chair before the table at which he had been writing. With the candles behind him, his face stood out from his dark red robe as if it were of ivory. And that sense of something smouldering within a husk of weariness which she had had before in his presence came afresh to Matilda.

"My lord, there is no one in the whole world who can so well do it," said Beatrice even more gently.

"God have mercy on His world then," replied the Pope. "But you know I should have preferred to work as I always had done, giving all my strength to the thing itself."

"I know," said Beatrice. For a moment the Pope waited for her to go on. But she, too, seemed to be waiting.

"But now they will think of me instead of the thing that must be done." Something lighter and tenderer warmed the ashes of the Pope's voice as he turned to Matilda, "You are young, Matilda, and you were born in the purple, and you bring such grace to the part that it would be niggardly of you to want to take yourself from it. So this must seem strange to you."

Matilda had listened with awe, the awe with which the young and the fearful learn of the uncertainty of the old and the strong, but now, an idea came to her. Two men hanged at Castellara—"I thought of you, Matilda, and I did not burn them as traitors should be burned," Godfrey had said to her lying at her side that night when he had returned.

There were no words for it; so now she said only, "I think I can guess, my lord."

"God grant that it be only guessing for many a day to come, Matilda," said the Pope with the same quick smile with which he had turned to her. And then the lines of his face fell back into their wonted sternness of mould.

"I need not tell you, my friends, that I have said nothing of this to the people here about me. They would only think that in modesty I was seeking encouragement, and they would flatter me with words that would shame me. You will not forget to pray for me, will you? For the work that is to be done, and of you I shall ask what I would ask only of old friends, for me, too?"

Neither woman spoke, but looking at their faces, the tired man seemed content, for his features again relaxed. And for the first time Matilda realized what mobility of feeling lay behind the harsh lines of Hildebrand's face.

"Do you think your son-in-law will serve me as the general of my forces?" He turned to Beatrice.

It was clear that this was the first time he had mentioned the matter to her, but there was no hesitation of surprise, only a slight added warmth of pleasure, as she answered, "I think he will."

"He is a good soldier," said the Pope.

"He is not like his father," said Beatrice quietly, "but he is a just man."

"I will speak to him when I see him after Mass in the morning." Then the quick mind seemed to veer again. "Gregory of Vercelli gave me private word this morning from Henry that he is sorry for the way he has behaved, using church offices at his pleasure and keeping evil men for counsellors, and that he means to be our loyal son and come and take his crown from our hands and be the sword and shield of the Church as a Christian king should. Do you think I may believe him?"

Beatrice smiled. "Yes, he meant it when he said it to Gregory of Vercelli. All the more because Gregory was so surprised to hear it, and he could imagine him telling you and your being pleased. But it will not last. That is what poor Agnes can never see. She goes down on her knees to Henry, and he is moved by her tears and makes the most beautiful speeches imaginable. And she, simple woman, thinks the matter is as good as settled when he has forgotten all about it."

The hope that had lighted the Pope's face faded as Beatrice went on. There was a tinge of bitterness in his quiet words, "He is perfidious."

"No," said Beatrice in her most matter-of-fact tones, "rather, he is not to be depended upon."

"If only he would help me drive the money-changers out of the temple," said the Pope wistfully.

"He can't afford to. He is making his own profit out of it." There was a grim finality in Beatrice's voice.

"But if there is any chance of winning him, God knows that I must. It is the salvation of millions if I can."

But Beatrice said no more.

For a minute, the three of them sat there in the growing darkness. Then the Pope rose.

"With help if I can, alone if I must, I am going to cleanse the house of God. That is why I am called to this work. If we can get the Church clean, then she can save the world."

"I think you will not fail, my lord," said Beatrice soberly.

"I must not." Matilda looked at him standing there, a slight, dark figure with the two candles behind him, his face white and grim against the shadows of the room, and knew that she would never forget the look of him seen at that moment.

"He will be a great Pope, Gregory VII!" she said to her mother when they found themselves alone again in their lodgings. When she had said it, it seemed a silly, a pretentiously obvious thing to have said.

Her mother looked at her gravely. "I am glad you think so, for he will look to you when I am gone."

That night as she lay awake beside Godfrey, she thought of Canossa. It seemed very far away. Even Godfrey breathing a little heavily at her side seemed suddenly a stranger. And then she remembered how the Archdeacon Hildebrand had talked to her of the Peace of the Church and of a dream of order in a terrible world. She would wait until her son was born—no, she must not let herself get frightened. There was an old poem which she had learned from her tutor as a child, a grace for living it had seemed to her with that final benediction of the sweeping appeal to eternity, dear to the child mind in its mesh of time and finitude. Softly she began to say it to herself until she fell asleep:

> "And after all this life's travail past
> To rest in Thee, alone, safe at last."

CHAPTER VI

It was with wonder and incredulity that Matilda remembered that night three months later. She was sitting on the western battlements of Canossa in the mellow warmth of the late September afternoon. Before her, the as yet unreaped fields of wheat lay in pools of bright gold between the somber olive trees. Beyond and above, rose the hills, deepened and burnished with the red and purple and gold of oak, beech, and chestnut, mantling the long slopes and leaning precipitously over the crags and scarps. Now and then the turbulent earth thrust its bare red-brown through the frail vesture of trees and underbrush. Yet even here something of the golden haze of September had mollified the fierceness of the earth so that like the cypress groves in the folds of the hills, these bare patches lay but as a shadow on the radiance of the harvest time.

"I think it is the most beautiful land that the sun ever shone upon, this Tuscany of ours," said Matilda, half to her mother at her side, half to the child asleep on her knees.

A sudden gust of wind shimmered through the long ranks of the wheat, and Matilda raised the edge of the shawl about the little head in her lap.

Without waiting for her mother to reply, Matilda half-whispered to the sleeping child, "It is a rich land you will be lord of, little Godfrey the Third, and a lovely one."

Then she turned again to Beatrice. "I am grateful to you, Mother, that you helped with Godfrey, for I did want my son to be born in this land of ours."

"Of course. It is no little thing to be Duke of Lorraine, but a strong Count of Tuscany can be the greatest prince in Italy. I think Godfrey appreciates that."

"Yes," said Matilda, softly, "but that all seems so far away. Just that I have him at my breast and in my arms is all that really matters now."

Beatrice smiled and laid down the strip of bleached linen that she was embroidering. "The years pass quickly, though. I remember sitting here with you in my arms…. Things were not so quiet then. Your father was away at Mantua. There was trouble all over, it seemed, and there had been stragglers roving in the hills. There was a report that they had taken the tower of Bianello over there. The men I sent out were cowards and oafs. They could find out nothing but the wild tales of the peasants, and they kept coming back at every word of a band in the neighborhood. I didn't dare send out more than a couple at a time for your father had taken so many with him that there were barely enough to man the walls if there should be real trouble. So I took you up here, and I watched the road until the sun set."

"Did he come that night?"

"No."

"She was younger than I am and new-come into a strange land," thought Matilda, wondering how she might put into words those things that between her mother and herself had never been spoken.

"I remember how when I was thinking that under cover of the night I would give you to Ermengarde to take to Reggio if anything should happen, you woke up and laughed at me and caught at my veil and pulled the chain at my neck. I hadn't thought I should sleep that night if Boniface did not come, but I did. And at noon the next day he came. I had my hands full then, for he was very tired and angry with the report of the captain of the castle and all for beating those timid scouts out the gate."

Matilda did not speak for a while. Then to chase away the shadows that were impinging on the rich content of the moment, she said lightly, "Well, I suppose the men for their part think we are foolish and soft-hearted."

Beatrice considered. "Not just that. They say we are always thinking of the moment and the person, and not of the longtime issues."

"I can't say that they solve their old issues," protested Matilda. "After all, we keep the families going when they are off at their meetings and their expeditions and the rest of it."

"Yes, it takes much labor for that, though there is no blowing of trumpets or waving of banners about it. There were three of you," Beatrice added soberly, "and you are the only one to grow up and have a child to carry on the family."

"It was cruel of the old Emperor to keep brother in prison," said Matilda. "Any one should know that a child shut up like that would sicken."

Beatrice considered. "Well, he had hoped to take my lands, or at least put a henchman of his here and make me marry him. When I married Godfrey, he knew I had a good man to defend me, and not a friend of his, at that. So in his anger he sent out men to waylay me. I didn't dare trust the boy to anybody. If he was with me, at least they couldn't kill him and pretend it was an accident."

"It is a terrible thing, the greed and tyranny of the strong in this world." Matilda held her child tighter in her arms.

Beatrice shook her head. "You must not forget that the strong are strong and the weak, weak. It would do no good to hand the world over to the weak. They couldn't hold it. It was then when your brother died," she added thoughtfully, as if for the first time she were thinking it out, "that I decided that I would do everything I could to strengthen the hand of the Church. There are bad and cruel bishops, and there have been bad popes, but that is the work of men. The pattern which they botch in their deeds is good. That is of God."

Something opalescent was coming into the golds and rose-russets of the scene before them. Invisible curtains were falling between the eye and the distances of the landscape, parting them into layers of tone and texture of color, staining the basic gold with the hues of the air. So it lay from fading saffron in the fields below the castle to the rose-purple of the farthermost hills, above which already the storm clouds were piling in billows.

"This here before our eyes is enough for the little Godfrey and me," said Matilda, looking down upon her sleeping child, and watching for a moment how the little lips sucked in and the little fists clenched in some passing restlessness of sleep. Then as the child relaxed again, Matilda looked up at her mother and smiled. "We are glad that we are not emperors or popes or bishops to have to make the bad world behave. Here in our own land we shall build bridges and make gardens and read the poems that gentle-hearted men have made in all ages, and we shall feed the hungry, and keep the peace, and worship God, and all who pass through our land will think that the Kingdom has come on earth."

"Kingdoms are not built by singing of songs or building of bridges."

But Matilda laughed gayly, "For us, Godfrey the Third, lord of Canossa, neither songs nor bridges matter yet. It is but sleeping and eating for us." Again the baby stretched, doubling his fists. Again he seemed to sleep the more soundly.

"If it does not storm tomorrow," said the Countess Beatrice, scanning the horizon critically, "I shall go back to Mantua. You're quite strong again, and anyway Godfrey will be back soon, and I want to be in Rome before the autumn rains make the roads impassable."

"Godfrey ought not to stay too long away from Rome," replied Matilda, holding the idea of Rome as it were at arm's length. "He was very proud to be made the Pope's general."

Beatrice gathered together the twists of bright-colored silk with which she had been working and rolled them up in the strip of linen. "Yes, Godfrey ought to go to Rome when the Pope comes back from the south."

"From the south?" Matilda looked at her mother. "I did not know the Pope had left Rome."

"We thought it better not to worry you. It is just the Normans again. You remember Pope Alexander tried to make peace with them without much success, for they are hard to bind with words. So now His Holiness has gone down to Capua to see what he can do with Richard the Norman face to face. Godfrey thought it unnecessary, but I sent him some of our men to strengthen the escort."

"I didn't know the Normans were making trouble again. I thought all was as quiet as our Tuscany here."

"Now that you are well again," said the Countess Beatrice gravely, "you must face the fact that things are not quite so quiet as they seem here today. They almost never are. This is not the Kingdom of Heaven, and there is no piety in shutting our eyes to the fact."

"But what is wrong here?"

"Godfrey sent word to a number of the lords and knights of our lands, bidding them go with him into Germany to visit the King. Some of them came promptly, as was right, but others made excuses, and some few refused to leave their lands because of the uncertainty of the times."

"But to say that is to imply that their lords would not protect them when they are in their service." Matilda felt her face flush with shame.

"Precisely," said Beatrice. "That is one of the problems when a woman is married to a man from a distance. So I went to Corvulus of Fregnano and I told him that your son was born here at Canossa and that both you and I expected your vassals to do their duty to your husband and lord."

"And the others?" asked Matilda, feeling suddenly a little sick as she saw the brittle peace of the moment crumble under her fingers.

"I charged him with seeing that his neighbors understood. Then I went over to San Benedetto and had a long talk with the Abbot and your old friend whom they've made their prior. And they promised to see that their visitors understood. Always remember that when it comes to public opinion, there is no friend like a monastery." Beatrice had risen and was standing now looking over the edge of the parapet into the distance.

"But everything seemed so quiet, so—"

"That was because you wanted it to be so," said Beatrice in her most matter-of-fact tone, holding her veil with a firm hand where the breeze was tugging at its edge. Then as if guessing Matilda's unspoken hurt, she added with her usual positiveness, "as was perfectly natural at such a time. But that is over now, and you must face the facts. Your maids may sleep quietly of nights in their chamber and the peasants in their little village, but in the rank of society to which it has pleased God to call you and me, there is no rest, no standing still. Not to rise is to fall."

"But all that," protested Matilda, "I thought that would be Godfrey's charge. He seemed so willing when we married."

"You are the Countess of Tuscany," said Beatrice firmly. "So long as I am here, I shall do my part, but when I am gone, then you are the lord of Canossa, and upon you depends the future of your family and the honor of your lineage. If God spares your son, you may look forward to his manhood."

"But," cried Matilda, quickly and impulsively out of her anxiety, "you have seen for yourself that Godfrey wishes to be master in his own household, and—"

"Not to raise any questions beyond the immediate one, Godfrey is at present in Germany. When he returns, we hope he will go to Rome and perhaps to the south, if the Normans do not keep the peace. In the best of times, he will be away half the time, and if we have trouble, more. There are lords who treat their estates as sheep to be shorn and then turned loose where the wolves may have them if they will. But that is not our way, as you know."

Then it was that Matilda remembered Gregory the Pope standing between the candles, and the terror of those hours when she lay awake.

"You make me think of the Pope," she said, trying to speak lightly. "He was very marvelous, but he frightened me."

"You sound like Peter Damian," her mother smiled. "He loved Hildebrand, but he called him his Holy Satan."

"I would trust him anywhere," said Matilda, trying to analyze the impression of that night, "but I should be afraid he would lead me into places beyond my strength to follow."

"I don't think that was what Peter meant. He was afraid neither of man nor devil."

But before Matilda could answer there came a long-drawn note from the pile of towers behind them. "Perhaps it is a message from Godfrey, saying that he is coming sooner than we expected." Whether it was the alarum from the watch towers, or the sudden movement of his mother's body, with a little cry the baby was awake.

"There, there," said Matilda lifting him up and swaying him slowly from side to side. "Don't get all red and angry-looking, my little Godfrey."

"My lady," came the voice of the steward from the stairs behind them, "it is the German Berthold, riding toward us alone."

"News from Godfrey," said Matilda. "You take the baby, Mother, and I will go down to the gate to meet him."

But as Matilda had half expected when she broke Godfrey's seal, it was not the hand of her husband, who had a soldier's contempt for the clerical arts, but of Egbert, his chaplain.

As soon as she had read the letter through once, she hurried back to the battlements.

"He will not be back this winter. The King is having trouble with the Saxons and has asked for his help. He thinks that perhaps I had better not travel with the child at this time," said Matilda, gazing at her mother with a deepening sense of alarm and oppression. "Berthold says that the King and his advisers are very much displeased with the new Pope and are resolved not to be put upon, as they say, by any of his demands."

Beatrice handed the child back to his mother. "I am not surprised. I will go to Mantua and then on to Rome. If both you and the Pope urge his presence, then I think he will come down in the spring."

"My lady Beatrice," the voice of Antonio the steward interrupted Matilda's preoccupation with the crying child. The man came up and stood against the wall, waiting. At Beatrice's nod he continued, "Berthold reports that he heard rumors of trouble on the farms of those who had gone into Germany with my lord Godfrey. He says that some of the bailiffs whom he saw also reported difficulties with the harvest collections. The peasants seem to feel that now that their lords are away, they need not be so careful."

Beatrice looked troubled. "They probably had to give extra levies before their lords went away. Matilda, I should have my bailiff ride through the farms, making it quite clear that there is to be no departure from custom, but that he will hear all grievances. You must see that justice is done, but there is nothing to be gained from breaking down old customs. Some of your vassals would take the chance to increase their exactions. It is the poor and the weak who always suffer most from disorder."

"It is not the peasants I fear, but some of our knights," complained Matilda, wrapping her son carefully in the woolen shawl as the breeze freshened.

"There is nothing to be afraid of," said Beatrice casually. "You can reach me in Mantua, and the Abbot of San Benedetto will be glad to advise you."

The sun was just over the horizon now, and the flame of the sunset was splashing the pale green western sky with its breakers of red and purple. Below, the slopes of the fields and the hills had darkened, with duller shades of mustard and blue-green filling the olive-guarded wheatfields.

The child was whimpering hungrily. Again, a deep content came into the heart of Matilda as holding him close to her breast she started down the narrow steps. It is the fullness of the year, she said to herself, and in peace with my son upon my knees I have looked out on the golden fields of Tuscany. Whatever the future brings, this day has been, and once I have known the fullness of life.

CHAPTER VII

It was, as Matilda had feared, spring before Godfrey returned to Canossa. He seemed very happy to be back, for he stood that night of his return in front of the fire in the middle of the great hall, with his legs stretched comfortably apart in the glow of the flame, tossing his son into the air and catching him again. The baby crowed with delight, and the men laughed with unrestrained heartiness at the child's pleasure.

"The baby should be in his cradle asleep," protested Ermengarde. "Men have no sense—"

She stopped, for Matilda had finally caught her eye. "One night will not matter. It is more important that the child and his father should enjoy each other." She pulled the thread with which she was stitching a scrap of red wool so tight that it broke. Ermengarde said no more but sat down on the wooden settle back of the fire where a couple of the other maids were sitting watching the play.

"My lady," said Alberic, leaning forward from the stool on which he was sitting next to Matilda's chair, "I saw your mother as I went through Mantua to meet my lord. She gave me this letter for you."

"Did you forget it, Alberic, that you said nothing about it before supper?" asked Matilda teasingly.

Alberic raised his eyebrows and smiled with a slight inclination of his head in the direction of the pair on the hearthstone.

"You were too busy."

"How did my mother seem to you? You know I have had so much to do that I have not seen her since the beginning of Lent. The hard winter has made much misery and discontent on our lands, and the rumors from foreign parts have been disturbing."

"She looked resolute as usual, but frail. I shouldn't think she ought to travel until the roads are clearer, and the air softer."

"She says she is feeling better," said Matilda, holding the parchment up to the candle to read it. "She has a letter from the Pope. He is well and Rome, praise God, is quiet, but he is troubled over the rumors that come out of Germany. Henry keeps promising amendment"—she lowered her voice—"but the Pope can hear no evidence of it. Henry has his excommunicated counselors with him again, and they are busy filling the churches of Germany with their men. He pays no attention to the Pope's legates or to the remonstrances of his own bishops." For a moment Matilda read on in silence. Then she looked up at her husband. He was still absorbed in his play. "He says the married clergy in Milan are still refusing to obey, and his agents report the Normans will move in the south as soon as the roads are open. Oh, that reminds me," she added, "I had a messenger this morning from Simone in Florence. He reports that the Arno is rising, and the poor along the banks are worried, but the wealthier merchants on the higher land will do nothing."

"That is the discouraging thing about it," said Alberic. "These Patarine friends of the Pope talk as if the only ones who ground the faces of the poor were those of noble birth, but I notice that when the base get together a little pelf and mount a horse, they soon forget the shops and farms from which they have come. The one thing the poor can be sure of is that whoever is in power, they will suffer."

"Who is a Patarine now?" asked Matilda in a low voice, so, she told herself, as not to disturb the play.

"Not I," said Alberic. "They think that if they can pull down the present oppressors and hoist themselves into their places, all will be well. As if it mattered who sat in the places!"

"See how straight the little rascal's back is," laughed Godfrey, as his son catching hold of his father's beard braced himself against his arms. The men drinking at the table a little back from the fire in the shadows of the night, laughed and clacked their wooden cups on the oak table in applause. The child heard the noise and looked uncertainly at his father. Amused by the child's wonder, the man opened his mouth and pulled his lips away from his teeth and made as if to snap at the child. Then he laughed, but the child began to cry, first a whimper, and then, as he seemed to work himself into a rage, he was yelling and beating his father with firm little fists.

"He is tired from the excitement," said Matilda, rising and taking the babe from his father's arms, and laying the hot little face against her own cheek.

"What a temper of his own he has!" cried one of the men admiringly.

Godfrey, who had stood for a minute uncertainly on the hearth, broke into a hearty laugh now and strode over to the table, his sword rattling in its sheath as he walked.

"Come, Alberic; homecoming makes a man thirsty. This is the King's own Rhenish which he gave me to keep warm in the cool Italian air, he said."

The whole company laughed heartily. The monk went over slowly to the table.

"Fill up, man," said Godfrey, jovially handing the leathern pitcher to his guest. "This is one place where a monk is as good as a man. God, how some of those German bishops in the King's company drank!"

"It is potent, my lord," said the monk, tasting the cup and putting it back on the table.

"Luitpold, what was that song that Ottilie, the Bishop of Regensburg's wench, sang?"

One of the men at the table looked around before he spoke: "I am not sure that your lady would like it, my lord."

"Like it! It was a brave wench who sang it, even if she is a churchman's hussy. Matilda, she had a voice clear as a bell. Even that milk-faced Bertha laughed."

Matilda smiled and went over to the bench on which the maids were sitting: "Help Ermengarde put the child to bed, and then go to your own chamber. I'll go right to bed, myself. Antonio, the fire needs mending, and it would be well to set out some of the wine that the monks sent us from San Benedetto last fall. You must tell your cellarer, Alberic, that it is ripening very well. And Antonio—"

There came a sudden blast on the trumpet, a little muffled as if overhead.

The wine slopped from the pitcher in Godfrey's hand and fell to the hearth.

"It must be a messenger from the King to come at such an hour. Here, some of you go out to the gate and find out who it is."

"Take torches from the wall," added Matilda. The men obeyed.

"I hope it is not the rising of the Arno," she went on, as they waited. "These heavy rains we have been having would swell any stream, and Simone's man says that the river was running high a week ago."

Godfrey set down the pitcher and faced his wife indignantly: "Well, if it is some of those damned peasants and peddlers you've been coddling while I have been away, they may look to be beaten from the bridge back into the mud from which they came. Disturbing their lords at such an hour with whines about their cowsheds and—"

"My lady—my lord," the steward Antonio corrected himself hastily, "they are men from Florence."

"What in God's name do they rouse us for at this hour of the night? Tell them to go back where they came from or—"

"The Arno is washing over the town, my lord, and—"

"Can I stop it?" asked Godfrey.

Even as he spoke, the wind which had been whinnying through the lantern of the hall for the last hour swept down in a sudden gust and blew the damp smoke of the fire in his face. Choking, he dashed his cup to the table and staggered into the clearer darkness.

Her eyes blinded, Matilda yet managed to reach for the copper jar of water standing by the fire. Clearing her own eyes, she took the handkerchief from her girdle and dipped the edge in the soft well water and went to her husband's aid.

"It's a foul night," he spluttered.

"My lady," said the steward in a low voice, "the horses are panting and the men are wet to the skin."

She nodded, and he slipped away.

"You are weary, my lord," she said gently, kneeling at his side where he sat on one of the chests by the wall. "You have had a long day's ride. Why don't you go to bed?"

"You are coming to bed?"

"There are some housekeeping things I must tend to first; then I will come." She had risen and now stood at his side, stroking his head. "How knotted your hair is! I will comb it out for you, tomorrow."

"Then be quick about it, my dear. Here, boy," kicking a youngster who had fallen asleep with his head on a low stool by the fire. "Oh, well, I'll get my things off by myself. Hurry, Matilda, or I'll be asleep before you come back."

"Antonio," said Matilda as she entered the kitchen, "warm a cup of Rhenish with a little sugar and take it to my lord." The steward bowed and hurried back to the hall.

There were no candles or torches burning in the kitchen, only a fire in the middle of the room, leaping up as if it had been freshly kindled and catching the gleam of copper in the pots and skillets on the walls. About the ash-strewn hearth three or four men were half-sitting, half-lying, with hunches of bread in one hand and brass-hooped wooden cups of wine before them. Half in the ashes and half on the hearth stood a copper flagon from which the steam of the warm wine rose encouragingly. One of the men who was not eating but who was apparently warming a chunk of meat on a copper spit, rose at her entrance and dusted his knees with his free hand.

"Don't let me interrupt your feeding of these men," she said, pulling up a stool and sitting down. As she spoke, two of the figures before the fire rose slowly and bowed low to her.

"Sit where you were and tell me who you are," she said.

But one of the men rose and came over and knelt down before her. Then he took her hand and kissed it. "I am Ubertino, the master of the company, and I am here to beg your help, my lady, on behalf of all the citizens of Florence. And he is Vincenzo, the curate of the parish priest of San Niccolo, that you might know that we are here out of no selfish interest of our own but for all the city."

"God bless you, my lady," said the young priest, coming over and bowing.

Matilda rose and reached for another stool.

"Do you sit here, Father."

The priest shook his head. "I am the son of your bondman, Leo, whom you made free."

Matilda smiled: "You are a priest, son of Leo. At least sit where you sat before. And tell me what has happened quickly, for my lord awaits me."

Again Ubertino took the lead: "Half the city is swept away, and as always happens, it is the poorest who lost their hovels first. Some of them have lost their lives, too, for the waters came in the night. It was still raining when we left, three days ago. The priest of San Niccolo has built a fire in the church and taken in as many as he can. The members of our company have opened up their houses, but we cannot hold all. Our grain is all wet, most of our wine is gone, and the fever has come. The cattle have been swept away, the pigs have run away. Your attendant refuses to let anybody touch your grain or wine. The priest has persuaded the people to leave it alone until we should come here and get your permission."

"Of course," said Matilda, "I will send him a line in the morning."

But though Ubertino kissed her hand again, he stood undecided as if not sure whether he should speak or not.

"Is there anything more? I must hurry."

It was the priest, Vincenzo, who now answered. "Yes, my lady, there has been trouble all winter. The poor craftsmen have blamed the rich, the rich have blamed the bailiff, the bailiff has blamed the merchants, the merchants—well, you know it is the second bad winter we've had, and God knows we have all of us our share of blame in our sins, but when men are desperate, they are not likely to be just. Father and I have had a hard time to keep the serfs from thieving, and one of the merchants was found dead, and his servant gone."

"What do you want me to do?" asked Matilda.

The priest hesitated. The layman threw himself passionately at her feet, and in the sudden light on his face and head she saw that his hair was iron-gray, and his face the grave face of a man used to giving commands to others.

"My lady, if my lord would come to us for only a few days, I think men would listen to him, and he could give commands, and they would start rebuilding. At present they are too discouraged to do anything but plot violence and curse their lords and betters. If—"

"I think you are right," said Matilda. "You are tired. Rest tonight, and in the morning, I will ask my lord to ride back with you."

Before the two men could complete their blessing, she was shivering in the great hall. The fire had died down, and the men who were sleeping there had crept almost on top of it, as they had wrapped themselves in their cloaks and turned to sleep. Overhead, the wind and the rain were beating like thunder on the tiled roof.

"God have mercy on all who are houseless tonight!" said Matilda half to herself.

"Amen," answered a low voice in the dark.

"Alberic, did they not give you a bed in the guest chamber?"

"Yes, my lady. But I wanted to remind you that I am at your service as early as you like in the morning."

It was too dark for her to see his face, but there was something gentle in his voice that in the storm and dark made her speak of the worry in her heart.

"They have asked for Godfrey to come back with them, to—" she hesitated.

"Do you think he will?" asked the monk.

She did not answer. Then wearily she said, "Good night."

"I will be lying here in the hall whenever you need me tomorrow." And Alberic vanished in the darkness.

Godfrey was already asleep when she crept in shivering, beside him. For a while she lay awake, going over in her mind the things she could get to the stricken city on the backs of half a dozen horses. Some herbs for the fever, but was there any use in trying to bring herbs when there would be so many? Some of Godfrey's Rhenish wine for the sick. Their own wine would be thin and sour and of little cheer. There were a score of extra coverlets in the store room. Some linen from the chests in her chamber, oil for the wounded—she would ask Donizo to pour the oil from the sanctuary lamp into it, for it would comfort them, poor things. Some sugar and spices, some salt. There were some woolen cloaks in the chests in the hall. She could wear one of her silver chains. For doubtless, some of the merchants had supplies hidden that a little silver would bring to light. Soulless things, some of these merchants with their itch for gain, and yet, where would dwellers in the hills be if the merchants did not bring their luxuries? So she fell asleep.

It was still dark when she arose and dressed herself. But when she reached the chamber in which her maids slept, she knew by the dim lightening of the one window under the ceiling that she was none too early. She roused the girl Maria and bade her wake two of her fellows.

She walked lightly, but it seemed to her that she had hardly entered the hall before one of the figures lying on the benches rose and came toward her. Without stopping to recognize him, she nodded and went on.

By the time the sun had risen feebly on a rain-soaked world, there was a heap of stuffed sacks and saddlebags on the kitchen floor, and outside in the courtyard, half a dozen horses were stamping their hoofs and whickering, as the blacksmith made sure of their shoes.

Godfrey was still asleep when Matilda returned to their chamber. She went over to the bed and shook him.

"Damn—" he stopped in astonishment when he saw her bending over him.

"Godfrey, I have everything ready for the trip to Florence. They beg that for the love of God you will come and help them." As she spoke, she lifted the curtains of the bed so that he might see the white light of the morning.

"For the love of God, come where?" He blinked suspiciously.

"They have had trouble all winter. The priests are striving desperately to keep order. You know the intendant, Simone, is faithful and honest, but he does not know when to give in, when to break the rules to keep order. I am afraid something dreadful may happen. If you just ride over, Godfrey, it will encourage them, and they will get to work on building. I know you are tired, Godfrey, and the roads are bad, but it will mean so much to the whole country if you go," she pleaded, sinking down on her knees and laying her head on his chest.

But he threw her off. "Such nonsense I never heard. I have come back to raise some more men to take to the help of the King. Such coddling of serfs I never knew."

"They are not serfs, my lord; most of them are not. They are freemen, weavers and merchants and workers in leather and metal—they are restless there, cooped up in their little town, and it is hard enough to keep them content. They will be desperate now, and I do not know—"

"Well, I know one thing, Matilda, I am not going on any wild goose chase down to Florence just because a couple of priests have taken to whining about their poor. If they'd leave the poor alone to do their duty and take what is coming to them, the swine, we would all—" He turned away from her and pulled the coverlet half over his head.

"My lord, if you don't go, I am going," cried Matilda, at last made frantic by the deepening of the light from the high windows.

"Go to the devil," retorted Godfrey and settled himself comfortably in his bed.

Outside in the courtyard, Alberic was waiting. Matilda pulled her mantle close about her neck. In spite of the sunlight the morning air was still cold.

As she looked around, Alberic led one of the horses to her side. It was her own favorite brown mare.

"How did you know?" she asked.

"I know Godfrey," he answered with a smile.

"Maria," she called to the girl standing in the doorway, "help Ermengarde with your little lord. Do not take him outdoors until it gets much warmer, and be sure the men do not tire him with too much playing."

For a moment, she was tempted to go in and look at him again, but he was asleep, and the horses were getting cold, standing here. So she turned her horse and rode to the gateway, with her company following behind.

CHAPTER VIII

"YOU came just in time, my lady," said the priest of San Niccolo. He had poured out some sour country wine in a wooden cup, and now he was cutting a loaf of gray bread into chunks. His face looked dirty and drawn in the light of the tallow candle he had set on the chest, but otherwise Matilda could hardly believe that less than two hours ago she had seen him pulled dripping from the flooded river, with hardly a sign of life in his spent body.

As she thought of it, again her own tired body shuddered, and she leaned her head against the damp wall. Even through her veil it was cold. She wondered if ever in the dark little house there had been a fire.

"But where were the better people, the men of property and of family? They know better than to let this ghastly thing go on." She talked to warm a little the dark and cold rather than for any desire of information. Every time she thought of those prosperous merchants asking for an ever larger and larger share of the tolls of their city, her anger returned. Bowing there in the sunlight in their pretentious robes and talking of the honor her city would bring her and the prosperity of her domain—for all the cold and damp she was hot at the very thought of them. It would be many a long day before she listened to those hypocrites again.

"It is not much to offer a lady, but it is all I have," said the priest, handing her the bread and the cup.

"No one can ask more than that, Father."

"But," he went on, sitting down on the chest beside the candle, "if you had accepted the hospitality—"

"No," said Matilda, biting firmly into the hard crust, "it was not the Bishop I found being drowned by those fiends."

The priest rubbed his head thoughtfully. "You must not be too hard on them, my lady. They were hungry and tired. Men do strange things then, you know."

"But what conceivable good did they think they would get from burying that poor old paralytic in the mud there?"

"Oh," said the priest, his rough face lighting up with understanding, "some old crone from the country told them that in ancient days men used to stop the floods by giving the river a life. Peasants, my lady, have a lot of tales gentle folks know nothing of."

"But why did they pick somebody helpless like that?"

The priest considered. "Old Filippo has a lot of queer ideas. I think he must have got them from some of the merchants who used to lodge with his wife. Merchants do pick up queer ideas, you know, traveling back and forth. And he has nothing to do but turn them over in his mind, lying there in the dark all the time."

Matilda shuddered involuntarily. She had thought it was dark here, but the priest must have seen the gesture, for he added gravely, "The poor are used to hard things, my lady."

"So they chose him because he had queer ideas?" she asked to relieve an unaccountable sense of embarrassment.

"No, not exactly, my lady. But you see he had been telling everybody who came by his house that God was angry with them for their sins and He was going to destroy them all for vengeance. Of course," he added hastily, "that was nothing for a man to say about the good God."

"I should think he would have left such sermons to you," said Matilda, amusement lightening her anger and pain.

The old priest folded his legs under his cassock and thought it over for a moment. "Perhaps, I should have preached to them, but it would not have been easy to get them quiet together. And there was so much to do taking the sick and the crippled out of the houses, and some of the worst of those people were robbing their neighbors, and I didn't want to see them hanged." He looked at Matilda anxiously to see if the excuse were good enough.

She leaned forward and patted the dirty hand. "Our Lord Himself would have done what you did."

"God forbid," said the old man with awe. "I'm glad, though, I thought of Pasco as I was coming home. I was feeling sleepy, but I said to myself, 'It has been a bad day, and maybe nobody will have thought of him.' When he wasn't there, I looked around, and then I saw that lantern down by the water."

Matilda rose. "How thoughtless of me. Here you have been feeding me, Father, when you must be ready to drop with weariness."

"Oh, no, sit down, my lady. It's funny," added the old priest with a chuckle, "but after that ducking I don't feel tired any more."

There came a knock behind them, and the priest took the candle and held it high so that its wavering and uncertain light fell on the opening door.

It was Alberic, with his cowl pulled over his head and a gleam of steel in one hand.

"Alberic," cried Matilda in astonishment. His eyes were shining, too, as if he had drunk of new wine. He laughed as he shut the door behind him.

"Don't look like the Abbot, Matilda. Yes, I've carried a sword, and I have used it. And I've sworn—I didn't realize I remembered as many words as I did. I shall have to confess it all and do penance, Matilda, but tonight Saint Benedict himself would have grabbed a sword."

He came over and sat down on the chest beside Matilda. "Sit down, Father, and look that you don't drop the candle. Those rascals of yours have this place quiet, Matilda. You needn't worry. But I found one of those damned merchants and his boy with a great bolt of woolen cloth, sneaking up the alley behind that pile of broken kindling down there. He had a sword in his hand, but I took it and stuck it into his buttocks just enough to drive home the point that this was not the hour for people with houses on higher ground to come down to the river. The boy carried the cloth up here to your church, Father, and I left him cutting off cloak lengths. It was damp, of course, but it will soften the pavement a little for their skinny ribs in there."

He flourished the sword to the left. The priest lifted the candle and, puzzled, inspected an oak door.

"They're asleep now, poor devils. You needn't worry, Father."

"Give me that sword, Alberic," said Matilda.

The monk laughed and held the sword high in the air out of her reach. "You have forgotten, Matilda, what a beautiful thing a sword is. Listen to what this sword did. There was another skulking miser—Lazarus will give his parching tongue no drop of water when he burns in hell, if my prayers have any power. He was trundling a cask of wine up from the water's edge. Ah, Matilda, there is no preacher that goes home so fast as a good sword. He stepped faster than he had ever gone in his life before, and he sweated wetter than the rain, but they were drinking his health over in that open market where the men are sleeping tonight under the tiled roof. They will not mind the wind through the empty stalls so much tonight with that fire inside."

"You are drunk, Alberic," said Matilda, reaching again for the sword.

"I swear, I am not," soberly enough. Then with a fresh spurt of mischief, "Unless you count being drunk with the astonishing satisfaction of having people actually do what you tell them they ought to do. Direct action is so much more soul-satisfying than exhortation, Matilda."

"Do you think you converted your friend who owned the wine then?" asked Matilda, amused at last by the complete resurrection of the old Alberic in the not always recognizable monk.

He shrugged his shoulders and laid the sword on the chest in the candle-light. It was, seen at closer range, a bent old thing, dull and thick of edge.

"There lie Charlemagne and all his paladins," he laughed his old mocking laugh. "As for conversion, Matilda, these swinish pot-bellies who at a time like this hoard their bread and wine and let their neighbors, not strangers but men whose faces they know, starve, they belong to the devil past redemption. All I care about is redeeming the good creatures of God, the wine and bread that, coming from His hands, should go to His use. That at least has been converted, Matilda."

"But the Bishop," said the old priest, at last finding his voice from the darkness to which he had retreated from the brandished sword.

"The Countess will assure him that I have always been a little mad. My lord Abbot will not mind. He thinks we are all mad, anyway."

But the old man seemed at last to have arrived at a decision. "Let me take this sword and leave it down at the bridge. There is no need of the Bishop's finding it in the morning."

"Yes," said Matilda, "do, for the Bishop will hear of a monk with a sword in the morning, though none of these friends of yours will care to identify him."

As the priest closed the door behind him, Alberic took the candle from the chest and held it high above his head so that its light illumined the whole dark little room—earthen floor tramped hard, two chests, a stool, a heap of straw in the corner, and a crucifix on one of the bare, whitewashed walls.

"Is this the whole house?" he asked.

"There is a little kitchen in a shack behind this, and a passageway into the church from that door."

"No problem of ecclesiastical riches here." Alberic set the candle down again on the chest. "I suppose he can just about manage the Mass and the prayers for the dying."

"But he knows every blind old woman and cripple in Florence."

"Does he know the rogues who were trying to drown him?"

"He said he was too dazed to recognize them. I have promised to tell the Bishop that I think that likely from the condition in which I found him."

Alberic laughed. "The lord of the city conspires with a peasant priest to hoodwink the bishop. Are you not a little drunk, yourself, Matilda?"

The door opened, and the old man entered, shaking the rain from his cloak.

"I am tired," said Matilda. "Take the light. Father Stefano, is there room in that little passage to the church for Prior Alberic, too?"

"Prior," repeated the old man with awe. "You can have all of it, and I will lie in the sanctuary."

"Are you sure you want to risk that straw?" asked Alberic, as he took up the candle.

"I can do no less."

Matilda had been under no illusions when she accepted the old priest's offer of his bed for the night. But she was still under the spell of the simplicity of mind that had alone in the half-light of the storm-drenched evening wrestled with the superstitious terror of his parishioners until, half in panic and half in anger, they had tried to drown him, too. And she was not sorry to administer the Bishop, whom she suspected of keeping his state at the expense of the emergency, a snub that he would be likely to appreciate. But now as she lay awake, first in the mouldy straw, and then, when she could bear its stench no longer, on the bare earthen floor, she began to appreciate what she had done, for, try as she might, there was no way of eluding the invisible life that bored into her itching flesh. Sometimes the rain pelting on the straw roof above her head seemed much the lesser of the two evils, but even as she sat up to consider, the damp air chilled her tired body, and she was not sorry to sink back where at least the heat of her own flesh had warmed the earth, and her woolen cloak shut out the sharpest edge of the night cold.

As the slow hours passed, she had plenty of time to consider what had been done and what still remained to do. She had been too angry with the intendant Simone to pay much attention to his complaints the night before. But now as she thought over at leisure the story of Alberic's exploits with the sellers of wine and wool, she wondered if perhaps there might not be more than she had at first thought to Simone's charge that the merchants were deliberately evading their taxes. And as she looked ahead to the tasks of the morning, she began to see that the Bishop with the protection of the unarmed clergy as one of his long-standing preoccupations could not be expected to take so lightly the palpable effort of the old priest to shield his disreputable parishioners. At best, authority was a brittle thing in this crowded, restless little town with its narrow streets and mean little churches and ugly, squalid houses. She remembered once looking down on it from the terraced gardens of the new basilica on the hill of San Miniato. Even in its prosperity it had looked raw and mean. Now in the disaster of the floods it was beneath contempt. Pity came to her afresh that men should be so poor as to be desperate for the loss of so little.

Shifting uneasily to scrape a little comfort for her aching muscles, she tried to think beyond the moment. It was more than wine and wool that was needed here. She found herself wondering if perhaps Godfrey would come the next day. It had been rash of her to come with so small a company. And the baby—would the maids think to see that he did not get overtired with the play of the men? Would they wrap him up warmly at night? How many nights she had arisen and gone into the chamber where he slept with his nurse, to make sure that he was wrapped up warmly! Did anybody think of it last night? It was foolish to worry. Several babies had been born since the floods began here. And the peasant babies died even faster than most babies, it seemed to her. But more than linen and shelter was needed. In a day or two the floods would be receding, and the sun would come out over the wrack of the river, and the townsmen would start again to build their wretched little town. It was at that point that an idea came to her, and, satisfied with it, she was for the first time that night able to sleep.

She had barely got the straw out of her veil and washed her face in a pail of water in the little kitchen, when the Bishop arrived at the door of the sacristy.

For a moment she wondered how he would approach the events of yesterday.

But when he sat down quietly on the chest and began to talk as if they had been sitting at Mantua, she knew why her father had years ago chosen him out of his company of young men and had him ordained and invested out of hand. For the Bishop seemed entirely unaware of the circumstances under which he encountered the daughter of his lord, and quite oblivious of the reception which his servants had obtained at her angry hands the day before.

"I am sorry that your ladyship finds our city in such grievous disorder," he began with courteous apology, as if he had been making his excuses for a hastily prepared banquet.

Without thinking, she replied in the same key, "In a disaster like this, my lord, one cannot expect men to behave as if things were normal."

"It depends on the men," said the Bishop gravely. "Any town, I suppose, is bound to have certain disorderly elements." Matilda was not quite sure whether the Bishop was looking deliberately or not at her host of the night before as he said this. "But at a time like this they get completely out of hand. I think it is now clear that what I have insisted on all along must be done, and these intolerable elements brought into some kind of order."

"What is needed," broke in the surly voice of Simone, who had followed the Bishop into the tiny house, "is that men should give up trying to dodge their just obligations to their lord and pay their dues as Christians should." Again, Matilda could not be sure that there was any particular meaning to the glance which Simone fixed on the Bishop's cross as he said this, but for a moment there was silence. Then the Bishop observed that the sun had risen and suggested that perhaps the Countess would do him the honor of accompanying him to his own house. He had horses ready without.

He waited patiently as she took leave of her host. Father Stefano was obviously embarrassed, but the Bishop paid no attention whatever to his stammering thanks for the honor she had done him that night, an honor which, it was obvious, he appreciated quite as highly as the fact that her arrival at the river the night before had saved his life. But Matilda was amused to notice that when she sent a message to the Prior, presumably busy with his patients in the church, the Bishop raised his eyebrows.

"His family are old friends of my father, the lords of Asti," she explained courteously to the Bishop, and she fancied a gleam of amusement came into his shrewd eyes.

"Your father made me bishop, my lady," he began as they rode along the muddy lanes, away from the river to the higher ground.

"I remember my mother telling what a splendid swordsman you were."

The Bishop bowed gravely as if there were no shadow of reservation in the compliment.

"They were bad times, even worse than these, and some fanatics under the cover of good men were making trouble, even as certain people are now. Master Peter Damian had been saying some pretty sharp things about the delinquencies of the clergy. You know how some of these saints talk—they expect everybody else to be cut out of the same piece of cloth they are. There were troublemakers in the town, too, and the monks were—well, you know how up in their nice, quiet eyries in the woods and hills they forget what the world is like. Peter Igneus, himself, pushed it rather far. So my lord decided that he wanted a sensible man who would help him keep order here."

Matilda wondered whether it would be wise to quote the praise her mother had often given the Bishop as an administrator. It seemed grudging not to, but she remembered also that her mother had agreed with the Archdeacon Hildebrand that Bishop Rainerius of Florence did better credit to Duke Godfrey's judgment of a soldier than to his taste in priests. Even as he rode here now in his bishop's mantle with his silver cross on his breast, he was a splendid figure of a knight, bearing himself with a calm pride and authority that seemed to find its fitting recognition in the bows and the scraping of walls that greeted his appearance on every hand. But the intendant Simone was grumbling behind Matilda, "You can't have order if people do not pay what they owe."

"I had thought," pursued the Bishop in his courteous tones, "that the Lord Godfrey might come, and we could talk over some matters of finance that it seems a shame to bother a lady with when she is, doubtless, anxious to return to her son."

"Would to God that he were here!" cried Simone, fervently agreeing with the Bishop for once. But Matilda hardly noticed him, for the Bishop's words had stirred the coil of fear which had beset her in the sleepless night but which she had been unwilling to admit to her consciousness. Then she saw that the Bishop was watching Simone, now plodding doggedly ahead of them.

"My lord," she said, turning to him as if to take him into her confidence, as they paused on a little rise of ground overlooking the desolation of the flood,

"I must go back to Canossa, for my lord has just returned out of Germany, and I am anxious about my child. But before I go, I want to talk over with you and my intendant here a plan I have. It would be possible to dike the river just above that point where the bridge was swept away, would it not?" She pointed up the river where, in a bend just below its confluence with a sudden torrent from the hills, the swollen waters had swept over the low banks and carried all before them. Such had been their force that now that they had fallen, the earth lay bare of anything but muddy sand. All the wrack of the flood in splintered wood and crushed pots and sodden hay and dead animals had been borne far below the vanished bridge. Only the broad tentacles of mud licking into the faintly green March grass told of the havoc which the still earth-brown waters had played.

The Bishop seemed uncertain. "It would take a great deal of labor, more than the town could muster."

"I should be ready to bear the expense. I was only asking if it were possible."

Matilda saw Simone rein in his horse as if he were afraid he should be carried out of earshot.

"Oh," said the Bishop charmingly, "that is munificent of you. The Countess Matilda will carry on the splendid tradition of her mother and the name of the family of Canossa—"

"But, my lord, is it possible?"

"Possible? Perfectly, my dear Countess. I think we can get the merchants to help us. And some of the nobility in the country about will doubtless be glad to give their aid, too," said the Bishop as he dismounted. He reached a gloved hand, with a cross sewn in gold on the back, to Matilda.

"Simone," she turned to the bailiff, still lingering uneasily. "Our dues in wine and oil and grain we will give to feed all who will work on the dike."

From the sudden whitening of Simone's face she saw that what he had been afraid of had now come to pass. "God forbid! My lady, you do not know what you do. Wait until my lord Godfrey can come. If you—"

"That is all, Simone," she said, laying the reins upon her horse's neck and patting it lightly as she did so.

"But, my lady"—the bailiff had flung himself on his knees in the mud and caught hold of her mantle—"if once you give up these dues, you will never receive them again. The rascals—"

The Bishop raised his whip and came toward the man clutching at his mistress' robes.

Matilda put out her arm over Simone's head. "I know you are loyal and faithful and will do as I tell you, Simone. Go now. I have told you what to do." The man let her dress drop. The last she saw of him he was picking himself out of the mud slowly, and the servants of the Bishop were laughing at him.

It had all seemed very simple and clear in the night, this project of hers, but face to face again with the jealousy and the greed and the callousness of men, she suddenly found herself tired and discouraged. They had reached the Bishop's palace by now. Without a word she sank into the high-backed chair by the fire in the great hall.

"You must be worn out after spending the night in such a hovel," said her host, as he brought a cushion and laid it at her feet.

"He is a brave man, that peasant."

The Bishop smiled. "They often have plenty of physical courage, these serfs. But what can you expect? That parish is a refuge for every scoundrel in the town. He will do nothing to help me clean it out."

"My lord, would a man of gentle birth be willing to live there?" It was, she knew, silly to argue, and perhaps hypocritcal as well.

"I tried putting a man of my own in there, but those rascals nearly killed him, and they threatened to burn down the church. I had to be away from home then at the Lenten meeting in Rome; so I let this rogue go back. Now I find him pretending that he does not know who they are who tried to drown him. Your ladyship, it is no sinecure being a bishop."

Matilda smiled wearily as she sipped the wine the Bishop set before her.

"A lord does not need to be told that. But I thought the Church had better discipline. At least you can threaten your rebels with hell-fire," she suggested lightly.

The Bishop sat down in the chair which one of his servants had put beside Matilda's.

"It takes imagination to appreciate that threat," he replied, pouring himself a goblet of wine. "This is Greek wine, my lady, from the island of Chios, from where the ancients, you remember, brought some of their choicest vintages."

"It still keeps the sunshine of the ancient world," she said, holding the bowl of the goblet in the palm of her hand and sniffing its fragrance.

"The goblet is ancient, too," said the Bishop, taking it from her and holding it up that she might see the carved ivory under the bowl. "It is said that the Emperor sent it for a gift to the great Pope Gregory."

"It is beautiful enough," she said, running her fingers over the satin-smooth ivory, "to make him repent his hard heart toward wine."

The Bishop frowned. "It is said that he sold it to one of his pious ladies in time of famine, and she heaped it with pieces of gold to feed his poor."

"I suppose beauty must always make way for necessity. I dreamed of building a bridge at Lucca, and to dike the Arno at Florence. It is a prosy world," she added as lightly as she could.

The Bishop rubbed his hands. "It is a magnificent thing. It will stop these floods, and it will give the whole town something to busy itself about and to think about now. I will have the masters of these companies of theirs called in this afternoon to make plans—"

She shook her head. "Simone will take it hard if we do not give him something to do, my lord. Besides, I could not dream of burdening you with this, too."

The Bishop took the world, as it came, it was easy to see. He would ask Simone to come that afternoon for supper. And meanwhile she was weary; would she not like to rest? His cousin, who supervised his household, would wait on her.

As she settled down comfortably in the fresh linen sheets of the Bishop, she reflected that though she did not like her host, she decidedly liked his bed. It was a relief to be free of her rain-and-dust-heavy robes and veil. If Godfrey should come this afternoon, as she half-expected, the Bishop would certainly do justice to the dike. For he would know how to put it to an ambitious man of the world.

CHAPTER IX

BUT Godfrey did not come. As she sat at dinner with Simone and the Bishop, trying to reconcile the surly suspicion of the one with the alert graciousness of the other, she found her thoughts going back to the same subject. Godfrey would be very angry when he finally woke up and found her gone. But before many hours were over, he would repent of his anger. He would still think it foolish of her to have come, but he would in a certain instinct of soldierly fairness feel that she had a right to her will and that in affection he should indulge her. There would be something a little contemptuous in his indulgence. For most of her purposes and motives, she reflected sadly, he could have no sympathy, but for the willfulness he would show a measure of generosity.

She was a little anxious when he did not come or send word that day, but she was so busy with plans for the new work that she found little time for actual worry. And the next day was quite as busy. Moreover, there was something exhilarating in the response of the various factions of the town to her plan. Simone, once he saw the plans under way, was reconciled to the loss of the grim eminence he had hitherto enjoyed in the eyes of the merchants of the town as the monster who threatened to devour all their substance. His new position as the source of supplies for the work on the dike gave him all the power he could want, and, Matilda suspected cynically, plenty of chance for a little profit of his own. As for the Bishop, though he would clearly have liked to supervise the works himself and play the almoner to his lord's bounty, yet he was quite intelligent enough to see that in a prosperous and hopeful town he would find it much easier to collect his rents and much easier to restore the order he so sincerely desired. The merchants and the craftsmen and the peasants were obviously enthusiastic about a chance to demonstrate their devotion to their lords in an enterprise which would redound so materially to their advantage. Though Matilda found herself more than once thinking of the blunt terms in which Godfrey would see the whole transaction, yet there was much satisfaction in seeing her plan materializing so swiftly, much quiet pleasure in the thought that here a little piece of the world's misery that had been given into her keeping was being relieved.

But not even this satisfaction could keep the worry at bay when the second day passed without any word from Godfrey. So, early on the next morning, she set out for the return home in considerable anxiety. Thoughts of her child were now taking the place of all others. It was the first time since his birth that she had left the precincts of the castle, and though he had been often in the hands of others, always he had been within reach of a moment's walk. In the lonely nights of Godfrey's absence his cradle had stood in her chamber, and his nurse had lain in her bed. And in the crowded days after her mother's return to Mantua, as she sat in the great hall by the fire, receiving and sending messengers to all her lands and keeping a constant eye on the work of her household, always one corner of her brain had been alert for his cry. Even when she had gone to visit the sick in the village at the foot of the hill, she had been alert for the treble blast on the watchman's horn agreed upon as the signal of trouble with the child. Now it was the third day that she had been without news of him.

Alberic must have divined her anxiety, for he rode up beside her and began talking casually about their visit.

"How sad the good Bishop was to see the last of my beloved habit!" he began with a touch of his old persiflage.

For a moment Matilda gazed at him without seeing him.

"I suppose," he added wryly, "most bishops have little love for monks."

With an effort she pulled her thoughts together. "Can you blame them?"

"Well," he affected to consider, "they are missing a chance to show their love of good men."

The incongruity between the habit and the tone of voice broke through her care, and she found herself smiling at this lean jester in black serge. "Especially with a sword?"

The laughing face sobered. "I suppose the less said about that, the less scandal there will be to worry my worthy Abbot when I return. But there's no use thinking of that. The good Bishop will obviously do his best with the material, and I cannot deny that it is promising. Still it was worth a good many days of bread and water to see that scoundrel pouring out his precious wine for those poor devils!" The muscles at the corners of his mouth quivered a little.

"Alberic, would you not like to be free again to do as you like?"

"I am doing what I want to do, Matilda."

She knew she was blushing. After all she should not have thought she could catch him unawares.

"Not just that," she said. "But, when you get back to San Benedetto, you will have to account for yourself to your Abbot."

His voice was gentle, and he watched her carefully as he answered; "And when you get back to Canossa, will you not account to your husband?"

"It's not the same thing."

She fancied that he looked a little ashamed. "No," he said, "I suppose not. But leaving out those personal things that enter into marriage, do you think I should be freer, say, if I were a knight? Do you think I could do as I liked, say, when my lord wanted me to do something different?"

But Matilda was not to be caught. "Oh, I know of course that nobody does just what he wants to do. That's not what you are trying to say, I hope."

"Well," Alberic considered, "I am not sure that all your friends take that for granted. The King, for instance, seems sometimes to have forgotten it, if he ever knew it. But to take less exalted and, I suspect, safer examples. Do you think that the Bishop wanted to see Simone put in charge of all this hurly-burly in Florence?"

"He accepted it readily enough," retorted Matilda.

"What else could he do? Every man of power like the Bishop must study to please his superior. To beg your pardon for a more personal reference, do you think that Godfrey when he is in Germany does what he wants to do if he knows that the King has decided on something else? At least my superior will not act on any whim. There are definite rules which he knows and I know, and everybody standing by knows them and will judge whether or not he has acted justly. Nor can he plead the necessities of his interests, nor cry that the order of society is in jeopardy if he finds that his subjects think he has been too severe."

"But the King must respect the rights of others, too," objected Matilda.

"If they are strong enough to maintain them or make it dangerous for him to disregard them. Not if they are weak or helpless." There was no mistaking the earnestness of Alberic.

But some blind instinct of loyalty to her own order stirred in Matilda.

"We all know that that is the way of the world, but tell me, sir monk, is this never true of the Church? Do you think that priest we found on the river bank would obtain justice at the hands of the Bishop?"

She was sorry that she had gone so far when Alberic shook his head somberly.

"God knows the world has taken possession even of the Church. You cannot expect an animal, like the Bishop, who has always lived by the law of the strongest to change his spots when he becomes a bishop. The names of the coins he handles now are different but the metal is the same."

"That is what the Pope was talking about in his last letter." But though she felt the curiosity of Alberic in the eyes he fixed on her, the effort was too great. Something must be wrong with the child. And riding along in silence, she began to think about it all again. Come to manhood, her son could do more than ever she could to see justice done, to raise up the oppressed, to comfort the weak. But would he want to? Maybe, he would be like her father and add fief to fief and realize his dream of all Italy under one rule. He might have some of his mother's and his grandmother's love of beauty and learning and build bridges and palaces and found monasteries. But he was his father's son, too, and suppose he cared for none of these things? But she would instill these things into him. Then she thought of Godfrey the elder. He might be gentle like him—for some reason she thought of her husband's sullenness when his will was withstood, and then she remembered the sadness of the elder Godfrey. Perhaps, he had not found it entirely easy to give his wife her way in so many things, and the gentleness which made it impossible for him to withstand the sharper willfulness of others yet gave him no peace.

So they rode all that day and the next two days, and into the fourth day. Sometimes they stopped to rest and to water their horses. Sometimes they stopped for food, and now and then they drank some of the Bishop's wine. It was warm and tasted of the leather bottle, but its fire drove them on afresh. For Matilda's anxiety had infected the whole company, and now, toward the end of the fourth day, they pressed forward as fast as they dared urge their tired horses.

Sometimes it seemed to Matilda in those last hours of their journey that her mind swam out of her body, and that, quite regardless of her will, her taut hands gripped the reins and her stiff thighs clutched the horse's back. Once, where some thick brambles reached out into the road, her horse nearly threw her. She looked up at Alberic to find his face drawn and thoughtful as he watched her. With a great effort, she loosed the tense muscles of her mouth, and she smiled at him.

At any moment now the road would open out, and the stone-peaked hill would swim into view. Ah, there it was now. The men gave a shout of relief. She nodded to them. And then she wondered if she had not been quite foolish. Of course, the child was all right. She could count on her household. It was simply that Godfrey was angry with her, piqued that she had run off like this so soon after his return. She must coax him a little.

Some peasants working in an open field rested on their plow handles and watched them ride by. She wanted to shout to them for news, but it would take too much time.

Far off as if out of the deeps of the sunset, she heard the sweet cry of the watchman's trumpet. If only the oaf would remember their signal of the winter before. He blew a second time, and she held her breath. But that was all.

They were in the muddy streets of the village, and some of the village folk now came to their doors and stared at them, but she was riding too fast to see their faces. Only, she noticed a couple of village girls with baskets of flowers on their arms, and some peasant women trudging after them with their heads huddled in short gray veils. They stopped as she came near, but they only stared, flattening themselves against the wall. Some of the castle people should be around the turn in the road.

Yes, somebody was coming around the turn in the road—a priest, Donizo. He reined in his horse and stretched out his hands to her. There were other figures riding out behind him.

"Father!" she cried and strove to check her excitement, for her hand was shaking so she could hardly hold the reins. And then she saw the priest's face, white and frightened. She took a firm grip on the reins and looked at him until his face had ceased to shiver in her frightened gaze. Slowly, he dismounted and came over to her. With all her strength she waited.

"It is the will of God, my lady. He gives, and He takes away." The priest was standing by her side now, his frightened face raised pleadingly to hers. She looked up at a fresh sound of hoofbeats over the drawbridge, and tried to focus her eyes so that she could see. It was Godfrey, bent almost flat upon the neck of his horse. She turned and looked into Donizo's face, white and still, as if he were waiting. Then slowly it swam from her sight.

Afterward she could remember a press of dim figures about her, of trying to answer Godfrey's voice calling her name from a great distance. She had not thought about it before, but suddenly she wondered. Again, she had a sense of coming from far off, of trying to focus her eyes so that they would catch what lay between.

It was the voice of Alberic that asked the question, but she was able to hear the answer of Ermengarde for all her sobbing. "A chill and then the poor little creature had the fever, and last night it choked up. Early this morning he turned black and gave up breathing. It was over as quick as that, my lady," added Ermengarde, turning to her mistress.

"I shall never forgive myself," said Matilda, lifting her head from the cushion on which it had been lying.

No one said anything, but Godfrey sat down on the edge of the chest on which they had laid her and took her hand. He did not look at her, but he stroked her hand slowly, and the rough tenderness filled her heart with sudden warmth.

"Oh, Godfrey," she tried to find words and could not.

He dropped her hand. "I did tire him too much that night and the next day."

She realized that he thought she was blaming him. For a moment she said nothing but looked at him, hunched up on the edge of the chest by her side. She heard the movement of the household falling back, she heard the voice of Alberic saying sharply, "Leave your lady alone with her lord now." She reached for Godfrey's hand, and she held it in her two hands as tightly as she could until she felt his sobbing breath upon her face, and then the world seemed to swim away again…

"It is so cold in here," she complained to Donizo as she entered the chapel.

She did not hear the pious murmur, for there before her stood the great mosaic candelabra which she had last seen burning about the tired face of Godfrey the Elder. Their gleaming reds and blues and golds looked astonishingly bright in the soft light of the great waxen tapers. And then she saw the wood snowdrops with their pale green stems and their frail white cups of blossoms lying in a heap on a little mound of silk in the mist of the candlelight.

Donizo was speaking to her, but she was gazing at the shadows on the closed eyelids. It was too late now to try to warm the cold little figure in her choking bosom. She heard a murmur behind her, and she turned.

It was a peasant woman with a little bunch of arbutus. She knelt down awkwardly as she pressed the flowers into Matilda's hand. Some of the damp earth still clung about their roots, but they seemed to fill the whole chapel with their fresh fragrance. In the light their flush of pink seemed a warm and living thing. It was with a sense of comfort that she laid them in the midst of the pale and scentless snowdrops.

"Do not grieve, my lady," said the woman, her eyes shining with tears and pride. "You will have other sons."

"You have lost, too?" Matilda asked, incredulously.

"Three blessed angels," said the old woman. "Ah, my lady it is as hard to get the children through the winter as the cattle. It is a deal of labor to go in a night." And the old woman put her arm about the waist of her lady timidly. But Matilda laid her head on her shoulder and wept without restraint. She had not thought how many dead children there would be in those great fields of heaven. She could not pray, but with a sudden impulse of supplication she took a sprig of the arbutus from the breast of the dead child and laid it on the stone of the Madonna's altar.

All the rest of that spring whenever she came into the chapel to kneel down by the fresh oblong of marble in the pavement, she noticed that whatever of the wood flowers lay on the new grave, one or two of the same kind lay also on the altar above. And touched afresh by the remembering of the humble, she was comforted.

✳ BOOK III ✳

ANOTHER CITY

CHAPTER I

"I thought," said Matilda to herself, as she rode along the way to Viterbo three months later, "that nothing would ever pierce this wall of grief. Blind with tears, have I lain down and risen all these weeks, and now, without a warning, beauty has come in again, and I am no longer one but two people. For I am still in that dark house in which I have dwelt, and here also am I in this sunshine."

But to her mother sitting on her horse at her side she said aloud, "I think the Pope was pleased. They are fine-looking men. Charlemagne would have been proud to call them his."

The Countess Beatrice looked again down the long line of horsemen, with the June sun running like a rill of pure light along their steel helmets and lifted swords. Here and there, the light broke and wavered, as a restless horse strained at his rider's hand or pawed the warm earth, but the accident deepened rather than marred the illusion. The movement of the light wind in the wood at their back filled the air, too, with the sound of running water on sea sand. But the sweetness of the air was wholly of the woods and fields, the warm, sun-distilled aroma of the cedars dominating the scentless freshness of beech and ash, and the elusive fragrance of the ferns and the mint and thyme, trampled beneath the horses' hoofs rising, triumphant over the light dust.

"You have done very well to gather them together in such unsettled days," said the Countess Beatrice judiciously.

"I could not have had a better cause. But still—of course, I am thankful for their loyalty."

Seen in that mighty cirque of hill and wood and field, with the green slopes of Monte Cimino at their back and the tower-crowned height of Viterbo on one horizon, and the ancient stone of Sutri on the other, the Tuscan forces seemed suddenly but a handful of men in a vast theatre. Yet of all the troops that had rallied to the Pope's summons, Matilda knew that the company that had flowed in from the four corners of the Tuscan lands and followed in the wake of her mother to the trysting place here in the hills between Viterbo and Sutri was the most numerous and the best-equipped.

"Arduino," said Beatrice, "do not let your men forget that this is not a raid or a feud that they are embarked on, but a holy war. There is food for all, and silver to buy more, and no need for any man to pillage or steal from the lands of Saint Peter."

Arduino bowed, his shrewd, far-set eyes fixed almost demurely on the face of his lady. Beatrice frowned, and her daughter smiled. For she knew that Arduino would agree to anything and do exactly as he chose with an enthusiasm and devotion to his mistress' interests that nothing could daunt.

"Did I tell you, Mother, that when Godfrey would not heed my prayers and stay to help the Pope, I had all I could do to keep Arduino from challenging him to a duel?"

Matilda found it impossible not to sympathize with the look of shock on her mother's face, but she hastened to add in justice to her general: "I have never been able to convince Arduino that Godfrey is his lord as well as mine. He has always looked upon him as something of a usurper against whom it was his duty to protect me."

Again Matilda found a certain grim pleasure in watching her mother's face relax. "There is something to that. His father was the gentlest of men, too," she added with a light sigh.

Before Matilda could reply, a low voice, clear and resonant, with a certain bell-like freshness in its volume, broke in upon the silence. "Are the two Countesses going up to Viterbo?"

She turned to look into the clear blue eyes of a monk, reining in his horse with bare brown hand. There was no mistaking the pleasure in Beatrice's voice. "My lord Desiderius! Matilda, you remember the Abbot of Monte Cassino."

"Did anybody ever forget the Abbot of Monte Cassino?" she replied.

The frank blue eyes smiled, as well as the thinly-moulded lips. "Is that to the honor of Saint Benedict or the present unworthy incumbent?"

Then to her courteous murmur, he retorted laughingly: "You have not heard then of the novice in our house who last Christmastide asked the novice master who was the strange old man who had stolen into the choir just before Vespers?"

Then as they laughed, he added gravely, "Ah, but there is worse to come. For the novice master answered, 'That is the peripatetic Abbot of Monte Cassino,' and the unhappy novice went around for the next day asking everybody he could where in the rule there was any description of that strange officer."

The clanking of steel, the neighing of the horses, the voices of the men, all softened as Matilda and her mother rode slowly away with the Abbot.

"Your men lined up there, Lady Beatrice, made me think of the first time I ever saw the Normans at close range. There was a company of them drawn up outside of the castle at Benevento. They grew weary of their waiting, and they began to sing. I have never heard anything quite like their singing. There they were lined up on their horses, those great fair-haired, blue-eyed giants, and they began to sing a low, monotonous, chant-like song in perfect unison. But the extraordinary thing about it was the way they looked. For though their voices swelled with unmistakable passion (you remember, I could not understand a word of what they were singing at that time), yet their faces seemed not to change a muscle nor did any man move from that soldier-like attention of theirs. It was extraordinary to hear that volume of sound surging from those impassive giants. I remember I forgot all my anxiety and just stared."

Matilda voiced a sudden wonder, "Will they not be troubled, these Norman friends of yours, to hear that you have taken the field against them?"

The Abbot of Monte Cassino smiled. "One need not worry about that with them. They expect to pay loyal service and to receive loyal service. You have heard of that old northern tradition of its being a disgrace to leave living the field on which one's lord lay dead? They know I am the liege man of Saint Peter, and they expect me to honor my fealty."

There was something in the sunny simplicity with which the Abbot spoke that made Matilda recall what she had heard of this man. A great scholar, a great administrator, a great builder—there was nothing of cloister pallor in the keen brown face poised lightly like a bird within the shadow of his half-fallen cowl.

"My lord Abbot," she began hungrily, "I have heard that you are doing wonderful things with your church at Monte Cassino."

Again, that note of simple pleasure in the clear laugh. "My lady, I should like nothing better than to show you our church. But I must not boast of it now, for in a few minutes you will see a man who is really going to do something with a church. You should see the columns on which Hugh of Cluny is planning to raise the roof of that new choir of theirs. Slender and white with carved capitals, they are lovely enough to bear the golden roof of the new Jerusalem itself. Only I warn you that once you have seen even the plan of them, all the rest of the world's pillars will seem gross and cloddish. They are like those nymphs of the springs that the old pagan poets sang of. So beauty worships clearly what once she groped for darkly in poet's dreams."

Halfway up the hill they stood and rested, looking out over the green country they had just left. Already one or two tents had been raised, and though the figures of the soldiers had blurred from the distance, there was an obvious going to and fro of the brown specks, with here and there a mirror-like flash of light as the warm sun caught helmet or sword or shield. They seemed curiously insignificant and transient in the encircling green, the dark purple greens of the wood behind them, the sunny yellow greens of the unploughed fields, the deeper, luminous green of the wheat, the soft blue-green of the oats, and everywhere the shadowy gray-green of the olives. All other colors, the white of the birch trunks, the tawny red of the rocks, the brown of the bare earth itself, seemed but accidents in that sea of veridian.

"The finest thing that I shall show you at Monte Cassino, my lady Matilda, when you come to see us, I think you will agree with me, is the view from our monastery over the valley. That we may boast of without fear of vanity or exaggeration, for that is the gift of God, and though we cannot better it save with good husbandry, neither can we harm it so long as we use it according to our rule."

"These last months, my lord Abbot, I have seen plenty of reason to feel that good husbandry is an art quite worthy to stand beside the building of churches—at least from the layman's point of view," Matilda ended humbly.

"From any point of view," said the Abbot heartily. "I am sure there is no worship more acceptable to God than the good use of his gifts. I heard, my lady, that your dike at Florence is finished."

She nodded, half-gratified, half-troubled that what she had held at arm's length came so close again.

"They call it the Dike of the Countess Matilda?"

"That is what they called it when the companies knelt down in the Cathedral and thanked me for it. But down on the river they call it the Dike of the Dead Child." She had not meant to speak of it so bitterly; indeed, she was surprised at the sound of her own voice.

But she need not have been concerned, for the Abbot said simply, "I was sorry to hear of your grief, Countess, and I have much admired the way in which you have gone on with your work."

It seemed ungrateful to say no more than the barest of thanks, but the kindness of the Abbot had gone to her heart.

Then with the same tact, Desiderius turned to the Countess Beatrice and began to talk of the meeting to which they were all going.

When they were just below the high brown walls of Viterbo, the Abbot began to talk to Matilda again. "This approach to the city seems to me always a parable. So far as we can see from here, there is only this pile of crags before us. It seems a dead-end against the sky. But, presently, when you come out on the piazza of the city, you will find a great expanse of beautiful country before you as if in truth all the kingdoms of the world were spread out there for your choice."

She smiled at the Abbot, "I shall not forget the parable, my lord Desiderius."

"By the way," he held her back for a moment as she started to pass through the gate, "is it true that my Lord Godfrey is not coming?"

"Quite true." And as the Abbot said nothing but simply nodded as if after all it were perfectly reasonable that Godfrey of Lorraine should have left it to his wife to answer the Pope's summons, she added: "He has gone back to Germany to join the King."

Still the Abbot said nothing but nodded again as if it were all quite clear. It had come, and now she felt a little surer of herself. For all the way from Canossa she had dreaded this moment—when people would begin to ask about her husband's absence, if it were true that the Pope's general had refused to answer his call for the defense of the land of the Church. It had been hard enough to face the world with its curiosity and its intrusive pity when her burden had been simply a matter of personal grief. She had blamed herself bitterly for the neglect of her child, but nobody else had reproached her. Indeed, there had been moments when it seemed to her that it would be easier to bear the aching of her conscience if her blame were openly acknowledged. She had gone so far as to ask Donizo to impose some extraordinary penance of pilgrimage or public devotion that would express her guilt, and he had refused, saying that it would be a sin for him to admit blame where no blame had existed. But this was even harder. For there was the bitterness of vicarious guilt in the broken fealty, and there was the shame of wifely failure in the memory of the violence with which Godfrey had repudiated her intercession. And there was, too, a sore conflict between honor and the pride of loyalty. She was bringing the Pope the most splendid assistance of any of the princes of Italy, but the greatest of all, the help of the ablest general of the empire, that she might fairly have been expected to bring, she was not bringing. In the days of her betrothal she had often heard men speak with pity of the wrongs of Queen Bertha, of the cruelty with which Henry treated her, and she had listened with contempt for the weakness and maladroitness of the abused wife. Now in justice she had to admit that Bertha was no more ineffectual, no more helpless than she. Well, she had met her shame face to face. And she still rode erect, with a firm hand on the rein down the streets of Viterbo. The bitterest was still ahead, when in the face of the Pope she should read the full extent of her failure, but she had tasted of the cup.

The people of Viterbo raised a shout, and there were many cries of greeting and acclaim as she rode down the street. But the applause seemed to her a bitterly ironic thing, and when from habit she smiled, it seemed to her that she had only drawn a mask over her face.

Perhaps the Abbot Desiderius guessed something of what was passing through her mind, for people said that he entered so fully into the interests of his fellow men that he was able to divine their very thoughts. At any rate, he leaned over to her as they came before the bishop's palace, and said so low that none but herself might hear: "It is more than youth and power and beauty that they acclaim today when they praise you, Countess of Tuscany. A prince who is true to his trust is worthy of the praise of all men." The last he added as an afterthought to himself.

Matilda felt her cheeks flame. The next moment she was kissing the ring on the Pope's hand and looking up into his face. It was careworn, anxious, but as always, steady. There was no shadow in the clear eyes that met hers, and there was a quickness of pleasure in his cordial greeting, "God bless you for what you have done, my child."

The cathedral was almost full when she entered it with her mother and the Abbot. It was a beautiful scene, full of life and color and animation. The standards of the assembled princes hung in blocks of brilliant color from the pillars of the nave, while underneath were massed all the colors of the autumn woods in the robes and mantles of their companies. There was a clanking of swords and a ringing of metal against metal and stone as the whole company rose to greet the Pope, waving their swords in the quiet church light. Then as the Pope took his place before the open gates of the marble sanctuary screen, with the clerical princes sitting on faldstools in the sanctuary at his back and the lay princes and their chief followers on long benches across the nave, the whole company seated itself again with another clanking of stone and metal down the long waves of color. At her mother's side Matilda took her place on a low stool just below the Pope's chair. From here she could see the entire lay company, headed on the one side by the nobles and knights of Tuscany, on the other by the vassals of Gisulf of Salerno.

Leaning forward, she could see the tall figure of Gisulf on the farther side of the Pope, with the haughty eye and the firmly pressed lips of the great commander. On the other side of him the Abbot Desiderius by contrast seemed a little casual, a little deprecating, with his finely moulded head drawn into the shadow of the lowered cowl so that his tonsure looked strikingly white in his iron gray hair.

The Pope spoke very simply and clearly, without any effort at emphasis, as he arraigned the Normans for their encroachments on the territories of the Church. At some length he described the various efforts he had made to recover the holdings of the Church to the south, the promises which the Norman leaders had made and never kept. As he spoke of the ambiguity and shiftiness of Robert Guiscard and his brother, Roger, Count of Sicily, Matilda looked again at Desiderius. His friendship with the Norman leaders was famous, ever since that first meeting when the charm of his personality had won upon the fierce hearts of the barbarian invaders. There had been whispers, that he had not sympathized too much with the Pope's efforts to bring his friends to book for their raids on the papal lands of the south. Men had talked, also, of the rich gifts which Robert and Roger had made to the treasure of Monte Cassino, of gems and manuscripts pillaged from Sicilian cities that had been sent to the library so dear to the heart of Desiderius, but there had been little malice in these reports, for all men knew that the heart of Desiderius was not set on the lands and gems and silver for which his neighbors strove so greedily, but on the paintings and books which the ordinary man did not covet. Matilda watched him as the Pope spoke with cold severity of the ill faith of the Normans, but Desiderius did not raise his head. He seemed the perfect figure of a Benedictine monk absorbed in meditation.

Watching him, Matilda for a moment lost the thread of the papal discourse, absorbed in wonder at the difference between the still white light of contemplation and the many-colored hues of reverie. "For," she said to herself, "Desiderius' mind is busy with one thing, but mine runs hither and yon, first from one thing glimpsed, like his face now, to wonder at what he is thinking, and back to myself, like a butterfly from flower to grass to twig on an aimless summer breeze." Then the voice of the speaker rose until in sudden power it rang through her idle ears, and again she was listening.

The Pope had drawn his slight figure to its full height and leaned forward from his chair. His face seemed blown clean of weariness, and his voice rang clear and strong through the great basilica. All the men before him, too, were leaning forward in their absorption in his words.

"It is no ambition of power that has moved us to recover what never belonged to us but to Saint Peter. These lands, these towns, these villas and churches are the gifts of centuries of pious Christians who have given their goods to the service of God. Even if we would, we have no right to allow what faith has given to that service to be appropriated by private and secular greed. We are not a rich lord who out of laziness or cowardice may let the heritage of our house be dissipated. We are a steward and a trustee, a servant into whose keeping has been given the materials for the worship of the altar, the bread of the poor, the sustenance on this earth of the Church which God has appointed to guide and to teach and to give law unto men. Thieves have broken in. They will not merely damage what they have stolen, but they will turn it against their neighbors and their lawful superiors to injure and enslave. If these barbarians are not stopped, they will use the patrimony of Saint Peter to lay waste this motherland of the faith and to make slaves of the people of God."

The great voice rang out in a final burst of eloquence and was still. There was a yell of approval from all over the vast basilica. Then another cry arose, "Death to Robert Guiscard and the Norman robbers." The Pope sat impassive, as if he did not hear what the crowd were saying. But Desiderius had heard, for he sprang to his feet, and folding his arms within his long black sleeves, he faced the Pope.

"My lord Gregory," the soft voice rose above the tumult. The knights sat down and waited curiously.

"My lord Pope," he began again, "are you telling us that it is your will that we should go to fight the Normans?"

From all over the church there came yells of, "Yes, slay the robbers. Drive out the barbarians."

A look of alarm came into the face of the Pope, but Desiderius did not wait for him to speak.

"My lord," he began, speaking in a low, earnest voice, while the whole company leaned forward to hear him, "these men, Robert Guiscard and his brother Roger, have invaded the lands of the Church, and we have a right and a duty to demand that they return what they have taken. But they have sworn fealty to Saint Peter, and they are Your Holiness' liege men, however remiss they have been. And though they are barbarians with the ways of barbarians, they are also Christians. I admit that they have not always dealt faithfully with Your Holiness, but when King Henry sent agents of his to tempt the Normans to swear allegiance to him, saving fealty to none, Robert Guiscard answered that it was to the intercession of the Saints Peter and Paul that he owed his victories, and he would not lose their help for any man."

A low rumble of protest ran through the basilica, and the mouth of Gisulf of Salerno tightened, even while the high look of disdain on his features deepened. This time the Pope had risen, standing very erect with his scarlet mantle stiff behind him.

"It has never been our intention at any time," he began in a low, harsh voice that carried sharply through the basilica, "to make war on the Normans. But since they understand neither the arguments of reason nor the persuasions of conscience, it has been our intention to invoke the only considerations they seem capable of understanding, the threat of armed force. If they see all of Christian Italy arrayed against them, they will listen with new ears to the voice of duty."

As he finished speaking, he looked sharply at Desiderius, who had not taken his eyes from his face.

The latter now bowed very low and answered so that all could hear, "Of that, Your Holiness, I have never made any question."

It was Gisulf of Salerno's turn now, and though he held his sword firmly to his side as he rose and bowed to the Pope, with the moving of his feet his helmet clanged against his shield on the stone pavement. He paid no attention to the noise, but plunged at once into his question, speaking in a high-pitched, severe voice that seemed to Matilda to be struggling hard for control. "But surely Your Holiness is not suggesting that after coming here to Viterbo, we should do nothing but march back to our own lands."

There was a low murmur of approval in the church, and the line between the eyebrows in Gregory's face deepened.

"My lord of Salerno, and our good son, I have from the beginning made no secret of the objective of this rally which you have so magnificently supported. It is the cry of the Christians of the East that has led me to summon you here. As I said in my letter of April, messengers have not ceased to come to our chair and to bring to us the anguish of these thousands who are perishing at the hands of the heathen.

"They dwell in those most ancient lands which Our Lord made holy by the scene of His Incarnation. And now under the sword of the crudest of invaders, they are being swept like beasts from the fields. Like beasts they are being hunted down and slain. And the land that the piety of generations has called holy is being made the spoil of men who know not God. There is nobody but us to hear their cry. The great King of the East has seen the barbarians spread over his rich lands like the locusts of Pharaoh, and his strength and his power have melted like dew from the morning grass. He has cried to us. The waves of the heathen are sweeping all before them. If we do not succor these helpless people, presently that sea of destruction will be washing our green shores and licking the walls of your own castles."

A great awe had come upon the host in the cathedral as they listened to the deep swell of the Pope's words, and in many of the faces before her Matilda could see the horror and fascination of the Pope's eloquence struggling with habitual indifference. Again, that terrible and beautiful voice rose: "But these are counsels of self-interest. Christian charity that bids all of the household of faith minister to one another's necessities will speak more directly to your hearts. And loyalty to the most ancient shrines of our faith will not passively see them destroyed by the powers of darkness."

Again, there was a yell of approval, knight and noble leaping from his seat to wave his sword, and the ringing of metal upon metal swelled the tumult. But there was no relaxation of the Pope's tense face, nor any faltering of the arm he lifted before them in command of silence. The noise died away, and the excited crowd waited.

"There is no man here," said the little dark priest, holding the crowd before him fascinated by his words, "whose heart has not swelled with the dream of glory. But every wise man knows that the glory of this world passes like smoke, and the longest memory of man is a swift oblivion. It is not to this brittle fame that the Christian knight looks in his dreams but to the glory of the soldiers of God for whom an immortal crown of victory and an undying peace are stored up in a world of which the splendor of this is but a shadow. To that glory no road is so short or so swift as this which I open to you. Soldiers of Saint Peter, take the path of God."

Then rose the wildest tumult of all, with some men shouting and waving their arms, and others kneeling and stretching out their swords to the Pope. For some moments the Pope stood there, watching the turmoil, apparently unmoved. Only, from where she sat, Matilda could see the muscles of his neck stand out hard and tense. Then when the first paroxysm of enthusiasm had a little spent itself, he raised his hand again, and while they waited with outstretched heads to hear him speak, he pronounced in clear, cool tones the papal benediction. As the company waited, too astonished to move, the Pope turned first to Beatrice, then to Gisulf with the same swift command, "Follow me to the Bishop's house." Then without a word, without looking to right or to left, he started down the main aisle of the church. As he came opposite the benches of the still kneeling company, they leaped to their feet and began to cheer wildly for the Pope and Saint Peter. But he made no sign of response, only strode with a firm step to the door.

The sound of the cheering still rang in the ears of the little company who had gathered in one of the smaller rooms of the Bishop's palace. Now in the quiet of the cool little painted chamber with the open loggia looking out on a garden, Matilda struggled to recover control of her feelings. Gisulf of Salerno strode back and forth nervously, the Abbot of Monte Cassino stroked his crucifix thoughtfully, the Bishop of Viterbo drummed his knuckles on the stone ledge of the window. Beatrice alone sat very still, her full face looking curiously long in her absorption in her own thoughts.

Moving very softly as if loath to break the silence, Hugh of Cluny slipped into the room and sat down on one of the stools about a long, narrow table, on the other side of which stood waiting a single, large chair. Then the Pope came in, shutting the door firmly behind him. Matilda looked at him curiously, but though her own heart was still throbbing with the excitement of his eloquence, his manner seemed as calm as if he had just risen from prayer. As he sat down in the chair on the other side of the low table, the company grouped itself before him on stools, only the Countess Beatrice sitting in a chair at the end of the table.

With a little bow to the company, the Pope plunged into the business of the hour: "I wish to take counsel with you, my sons and daughters. For it is in your loyalty that under God I put my trust."

For a moment no one spoke. Then Gisulf of Salerno broke the silence with a certain air of pent-up impatience, "Do you seriously propose, Your Holiness, that we should start out on this crusade now?"

The Pope folded his hands on the table before him and looked up at Gisulf for some moments. Then he spoke, "That is a question which I hoped you would answer for me, my son."

Gisulf was on the point of replying. Then he hesitated as if reconsidering.

"I have given you the reasons why I think we should go to the aid of the Christian peoples of the East," said the Pope quietly.

"But, Your Holiness," exploded Gisulf, unable to contain his impatience any longer, "you don't think that we could meet those hordes of pagans with the forces we have here?"

"No," said the Pope, leaning forward and speaking with great frankness of manner, "I don't, but I had hoped there would be more of you." He did not take his eyes off Gisulf, but though Matilda did not flinch, she felt her cheeks burn.

Gisulf turned to her. "Countess, I am sorry, but isn't your husband coming at all?"

Before she had time to think, she heard her own voice saying very calmly, "I am afraid not, my lord of Salerno. He has gone into Lorraine."

For a moment Gisulf stared, but though her heart was beating furiously, she met his gaze steadily. At last, his eyes fell. He turned to the Abbot Hugh. "My lord of Cluny, are none of the lords, secular or spiritual, of the Frankish Kingdom here?"

The pale face of the Abbot of Cluny flushed, and he rose quickly to his feet. "The Frankish Kingdom is a," he hesitated and considered the word, "troubled and uncertain place, my lord. I have no doubt that we could raise a large company among the Frankish lords, but it would take time for these men to set their domains in order and to make certain that no one would vex their lands in their absence. I have wondered," he said a little timidly, "if my lord Pope were to come into France, if he could not raise the Frankish nobility sooner than anybody else."

But Desiderius shook his head vigorously. "My brother of Cluny, Italy is not so quiet a place as that. We need His Holiness here."

"Ah, your Norman friends," said Gisulf, with a scornful flash of dark eyes under long lashes. Then as Desiderius flushed, he turned to the Pope again, "My lord Pope, there is no help from France, there is no hope of help from the King of Germany. Even your own general, Godfrey the Hunchback, has turned his back on your summons and taken refuge in Lorraine."

Matilda opened her lips to speak, but no sound came, and she struggled helplessly with the hot sobs in her throat.

"My lord of Salerno," said Beatrice coolly, "nobody has ever called Godfrey of Lorraine a coward, or had cause to."

"I withdraw the imputation if the Countess Beatrice prefers to have her son-in-law called recreant to his pledges and his oaths—" Gisulf paused, for the corners of the Pope's mouth had straightened dangerously.

"For the matter of that," said the Bishop of Viterbo, speaking lazily from his corner where hitherto he had said nothing, had indeed seemed to devote all his attention to the butterflies fluttering in the sunlit garden without, "the captain of the Pisans told me just before we came here that under no circumstances would the people of Pisa fight with the Lord of Salerno. It is some old grudge about the seizure of merchants and their goods, isn't it, Gisulf?" he asked, leaning across the table.

The indignant soldier leaped to his feet, but before he could find words, there came an insistent knocking at the door. The Pope nodded to Hugh, who sat nearest the disturbance.

It was Arduino della Palude who stood on the threshold, bowing to the Pope. With bulging eyes he searched the company until he found the Countess Beatrice.

"My lady, I must see you at once."

"You may say here whatever you have to say," said Beatrice, with obvious scorn of his excitement.

For answer Arduino looked helplessly to Matilda, but though Matilda saw his fright and anger, she was too sick at heart to interfere.

"As soon as your ladyships' backs were turned, the Lord of Baggiovara invaded the lands of the Bishop of Modena. Word has just come to the camp down there, and those blasted traitors of Modenese have ridden off, though I told them your ladyship would hang every man of them. The Lord of Camaldoli laughed when the Bishop threatened him with your ladyship's—" But Beatrice had risen and taken Arduino by the shoulder.

"You fool, to bother us with such trifles! Your Holiness, will you excuse me until I shake this coward out of his panic?"

As the Countess Beatrice swept majestically from the room, followed by the cowed Arduino, the whole company looked at each other. It was Hugh of Cluny who broke the silence, "Time is passing, and we are all tired, Your Holiness."

Suddenly, the Pope seemed very weary. "Until after Mass tomorrow then," he said, raising his hand to dismiss them.

Without a word, Gisulf of Salerno strode from the room. The Bishop of Viterbo chuckled. "It is one thing, Your Holiness, to attack the Normans with the hope of their lands to carve fresh fiefs from, and quite another to march against the Turks with nothing but wounds and the pains of travel to look forward to."

The Pope's eyes glittered, but he made no answer. Only, as Matilda came round the corner of the table, he lifted his hand to stay her.

When they were alone, he motioned to her to sit down.

"You are my beloved daughter, Matilda, and there is no shame in what a daughter tells her father." For a moment he paused as if uncertain, and Matilda fixed her eyes upon his face. Then he said very gently, "Godfrey has left us, hasn't he?"

"Yes."

"I thought that letter sounded final. I wonder if Henry has spoken more plainly to him than to me. In all he has written to me he has been a model of obedience and cooperation, but so far I have seen no evidence of more than words. When I knew Henry in Germany, he was always quite ready to agree with whatever you had to say." He paused.

"My lord," said Matilda, folding her hands tightly in her lap, "I am afraid I have not the honor of my husband's confidence. When he wrote that letter to you, he told me that I was more interested in your—" she hesitated, but it seemed to her that she was now far beyond either courtesy or loyalty—"in your schemes than in my husband's or my family's aggrandizement. His father had been his wife's slave. He did not propose to be mine." Her eyes filled with tears, and she strove frantically to check them. Gregory seemed absorbed in the problem. Not even to her mother had she said so much, but the least she could do, it seemed to her, was to put the Pope in full possession of the extent of her failure.

"He believes, then," said Gregory thoughtfully, "that his loyalty to the King of Germany would be jeopardized by my service. He is an honest man, your husband, Matilda."

Then, suddenly, he seemed to be aware of her pain. "Things seldom work out as we plan."

For the first time Matilda noticed the flush in his hollow cheeks. This was something more than weariness. But he seemed unaware of her scrutiny.

"Tomorrow," he went on, "your mother will have to go back and you with her. For now we will have to give up our purpose. Later perhaps when God wills, we can do it. For now, you will not forget to pray for those who are suffering so sorely, will you?"

He must be disappointed, she said to herself, and out of her own misery, she yearned to say something of reassurance, but she could find nothing that she could say with any confidence. He seemed to feel something of her unspoken sympathy, however, for when she knelt down to kiss his ring, he looked into her face, and there was pity in his voice as he said, "First your son, and now your husband. God is trying you in his fire, my lord of Tuscany."

As her lips touched his hand, she was shocked at the heat of fever. "You are ill, Your Holiness."

"Just fatigue," he smiled at her. "I will rest now."

But ten days later when Matilda and her mother reached Modena, weary and sore from their journey and from an inconclusive skirmish with the rebellious troops of Baggiovara, they found a messenger from the Pope waiting for them. He was grievously ill, and he asked their prayers. If he should die, they were not to forget the harassed Christians of the East. Living or dead, he would pray for them who had been his faithful daughters. There were tears in the eyes of Beatrice as she read his letter.

CHAPTER II

BUT Gregory did not die. Some three months later, Matilda waited in the reception hall of the monastery of Saint Mary on the Aventine.

"He has been asking all day, my lady, if the Countess of Tuscany has not come," said the Prior, standing above her and rubbing his thin hands with pleasure. "But this Archbishop of Ravenna insisted on seeing him, and black as heaven knows his heart is, yet the good Pope would not let him be turned away."

"Perhaps, Prior Bonizo, Guibert of Ravenna has seen the evil of his ways and has come to do penance," said Matilda idly, watching the warm September sunshine flicker through the moving screen of the vine leaves across the open window.

But the Prior shook his head. Quite obviously, the good old man liked his villains as strong and black as he liked his saints shining and white. "Not he," he insisted with the gusto of quite impersonal reprobation. "The mark of the devil is in his smiling eyes—"

But more Matilda was not to learn, for at this moment the inner door opened and a large man came out, his dark features fixed in a rather puzzled frown. Without looking at the Prior, he strode almost past Matilda, and then he halted, and in a flash the frown had vanished, and the smile of which the Prior had disapproved, filled not only the eyes but the whole full, handsome face.

"Ah, my lady Matilda, it is you of whom the Pope has been thinking while I have been trying to talk to him. So the world goes. Here even in Rome the face of a beautiful woman is worth all the ecclesiastics in the world."

Soberly, Matilda kissed the beautiful emerald ring on his right hand.

"I am quite sure," she said gravely, "that my lord of Ravenna has things to tell the Pope of far more importance than anything I could ever say."

Guibert laughed. "Not that I blame His Holiness. If you would come to Ravenna to see me, I should turn all the bishops in Christendom from my door. There are many points on which the Pope and I do not see eye to eye—don't look worried, my beautiful Countess; it is politics not heresy that divides good churchmen. But in the matter of visitors, there my taste is at one with his."

"No, my lord Bishop, I bring His Holiness nothing more than the humble congratulations of my mother and myself on his recovery." Involuntarily she found herself edging away from the importunate smiling of Guibert. The corners of his mouth rose, and the lower lip pointed slightly. Gratefully, Matilda saw the door behind him open, and with a curtsey she slipped through, but not before she heard the light laugh of Guibert as he went his way.

There was still an unpleasant taste in her mouth when she looked around the cloister. It was empty. So she went to the arched doorway into the courtyard. For a moment she blinked in the bright sunshine that poured down the golden marble of the cloister walls.

"Over here, my child," said the familiar voice, slightly husky as if spent with talking. "And God bless you for coming."

In the corner of the cloister garden where some late red roses were blooming in a cluster of earthen jars, the Pope had set his chair in an angle of shadow from the vines. In a dark monk's habit such as he had worn in the quiet days of his youth, with a purple rug thrown across his knees, he looked worn and pale, his large eyes shining out of deep caverns of shadow.

As she knelt to kiss his ring, Matilda could not repress a little sob, whether of grief or pleasure she could not have said, herself. For some moments neither spoke. Matilda raised her head. The Pope was not looking at her. His eyes seemed fixed on something behind her back, and she turned her head to look.

There was no one there. Only from a poplar tree in the opposite corner of the garden the slim, golden leaves were falling slowly in the sunlight, lying flat on the windless air of early September like bright coins. They seemed to make the stillness of the warm sunshine more still, even as the soft falling of the water in the foundation below but deepened the silence of the empty garden.

"Their day is done, and they fall without haste and without repining," he said softly. "So it is in all this world we call insensate, Matilda. Only we to whom the Creator has given the gift of reason quarrel with His will."

She dried her eyes and, still kneeling by the sick man's side, she said as lightly as she could, "This time we are giving thanks that His will was as we prayed, and that He spared you to us, Holy Father."

For a moment, the firmly-held lips pursed ruefully and then straightened: "I thought the days of my service were done, Matilda, and that presently I should be home in my Father's house. Even now as the strength of my body rises in me, I can hardly bear to think that I must carry the burden of this life, God knows how much longer. To lie down to sleep, tortured with the things I have not been able to bring to pass, to rise overwhelmed with the things I must do and cannot—do you wonder that I prayed that my Master would call His servant back?"

Matilda shook her head, and suddenly she was very sure. "To whom then should we turn?"

"No," said the Pope, "that is small comfort. For one's own affairs one can take comfort that one has done one's best, but in God's the best is only the beginning. Have you ever heard the story of that Pope whose name I bear, of him who made it after the name of Peter the greatest of titles for his successors? It was in a time of famine and invasion. He had done his best to look after his flock, to strengthen and to feed and to comfort them. But one morning in the desolate streets of Rome a man was found dead of hunger. Gregory wept that he had failed in the charge which God had given him, and that day he forbore to say Mass because his hands were stained with the death of one of his children."

Matilda shivered. "Then, Holy Father, it will go hard with the rest of us. For who of the princes of Christendom can say that none of his subjects has ever died through his neglect?"

But the Pope smiled, and leaning on his elbow, he drew himself up and smoothed the rug across his knees. "Forgive me, Matilda, for troubling you with these complaints of mine. It is His will that I live and bear my burden. You must not sympathize with me when I grumble, or I shall be tempted to lay on your young shoulders a load for which they are not yet braced."

She yearned to tell him that never had she been prouder of anything than that he should turn to her for comfort in facing trials which she could only dimly understand. But she hesitated to put even this much into words. He seemed, however, to sense the unspoken sympathy, for his voice softened as he said, "Now tell me how you are."

"What shall I say? I arise in the morning, and I take what the day brings, and at night I lie down, and if you brought them to me, I could not tell the face of one of my days from another," she replied passionately.

For several minutes he did not answer. Then he spoke in low and measured tones: "That is not the whole story, Matilda. From many people have I heard news of you these last months. I heard that after he had drawn his sword against you and made war on you, you forgave the Lord of Baggiovara and out of your own stores you fed the castle and town that had rebelled against you. And when you and your mother were at Pisa and gave a princely gift to the cathedral there, it was given in prayer not only for yourselves but for the husband who had left you in anger. And when there was the sickness at Terni, you went yourself with spices and medicines. And the drunken priest at Bobbio you sent to his bishop, and the Lord of Narni, who had abused his serfs, you threatened to kill with your own sword so that he was ashamed. These are not the things one hears of most of the princes of this world, Countess of Tuscany."

Matilda laughed grimly. "These are the kind people you have listened to, Your Holiness. There are other tales, too. And the voice for which I would give all the world's voices is silent still."

The Pope shook his head, and with one thin hand he rubbed the rug over his knees slowly. "Have you written to your lord?"

"Yes, humbly and dutifully. But I still did not feel that with all so uncertain in my lands I could leave them now, and I did not feel that in conscience I could forswear the pledges I had given or promise that his allegiance should be mine."

A look of great pity came into the Pope's face. "When there is division in the high places of the world, then all relations are vitiated where peace should dwell."

"No," Matilda hastened to object, "sometimes I wonder if perhaps I am wrong to set up my will against my lord's, and yet though I am a woman and subject to authority, I have been given this trust of my lands and my power, and I do not see how I can let that power be alienated from the loyalties to which my family and I have always held. It isn't just willfulness as I am afraid Godfrey thinks."

"Your mother agrees with you, doesn't she? I am sure you are right, for, as lord of Tuscany, you have responsibilities that transcend your obligations even to your husband," said the Pope gravely, as if speaking to a child. And then as a sudden thought came to him, he added, "If I had realized that my request of last April would precipitate such a crisis in your relations with your husband, I should not have sent to you, sorely as I should have missed your support."

"No," said Matilda, refusing to snatch at the offered comfort, "I had pledged my help. What are our resources if we do not spend them in the service of God?"

"There are of course a good many ways of doing that," said the Pope, as if thinking aloud.

"No. The issue had arisen already more than once, and I am sure that we should have had to face it finally." She hesitated over the word, and then went on steadily, "My lord is a just man and honest, and that in spite of bad faith to you.

But he thinks that this world is made for the opportunity of the great, and that the crumbs that fall from the tables of the rich are all that the poor have a right to. He counts himself a loyal Christian, but he objects to any restriction that the Church seeks to impose upon the great. He honestly believes, Your Holiness, that everybody in the world cares as he does for power and honor and magnificence, and for these things first and foremost. That is why when you insist that the King should not sell benefices, he thinks you are simply interfering with the King's right to act as he sees fit with the power God has given him."

"He is not alone in that, Matilda," said the Pope sadly. She had become so much absorbed in speaking of the things that had troubled her day and night for so long, that she had forgotten she was talking to a man who had been at death's door.

Now she leaned forward from her seat, and she spoke eagerly, and as lightly as she could, "But I did not mean to vex you, with all these problems you have worried over so much more than I."

"You have a right to, if any one has, and it comforts me to find you, in whom I have so much confidence, agreeing with me. It is no little thing," he added with a touch of whimsy that Matilda had never noticed in him before this afternoon, "for me to know that the prince whom everybody considers the most promising of all the princes of Italy agrees with me in these first principles of my faith."

But Matilda shook her head, and then, moved from her hard-held control by his kindness, she knelt down beside his chair, and she cried passionately, "Oh, my lord, what I really wanted to talk to you about this afternoon was none of these things but only this—I want to leave this world in which one either beats or is beaten, in which one either surrenders his conscience or strives for his own will as no intelligent mortal would, I want to give up this fight in which there is no surety or peace."

"My poor child," said the Pope tenderly, "I do not blame you."

"But, Holy Father, I mean it." Matilda felt her throat dry and her heart choking her even as she spoke.

"You don't mean that you wish God would let you die?" he asked.

Matilda's laugh rang bitterly in her own ears. "I have thought of that many times, and I have wished that I could honestly ask for it. But I can't. I don't know what it is, Father, but though I have seen the light of the day come in agony and have watched it go in despair, yet I can't ask God to let me die."

She looked up through her tears to see the Pope's eyes fixed upon her with unwavering keenness. For a moment, she thought he did not believe her, and her control gave way. "My father, I hate and despise myself beyond anything I can tell you."

Still the Pope said nothing, and the despair which had risen around her as she talked overwhelmed her. Then he spoke with a matter-of-factness for which her raw spirit blessed him. "You are young, and this unwillingness to surrender the glorious possibility of the future is God's gift to help you to bear the bitterness of the present and to face the darkness of the days to come. It is not lack of courage or vanity or folly but it is the evidence of health in you, Matilda. It is something for us both to trust."

"But I have not said all," insisted Matilda, realizing that in her half-demented anguish she had not said what she most wanted to say: "What I want to do, Holy Father, is to give up my lands and to free my husband, to let him have this divorce I have heard he wants to get, and to go into a convent, and there, without distraction or vanity or compromise or yielding to the temptations of this world, I want to give myself wholly to God."

The Pope said nothing. The sunlight was slanting over the warm yellow marble of the walls and throwing delicate traceries of leaves and flowers and tendrils of vines upon their bright surfaces, and within the arches of the cloister the shadows were deepening. There was something sharper now in the tinkle of the falling waters, and the golden leaves trembled a little now in the moving air.

"It would be simpler—for you, Matilda," he said at last.

She felt the shamed blood burn in her cheeks, but she held her ground obstinately, "I am not a coward or a runaway, Holy Father."

He smiled. "You need not tell me that, my child. For you, as I know you with this tenacity of life and purpose of which you have just spoken, there would be no surrender in the personal sense in this course you contemplate. If you were the person you are afraid I think you are, I would tell you how monotonous you would find life in a place like this when you saw it not as a refuge of a few hours from a troubled world but as the bound and limit of your physical life. I would ask you whether you thought that wide-roving imagination of yours would be able to check itself and hold itself to the strait grooves of each day's meditation. I would ask you, Matilda of Tuscany, whether you would be content to give over your will in obedience to a judgment less ample than your own, to an imagination less generous and quick. But I know you, and I know that you have taken the measure of these things, and where the woman you are not would have seen a closed door to be hugged by weakness and despair, you have seen a gate opening upon eternity."

"God bless you, my father," she said humbly.

"No, rather God bless you, my child. But this is what I should say to you. Some things we can give up because they are ours to give up. Others we cannot, because they do not belong to us. They are entrusted. In some situations we can fulfill that trust more clearly than in others. And at some times rather than at others. Do you follow me?"

She nodded soberly.

"Whether at the end of your life you lie under a long Latin inscription with your fathers in the chapel at Canossa or lie under a wooden cross in a convent cemetery will not matter much. But whether you have used the resources God gave you to the best possible advantage for His service will matter, will it not? Neither you nor I have any doubt of that. The question is rather as to the how. All human vision is limited and fallible. But, for whatever my judgment is worth to you, Matilda, I give it to you, that at the present moment, you can do more for what this world needs, for what is necessary to God's service, so far as we in our human infirmity can understand it, at Canossa as lord of Tuscany. The world has many noble nuns—not more than it needs, and I am not saying that you would not do valiant service as a nun, but the world has not nearly so many good princes. There is where the need is greatest, and there is where you are, I think, needed most, where you with the gifts God has given you are needed most."

She stood up, and for a moment she gazed down upon him without speaking.

"You need not answer me now, my child. Think it over and pray it over. Do not worry. The work you will offer for worship. The pain for atonement."

Still she stood without saying anything. And then she remembered what it was so easy to forget even when Gregory looked weary. "Again I have taxed you when I would have brought you rest."

"No, my child, in bringing this to me, you have brought me something larger than either of us. It is in carrying each other's burdens that we take rest from our own."

For a moment his eyes rested on the stone in the pavement at her feet. A ray of sunlight lay softly on the gray white marble. "Do you see that marble there? It is worn with the passing of many feet even in so quiet a place as this, and with the rain and the sun, and it has lost that first dazzling whiteness which it took from the hills of Carrara. But do you see those little veins of color in it—purple and rose and tawny amber? As the years pass, they will deepen and grow more beautiful to the eye that looks for them. It does not matter where we are for that which matters most. In the end we shall come home to God."

She did not try to say anything more to him of thanks or of apology, but, choking back the tears, she kissed his ring and left the little garden in the gathering twilight. Two weeks later at Canossa she was astonished to receive a letter from the Pope, thanking her for her visit and telling her that from that day he had grown really strong and well. She wept over the letter, remembering its cause, but there was no sting in the tears, and she wiped them away without shame.

CHAPTER III

"I am glad Mother did not try to come," said Matilda, drawing her woolen mantle more tightly about her as, sitting on her horse, she waited for the gates of the Lateran Palace to swing open. "The snow of the hills is still frozen here on the edge of my saddle."

"It was a good deal for you to try to come, yourself," said Alberic, patting his horse's neck to still its impatience.

Idly roaming over the deserted square of travertine pavement and high brick walls, Matilda's eye came to rest on a rill of dry leaves dancing in a funnel of wind. The crisp rattle of their frozen edges dusted the silence, and their gay futility seemed to her to mock her own preoccupation.

"It was the least I could do," she answered simply. "The Pope likes to have a few of his princes here for counsel and support. After all, the layman should not leave all the problems of Christendom to the priest."

"God knows I shall not argue with you there," said Alberic. "And there are few enough of you to see it. But tell me, Matilda, did Godfrey ask you no favor when he wrote to you at last?"

Matilda hesitated. She was quite aware of the fact that Alberic had been curious all the way as to the letter which all Tuscany knew its lady had received a month ago from her estranged lord. He had given her more than one chance to confide in him. His was no idle curiosity she knew, nor frivolous impertinence. Though Alberic would take no part in the public discussions, he would be free of the counsels of the Cluniac leaders. For his gift of shrewd insight and quiet suggestion was known and appreciated by men who from their basic point of view would cherish the inconspicuous and the unobtrusive in preference to some of the showier figures who would dominate the public scene.

It was like Alberic, she reflected, in no way to explain what he knew she knew or to seek to palliate the seeming intrusion.

At last the gates were swinging open.

"It has taken them long enough, even if everybody is at Mass," grumbled Alberic.

As he helped her from her horse, Matilda decided to confide in him. "Godfrey has asked me to do all I can to see that nothing is decided against Henry. He pleads that the Pope give him time."

The monk lifted his eyebrows.

"I think he is sincere. I mean the King," she added with embarrassment.

Alberic chuckled. "Doubtless; the Saxons are certainly pressing him hard enough for him not to want the Pope to throw any more weight into the scale against him."

"Oh, just a moment," Matilda called to the grooms who had run out to the horses. "They have come through much snow and cold, and my grooms are too weary to treat them properly." The men in their short tunics and great hoods nodded, and with a gesture of dismissal to her companions, Matilda joined Alberic and the steward who stood bowing in the courtyard.

"There is bread and meat and wine set out in the chamber of the Virgin," he said.

As she slipped into the low chair set beside the papal throne, Matilda took a quick look at the man whom she had found so frail and tired five months before. There was no question of his recovery now. A larger man, physically, than Gregory might easily have been swallowed up in the shadow of the great stone chair, and dwarfed by the stiff crimson cape half flung over the back of the throne and the heavy robes of linen and brocade, but on Gregory, as always, splendor seemed the insignificant vehicle it was, and the eye rested undistracted on the drawn, dark face, so sure, so resolute, so self-contained.

Although when she knelt before him, he had thanked her graciously for coming, the Pope now seemed completely absorbed in listening to a speaker in the front rank of the seated ecclesiastics. A tall man in a monk's dress, with head slightly inclined as if to hear better some smaller companion, he was talking very earnestly with his eyes fixed on the Pope.

"In the meeting of last April, my lord, we all agreed that these two things were intolerable, that gold should be given for the gift of the Holy Ghost, and that he who offered the sacrifice of the altar should be stained with incontinence. And we swore, all of us, regular and secular alike, that we would neither commit nor suffer these abuses in any place in our charge. Before we consider what more to do, would it not be wise for us first to ask what fruit these promises we have all made, have borne?"

"Don't you think he puts a matter very well, this Odo of ours?" asked a gentle voice in her ear. She had returned the greeting of the Abbot of Cluny when she came in, and then she had forgotten that quiet presence at her side.

"I remembered seeing him at the Lenten Synod of last year, but I had not known who he was. He is your prior, isn't he?"

"Yes," said Hugh proudly, "he is the most promising of our younger men. He is moderate not for lack of zeal but out of charity. The Cardinal of Ostia already speaks of him as his hoped-for successor."

"You monks," she said teasingly, "take as much pains with your succession as do we lay folk."

He smiled and serenely folded his hands within the wide sleeves of his habit. "We have at least as much reason, for we too, look to a larger increase. But we are not tethered within the flesh, but are made free of the larger succession of the spirit."

"That is true," she said sadly.

But a tumult had arisen while they were talking in low tones with each other, for all over the great nave, men both monks and bishops were rising and trying to speak. Finally, the Pope arose, and there was silence.

"My lord of Bremen," he bowed courteously to one of the bishops sitting in the front ranks. "You have come farthest of all this company, and it is only fair that you should speak first, especially since you speak not only for yourself but also for the other bishops of the north."

The present Bishop of Bremen was very different from the impressive figure that Matilda remembered from earlier days in Rome, but though slighter of build he was obviously a proud and resolute man.

"My lord Pope," he began, speaking in a dry voice that filled and swelled as he warmed to his subject, and turning sidewise so that without any rudeness to the presiding officer, he yet addressed the whole assemblage, "I don't know that I need to speak at any length, for all Germany knows what happened when the primate, the Archbishop of Mainz, tried to enforce the decrees of the synod in his diocese. His priests cried, 'We will give up our orders before we give up our wives. If the Pope will not be content with men, then let him find angels to do his work.'"

Though the speaker kept one eye on the Pope, his voice yet rose challenging-ly on the last words, and the reaction was instantaneous. There was a low murmur of applause among the front ranks where most of the bishops sat, and there was a stamping of feet in the rear where the majority of the monks were congregated. Matilda saw the face of Odo of Cluny flush, and she heard the hard breathing of Hugh at her side, but the Pope had lifted his hand for silence, and the incipient uproar died almost as soon as it had arisen.

"Go on," he commanded Liemar of Bremen with a dangerous glitter in his voice.

For a moment Liemar gazed at the Pope as if measuring his man, and then he resumed his speaking in a calm and steady tone: "The Archbishop of Mainz persisted in spite of all the warnings we could give him. The result was a riot in the cathedral. He was able to quell the disturbance only by listening to reasonable men who urged him to do no more until he should have sent word to Rome."

Again a buzz of voices rose, and again the Pope fixed his eyes on the speaker. Now a note of pleading came into the voice of Liemar: "Everybody knows that Altman of Passau is a saint, but when he tried to suspend some of his married clergy, they raised such a tumult that only the quickness of his cross bearer saved him from being slain on the spot. As for the giving of gifts in the German church, it is universal, and no man can with a stroke of the pen—"

But Liemar had been carried a little too far. There were cries of "Shame," and though for a moment he glared at the disturbers, he apparently thought it the better part of discretion to sit down.

"My lord Pope," Matilda heard a familiar high-pitched voice from the other side of the papal throne. She leaned forward to see. It was the Empress Agnes, clad in a plain gown and veil of blue wool such as a nun might wear. She repeated her appeal, but the Pope was too absorbed in gazing sternly out over the rows before him to hear. Timidly, she put out her hand and plucked at his sleeve, but he seemed quite unaware of the interruption, and, apparently frightened at her own temerity, she shrank back into her chair, gazing up at the tense face beside her with frightened eyes.

Then one of the gorgeous purple figures sitting in a large semi-circle below the Pope's throne to the right and the left, rose and faced the Pope. Matilda fancied there was a slight relaxation in the Pope's face as the Archbishop of Salerno, pulling his gown back and planting his feet firmly on the pavement, began to speak. He was a heavy-set man with a large, dark-fringed head and heavy-lidded eyes, and there was a certain ponderous slowness in his voice as he began to speak, but the whole company turned towards him at once, and bishop and monk alike leaned forward to listen. "My brother of Bremen is quite correct in his report of the disturbances at Mainz and Passau. But I am sure he does not mean to have you think that all the clergy of Germany are incontinent or stained with simony. When Cardinal Gerald of Ostia and I went into Germany last spring, we found a hearty welcome at the hands of many good men who said that the laws we came to promulgate would be the saving of the Church in Germany. At any time and in any place a handful of willful men can make a riot that the peaceful tempers of the law-abiding will have a hard time to quiet. I am sure that my brother, the Pope's legate to France, will bear out what I say." Alfanus of Salerno sat down, spread his purple robe over his knees, and, leaning back easily in his chair, shut his eyes.

No contrast could have been sharper than that between the man who had just spoken, and the man who next rose. There was a nervous vigor apparent even in the way Hugh of Die, the Cardinal Legate of France, sprang to his feet, and as he began to talk, he raised a slender hand that seemed in its gestures to follow the slightest impulse of the vivid mind behind the flashing eyes and the mobile lips.

"It is the same story for France," he began. "Every serious Christian in the Frankish Kingdom agrees that it is the death of religion to see priests buying their orders with gold and spending the patrimony of the poor for the advancement of their sons. The men who are doing these things know that they are transgress-ing every rule of canon law and betraying every obligation of their calling both human and divine. The lords of France used to say, 'If my son is a weakling or a coward, I will make him a priest.' Now they say, 'I do not want to divide my lands; so I will buy my youngest son a bishopric.'"

Several times a short, stout man in the episcopal purple had tried to claim the attention of the Pope. Now, seeing Hugh of Die pause for breath, he jumped up, crying at the top of his voice, "My lord Pope." For a moment the Pope looked at the Cardinal, and when the latter sat down again in some confusion, Gregory recognized the interrupter, "Cunibert of Turin."

"My lord Pope," he repeated explosively, "it is easy for these monks to talk as they do. They are safe enough in their snug little cloisters high up on the moun-tains with serfs and peasants in the valleys to feed them while they dream away over the writings of the hermits of the desert. All they see of the world is when the world comes up and offers rich gifts at their shrines and kisses the robes of their holy men. They can take any feeble leaving of humanity and put him in a cowl and march him in a line to chapel and to refectory, and the world will never know that he hasn't brains or guts enough to say boo to an old woman's goose."

There was a roar of indignation from the ranks of the monks, but the Arch-bishop of Salerno, who on occasions like this delighted to recall his monastic days at Santa Sophia, and the Abbot Hugh, after a first exchange of glances, had the presence of mind to burst out laughing. The Pope's tightly drawn lips twitched, and presently even the bishops were laughing at the mirth of the two monks, of whose brains or courage no man had ever dared to make question.

The Bishop of Turin was not to be laughed down, however, and the whole company leaned forward to listen appreciatively to his wrath.

"But a bishop, my lord," he shouted, "has to meet the world as it is, and all kinds of men. How do you think the Church is going to make herself respected if she staffs her armies only with weaklings and peasants? Let the men of birth and of strength and of intelligence and of capacity come into the service of the Church, and the Church will be able to hold her own with any power on earth. But you can't get the right kind of men to live on a beggar's alms in a barbarous hole of a parish. If the Church is to have the men of blood and of ability, the no-ble and the great, for her leaders, she must make her service attractive to them."

As the Bishop of Turin sat down, still looking hot and indignant, Hugh of

Cluny shook his head. "He has really put it very well, and most of the bishops, God help us, would agree with him."

"There speaks the monk," said Matilda, who had begun to enjoy the debate.

"I admit that the Bishop has his side, but wait, Hugh of Die is not going to let it pass. Alfanus has been trying to hold his gown, but it would take more than the bulk even of Alfanus to smother Hugh."

There was no mistaking the fire in the eyes of Hugh of Die or the passionate thrusting-out of his arm as he began, "My lord Pope, our brother of Turin has put the whole case in a nutshell. The world has taken possession of the Church. And the Church has ceased to say with its Founder, 'My kingdom is not of this world', but in order to win this world it has studied the ways of the world that it might use them. And in so doing it has become like the world until now; who shall tell the difference between my lord the count and my lord the bishop?"

There was a terrific uproar, in all parts of the church, men jumping up and shouting at the top of their voices. But Matilda heard clearly only the low voice of Hugh of Cluny murmuring at her side, "He that loveth his life shall lose it."

With a gesture of despair Gregory arose from his place and began to pronounce the benediction that dismissed the first meeting of the Synod of February, 1075.

That afternoon, in the library of the palace of the Lateran, Gregory faced a small group of his confidential advisers and most trusted supporters. Sitting in a corner beside the Empress Agnes, Matilda followed his eyes as they swept over the company gathered between his chair and the shelves on which lay the scrolls and volumes of the papal library. To begin with, that assembly, small as it was, bore out the oft-repeated charge that Gregory was a Pope of monks. For though the episcopal purple brightened the monastic black, yet everybody knew that the Archbishop of Salerno had spent some of his happiest days writing music in a monastery and the Bishop of Lucca had been with reluctance torn from his conventual retreat to give advice to the Countesses of Tuscany. Hugh of Cluny and Desiderius of Monte Cassino were the most famous monks of the day. Only Agnes the Empress, Gisulf of Salerno, and Matilda herself represented the laity. She wondered if Gregory were troubled by this fact as his eyes moved restlessly over the room. And then she asked herself who of all the princes of Italy was not there whose loyalty and support could be counted on. With a heavy heart she watched the Pope seat himself and turn to the Abbot Bernard at his side.

It was a moving contrast to observe, this between the Pope and his friend. Physically there was much in common between the Abbot of Saint Victor in Marseilles and the other great Cluniac rulers. Tall and spare, with the distinction of asceticism without that sternness that sometimes marks its less sure manifestations, the Abbot of Saint Victor had also the same simplicity and the same serenity. But here the resemblance ended. For the luminous directness of the Abbot of Cluny that revealed itself in the grave sweetness of his manner seemed to take on in the personality of Bernard the subtler stain of a more complex temperament. And though Bernard shared the unhurried ease and spaciousness of manner of the Abbot of Monte Cassino, there was in his reserve little of the radiance of Desiderius. It was as if the pure light of the original Benedictine inspiration had passed through three windows of different dye and taken the peculiar stain of each glass as it passed. Yet, through all three, the light shone without shadow or deviation.

Nor could Matilda find it in her heart to wonder that the larger, more troubled, more hard-driven spirit of Gregory should turn to these children of light for comfort in his doubtful and tempestuous days.

The Abbot Bernard was nodding almost imperceptibly as the Pope talked, searching his clear face for every shadow of feeling. With that swiftness of change of look so characteristic of him, Gregory glanced suddenly at Matilda and surprised the intensity of her observation. She felt her cheeks burn, but there was a flash of amusement in his look that passed as quickly as it had come. Then he gathered up the attention of all the company, as he began to speak.

His voice was low, and he spoke obviously with every intention of eschewing any appeal to sympathy or feeling. "You all heard what was said in the Synod this morning, and you heard for yourselves the reactions of the men who listened to those speeches. The feelings of the moment that prompted some of those demonstrations of sympathy or objection will change with the passing of the hours. Tomorrow morning those in whom the spirit of levity was today most apparent will be most eager to show their capacity for responsibility. Those who were today most insubordinate will tomorrow be most ready to follow leadership if that leadership can commend itself to the common sense of reason and justice. I am convinced that the promise that Our Lord gave to His first apostles, that until the end of time He would abide with them, will be fulfilled for us, and so I know are you. There is only one thing I want to remind you of as we take counsel together.

"You will all remember the two cities of Augustine's book. The one city, the city of the power of this world, the other city the City of God. We are citizens of both cities, you and I. It is our duty as Christians to do everything we can to make the city of this world's power the body of the City of God. But we must not deceive ourselves. The city of this world is built by force on the inequalities of men. He who has power can silence all objections to his ruthlessness, his lawlessness. Very literally most strong men believe that might makes right. That is the source of all the sin and misery we see about us so that a man could not be blamed who said that this world as we see it in the hands of the princes of this world is the kingdom of Antichrist. It is terrible enough that the city of this world should be in such hands. But if men should surrender the stronghold of the City of God on this earth, the Church, to the powers of this world, if forgetting the love and the justice of God, they should worship force alone and sacrifice the hope of eternal life for the dubious power of the moment, then indeed would the race of man have fallen on such darkness as the mind shudders to contemplate. There are two powers, and one is of this world, and one is not. It is tragic that the law of God should not rule all things in the world He made and His will be fulfilled in priest and prince alike. But if, in fear of violence or through sloth, we suffer the power of the kingdom of God to pass into the hands of the princes of this world, then is the light of the world gone out, and chaos come again."

More than once the voice of Gregory had risen throbbing with passion, but each time it had fallen as if suddenly he had heard his own voice and scorned to make any appeal but to the cool judgment of his auditors. It was as if he had decided that in the bare idea there inhered a strength beyond that of any gust of passion or feeling. When he had finished, however, he sat down, still with his face dark and expressionless as if the fire behind its volcanic animation had suddenly failed for breath.

Matilda looked to the Abbot Bernard, expecting that he would speak, as she fancied it had been agreed between Gregory and him beforehand. But he said nothing. "There are two cities," she said over and over again to herself, the delight of the sweeping periods of Augustine coming back to her with a rush that swept away all the pain and uncertainty of the last months.

It was Gisulf of Salerno who at last broke the silence. "I am not sure I quite understood what you said, Your Holiness. Did you mean that the Church should manage the affairs of the Church, and not the King, or any prince?"

"Yes," said Gregory, looking up and scrutinizing the honest face of the knight.

The face of Gisulf cleared, and he looked around the room. "That seems fair enough to me."

The Empress Agnes leaned forward eagerly from her place beside Matilda, speaking with animation and anxiety, "I am sure it is the bad advisers of Henry who make all the trouble. He is not a bad boy at heart at all."

The Pope smiled, but there was something in the gentle look he gave the Empress that silenced her.

"I don't suppose a woman should speak out," she whispered nervously to Matilda.

Only a moment later did Matilda hear what she had said through some echo that pierced her abstraction.

"What do you think we should do just now, Your Holiness?" asked Cardinal Hugh of Die.

"What do you advise, Hugh?" countered the Pope.

For a moment Hugh hesitated; then he seemed to take the plunge. "I don't think we are ever going to advance this reform of the Church that everybody, cleric and layman alike, agrees must be accomplished if we are to save Christianity, until we strike at the root of the whole thing. As I have found it in my experience in France, it is simply this. The prince, lord or king or emperor, claims and is accorded the right of investiture. The result is that he uses the bishopric or the benefice in question as a possession of his to be disposed of like any other fief, in his own interest. He wants a man who will serve him first and foremost, who will use whatever resources are at his disposal to further his lord's interests. The result is that he puts into important Church positions the only kind of man he knows, a man like himself. That is why we have some of the finest warriors in the kingdom of France among her bishops and some of the most unscrupulous adventurers in the world among her priests. And never will you have better priest or bishop so long as this custom is allowed to stand."

The Pope raised his head and looked sharply at the Cardinal. "You are aware that this custom, as you call it, is against every commandment and law of the Church, express and implied?"

The Cardinal flushed as he replied, "I know, my lord Pope, that it has worked the devil with the Church of France."

Then the slow voice of the Archbishop of Salerno rose from his corner, "Are you ready to anathematize lay investiture, Your Holiness?"

There was silence for some minutes, and all eyes turned to the Pope. Presently he spoke, slowly and distinctly: "That is why I have asked you to give me your counsel today."

"It is war, my lord," said the Abbot Bernard, speaking for the first time.

The Pope said nothing, but Hugh of Cluny looked at his colleague of Monte Cassino. Matilda could not detect any sign of anxiety on the clear features of Desiderius, but he spoke before any one could answer the Abbot Bernard, "Isn't there perhaps some just interest on the part of the princes that we should not overlook? After all, the bishop, for instance, often holds some of the most important lands of his prince, to say nothing of offices. We can hardly expect the latter not to be concerned about the devotion of perhaps the richest and most powerful of his vassals to himself."

"That is true," said the Pope, "but which interest is to be put first, the interest of the prince in a faithful and subservient vassal or the interest of the Church in an honest and faithful bishop?"

Desiderius agreed with that fullness of concession that had always seemed to Matilda one of his greatest charms. Then half to himself he asked, "Is there no compromise possible?"

"A compromise with what?" asked the Pope.

Desiderius subsided. Hugh of Cluny nodded his agreement with the point of view implied. So did Bernard when Gregory finally appealed to him with a look.

"What do you think, my lord Gisulf?"

For answer the Lord of Salerno drew his sword and stretched it out to the Pope by the handle. The simple soldierly gesture drew a round of applause from the churchmen.

"And you, my daughter?"

Matilda felt suddenly hollow, as the Pope looked around the intervening heads to her corner. It seemed to her that she had come down from the heights with a thud. "My lord," with terror she heard herself speaking as if from afar off, "Your Holiness, I think the freedom of the Church is as essential as you do." The whole company had turned round to look at her. Driven back against the wall as she felt herself by the impact of all those eyes, she yet stuck doggedly to her task: "I am prepared, and I know that here I speak for my mother as for myself, I am prepared to give myself and everything I possess to your service in this. But I have a letter from my husband, the Lord Godfrey, and he has bidden me to ask you to do nothing that will put up a bar between Your Holiness and the King of Germany."

Matilda read the alarm on the face of Hugh of Cluny, the pity in the eyes of Desiderius, the half-suspended concern on the placid features of Alfanus, but the face of Gregory was inscrutable.

It was the sight of his expression, more than anything else, that nerved her to add, "I am wondering, Your Holiness, if it would be possible for the Synod to agree on the principle of the prohibition of lay investiture and then when you send word to the King of Germany and the princes of Christendom, invite them to bring forward any claims that they may wish to advance, that no injustice may be done in a reform that everybody knows is essential to the Church."

She paused, overwhelmed with the consciousness of her own audacity. It was the Abbot Bernard who broke the silence, "I think the Countess has made a suggestion that will get us out of our difficulty for the present."

"For the present, Bernard," agreed the Pope, it seemed to Matilda bitterly. Then with a light sigh, he added, "I think that is the best we can do for now."

When Matilda went up to kiss the Pope's ring, he said only, "You may tell your lord that you have done his errand well." Then as he saw her wince, he smiled his most charmingly. "I have a new book to show you on the shelf here. It is a Gospels which the King of the East has sent me for a present. It is not work of Constantinople but of the Western Isles." As he spoke, he went and took from the shelf by which she had been sitting a volume richly bound in gilded boards of cedar wood with five great gems set in the middle of the front cover in the form of a cross. He opened it and held it out to her that she might see the rich page glowing with red and purple and blue and gold, gemlike colors twined in an arabesque of tracery that covered the entire page.

"Why there are all sorts of fantastic beasts hidden in the twining of the flowers," she exclaimed with delight.

"Look again," he said. She took the book into her own hands, and then she saw what she had never seen before.

"And they have twined funny little men into the pattern as if they were no more than stem or leaf or beast."

"Yes," said the Pope, closing the book and giving it back to her, "all the countless differences and clashes of will and intractable individualities of men, and, lo, they are but twists and curls in a craftsman's design. Take the book back to your lodgings, and if you have trouble sleeping tonight, look at it."

But she was so spent that it seemed that when her head touched the pillow, she slept.

CHAPTER IV

MATILDA was not sorry that the Pope could not see her mother and her at once. The library of Pope Zachary was as cold and bleak that first of October as it had been nine months ago when the Pope had called his closest friends and supporters into conference in the middle of the Lenten Synod. But she was tired enough to welcome a rest even in the least comfortable of surroundings. Moreover, try as she would, she could not quite free herself from a sense of disappointment and even of irritation at this disturbance of her plans by the Pope's summons to Rome. For she could not pretend to herself any longer that the work of conciliation to which she had devoted all her efforts these last months would go on. She knew that she could not reasonably expect the Pope to disregard the ominous trend of recent events, but she had been hoping that the outcome might prove less alarming than she had feared. And she had hoped, now she realized with a sudden feeling of emptiness, that she might succeed in bringing the Pope and the King of Germany into an understanding of each other and of each other's problems that would make it possible for the two controlling powers of her world to cooperate for the welfare of Christendom.

It was the willingness with which the Pope had listened to her suggestion of leaving open some margin for adjustment and for ease of transition in the promulgation of the decrees of the Synod that had given her the hope of reconciliation and the chance for mediation. The first letter which Godfrey sent after the papal letters reached Germany had been warm in its approval of what she had done and cordial in its appreciation of the Pope's understanding of the ruler's problem. But when she had taken this opportunity to send Godfrey a very graphic account of the circumstances which had led to such seemingly drastic measures, he had replied less warmly. Still, even then, he had referred appreciatively to what she had said of the Pope's paternal interest in the personal welfare of the King, and though he had somewhat gone out of his way to make clear that he must pursue his own line of policy in these great issues, he had obviously spoken to the King with pride of his wife's help. For Henry himself had sent a messenger to her as well as to Beatrice, announcing his progress with the conquest of the rebellious Saxons and asking her continued help in the promotion of that understanding with the Pope which he professed to desire more than anything else in the world. She had taken advantage of this letter to write directly to the King, setting forth the problem of the Church as it must commend itself to any enlightened ruler.

It was right after she had finished that letter that she received word of the latest troubles in Milan. At first she was not particularly worried, for trouble was endemic in that city. Even when details of the killing of the Knight Herlembald had drifted down to Canossa, she had not anticipated any immediate threat to the peace for which she had been working. It was a sobering thing for a lover of justice to reflect on, that the great leader of the Patarine party, after twenty years of fighting for those reforms for which on a larger scene the papacy was now striving, should have been murdered in a tumult of clerical rabble. But, after all, the defeat in Milan was but one episode, and not even the most ardent sympathizer could pretend that the Patarine reformers had always been either temperate or reasonable. The news, too, that Henry had sent his agent, the Count Nellenburg, into Milan, had been in no way alarming at first, for it had followed upon the cordial letters in which Henry had notified the Pope and the princes of Italy of his victory over the Saxons.

But the last weeks had brought first one disquieting rumor then another of the favor which the imperial agent had shown to the disturbers in Milan. Matilda had sent a letter to Godfrey imploring him to use his influence with Henry to enjoin discretion upon Count Nellenburg. But Godfrey, whose military prestige had been enormously enhanced by his share in the Saxon victories, was apparently being sent to various doubtful quarters of the kingdom to cement the allegiance to the King. Beatrice wrote to Henry pointing out the possible consequences of the indiscretion of Nellenburg upon the hoped-for alliance between Pope and King. There had been no time to hear from that remonstrance when the Pope's message had arrived asking for a conference in Rome. Gregory's anxiety over the state of the Church of Milan was the ostensible occasion of his letter, but both Matilda and her mother had agreed that nothing short of anxiety about the King's behavior would have prompted Gregory to summon his friends at so awkward a time.

It was in vain that Matilda tried to shake off that mingled sense of helplessness and irritation that had beset her ever since she had started south on the prematurely autumnal roads. She rose restlessly from her chair, and going over to the low door in one of the corners of the room under the high windows, she opened it slightly and looked out. The courtyard before the library was as bleak as in February, and the sky above was of the color and the seeming impenetrability of slate. Suddenly her eye was caught by the sight of a solitary figure wrapped in a riding cloak crossing the pavement in front of her. As if he had been watched for, another figure appeared from an opposite corner of the courtyard and hurried to his side.

"Those must be the Pope's visitors leaving now," she said idly to her mother, who had sat more composed with a book on her knee.

"Anyone we know?"

"I can't see their faces. Why," as the first figure suddenly looked back at the palace which he had just left, "it is Guibert of Ravenna. What can he have been doing?" And then as the figure at the gate turned back to wait for Guibert, Matilda could not contain her astonishment. "And Hugh Candidus has just joined him. I did not know they were friends."

Her mother's mouth straightened. "They are a precious pair. But this is the first time I ever knew they hunted together."

"But the Pope has always trusted Hugh Candidus, and until recently he has not thought badly of Guibert. I remember with what surprise he spoke of the reports that Guibert had been trying to obtain possession of some of the towns that belonged to the Exarchate," answered Matilda.

Beatrice's voice fell so that at the door her daughter could hardly hear her. "Sometimes I think the Pope is too trustful of men. He can never quite believe that they are such liars as these two are." She stopped suddenly, for a servant had come in.

With apologies he closed the door behind Matilda, and then returning to the door by which he had entered, he held it open for another servant, who brought in an open brazier of charcoal and set it down in the middle of the room. With the shutters closed, and now only the light of the bleak October day to come through the yellow opacity of the glass in the windows high on the walls, the library was in a dim fog that did nothing to increase the comfort or cheerfulness of Matilda.

"There is no use being so fidgety," said her mother. "You'll know soon enough how things are."

"I wish Henry had had more sense than to send Ebehard of Nellenburg into Italy now when we are having our hands full to keep up the Pope's confidence in him any way," Matilda complained, stretching out her hands over the brazier and shivering a little with the sudden warmth.

Her mother laughed grimly. "When you have had as much to do with Henry as I have, you'll know better than to expect Henry to have any discretion. I should have known that as soon as he had the upper hand of the Saxons, he would not be nearly so concerned about what the Pope thought."

"Yes," said Matilda, rubbing her hands, and raising one foot to set it on the edge of the brazier, "he was pretty frightened when he wrote the letter to the Pope that you and I have stressed so much. He was sincere at least when he wrote that; he did not know where else to turn."

But here with her usual concern for justice Beatrice suddenly came to the aid of the man whom she had been criticizing: "I hardly blame him. The man he sent to me said that those savages had fallen upon the bodies of the dead and scattered the bones of Henry's own son and brother there in the chapel at Harzburg before they set fire to it."

Matilda shuddered. "From what one hears, the things Henry has been doing do not make pleasant things to think about either."

"War is war." Beatrice shrugged her shoulders. "It is what Henry does at home in peace time that I find hardest to get over. And yet," she added with a sigh, "it will do no good to have trouble between the King and the Pope. When the rulers of the world disagree, it goes hard with those in the lower ranks of society. Anything you and I can do for peace will help. God knows there are enough men who will try to make their profit one way and another out of trouble."

The door opened, and the Pope in his red dress, and two dark figures stood in the doorway.

"I am sorry, my friends, to have kept you waiting in this cold place," he apologized, seating himself away from the brazier and motioning to his friends to resume their warmer places. "But this is the room where we are least likely to be disturbed."

He looked up, and the two figures by the door came over and bowed to the women, and Matilda was not surprised to hear the welcome voices of Hugh of Cluny and Bernard of Saint Victor.

"I came as soon as I could, Your Holiness, for there were some difficulties with the harvest that kept me," said Matilda, folding her hands in the sleeves of her mantle like the monks.

"Even so, you came a day earlier than I expected," replied the Pope graciously. "I hope the harvest has passed without trouble, and that men are more settled and content."

It was with deep satisfaction that Matilda answered that question. "The harvest was good, thank God, and we have been able to change some of the bailiffs so that I think our people have little to complain of in the way of oppression."

"The times are bad," said Beatrice, "and everywhere men are trying to lay hands on more than is their due."

The Pope smiled. "That is hardly news in Rome, is it?" He turned lightly to the two abbots as he spoke. Then his face sobered, and Matilda saw that though now his features had recovered their wonted firmness, there was an unmistakable look of care and anxiety in his face. "I was sorry to ask you two ladies to make this trip to Rome at this season, but most of the friends on whom I depend are far away. Desiderius is visiting his friend, Robert Guiscard. It is a long-standing invitation, and when I heard of the coming of the King's agent, we both agreed that it might be a good time to accept it. Hugh of Die is as busy as ever with those problems of the Frankish kingdom that never seem to sleep. Cardinal Gerard is visiting some of the Lombard princes, and so it goes."

"You know, Your Holiness," replied Beatrice, "that you have only to tell my daughter and me how we may serve you and the Church to command our immediate help, such as two women may give."

Again the Pope smiled with pleasure. "Both of my brethren here will bear witness that I have never forgotten that when the crisis came and most of the men got out of the reach of trouble, it was the women who followed Our Lord to the Cross."

"And especially," added Matilda, "when it is anything that will promote peace in this troubled world."

The smile faded from the Pope's face as he answered gravely, "It is for the sake of peace that I have asked you to come here."

There was silence for a moment, and then the Pope, leaning forward and folding his hands on the table before him, began to take up the business in hand in earnest. "You have heard of the trouble in Milan after the murder of Herlembald?"

Matilda nodded. She thought of Herlembald as she had seen him once years before on a visit to Rome, a giant of a man with a red beard and a deep passionate voice, and a certain look, as if he had drunk of something bitter, about a gentle mouth.

"I cautioned him when he was last in Rome," said the Pope, "that the Milanese are very proud of their ancient liturgy. It seems a pity that he could not give them time on the less important things when he had done so much in the essentials."

"Oh," said Beatrice, "I had heard that it was on the old issues of the buying and selling of orders and the marriage of the clergy that the nobles and the rebel clergy attacked him."

"Basically, yes," said Gregory. "But when Herlembald tried to get the clergy to substitute the liturgy of the universal Church for that of Milan, then these men saw their chance, and they stirred up the mob of the city to attack the reform party in defense of the ancient liberties of the Church of Milan."

"It is hard to be temperate in reform. And I think Herlembald never forgot that day so long ago when he learned that the girl he loved had been seduced by that wretched clerk." There was great pity in the voice of Hugh.

"I have never been sure, either," broke in Bernard, "that it was a wise thing to let the laity judge the clergy as these Patarines have done."

But the voice of Gregory was like steel as he answered: "What then do you think of the King's agent? He has congratulated the rioters on their murder of Herlembald, and he has urged them to depose even the usurping archbishop whom these rebels have hitherto supported and to intrude still a second pretender upon this distressed church."

"But surely," interposed Matilda, "no one will be found so foolish and so abandoned as to accept such a nomination."

Gregory smiled, "My dear Countess, someone has been found already. And what is more, he has gone into Germany, and I have been just informed today that the King has invested him with the ring and the staff. It is Tedald, of good family, but a man brazen enough even for this."

Matilda looked at her mother. She knew that Beatrice had always kept some hope of Henry's ultimate reform. In the case of any other woman she would have suspected that her girlhood affection for his mother was largely responsible for this optimism, but such sentimentalism was quite out of character with all Matilda knew of her mother. More likely it was some instinct of justice to a man at the hands of whose father she had suffered so sorely in times past. Then, too, as Matilda well knew, Beatrice dreaded the possibility of conflict between the papacy and the empire. Part of her fear was obviously due to the exposed position of the Tuscan lands, which would inevitably force her house into the very center of the conflict, part to her horror of war and its accompanying disorders as the ruin of the work she had done for the security and prosperity of her lands. But most of all, Matilda realized, Beatrice dreaded the possibility that the secular power to which she was bound by so many obligations might sacrilegiously set itself against the spiritual.

Matilda found herself looking enviously at the two monks. For them the issue was simpler, however distressing, in its very nature less harassing. They had no loyalty to family—for the first time the full significance of the death of her son came over Matilda, and for the first time her grief found a moment's assuagement. In this civil war her mother would be grieved to contemplate what would happen to her daughter, but she herself had no child to darken the future for her. She was turning over in her mind the bitter comfort of this realization when she heard her mother speaking.

"I wonder how much of the blame for this must be placed on Ebehard of Nellenburg. He has, ever since Henry was a boy, been one of the worst of the many bad influences about him."

The Pope shook his head. "We have done everything possible to make the dangers of Ebehard's company apparent to Henry. Pope Alexander excommunicated Ebehard. In spite of all our admonitions and reminders Henry has persisted in associating with him, even though we have reminded him that he was himself incurring the penalty of excommunication by such association. I don't see how he can hope to escape the consequences of a relationship in which he has persisted in the teeth of every form of warning."

It was growing dark in the room, and the open edges of the books stood out in ghostly pallor against the dark edges of the bindings and the shelves. But it was not too dark for Matilda to see the deepening frown of thought on her mother's face.

"Henry was always willful," she said at last. "If you told him not to do a thing, he seemed determined to do it."

"So I have observed," responded the Pope dryly.

"On the other hand," said Abbot Hugh, offering his suggestion with an air of deprecation, "men as willful as he have sometimes come to see the light and turn that very obstinacy to the service of God."

There was no hint of impatience in the voice of the Pope as he answered, but there was a certain weariness that seemed to Matilda significant: "It would be lack of faith in the grace of God to doubt that, Brother Hugh, but it would be a rash presumption on the goodness of God to count on it."

"But," said Matilda, now thoroughly alarmed, "I have had a letter just this fall from Henry himself in which he expresses the deepest veneration for the chair of Saint Peter and for its present occupant, whom he refers to as an admired friend from his boyhood days." Even as she said it, she knew that the letter was but slim evidence to offset the undoubted fact of the investiture.

It was now too dark for her to see the face of the Pope clearly, but she could hear the short laugh, so grim in its implications. "The letters I have been receiving from Henry for the last two years might be included in any manual of letters as the ideal model for a young king to a pope. If you were to trust them, you would think that all I had to do would be to suggest what I would like to have done, and it would be done. But you are as familiar with the results as I am. So far as personal reform is concerned, there has not been one actual piece of evidence from the beginning to the present. All Christendom knows that he has been warned to give up his scandalous counselors, and now he sends one of the worst of them into Italy as his official envoy and gives him authority to make and unmake bishops. And then without a word to us he invests this usurper of the chair of Milan with the symbols of his office. As for his personal life and the example he gives in his high place, you have only to ask anybody who has been into Germany these last two years to learn the whole sorry tale."

"But," asked Matilda, snatching at a sudden straw that swam to the surface of her frightened consciousness, "is there no conscience in Milan? Will the people, will the Patarines allow this investiture to pass?"

"The people!" said Gregory still more wearily. "How much can you ask of the people? They are trained to follow their leaders. Society depends on authority and obedience for its security. Moreover, let Tedald distribute a sufficient largesse of silver—his family are rich enough, and the revenues of the see of Milan are large enough to enable him to recoup in a year or two—and the very people who talk loudest about the faithlessness of the Church will shout most noisily for him. As for the Patarines, at the instigation of Ebehard, they are being hunted down like vermin. I have seen several of them here in Rome, as ragged and miserable as their name of ragbag. No, for the present the Patarines have done all they can for the Church. Just now, all they have before them is flight or martyrdom."

It was that grim picture that resolved Matilda. "Your Holiness," she said, speaking very slowly that in the growing darkness her words might be the better heard, "if Henry is as faithless and conscienceless as this indicates, then there is very little hope of our doing anything with him but fighting him. That is a dreadful thing to contemplate. Won't you let me make one more effort to see if I cannot bring him to a sense of his obligations? Even Godfrey admits that there is an element of levity in his nature as well as willfulness. It may be that when he sees more clearly what he has done, he will try to make amends."

"God knows," said the soft, thin voice of Bernard, "we all wish that were so, and as the Countess suggests, we have nothing to lose by making the attempt."

"Very well," said the Pope. "Do what you can, through Godfrey or directly. You might try, Countess Beatrice, to see what can be done with the help of the Empress, though I cannot see that she has much influence with her son."

"But how about Tedald?" asked Bernard. "He knew the decrees against investiture by laymen, and there is no necessity of special interest that can be pleaded in this case."

"Well, I don't know about that," objected the Abbot Hugh. "You see, things have been pretty upset there in Milan for some years now, and I suspect that the recently-deposed pretender did not pay much attention to messages from Rome anyway. And Tedald—well, as you know, he certainly did not move in Patarine circles."

"No, Hugh," said Bernard, "that won't do. Tedald may be a little thick in the skull. His kind certainly do not devote much of their time to literature or theology. But he knows what everybody knows, that the elected Archbishop of Milan is a fugitive in Rome, and that the pretender has been deposed."

There was a knock at the door, and it opened to admit a servant carrying two lighted candles. These he set on the table, and then he withdrew. In the sudden light Matilda saw the face of Gregory frowning and tense.

"God knows," he said when the door had closed, and the steps of the servant had died down the passageway, "that men like Tedald are muddled enough to be capable of any confusion. Moreover, the name of the King would have power in the world in which he moves. I will write to him as to an erring son, and I will see if he can be brought to understand what he has done. As for the King, we'll let the young Countess see what she can do. Anything you think fit to do will have our blessing, Matilda, and we will stay our hand. Only it would be negligence not to take some notice of what has happened. So I will write a letter that will be unmistakable in its protest, but that will leave the door open if, by the grace of God, he should choose to return to his father's house."

That night Matilda could not sleep. At first she lay very still so as not to disturb her mother who was sleeping in her bed. But presently she thought she heard her mother sigh.

"Are you awake?" she asked softly.

"Yes."

"Do you think anything is to be done with Henry?"

For a moment her mother seemed to consider. Then she countered with another question, "What do you think can be done?"

"Nothing," bluntly. "But I have promised to try. Mother, I am going to Germany myself." She held her breath to catch her mother's expected start of surprise. But in the dark she heard nothing.

Then when she had decided that her mother must not have heard, Beatrice turned over heavily, saying with her accustomed finality, "I think you are right to try, and I don't think anything can be done. It is really beyond worry now. You can only do your best."

Curiously enough, Matilda found herself comforted, and she slept.

CHAPTER V

THE journey into Germany proved harder even than Matilda had anticipated. The early snows had nearly blocked the passes, and various lawless knights had taken advantage of the absence of the more important lords of Germany in the Saxon wars to waylay travelers. Twice Matilda had been forced to leave a wounded man at a friendly monastery, and the escort which she had sent a messenger ahead to request of the Bishop of Augsburg at Trier did not put in an appearance. She had comforted herself with the reflection that Godfrey, now that the Saxons had submitted, would be free to escort her back to Canossa. The worst of her journey, therefore, would be over with her arrival at the King's court.

Meanwhile, she had counted on getting exact information as to the King's whereabouts from some of her friends among the Bavarian barons, but the reports she could pick up varied so from town to town and monastery to monastery that it was soon clear that the King was moving from manor to manor, partly no doubt to make sure of the loyalty of his vast estates, partly also to replenish the stores of supplies which had been exhausted by his campaigns. Several times she was tempted to accept the invitation of friends of her husband and mother to spend the heart of the winter in storm-fast castle or well-stocked manor, but always she reflected that after what had happened in the affair of the Milan bishopric, there was no time to be lost. Sometimes as she urged her horse along a nearly invisible road in the teeth of a stinging wind, she was sorely tempted to yield to the prayers of Arduino and take refuge, but even then, she knew, Henry might be perpetrating some outrage that would at last break the patience of the Pope.

So she rode on until with her small company she had penetrated almost to the Thüringer Wald before she received certain news of Henry's presence at an ancient hunting lodge, to the east of Mellrichstadt.

It was with a sense of relief and of triumph, therefore, that she finally rode into the stockade of Kaisershof, and found herself standing on the broad porch that fronted the great manor house of unhewn logs. Although it was still only early afternoon, deep purple shadows lay on the piles of snow about the manor yard, while behind the house the hemlock and spruce forest hung like the curtain of aboriginal night.

Inside, however, the great hall was warm and cheerful. A fire blazing in the stone fireplace in the middle of the hall nearly hid from view the dais at the farther end. But the light of the flames touched the metal of swords and shields and spears and axes hung along the walls, and the copper and silver of the pitchers and goblets on the table at the back of the hall glinted through the firelight. Down both sides of the room ran long benches with trestle tables before them, and at these sprawled and lay and sat a numerous company of men with here and there a serving maid in a brightly colored and tightly girdled dress, pouring beer from a black leather pitcher into the copper and leaden cups. The air was heavy with wood smoke, and the green aroma of burning pine knots, and the stench of damp leather drying and the warm bodies of the drinkers and the hunting dogs dozing in the straw on the floor.

As Matilda stood at the end of the hall, trying to slip her frozen gloves from her hands, there was a stir among the men, and one or two of the serving maids who had been sitting on the table slipped to the floor. Then there came a roar from the other end, and a tall, handsome man in a loose mantle over a short tunic and a fur vest leaped from the dais and strode down the hall.

Tall as Matilda was, he towered above her with his arms outstretched to embrace her, a strikingly handsome man with reddish-brown hair and a reddish beard, and bold, laughing eyes.

"I did not expect you for another week at least, my brave little cousin Matilda. Godfrey told us that when you had set your heart on a thing neither God nor man could stop you. And now I see that not even the wind and the snow can hold you." He was fuller of figure than he had been when she had last seen him as a boy in his father's train, and the lines of his face sagged a little, but the general impression of it was as laughing and as careless as what she had remembered.

"I was anxious to see you, Henry," she said, slipping lightly from his clasp.

"I have told you for years," he laughed, "that I was at home to you any time you would come. God, Matilda, but you've grown to be a handsome woman. No wonder I had such a time getting that rogue Godfrey up here."

He slipped his hand through her arm, and kicking the benches out of their way, he took her down the hall. Halfway his steward scrambled out of their path.

"Here, Gunzo," the King gripped his shoulder with his free arm, "put a fire in the bower"; then in a whisper which Matilda yet caught, "and for God's sake kick these damned sluts out of here."

He laughed apologetically to his guest. "We are a camp here and not a court, Countess Matilda."

The woman who waited for Matilda in the hastily prepared bower was a sober matron, the wife of the steward, she hastened to explain. At first, she gazed with some awe upon the beautiful gowns and mantles which the maid Maria had borne before her on her horse, but presently as she helped Matilda change her heavy, mud-stained riding clothes for a gown of dark red wool with borders of heavily embroidered gold and silk work and a mantle of blue-green wool with a scarlet veil, her tongue began to loosen. And though Matilda thought it ill-becoming a guest to listen to any gossip about her host, she found it difficult to silence the woman without unkindness.

"I am glad that a lady has come to the manor, for now those hussies from the neighboring villages will be driven out, and we can get something like modest behavior and decent service from our own girls. I assure your ladyship that you must not judge German women from those you saw in the hall," said the woman kneeling down to warm the soft leather slippers which Maria had produced from her pack before the fire.

"You must not forget," said Matilda, smiling gravely, "that the King's mother, the Empress Agnes, is one of my mother's oldest friends."

The woman shook her head solemnly in its stiff white kerchief. "And your ladyship's own mother was a German lady, was she not?"

Matilda nodded.

"It is a pleasure to have a lady here," said the woman, "for the Queen has never been here. Only a Saxon lady whom the King had taken in one of those castles which were burned was here, but the King would not let her out of his sight, and she did nothing but weep. Even though the Saxons are wicked people to rebel against their King, one could find it in her heart to be sorry for her. She was so young, and she wept so."

"What happened to her?" asked Matilda curiously.

The woman shrugged her shoulders and rubbed her hands on the corner of her apron.

"All I know is that when the Archbishop of Cologne, the stern, old one—do you know him?"

"Yes," said Matilda, "the Archbishop Anno. He was once the King's guardian."

The old woman considered gravely. "I should have said there was no love lost between them, but then it is not for me to judge. At any rate, he took the part of the Saxon lady, and when he went away, the Saxon lady did, too, and the King was so angry that he knocked a man down for—"

There came a sharp knock on the door, and the steward entered. He bowed ceremoniously to Matilda, and then he looked suspiciously at his wife.

"My old woman here is a terrible one with her tongue, I know," he began, uneasily, "but the King is very anxious to offer the Countess some entertainment."

Matilda smiled at the embarrassment of the man and the indignation of the woman, an indignation which she obviously thought it wise to restrain in the presence of her betters.

"It is my fault," Matilda hastened to explain. "I was so tired that I am afraid I have dawdled."

When she emerged from the bower, Matilda was astonished at the change in the aspect of the hall. Half of the men who had slouched up and down its length had disappeared, and all of the girls. A couple of older women were spreading fresh linen on the table on the dais, and a second high seat had been set beside the King's. Several older men had appeared on the dais, and two ecclesiastics were now talking with the King, one a man nearly as tall as Henry and in a totally different way quite as striking in appearance.

"I don't know, Matilda, whether you remember Ebbo of Naumburg? You see, I have not forgotten your taste for the Church, and Ebbo is quite the pleasantest wearer of the purple that I know."

The Bishop of Naumburg laughed, showing white teeth in a full, easy-going face. "I am not sure, Countess, that your friend the Pope would agree with the King, but I am at your service."

"And Luitpold, Count of Merseburg," went on the King, laughing gayly at the Bishop's sally.

A grave and very dignified older man bowed and kissed her hand. "I met your father once, when I was a lad, Countess. He was the perfect figure of a lord."

"And Frederick, Count of Bergen," Henry laid his hand lightly on the arm of a young man with a very homely but exceedingly expressive face. "You ought to know him, because he likes Prudentius and Virgil, and for a soldier is a very good scholar."

"Indeed," said the Bishop of Naumburg, "I should be more than satisfied if my clergy were half as well-read as Count Frederick."

"It sounds scandalously clerical, doesn't it?" Frederick executed a brilliantly mocking caricature of a pious expression. "But I was ill for a long time when I was a youngster, and then we stood siege. So the old chaplain amused himself by sharing some of his superfluous Latin, and having nothing else to do, I lapped it up."

The King roared with laughter. "I suppose then that I am not giving you enough to do that when the other men go out for a stag, you hug the fire with a book, like any priest with his breviary."

With a stately gesture that transformed the hunting lodge into a court, Henry handed Matilda to her chair, and poured out some of the contents of a tall silver pitcher into a chalice of ivory and gold.

"Godfrey tells me, Matilda," began her host charmingly, "that you persist in drinking that thin Italian wine of yours and leave all the good Rhenish to him. It is a modest thing in a wife, that, but not befitting the honor of a great princess not to know good wine when she sees it. So I told Godfrey that he kept his wine but carelessly, and that really your scorn of the best wine in the world was nothing but your unwillingness to suffer the corruption of a good thing."

It was good wine, Matilda agreed, warm and potent and pleasantly dry. She returned Henry's pledge, and then the company settled down to more steady drinking, while the servants from the kitchen began to bring in one platter of meat after another. Henry was, Matilda soon discovered, a perfect host. He cut the choicest portions from each successive dish and laid them on her side of the large silver plate he shared with her. And though he drank a good deal, he yet never forgot to be even dainty, after he had drained his cup wiping his upper lip on the edge of the napkin which a boy held in readiness behind his chair, and neatly throwing his bones into the straw beneath the table, where already the rustling and low growling of the hounds could be heard.

Throughout the meal he kept up a running flow of compliment to his guest, of courteous inquiries about the health of old friends in Rome, of chaffing of his companions, with not a word of war or politics. Never had Matilda encountered so charming a host, and she was reminded of how years ago Henry had won the stern heart of Peter Damian in the days when the exploits of the young King of Germany were first beginning to be one of the great sources of gossip for all Italy. Several times Matilda tried to bring the conversation round to business, but without success.

"My lord," she began once, "I saw the Empress Agnes when I was last in Rome, and she—"

"Wept," interrupted Henry, with a mock-sheepish hanging of his head, "and prayed God I might be a good boy."

There was a hearty burst of laughter among the royal table guests and those of his company who were serving.

"The Empress Agnes is a very pious lady," said the Bishop of Naumburg courteously.

The King made a wry face, "Almost as pious as my wife," and then seeming to recollect the presence of his guest, he hastened to add, "Not that all the models of feminine piety are to be deplored. The Countesses of Tuscany have afforded the world an example that would convert the most obstinate heathen."

So it was with every effort she made to broach the subject that had brought her north. Not until the next day was she able to persuade the King to consider her errand.

"If you will, though I can't think of any worse waste of a beautiful woman than to talk business with her. Let me make love to you, Matilda, and that will do justice to the talents of both of us," he suggested, leaning over and laying his hand on the arm of her chair.

"If my lord were here," said Matilda, trying to keep the tone of her voice light enough.

The King laughed. "I'm not afraid of any competition Godfrey could give me. He is the best general I have, but as for love, I shouldn't say he had the temperament, should you?"

The Bishop laughed and shrugged his shoulders.

"Now the Bishop," said Henry, leaning over again and speaking in a loud whisper, "has. You mustn't judge the art by the performance of that gruff Godfrey. Besides, I have given him enough to do in the Low Countries to keep him busy till after Christmas. So you had better not look so coldly on me."

"Perhaps," said the older lord who had listened with rather a thin smile to the King's persiflage, "the Countess brings you some message from His Holiness, which you would like to hear."

Frederick laughed. "It isn't often that the Pope sends so charming an ambassador to us. It would be a pity to discourage him."

The King frowned at Frederick. Then he turned to Matilda with his most charmingly open and winsome manner. "But why didn't you say you had a message from the Pope, my dear Matilda? You know I have a special veneration not only for his office but for the person of the man himself. When I remember how my father used to worry about the sort of pope that those degenerate Romans were in the habit of foisting upon the Church, and how finally even Rome revolted and asked my father to come to the rescue, then I realize how fortunate we are to have a man like Gregory. He brings to the papal chair a luster it has not enjoyed since the days of his great namesake."

For a moment, Matilda was completely enchanted. How stupid she had been to listen to the rumors that floated around Rome, the countless stories that only the corruption to which Henry so feelingly referred could possibly bear to circulate. And how pathetic that one so generous in his expectations of human nature and in his trust as Gregory should be deceived!

"I am delighted, Henry, to hear you say so, and I know that the Pope will be, too, for in spite of all the alarming reports that drift to Rome, the Pope has the highest hopes of you."

After the words had come tumbling from her lips in her pleasure, she wondered if she had not somewhat exaggerated. It troubled her, and perhaps Henry caught the hesitation in her face, for he exclaimed indignantly, "There are always people who are trying to make trouble between the great. I think it is because they hope to make their profit out of a time of anarchy. I assure you, Matilda, that I have not the slightest intention of infringing on the rights of the Church; I am only trying to restore the power of my fathers. You see, Matilda, in the long years of my minority the nobility of the kingdom, both lay and clerical, took the chance to rifle my estate, stealing lands, and towns, and market rights, and tolls, and all sorts of valuable possessions and rights that belonged to the crown. Now that it looks as if I might be soon able to complete this task of recovery, I am looking forward to going down into Italy to receive the crown of the Empire. I want personally to assure the Pope that I desire nothing so much as that the two swords of society, the secular and the spiritual, should together rule the world in peace and amity."

"But that is the thing that the Pope wants, too, Henry. Now take, for instance, Milan. We hear that you have invested Tedald as archbishop without any word to the Pope."

The expression of innocence which Henry's face now assumed astonished Matilda. "But Count Ebehard sent him to me as the choice of the canons and the people. I was assured that everything was in due order, and since the lands of Milan are really an imperial fief, why, naturally, I invested Tedald."

"But didn't you know that Atto has never resigned the see, and that consequently it could not be vacant?" Anxious as she was not to have her faith in her pleasant host proved untenable, Matilda found herself puzzled.

"But I was told that Atto was in Rome hiding from the people, and that the bishop who had been taking his place was no longer able to keep order in the Church, that the whole situation was a menace to the order of the state as well as the Church. Matilda, if you had been through what I have just been through with the Saxons, you would not face the prospects of anarchy so calmly. Those sacrilegious savages desecrated even the graves of the dead."

"Still, you could have sent to Rome and got the approval of the Pope. You know, Henry, that the Lenten Synod of last year expressly forbade lay investiture."

But the King only laughed. "My dear Matilda, that is just an ideal which everybody knows cannot be put into effect. Gregory is a saint, and he dreams of a Church ruled over and staffed by saints who will have no thought for anything in this world but the spiritual welfare of their people. But the bishops he has in fact are no such saints. No, I am not any Patarine," the King hastened to explain as Ebbo of Naumburg looked up sharply; "I think the bulk of the bishops are fine fellows. But they are holders of land and engrossers of privilege just like the lay lords, and it is no use pretending they are not. When war comes, like what we have just been through, you know a king can't have half his kingdom in hostile or idle hands. A fief is a fief whether it be held by priest or layman, and it owes loyalty and service like every other fief. What would become of society if this loyalty and service were withheld? You can answer that question, yourself."

The full, laughing face of Henry had sobered, the relaxed muscles tightening as he spoke. And Matilda realized that here for the first time was something indubitably sincere and genuine—this determination to make of the power he had inherited a reality. For some moments she said nothing, looking thoughtfully at the charming, ambiguous face that in a flash had undergone so complete a change.

"That is the side of the lord who invests and of the King," she said, at length, "but how about the Church?"

"The Church has everything to gain from being strong and prosperous; you know that yourself, Matilda. Do you think that in this world men are going to respect an institution that is beggarly and weak and without power? Are priests and monks and bishops and popes angels that they can live off the air?" Again there was no mistaking the sincerity of Henry, but, Matilda reflected, he had not faced the question.

"Granted," she said, "but you know that it depends on the type of men the

Church has to work with. You yourself do not choose ignorant men to counsel you in the more complicated business of your realm. You do not choose stupid or cowardly men to lead your armies. Every office in society requires its own gifts, its own training, its own experience. Do you think that letting a lord choose the most satisfactory vassal is the best way of making sure that the Church will have the kind of bishops she needs?"

Henry scowled. "Oh, Matilda, there is a lot of rot talked about that. I know that a lot of these rich clergy are nothing but landgrabbers, and a lot of them are married, and all that. But look at the people who are making the fuss, like those miserable Patarines in Milan. The first thing you know they are rebelling against all authority, secular or civil, and where are you then?"

So the argument went on for the rest of the day. Henry was ready to make any concession that could be asked of him. He was quite ready to live like a monk himself, he averred—at that moment Matilda looked up and caught a cynical smile fading from the face of Frederick—and he would do everything he could to make sure that his companions kept the laws of God—it was at this point that the Bishop of Naumburg whose head had bobbed forward several times over the beautifully illuminated breviary he had been reading with an occasional tolerant glance at the disputants, gave up the struggle and fell peacefully asleep. In all the discussion Henry never ceased to reaffirm his veneration for the Pope. According to his own showing, he was the most misunderstood of men, and not a more loyal son of the Church was to be found in Christendom. But whenever the question of the selection of the officers of the Church arose, he insisted that it was sheer nonsense to put into such crucial positions the type of man who would be entirely useless in an emergency and in the best of times impractical.

It was then that a sudden fantasy came to Matilda. "But suppose the Church should surrender these lands and let laymen have them subject to some sort of additional tithe so that they might not be so encumbered with war and politics and could give all their energies to the service of God?"

For a moment, Henry gazed at her incredulously. "You mean that the great churchmen should live on such pickings? What sort of men do you think would consent to such meanness? You know what the priests are like in villages, ignorant, uncouth peasants?" He laughed and nudged awake the Bishop to share the jest. The latter gazed solemnly at Matilda; then he, too, laughed.

"If you were not a great Countess, I should think you a heretic," he said.

"But there are bishops who live as meanly as that and give their wealth to the poor even now, like Anselm of Lucca. And the Pope himself for all the public splendor and the palace lives as austerely as a hermit," she persisted stubbornly.

The Bishop shrugged his shoulders, "They are saints. There was Peter Damian, too. You cannot ask that of every man. What would become of the work the Church is doing for art and learning and civilization if all men did that?"

The King's face had sobered as the Bishop explored the possibilities of the suggestion which, Matilda admitted to herself, had been made in the heat of argument and without thought that it would be seriously considered. Now he shook his head decisively. "No," he said. "Secular vassals are always making trouble and intriguing like these rascally Saxons. The clerics are often enough nuisances, but they are more dependable; they'll do more for you, stick by you better, keep things in better order. No, my dear Matilda, you may assure His Holiness from me that I am always a grateful supporter of the Church. He can always count on me. And," he added, rising from his chair and taking Matilda's hand and kissing it, "I am all the more grateful to him for his solicitude because it has given me the pleasure of this visit with the most charming woman in the world."

It was clear to Matilda that there was nothing more she could do. And this feeling of futility was deepened to a general sense of frustration by her disappointment at not seeing Godfrey. Now for the first time she realized how much she had counted on the long hours of the return journey for the establishment of that understanding of which she had so long dreamed.

That night she announced that she must begin her return journey early the morning of the day after. To her surprise, Henry made no effort to detain her, but called his steward and gave him directions to see that everything was done to make the Countess' return as comfortable as possible. The next day he gave presents to every man in her company and to the maid Maria he gave a rich jewel and some gold to have it set for a clasp. To Matilda he gave the breviary in which the Bishop had been reading his office. It was a beautiful book from the scriptorium of Saint Gall, bound in jewel-studded boards. This final evidence of the King's tact moved Matilda afresh, and she set out on her return to Italy in very considerable confusion of mind.

Nor was this uncertainty in any way relieved by what she learned during the long and painful weeks of her journey back to Italy. For when she reached the hospice near Brixen, the sociable Abbot informed her that only the day before he had had the honor of entertaining the Cardinal Hugh Candidus and the Archbishop of Ravenna. One thing, however, was clear. Henry had had good reason for not regretting her departure. This suspicion was confirmed when she learned from the same loquacious source that the two dignitaries of the Church had honored his house by resting there a month before, while they sent messengers to the King.

CHAPTER VI

So anxious did Matilda become, the more she thought of the possible implications of what she had seen in Germany, that she stopped in Mantua only for the night. She was shocked to find how ill her mother had borne the ravages of the cold and dark of the winter, but when she had recounted the story of her visit in Germany, Beatrice would not hear of her stopping longer.

"I am really quite well," she insisted, the dark circles under her eyes belying her words. "You know I never have looked as flourishing when I had to be shut up in the winter as I do in the summer, when I can be out on my horse. I'd go with you to Rome, but I cannot ride as fast as I used to."

So Matilda left the majority of her company with her mother to rest from the labor of the journey over the mountains, and accompanied by two of Beatrice's best and most trustworthy fighting-men, she set out on her forced journey for Rome. At her mother's suggestion, she had donned an old riding mantle of sober appearance, and she had forbidden her companions to drop any hint of her identity. For Beatrice feared that the absence of an escort, which speed made imperative, might possibly expose her to the enterprise of some of her disorderly neighbors and even of her uncertain vassals if her journey were widely reported.

The twelve days on which she had counted to get to Rome, as it proved, had to be extended to fourteen. In the hills the snow was falling, but farther south the snow and ice gave way to sleet and rain; so though the horses often sank to their knees in the mire of the road when they were riding through the lands of some careless lord, it was possible to keep on. It was, however, late in the afternoon of the day before Christmas when Matilda and her companions reached the gates of the Lateran Palace. The wind had risen and sent the rain battering in great sheets against the stones of the outer wall. As Matilda waited with her companions before the gates, she felt the tight clench of her lips give way, and in a moment her teeth were chattering.

It was so dark when the gates finally swung open that the men accompanying Matilda had some difficulty in making their identity clear. By the time she found herself sitting over a brazier of burning charcoal, she was so exhausted that she could only lay her head back upon the chair in which she sat and shiver. All her remaining strength passed into irritation, as she felt someone remove her wet cloak, and choked in a moment of keener consciousness over the cup of hot wine she found pressed to her lips.

She must have slept, for she came to herself presently to find the Pope standing in front of her, looking down at her. He merely nodded when she opened her eyes, and turned to slip the dripping cloak he wore over his red habit into the hands of the servant behind him. Then he pulled another high-backed chair up to the fire and sat down.

"What has happened?"

Slowly Matilda told her story, the Pope listening gravely to each detail of her report. Once or twice he rose and stirred the charcoal fire between them, but he made no comment. Only when Matilda repeated the King's protests of personal admiration for him, did he raise his eyebrows and follow her words with fresh vigilance. Once he asked her to repeat, when she came to what the King had said on the subject of investiture. This he considered so carefully that for some minutes she said nothing. Then he looked up and nodded at her, and she went on with her story.

When she told of what she had heard of the journey of Guibert of Ravenna and Hugh Candidus, he looked startled, but the speed with which that expression yielded to one of critical speculation suggested that what he had heard fulfilled a suspicion rather than astonished by its novelty. Then for the first time she remembered the figure of Guibert of Ravenna crossing the courtyard while she and her mother waited for the Pope, on her last visit to Rome. So startled was she by the memory that she looked up at Gregory. He caught the glance and smiled.

"That explains the very confident line Guibert took with me that day you and your mother came to see me. Where before he had been plausible and insinuating, now he was openly threatening. It was over those towns of the Exarchate he had taken. They have been in the inheritance of Saint Peter from old time, and so I told him."

"But," said Matilda, "I thought Hugh Candidus was a warm supporter of yours."

The Pope hesitated. "Hugh and Bernard told me I was wrong to trust him. But it seemed churlish to suspect him."

For the first time Matilda found herself wondering how many disappointments must have come to this ardent and enthusiastic man in the last two years, and how bitter to the incorrigible idealist must have been the disillusionments of power.

The Pope seemed to read her thoughts, for he said gently, "It is good of you to have hurried back here to me in such weather and at such speed. You deserve some rest, and it is Christmas Eve. Now, if ever, Christians should make some truce with their worries and suspicions."

The reaction to the excitement of the last weeks had set in, and Matilda discovered that she was not only tired but sick of herself. It had seemed so important that she should hurry back, and now it did not seem to matter much. Wearily she wondered whether, after all, she had not been a little hysterical.

If Gregory divined her mood, he gave no sign, but lightly, and for him gayly, he began to talk to her of the coming feast.

"It will be pleasant to have you here for my Midnight Mass, Matilda. I will say it at Saint Mary's on the Esquiline, you know."

"Isn't there a banquet there at the monastery tonight to which you should go?" asked Matilda, suddenly suspecting that he was lingering to talk with her out of sympathy for her weariness.

"I have just come from there," he said. "The Cardinal of Albano's dinner was very good, but I had had all I wanted of it some hours ago. Our good friend William of Hirschau had sent us some excellent wine, and priest and layman pledged each other peace and joy for the Holy Season."

"Rome has been very quiet, hasn't it?"

His dark face lighted as he answered, "Yes, thank God. There was a report a couple of months ago that that Cencius whom you saved a year ago from hanging for his forgeries and thefts had been trying to stir up trouble, but I have heard no more of it. God has been very good to us, Matilda, this last year. The people of Rome seem to have given over their bad habit of rioting on every occasion and busied themselves with their various callings, and I think they have prospered as never before. And the unruliest of the nobles have been leaving their neighbors' possessions alone and enjoying their own. There have been some new houses building, and there have been some handsome gifts to the Roman churches, frescoes and candlesticks and vessels of silver and gold for the altars."

"You may be proud of your good government," said Matilda with a smile.

"We have labored but God has given the increase," replied Gregory promptly. "But I am grateful, for it is in law that I am trying to build these troubled years where in happier times my predecessors built in marble and in silver and gold."

"Yours is the harder," said Matilda wistfully. She wondered if the Pope had ever dreamed of building a church beautiful enough to be veritably the house of God. Ever since she had heard of Hugh's plan for a new church at Cluny with white pillars rising like tapers about the high altar, she had been haunted by a vision of tall, slender columns marching down a long nave to an apse as rich in color and stately figures as the ancient church of Theodoric at Ravenna, which for so many years had been the source book of all her dreams of the Heavenly City.

"Yes," said the Pope, after some minutes, "it is harder because one is working not in the more pliant textures of stone and wood and metal but in the hardest and most resistent of all mediums, the fallen nature of man. And yet we must not forget that God so cherished that nature that He put it on that He might show us what He meant it to be."

Matilda wrapped her cloak more closely about her and sighed.

The Pope stirred the fire again, and the charcoal smoldered red. "But let us not talk of these things today, which Our Lord gave us for rejoicing. You know, it has been much in my thoughts today how we used to keep Christmas at Soana when I was a child. The day before Christmas always seemed to us children the longest day in the whole year, for my mother would roast a goose that day, and we children would sniff it with our tongues hanging out and watch the rich fat fall into the copper basin she had set underneath the spit that nothing might be lost. Sometimes some of the fat would sputter into the flames, and they would leap up around it until somebody cried that the goose was lost. But it always escaped. Once I put my finger into the edge of the basin, and though it burned,

I licked it with delight until I remembered the fast, and then how I scrubbed my mouth. I resolved not to eat any of the goose on the morrow in penance for my sin, but my mother found me scrubbing, and she cried, and told me that since it was in forgetfulness and I had tried so hard to scrub out the savor, she thought I might eat."

So they talked of the holidays they had known, and Matilda found herself thinking of Christmas long ago when there had been three of them children at Canossa. And presently she was talking even of the Christmas feast she had made in honor of her small son, when friends had come in from all the land about to admire the babe as he lay on his grandmother's knee. For the first time she found herself thinking of him only with delight in the bright baby wonder, unshadowed by the pain to come. Outside the storm rose to a tempest that beat upon the shutters of the windows and roared in the chimneys and swept the lead-covered roof with great surges of sound. But within, wrapped in their cloaks, with the great cauldron of smoldering charcoal between them, they talked peacefully until the Abbot Hugh came to tell them that it was time to get ready for the long ride to the Esquiline.

"There will be very few people out tonight," said Hugh, as he helped Matilda mount her horse.

The streets were quite deserted, and since the rain soon blew the torches out, they rode in almost unbroken darkness. Here and there a faint raveling of light might be seen where folk still drank in the Christmas Eve with ill-fitting shutters. But for the most part the storm held sway, and even the large company that escorted the Pope seemed lost in its more majestic violence.

When they reached the basilica of Saint Mary, there was something ghostly in the faintly luminous windows high in the clerestory and the stains of light that lay in the porch. By contrast with the pit of night out of which they had just come, the candles in the sanctuary made a blaze of light in the cave of the church. And to Matilda there seemed something almost recklessly lavish in their magnificence with the wind booming out of the dark on the high wooden rafters overhead.

But the church was practically deserted except for the guests who had lingered late at the Cardinal of Ostia's banquet, and the guards who had come with the Pope. Matilda was therefore surprised when the two of her mother's men who had ridden with her from Mantua came and knelt down a little behind her, instead of staying respectfully in the rear of the basilica. As she turned her head again, one of them, a taciturn northerner with grizzled hair but still of a frame to make younger men look upon him with awe, leaned over and whispered, "The Pope has given orders that because of the storm his men shall come into the church."

Matilda looked at him in astonishment. He shrugged his shoulders, "This is Rome, Madonna. It is crazy to take such chances."

For a moment Matilda was angry at the impertinent intrusion of habitual suspicion on the peace of the evening, but Wolfgang had come down from the north with her mother on her bridal journey, and though he never had anything to say for himself in the more expansive south, he was a privileged character. So she returned his shrug of the shoulders and tried to focus her attention upon the lighted altar. In the night the misty radiance of the tapers was not potent enough to dispel the shadows from the many-hued mosaics of the apse. Only the sheen of the gold emerged distinctly from the dim blur of color.

The church was still full of incense from the day's services, and between the sweetness of the air and the brightness of the lights in the enveloping darkness, Matilda found herself very weary as she rested her head for a moment on the marble railing before her. When she awoke, the sanctuary was filled with the gold and silver vestments of the high clergy of Rome, and the Pope, an almost insignificant figure in that dazzling throng, was intoning the opening words of the Mass.

Matilda was still absorbed in the level stillness and concentration of her Communion prayer when a sudden jangling of metal on stone broke into her consciousness. Slowly and reluctantly, she opened her eyes. The Pope had just set the chalice back on the altar. Then before she could move, there was a wild rush out of the darkness, and a mob of armed men hurled themselves into the stillness of the sanctuary. Frozen with horror, she watched the Pope cover the chalice and then turn to face the mob. For a moment she saw his face very white and calm in the candle-light; then there was a flash of silver as one of the intruders swung his sword high over his head. Involuntarily, she screamed as the blade swept down, but it grazed the Pope's forehead, and in a moment as the man fell back on the rebound of his own blow, she saw the Pope again, standing in the same place on the second step of the altar, very straight with the blood from his forehead streaming down his face.

Then the hot anger surged through her body, and flinging off the encumbrance of her long mantle as she ran, she dashed into the mêlée. Unarmed as she was, she knocked one of the rioters down and seized a candlestick from a pedestal at the entrance to the sanctuary. The burning taper she tossed to the ground, and swinging the huge bronze holder like a battle mace, she brought it down on the head of the man who had tried to behead the Pope, stretching him flat on the marble pavement. As he fell, two of the other invaders rocked unsteadily on their feet, and between them she caught a glimpse for a moment of the Pope now on a lower step yet still erect with the same look of unearthly calm on his blood-streaked face. Then snarling with rage, one of the knights who had teetered, perilously recovered his balance and lunged at her with his sword. His lips had curled away from his mouth, but even in the foaming mask she recognized the face of Cencius. Anger at the man's ingratitude to the Pope who had forgiven past outrages and had spared his life gave her desperate courage, and with her improvised weapon she knocked the sword from his hand.

Again she raised the candlestick and fixed her eyes on the man's rolling eyeballs. Then it seemed to her that the weight of the bronze was but as air in the fire of her anger. Indeed, for one moment she hesitated, tempted to fling away her weapon that she might feel the wild delight of crushing out his warm life with her own naked fist. She raised the candlestick again, but strong arms had seized hers, and a low voice cried remotely, "For God's sake, my lady!" Then her head rang, and still struggling she went down into the dark waters that were rising about her. But still she seemed to see the face of the Pope calm and for all the blood streaming down its pallor, untroubled, like a presence from another world...

When Matilda came to herself again, her head was burning with pain, and her closed eyes were dazzled with fire. Slowly, the fire faded, and her consciousness seemed to slip out from under the pain. With a great effort she opened her eyes, blinking as she did so.

The red light faded, and she heard a familiar voice say in low tones, "You are quite safe, my lady."

Painfully, she struggled to one elbow and looked about her. Just in front was a wooden chest with a candle set on the edge, and in the light of the candle she saw the face of Wolfgang, drawn and gray.

"Where is the Pope?" she asked.

"God knows," he answered soberly. "They have carried him off."

The fire rose again, but he laid a strong arm on hers, and she fell back. With the realization of her weakness, the terrible lust to kill burned out and left her sick and choking with sobs.

"For God's sake, my lady!" pleaded the man huskily. "There is nothing you and I can do against so many. The Pope's guard could do nothing, and the bishops and cardinals who tried to fight were overpowered. Cencius must have planned it carefully, and if the Pope is still alive, he will be in some stronghold of his. Listen!"

For the first time Matilda heard the wind and the rain still beating against the leaden roof high overhead, and now above the sound of the tempest rose the tolling of a bell, loud as the sound of the storm fell in its tempestuous rhythm, muffled and far away as the wind roared and the rain beat against the metal in sheets. Now there were other bells swinging into the loud, steady beat of the alarum.

"They are raising Rome," said Wolfgang.

Matilda tried to rise. Her head still ached, and she was sore all over. Wolfgang helped her to her feet, and then firmly drew her down on the chest and stood over her, watching. She raised her hand to her head and for the first time she realized that it was bare. She looked down at her body, and opening the mantle in which she was wrapped, she saw that her dress was torn and wet, and the girdle at her waist cut to shreds.

She drew a deep breath, but it seemed to stick in a gasp. Wolfgang shook his head. "Here, behind the sacristy you are safe, my lady. Everybody in the church has gone, who could." At the grim qualification, Matilda shuddered.

"But how did you get me here?" she asked, rubbing her head to see if she could get her wits clear enough to consider what she should do next.

"One of those ruffians knocked you down just after I came up. I dragged you off, and he laughed, when he saw it was a woman, I think. By that time most of the candles on the altar had been struck down and all the candles around the sanctuary. It was dark, and they were all fighting each other; so I had no trouble dragging you into one of the aisles. Then as the mob swept out of the church, with their prisoners, I came here." At the word "prisoners" Matilda covered her face.

"If only you could have reached the Pope," she sobbed to herself.

"I had my lady to think of," and then, as if touched by her anguish, the man added more gently, "It was impossible. There were too many on him."

As she looked at him, he added hastily, "He was still all right except for the head wound. It did not look serious, for he was still standing when they seized him."

As that calm face came again before her eyes, it seemed that her head cleared a little. She rose and stood by the chest, alone. "We must go and help, Wolfgang," she said resolutely. He stared at her. "You have no company but me. Hermann was knocked down, trying to reach you, and I had to leave him. It will be dark in the streets, and God knows what ruffians will be out."

For a compromise and to gain time she insisted that they return to the church and look for the wounded Hermann. But when they opened the little door from the sacristy into one of the side aisles, the great building was in such darkness that all they could see was a single taper guttering feebly on the high altar and the dusky flame of the sanctuary lamp in front of the ciborium, still swinging slowly in the wind from the open doors. For a minute they stood there, listening to heavy breathing from the pile of shadows beyond the wavering circle of the light. Matilda moved forward, but Wolfgang laid a firm hand on her arm.

"Let me go, my lady," he whispered. "You can't tell what vermin may have crept in to rob the wounded."

She hesitated, and then taking his hand in hers, she went up to the high altar. There she picked up a candlestick that had been overturned, and set a half-burned taper in it and lighted it from the candle already burning. Holding it in her hand, she threw its light down the altar. It was strewn with the debris of overturned candles, lumps of melted wax and shreds of charred linen, but the chalice still stood upright, covered with the veil as Gregory had left it when he turned to face the intruders. She knelt down, and for a moment she prayed for the safety of the Pope.

There was a scuffle as of rats when she lifted the light of the candle upon the scene in the sanctuary. It was a feeble and flickering beam in that huddle of darkness, but it was enough to send several dark figures out the gates and slinking into the aisles. Handing the candle to Wolfgang, she knelt down and turned over the first body lying in a heap on the steps before the altars. He was quite dead, but the next stirred uneasily in his stupor. At a sign, Wolfgang brought wine and water from the table by the altar, and she washed the wound in his head, and with a strip of the linen vestment the injured man had been wearing, she bound it up.

There came a sudden noise in the back of the church. Wolfgang dashed the lighted taper to the ground and drew his sword. Then a loud voice rang through the church, "The dirty bastard told the truth. There's nobody here." The clatter of arms on the marble pavement of the porch ceased, and Matilda returned to her search for the wounded.

Several times she was interrupted by the intrusion of armed men, but each time the presence of mind of Wolfgang saved them from disturbance, and the clatter of arms and of angry voices faded without molesting them.

There was no sign of Hermann, but before the night was over, two of Matilda's patients had recovered enough to help her in her labor, and two more were sitting up, rubbing their polls. Now for the first time, Matilda, listening to the wind surging above their heads on the leaden roof of the basilica, and the rain beating in the open door, realized that the air in the sanctuary was bitterly cold and raw. So half-dragging, half-carrying the helpless, she and her aides removed them to the comparative comfort of the wood-sheathed sacristy.

"It is coward's work," she said bitterly, sitting down on the edge of a chest to catch her breath.

"No," protested one of the rescued priests, who, white and tottering, had yet helped in carrying the injured. "Listen!" As he spoke, Matilda realized that the clangor of the bells had never ceased through the seeming hours of her labor in the sanctuary.

She rose from the chest and moved to the door.

"Wait, my lady," cried the priest, "all Rome is out and armed tonight."

"But the Pope?"

"If he was not killed in the first madness, he is safe. Even Cencius would hardly dare that. Every honest man is out looking for the Pope, and the streets will be full of rabble."

So Matilda was forced to wait, but though her companions protested, there was one thing they could not keep her from doing. While the men swung the doors of the basilica shut, she cleaned up the wreckage of the sanctuary and tidied the altar.

It was nearly dawn when the first news began to come in from priests and servants of the monastery who, wounded, had been sent back to their house, and whose first thought had been of those whom they had left behind in their church. To begin with, they brought the news of the imprisonment of the Pope, still living, in a tower which Cencius possessed among the ancient buildings on the edge of the city. One of the monks had heard the voice of Cencius shouting at the Pope his demands that the papal strongholds of the city, especially the fortress of the Castle of Sant' Angelo, be turned over to him as ransom for his release. The man had also heard the Pope refuse to offer what he did not own but held only in trust, as ransom from a robber and a bandit. The sister of Cencius had come and stood at the door and shouted curses and imprecations at the imprisoned Pope, which the bystanders had shuddered to hear.

Another refugee brought a stirring picture of the mobs roaring through the dark and rain-drenched streets and converging upon the Capitol to exchange rumors and reports as to the whereabouts of the Pope. Still another had to tell of the discovery of the tower of Cencius, of the horde of knights and soldiers who had rushed upon the tower, of their vain beating against its stones until someone brought up an old battering ram from his own stronghold hard by in a corner of the ruins. But even the sensation which this chronicler produced was eclipsed by another monk who rushed in with the story picked up from some of Cencius' men who had prudently fled before the mob should break in. As the stone tower reverberated with the thrust of the battering ram against its gates, Cencius had flung himself at the feet of the Pope and had besought him to spare his life. This the Pope had promised, with the mob outside yelling to Cencius that they would tear him limb from limb when they reached him.

There was another story, of one of Cencius' men who had leaped upon the helpless Pope even as he stood on the battlements to speak with the besiegers below. The man had his sword at the Pope's throat, when a knife thrown from a height near the tower pierced his own throat, and, dying, he toppled back and plunged headlong from the battlements. There in the courtyard he lay on the cobblestones, with the dogs that had come out with the mob nosing curiously at the bloody heap until a priest took off his cloak and covered the broken body.

So the dawn came, and with it a mob of all ranks and classes of men and even some women. The rumor had spread over the city that the Pope was coming back to Saint Mary's on the Esquiline to give thanks for his escape, and curiosity and enthusiasm had drawn all, from beggars and thieves to ladies of the proudest families of Rome. The latter, wrapped in richly-embroidered mantles hugging the walls, with bodyguards of servants between the mob in the aisles and their own delicate figures, made a striking contrast to the half-naked and mud-and-blood-stained men-at-arms that jostled each other in the nave side by side with their lords, whose bright armor and rich mantles had left their luster in the mud of the night before.

With a beating heart, Matilda watched the mob, from the shelter of the carved screen before the entrance to the sacristy. Behind her she could hear some of the servants of the monastery stealthily bringing out swords and shields, for it took little imagination to see that motley throng breaking all bounds and leaping into the sanctuary. But at present, with every degree of hoarseness and exhaustion and wild frenzy, they were yelling acclaim for the Pope and curses for Cencius. Overhead and on all sides came the sound of church bells tumbling over each other in wild and resonant confusion, but quick and joyous in their varied and unstudied dissonances.

Two of the priests of Saint Mary's went out to the high altar and began to light the candles which Matilda had set again in their candlesticks. A roar went up from the nave of the church as the first lights flickered and swelled. Matilda saw the two men look at each other, but they went on lighting taper after taper until the whole altar was ablaze. In the half light of the early morning, there was something incredibly white like marsh mist in that waxen radiance.

Then came a sudden blast on the trumpet, and a great scuffling as the whole mob strove to turn at once. The cheers rose again, and the vast throng seemed to go mad. Matilda stretched her neck around the edge of the screen, but all she could see was a company of knights in shining shirts of mail with raised swords, making their way down the church. As the first of the escort opened the sanctuary gates, Matilda shrank back.

The cheering died down suddenly, and she looked out again. The Pope was mounting the steps of the altar, slowly, deliberately. His head was bound in dirty linen, and his vestments were torn and stained with blood and mire, but his face was perfectly calm and collected. For a moment he knelt down and prayed. Then he laid his hand on the veil of the chalice, and with a clear voice that rang through the church he went on saying Mass at the point where he had been interrupted in the night. The great throng grew still, and Matilda sank to her knees.

CHAPTER VII

"THIS fellow seems in a hurry," said Alberic, drawing his own horse to the side of the road and motioning to Matilda to do likewise. His warning came just in time, for the newcomer who had scattered their company to the ditches on either side of the narrow road, made no effort to slacken his speed. Rather he seemed to put spur to his horse, for the panting creature almost flew by them, kicking up the mire of the spring rains and covering Matilda's purple-blue riding mantle with mud.

"Damn your insolence," cried Alberic, starting his horse after the offender, but the latter only waved his arm tauntingly and rode the faster, his light laughter drifting back to his victims on the teasing breeze of late February.

Amused by Alberic's wrath, Matilda laughed, "There spoke a gallant knight, but was it quite, let us say, prior-like?"

"I don't care what it was," exploded Alberic.

"He looked clerical, too. He must be in a great hurry to get to Rome. You may get a chance at him at the Synod, my dear Prior of San Benedetto."

The corners of Alberic's mouth quivered, and involuntarily he looked back to where two of his own monks were plodding along stolidly with some of Matilda's men-at-arms. But there was a hard look in the eyes he brought back to his companion, and again she was amused by the flatteringly unregenerate behavior of the new Prior.

"I suppose they choose priors for their piety," she said impersonally to the air.

"Piety—oh, well I have to set a good example to those wooden heads of mine back there. But, thank God, they are not canons of Parma."

"Oh," said Matilda, trying to steer her horse clear of the worst pools in the road, "so you know him."

"I've seen him in action once or twice. You know I have never been one of those who thought that the service of God should be the perquisite of those whom He had blessed enough already with possessions and family. I suppose if I had had enough land myself to live like an honest man without robbing my neighbors, I should have been too comfortable to ask myself what life was all about anyway. But when a base-born man chooses the Church as the readiest way to live by his wits, then my gorge rises, and I begin to sympathize with those old dodoes who at every general meeting ask for the family trees of all the new recruits."

Matilda sighed, "I suppose being a prior has its own worries."

It was Alberic who laughed now. Then he sobered: "But Roland of Parma isn't anything to sigh over. He is a perfectly clear type. He's quite reckless. Born a little higher in society, in a part of the world where the Countesses of Tuscany had not been striving for twenty years to establish law and order, he would have been an admirably successful robber baron. As it is, well, he is right-hand man to Guibert of Ravenna. Give the devil his due, he will carry out anything he attempts, but you can count that he will not attempt anything of which he is not sure to make his profit."

Matilda nodded absentmindedly. She was not in the least interested in the insolent and rude ecclesiastic who had awakened the wrath of Alberic, but she found it hard to keep up her share of the light banter with which her companion had been entertaining her all the way from Mantua. It was not really that she was tired, as her company suggested by the solicitude with which they watched her every move. It was not simply that she was worried by the last letter which she had received from the Pope, with its disturbing confirmation of her own impression of the King's state of mind. It was not even that she was worried by the disquieting rumors that every day brought of restlessness and intrigue and bitter calumny in her own lands. It was not even her anxiety over her mother's obviously failing health—for the first time in her life Beatrice had clung to her daughter as she set out and begged her to return from Rome as soon as possible. Matilda felt her eyes fill with tears again as they had when she suggested to her mother that after all she need not leave her this time. But the habit of a lifetime of answering the call of duty had been too strong even for loneliness and infirmity, and Beatrice had proudly reminded her daughter of the position which the house of Tuscany had always held at the Roman court and the faithfulness upon which pope after pope had relied.

Nor was it even the bitterness of Godfrey's continued absence and the sense of estrangement in his infrequent letters. For if she had not become reconciled to that failure and privation, at least she had become inured to it. Not even the repeated rumor that Godfrey was seeking a divorce had broken down her pride and her hope against reason and every shred of evidence that perhaps even yet... But sure as she felt in her own resolute facing of the fact that she must not ask for happiness, she turned her thoughts from that torturing and delusive vista.

It was none of these things. Rather, she saw it now, it was that in the more than two months that had elapsed since her departure from Rome, she had not recovered from the shock of what had happened on Christmas morning. Now as she rode along on this gray afternoon of mid-February with Alberic absorbed in his own thoughts, and the company riding silently in the weariness of the journey nearly finished, she tried to get hold of this feeling of hers. It was not just the horror of the thing. That had been exorcised by the fierce anger that had filled her with the madness of killing. It was something deeper than that, burrowing like a worm into the groundwork of her peace and confidence. Anxiety? Perhaps—but the Pope had shown no fear either then or later. It was something deeper, something that would not seem easier on the morrow, something beyond comfort. She had carried it in the back of her consciousness all that last month in Mantua. It had been gnawing all the way now from Mantua to Rome. But in neither case had it occurred to her to confide in her mother or in Alberic.

And yet it was Alberic who gave her the key. He had begun to talk as if to distract her mind from her care by approaching it from another angle.

"Most of the things one pretends are important, really are not," he said half to himself. "We only justify our preoccupation and our sense of importance in thinking them so. But this meeting is something more. For good or for evil what we decide in Rome will make a difference."

Something of the anxiety his first words stirred in her must have appeared in the quick look she gave him, for he went on quietly and gravely: "What is the true solution of all these problems of authority and allegiance, I, for one, do not pretend to know. You certainly could not suspect Peter Damian of any doubt as to the relations of the two swords. Yet he thought there was something to the King's case. He used to say that you could not blame him for wanting to make sure of the loyalty of men he relied on as heavily as he did on his bishops. Hugh, who thinks Rome the one beacon light in a great storm, yet wishes there were some way in which both lay and spiritual interests could be recognized."

Involuntarily, she shuddered, and it seemed as if deep within, her whole being went cold. But Alberic seemed unaware of her distress, for he went on in the same tone of thinking aloud: "And certainly the man Gregory is about as different from what I am as could be imagined. For an ordinary fellow like me, his concentration, his devotion, that vision of his that takes the whole world into his view, the steadiness of purpose, the sureness—God, it is beyond anything I can imagine! And yet I should go anywhere he led. I suppose that is the way those Greeks and Romans felt when they heard Saint Paul preach."

She caught herself breathing with sudden relief as if a pressure that had been choking her had been removed. Then she knew. It was not fear that the Pope should be attacked, nor even that he should be worsted. It was not that Cencius had struck him and carried him off that had shocked her so, for Gregory himself had said that it did not matter. But that Cencius should have wanted to hurt Gregory, that he had not known him when he saw him just and forgiving, when at her suit he had remitted the just penalty of his misdeeds, that anyone who had had a chance to know what sort of man Gregory was should not understand him—it was this that gave her a sick feeling as if she had just witnessed sacrilege. And now she knew that she was afraid that the sacrilege might be repeated. Ah, there was the heart of it—the sacrilege was being repeated in all these rumors they had been hearing of the meeting of bishops that Henry had called at Worms. She tried to look her fear steadily in the face, but she could not. Irrelevantly, she thought of that night at the banquet in Rome when she had been so terribly grieved by the anecdote of the rotting noses which her father had cut from the faces of his enemies. No, she had no fear that she would ever revolt at anything the Pope did, but that anybody should fail to see...

The Pope was very gentle when he greeted her, but there was a large company of bishops and cardinals and other church notables in the library of Zachary where he received her, and he spoke with her barely for a moment. His face looked very tense, only the eyes seeming to smile. She could not have said whether the tension was anxiety or simply concentration, but she had a feeling as she watched him for a moment that while he moved slowly through the room, speaking with first one and then another, his thoughts were really not there at all.

Although Matilda remained in her lodgings all the rest of the day, declining all invitations to visit the palaces of friends, she received no word from the Pope. She was puzzled, for she had heard repeated rumor of impending trouble. Several of the friends who called that afternoon had actually seen a copy of a letter which a canon of Parma was supposed to have brought into the city. The accounts varied. Some said that the letter invited the Pope to abdicate; others that the letter declared that the Pope was deposed. All agreed that the letter purported to come from Henry. Rumors had come, too, of the charges which the King had preferred against the Pope in the meeting of the German bishops which apparently had taken place at Worms during the last month.

This part of the gossip Matilda tried to dodge. There was no one in the company who did not know of her hereditary and personal devotion to the Pope. It seemed incredible that civilized men should take satisfaction in telling her of such calumny. But still they persisted in telling her of the charges of heresy, of tyranny, of usurpation of power, of stirring up war and rebellion against civil authority, that the King of Germany had made against the Pope in the assembly of his bishops. There were also charges against his personal character, but here at length some shred of decency seemed to restrain the officious tongues, and the voices fell, and the subject was changed. At such moments she felt the thrust of curious eyes on her, and her whole being went sick within.

She tried to tell herself that it was the nature of greatness that it should draw the shafts of the base, but common sense told her that this comfort was a very sentimental form of pride, of dodging the full impact of the facts. It was a wretched afternoon for Matilda, and she was glad when it was over. But when the maid Maria, as she lifted her veil from her tired head, said gently, "Madonna is very weary from her journeys," she was angry. For it seemed to her that her very pain was in itself a failure of the indifference that pride and loyalty alike prescribed.

The next morning the Pope opened the Synod by himself intoning the Mass of the Holy Ghost, and in the two hours that followed Matilda found release. It was as if she had been shut up in a little room, and now she had come out into a great basilica. She had been imprisoned in her own life, and now she was free in something greater. What she knew at that moment was not comfort. The world she had found so bitter was just as hard and cruel and malignant as she had found it. So abandoned had it seemed to its Maker that only the suffering and death of His Son would have power to redeem it. In the contemplation of that larger mystery of pain, lifted up by omnipotence and cleansed by universality, she found neither peace nor comfort but release from the stifling particularity of the single mind in something too vast for hurt pride or outraged loyalty.

Once she saw the mystery as clearly as she had ever seen anything so great. The choir of the Lateran was sweeping through one of the majestic sequences of Saint Gall. For a moment she listened to the naked music, the organ rolling in a low monotony like the incoming waves of the sea on a smooth beach, the voices breaking through that surge, brittle and many-pulsed like the spent foam seeping back through the long fingers of the shingle. And then the passion of it laid hold upon her, and she heard no longer the soulless beating of the sea but the cry of all the world's need and grief and fear and wistfulness rising in flames to the high wall of heaven. There was something almost angry in that lashing of complaints and tears, but as it fell back into silence, there came that same sense of release. Not a featherweight of that grief would be minimized nor any of its bitterness disguised, but God himself had taken up the burden of His creatures, and it could be borne....

The Pope had barely concluded the speech with which he had opened the day's session. He had been very brief, and very temperate. He had merely reported the failure of his emissaries to secure any satisfactory answer from the King of Germany as to whether or not he intended to observe the decrees of the Synod of the year before. Still more disquieting had been the reports which for some months had been drifting back from Germany. The excommunicated counselors were still at the King's elbow, and the strongest and most faithful of the Saxon bishops were in prison, though the Saxons had submitted months ago. As for the private life of the King, it was still such as to bring down upon any man in any rank of life the severest censure of the Church. Gregory had concluded by repeating his oft-expressed hope that the King would in repentance return to the observance of those laws of Christian morality from which even the highest of earthly rank could not plead exemption.

For a moment there was silence in all that vast throng of laymen and ecclesiastics. Then a man rose from the end of one of the benches in the middle of the nave of the basilica and with a heavy step strode down the aisle between the forms. Startled, everybody watched him in silence until he stood before the throne in which the Pope had just seated himself. Then he turned sidewise so as half to face both the Pope and the meeting before him. Astonished, Matilda recognized in him the man who had passed them on the road yesterday, jeering at the damage his reckless riding had done. Drawing himself up without any gesture of reverence, he began to address the Pope in a loud, defiant voice. In the name of the King of Germany and the German and Lombard bishops he bade the man Hildebrand of Soana come down from the throne he had usurped. Then in a voice that rang through the basilica, Roland of Parma went on to remind the Pope that the honor he had usurped could belong only to him who had been chosen by the bishops and approved by the King. Then he turned his back on the Pope and faced the stupefied nave.

Again his voice rang out as he cried to the bishops that the King bade them all attend upon him on the Feast of Pentecost when he would give them a real pope and father of the faithful, "for this man"—he raised his arm in the same large, contemptuous gesture of the afternoon before—"is not a pope but a ravening wolf." As his voice rang through the church, Matilda covered her face with her hands, but right in front of her, she heard a yell, "Take him there," and looked up to see one of the cardinals on his feet. There was an answering roar, and on all sides swords flashed, and men, priests and laymen alike, leaped to their feet, yelling, "Kill the insolent rascal!"

For a moment Roland stood there uncertainly, his bold face white and surprised. But before any of the swords could reach him, the Pope had sprung from his throne and put his arm in front of the man who had insulted him.

"Traitor as he is, he is yet a messenger," he cried, lifting his free hand to still the frenzy.

When order was at last restored, he turned to the frightened Roland and bade him read the letter he held in his hand. Then he seated himself on his throne again to listen quietly and attentively to the reading of the letter.

Silenced, but still flushed with anger, the company listened. There was no doubt about its being the document with which rumor had been busy for the last day, and for once report had not exaggerated the sensational character of its object. It was addressed from Henry "by the Grace of God King" to "the false monk Hildebrand." There was a growl from the whole church at this, and Roland had the grace to stop and look around. The Pope bade him proceed. His voice still bold but, Matilda noted, much less resonant, Roland read the categorical charges of the King against the Pope. Hildebrand of Soana had procured a fraudulent election to the seat of Saint Peter by violence and gold, he had trampled on the bishops, he had tried to deprive the King of Germany of the power which God had given him, he had promoted war instead of peace. Therefore, the King with his bishops declared the usurper damned and deposed.

When Roland had finished the letter, he shrank back from the yells that rose all over the church. With difficulty the Pope thrust back the swords from the terrified canon, and strove to quiet the mob. But in vain. So presently, seeing that the tumult of wrath and indignation was beyond control, the Pope lifted his hand high above the seething mob, and hastily pronounced the benediction. Then calling his guards about him and bidding them protect Roland on penalty of their own lives, he gave orders that the messenger was to be escorted to the gates of the city and, with all necessities supplied including a fresh horse, he was to be set upon the road to the north.

"And," added the Pope grimly, "I hear that the King has gone into Lorraine; so don't waste any time going farther north." Then he left the still tumultuous church and hurried back to the palace.

That afternoon word came from the Lateran asking the Countess of Tuscany to join a conference of the Pope's most trusted counselors. When she arrived, Matilda found the rest of the company assembled. Hugh of Cluny was on his feet speaking when she entered the library of Pope Zachary. He paused, and several of the priests rose and made way for her about the table at which the Pope sat. The latter nodded gravely to her, and she sat down in the place made vacant for her at the end.

The atmosphere of the great room was charged with excitement as she soon saw in flushed faces and gleaming eyes. Only the Pope sat as calm as usual with the tension of perfect absorption in his lean face. But the dark eyes were heavily shadowed and inscrutable, and in the corners of the taut mouth lurked some invincible shadow of repugnance as if he had recently drunk of gall. The whole poise of the head, however, was firm and resolute as always.

Steadied by his look, she turned her attention to Hugh of Cluny. He was speaking in his usual low voice, but he was clasping his long hands, strikingly white against his black robe, and unclasping them, oblivious of the fact that the full sleeves fell farther and farther back on his lean arms.

"Mind you," he said with the slight insistence of the man who goes again over the ground he has already covered, "mind you, I agree with the rest of you that it is unheard-of blasphemy, but to excommunicate the King of Germany is to dissolve the bonds of Christian society."

Hugh looked anxiously at the Pope. Gregory nodded to him, and, obviously reassured, he sat down. There was an excited mutter of dissent, and the Pope looked around the company.

It was the Archbishop of Salerno who voiced the popular disagreement. Rising in his slow fashion and speaking even more slowly, he drew the restless eyes of the whole company to himself. "Wouldn't you agree, Hugh, that the bonds of Christian society had already been somewhat stretched by the King?"

Matilda watched the color mount in the thin cheeks of Hugh. But he said nothing.

"The insult to the Pope—"

But the Pope shook his head: "No, Alfanus, I have said that there can be no question of insult to me or of punishing or avenging insults. What we must consider is first the principle, and second, if we agree on the principle, as I think we do, how that principle is to be established."

The Archbishop Alfanus was not to be brushed aside, however, for in his slow moving way he persisted: "But the majority of men are not aware of principles. What they see is individuals and deeds. The King has attacked the Pope. The question is do we allow him to attack the Pope or do we do something about it?"

But Cardinal Hugh of Die was on his feet, trembling with excitement: "Whatever the Archbishop's majority of men may say, the question is who controls the Church? If we suffer this outrage to pass without some signal mark of reprobation, we have given the Church into the hands of the King."

Hugh of Cluny leaped to his feet. "You know how likely it is that I should want to give anything of the Church out of the protection of Rome." There was a loud laugh at this, particularly from some of the bishops present, and, anxious as she was, Matilda found herself smiling, for as everybody knew, Rome had fostered the Cluny empire in the teeth of bishop as well as prince.

Hugh was not to be daunted, however, for he went on doggedly, "But it is one thing, I think, to say the King shall not rule the Church, and another to say that the Pope shall rule the King."

There was a moment's shocked silence, and some of the bishops whom Matilda had not seen in Rome before looked anxiously at the Pope. Perhaps it was because he felt their eyes on him that Gregory answered that challenge himself, speaking in a low, cordial voice that left no doubt as to his feeling for Hugh. "You are quite right, Hugh, that the sword of Caesar belongs to Caesar and not to Peter. But now, thank God, Caesar himself is a Christian and a child of the law. To say that a king is above the law that binds all believers is to destroy the fellowship of the family of the faith. What is sin for the meanest of his subjects is sin for the King or for the Pope, for that matter. To say that is not to set the Pope over the King in the things of this world. To deny it is to set the State above the law and to make the laws of God bow to the powers of this world."

There was a spontaneous burst of approval as the Pope finished speaking.

"Your Holiness," said the Abbot Bernard in his quiet, matter-of-fact way, "I do not think that we need to spend much thought as to whether we should advise the Synod tomorrow to condemn Henry. You would have something very close to a riot if you made any effort to stop them."

For the second time that afternoon there was a decisive note in the Pope's interposition, "There is no doubt about that, but whatever the Synod asks, we are responsible for not yielding to it unless it seems just."

When the whole company had agreed that on the morrow the Pope should excommunicate the King, the Pope rose and solemnly prayed that the Church might have peace and that all her enemies might quickly be made of a better heart. Awed at the possibilities of their decision, the members of the informal council did not linger about their leave-taking but went quickly out in silence.

The meeting in the Lateran Basilica on the next day opened as Abbot Bernard had predicted, and from all over the great edifice rose cries for the excommunication and the deposition of the King of Germany. For the first time the Pope seemed deeply moved, and when the Synod voted the petition for excommunication, he read with great sadness but with firmness the decree formally declaring the King of Germany excommunicate and absolving all Christians from the observance of their oaths and obligations to him. When he had finished, there was a great silence and then acclaim.

Before she took her leave of the Pope for the journey back to Mantua, Matilda suggested that she send a messenger to Godfrey urging him to do all he could to bring the King to a realization of the wrong he had done. A queer look came over the Pope's face, not so much of disapproval as of wonder, it seemed to Matilda, and he replied that it would not be necessary. His own messenger to the King would bring him his personal assurance that the Pope was waiting to absolve him as soon as he manifested the spirit of repentance and a readiness to make satisfaction for his sins. "He has only to take the measures that any Christian would take for the mercy that is open to any penitent to be shown to him." Then he added gently that he would himself pray for the conversion of the King, and he asked the help of her prayers in this, his dearest intention. He did not look at her as he spoke, and Matilda left him with a desolate sense of incomprehensible estrangement.

CHAPTER VIII

THAT sense of something wrong and of complete helplessness to put it right came back afresh to Matilda one evening nearly a month later. She was tired, and it seemed to her that she could not bear any longer the eyes of her mother's household upon her, watching her every movement with affection and solicitude, it is true, but still with unremitting vigilance. She knew that she would not have minded it so much if she had not been exhausted from the cares of the spring season, with the accompanying restlessness throughout her lands and all the decisions to be made as the life of the awakening countryside stirred again. Then, too, in spite of all that her mother said about feeling better now that they had come to Pisa with the softer air of the seacoast about them, she knew that Beatrice was not getting better.

Most of the time the old Countess of Tuscany sat by her window overlooking the Arno, watching the boats going up and down the river and the March sunshine playing on the water. She who had never sat idle in her life would spend long hours thus, and when some question of the household or her lands was brought to her, she would bid the intruder carry the problem to her daughter. Even when Matilda would bring to her the latest messenger from Florence or Rome, she would hardly turn from her window as she said, "You will have to abide by the consequences of the decision, not I. Do as you think best. Come, look at the queer way those sailors have twisted the bright scarves round their heads. If you didn't see the cross on their sails, you would think they were Saracens, wouldn't you?"

It was as if Beatrice who all her life had devoted her great energy and versatility of power to the service of large interests and more remote purposes, now as she felt her days drawing to their close, was devoting all her vast resources to the enjoyment of the little pleasures of the moment. A cup of the golden Greek wine which Desiderius of Monte Cassino had sent to cheer her illness would give her many minutes' quiet pleasure. By the hour she would listen to a jongleur singing long tales of battle and sudden death, or the chaplain Donizo reading in a low voice with a delicate sense of rhythm some of the verses of Fortunatus or Paulinus of Nola. So she would sit with the warm spring sun from the open balcony falling about her chair, and her maids weaving quietly in their bright-colored tapestry the story Beatrice herself had chosen, of the first lord of Canossa who had sheltered a queen from her enemies and so laid the foundation of the great destiny of his house.

Once when Matilda sought her out with the latest message from Henry, demanding that his liege vassals Beatrice and Matilda execute his will in the driving from Rome of that impostor Hildebrand, she found Beatrice listening to a little girl she had picked up in the kitchen. She was a bright little creature with black braids standing out stiffly from her head and big eyes that opened in a perpetual astonishment at the world. Now she stood looking up at her mother's mistress with her hands folded behind her back, talking with great animation: "But you remember the little black kitten, the one that flew like the Evil One himself? And his funny little screw of a tail that went high up in the air whenever you came near him—he's getting fat now, and he lies still and lets you touch him."

Beatrice laughed, and when her daughter laid the letter open in her hands, she looked up at her wistfully and said, "I like to hear her talk. She reminds me of you when you were little."

But it was not the burden of so many things to see to that wearied Matilda. It was rather the bitter sense of hollowness, of cruelty and falsity, in everything that she looked upon. Ever since that afternoon in the Campagna just outside of Rome, when she had faced her fear and uncertainty and had asked Alberic if in his conferences with the other members of his order, he had picked up any rumor of an effort to discredit her with the Pope, she had felt thus. She had not spoken to her mother or to any member of her household about what Alberic had at last told her. She could not bring herself to, but she knew that they all had heard that the King of Germany before all his bishops and barons had accused the Pope of scandalous relations with the young and beautiful Countess of Tuscany.

Now, this evening, it seemed to her that she could not endure any longer the close and whispering air of the great house. She wanted to escape, to go out just anywhere into the coming night, and alone with the indifferent spaciousness of the vanishing world, recover something of her old integrity of freedom and peace. But she had promised her mother that in these unquiet times she would not leave the house without some protection, for as Beatrice had reminded her, a great lord had no right to think that in this world of ruthless enemies and turbulent vassals he could move about as casually as if he were a peasant. So now she went to the stable and bade two of the men saddle horses for a short ride before supper.

In a few minutes she had reached the edge of the city, a little rise of ground just above the city wall, looking away to the hills on the north. Here she halted her horse and turned back to see if the two servants who had followed her had stopped, too. They had already dismounted. The promptness of their action with its silent evidence of the fidelity with which they had watched her every movement gave her again that choking sense of being constantly watched.

She knew her resentment was unreasonable. But it seemed more than she could bear, this consciousness that every least motion even of her effort to escape from the crowded house into the peace of the hills was being watched, doubtless to be discussed in kitchen and stable, and now, she was afraid, elsewhere. It was that sense of the endless repercussion of one's lightest motions and the limitless possibility of misconstruction that weighed on her now. She tried to choke down the burning tightness in her throat.

She tried to tell herself that Godfrey had been far away in Lower Lorraine when Henry made those dastardly charges. But she knew that rumor would not spare Godfrey, and no instinct of delicacy would restrain Henry from mocking his best general. She thought of Godfrey's last letter. It had been curt and wholly occupied with business, with requests for certain supplies, with expostulations on the Pope's treatment of the King. She tried to think of how Godfrey would receive the report of Henry's charges. He would not lightly believe them; of that she felt sure. But when she sought the grounds of that certainty, she could get nowhere. For in most of her relations with people she had assumed that their minds would work much as hers did, and she had known now for some time that Godfrey's worked quite differently. What he valued was entirely foreign to what she cared for—she brought herself up with a start. For the new grief was bringing the old grief in by the hand. She felt weak and ashamed of herself as she realized, not for the first time, that every fresh prick made the whole wound smart.

She looked down at her men. It was so dark now that they were but darker
and taller shadows at the base of the bare knoll on which she stood. She looked
out over the dim meadows at her feet, to the hills. Like some long-extended
leopard dozing against the sky, they lay, a dull blue against the fading after-sunset
glow. As she turned to bring a fuller circle into view, the figure changed, and they
stretched out in long restful curves of solid shadow against the flaked sky, the
tension of the first view relaxing into the slow rhythms of the larger movements
of the world. Looking on them, she felt the muscles in her throat and breast relax,
and she breathed more deeply of the March wind fingering its way through the
dry grasses where as yet the green of spring had not come. With the city at her
back, she seemed alone with the sky and the hills and the wind, and her cramped
and huddled spirit flew free like a standard unfurled on the wings of the moment.

As if from a great distance she heard a step behind her, but she was too loath
to yield the peace of the moment, and it was only when the step multiplied and
came up behind her that she turned.

For a moment she stared incredulously at the figure in heavy dark riding
cape and thrown-back cowl. Then, as Alberic bowed, she put up her hands before her face. For the horror had come back of that moment on the edge of the
Campagna when at last he said he would tell her, to save her from others less
understanding and less devoted. Shuddering, she looked at him, standing there
without moving. It was too dark for her to see his face, but even without seeing
she felt a gravity and a reserve in his demeanor that made her cheeks burn.

"Your name will be compromised, if you are seen talking here to me," she
cried sharply.

Alberic laughed. "Put down your hands, my lady. The man at the North
Gate, as he closed it behind me, told me that he had seen the young Countess
ride to the hill above the wall. My two brethren are down there now with your
men. So I think that there is no danger of anybody calling my escorting you back
to your house a tryst."

"God knows, Alberic," she said bitterly, "what they will say of a Pope's harlot."

He stood still for some minutes, while the breeze blew lightly on Matilda's
hot face. The hands she had clenched under her cloak relaxed.

"You have forgotten what I told you. There is nobody so high-placed in this
evil world that he is beyond the reach of calumny. And this is even more true in
time of war like the present. I don't think Henry himself for a moment believes

what he said, though we must not forget that his determination that nobody shall curb his vices makes him eager to believe that all men are as bad as he. It's to his advantage, too, to make out the Pope as black as he can so he may with the better credit fight him. That your name is sacrificed can not matter to a man who never stopped at any means to get his ends, and who has never had a chance to learn the value of a fair name, himself."

"But that none of those bishops should say a word!" she protested.

"They're used to doing what the King wants. That is the end for which they're chosen, and they know how unwise it is to thwart him. Then, too, Matilda, you must not expect men to understand what they have never had any chance to experience. Most of those men have never known what it is to be devoted to anything beyond their own interest or, the best of them, their own personal activities. That is why they think Gregory is simply ambitious to put his hands on all the power he can get. And for a pure and selfless devotion, they have spent their lives conspiring against their neighbors and trying to keep their vassals from conspiring against them. It is the final judgment of such a world that it can only throw mud at a beautiful thing."

If his words did not fully comfort or reassure her, they at least touched her heart enough to break down the guard of her pride, and before she knew it, she had said, "But it isn't what they say that I mind so much as what Godfrey must have thought and felt when he heard it."

She saw him start at the mention of Godfrey's name, but it was too dark for her to see his face. She knew she should not have brought him into the discussion, and she was silent with embarrassment.

But there was no trace of disapproval in Alberic's mouth, only great gentleness as he answered, "You must not assume, Matilda, that Godfrey felt—feels about these things as you do. He is a soldier, and for him it is the faith he gives and the faith he receives that matters. He would not lightly believe that you or the Pope had broken faith with him. If he did believe it," his voice sank, "he would kill you, but he would not spend much time in grieving or in blaming. It would be one pledge more broken, and he has seen too much faithlessness to look for perfect faith on this earth."

Again, Matilda's heart warmed in gratitude that in spite of the veil of words Alberic had understood what was in her heart, for it was not about what Godfrey might do or even think that she had been so concerned. It was simply that knowing in what things Godfrey put his trust, she could not bear the thought that he might be hurt or disillusioned.

She said nothing, for now she saw with grim lucidity that Alberic was right. She had known from almost the beginning that Godfrey would not be jealous, for her beauty meant no more to him than the learning which he despised in man or woman. She was his wife, and he would keep faith with her as he expected her to keep faith with him. That she was rich and powerful made her a masterpiece of her kind. Were she ever in real difficulty, he would cross Europe to her defense, and he would expect her to do the same for him. She had rather a feeling that he would no more distrust her than he would distrust the sword in his hand when he knew it was the best steel that Spain could afford and held in its guard relics that might have made a King's ransom.

No, she said to herself as she took one more look across the hills now fast melting into the night, this is not the day of our judgment. It is rather when the Pope and Henry come to open war, and each side musters his forces. That, thank God, has not come yet. Then for the first time she wondered what had brought Alberic to Pisa.

CHAPTER IX

BUT Alberic gave no hint of his errand until they stood in the great hall of Beatrice's house. She had brought him aromatic Moselle for the chill of the evening, and he had insisted on her taking a cup with him. Wondering on his so standing on the point of courtesy, she had complied, while he chattered lightly of the spring plowing and sowing on the lands of San Benedetto and of the new cloister that he was building. His two companions said nothing, but when she looked at them once or twice, she found their eyes fixed solemnly upon her. Behind them, Matilda could see a couple of her maids setting out food on the dais table.

When her guest had emptied his first cup, she could stand the mystery no longer. "Alberic," she began with all the finality she could muster out of her worry, "what has happened that you are so loath to speak of your errand? Is it news from Germany?"

"No," said Alberic, looking at her quickly and looking away, "it is from Lorraine."

"Ah," she nodded, "Henry had gone to Utrecht, I remember."

Alberic looked at her sharply. "It isn't Henry; it's Godfrey."

She rejected her first thought. She had heard of no fighting in the Low Countries. But there had come, weeks ago, that rumor that Godfrey of Lorraine was planning to divorce his wife.... With her heart beating she looked up at Alberic. He took a step toward her chair. No, it was not that—she knew from the look on his face seen even by candlelight. "He is hurt?" she asked, ashamed of that first fear.

Alberic nodded with a compassion in the simple gesture that suddenly terrified her.

"How?"

He did not answer but only watched her. Then she knew.

"Dead!"

She was stunned, but quite in possession of herself. She even noticed that the maids had ceased their work and were listening; at least they were making no sound. The two monks behind Alberic were staring at her as if they could not quite make out her features.

Alberic barely moved his head, never taking his eyes off her face. Then those watching eyes seemed to swim and his face blurred, but he had not reached her chair, when she raised a hand and asked, "How?"

"He was stabbed by a couple of ruffians."

"Then?"

"Yes, he was murdered."

"Murdered!" She heard her voice shoot up in a sudden spiral of a scream. She strove to stop it, and then there was silence.

She opened her eyes to find Maria rubbing her hands and crying. Alberic stood in front of her with a cup in his hands.

But she looked beyond him, for in the doorway at the side of the dais stood a tall white figure. It was her mother in her night robe. She recognized her, but she seemed too remote to make the effort of speaking.

"What is it?" asked Beatrice querulously, like a child waked suddenly from sleep. It was the childishness that roused Matilda.

"Oh, Mother, I'm sorry I waked you." She was across the hall and had taken her mother's hand from Ermengarde's arm and slipped it through her own.

"Alberic?" The Countess Beatrice, holding the shawl over her head together under her chin with her free hand, advanced into the room as stately in her night robe of white wool as if she were dressed for an imperial banquet. Alberic stood unmoving, while Matilda led her to the chair in which she had been sitting, and taking her own mantle from the chest where she had dropped it, wrapped her mother in it.

"I thought you screamed," said her mother with relief. Then as she looked around the silent circle, she asked impatiently, "Why do you all stand round like statues?" Matilda tried to speak, but a scene from her childhood had flashed into her eyes, and she could not. She remembered a covered bier being brought into the great hall at Canossa, and her mother falling sobbing across the foot of it, and the singing arrow that she could never afterwards wholly believe she had not heard herself, though the wood in which that arrow had sped to its bloody mark was miles away.

But nobody spoke, and in the firelight Matilda saw her mother's face blanch. She took her mother's hand in her own, and she said simply: "Mother, Godfrey is dead." She heard her own voice speaking as calmly as if the news had been no concern of hers.

She saw her mother's lips twitch. "Godfrey? Not young Godfrey!"

Matilda tried to keep steady the hand that held her mother's, but presently her lips were quivering so that she forgot.

"God have mercy on us all!" said her mother, crossing herself. All in the room made the same sign and a low murmur of "Amen" rose from the farthest shadows. Matilda felt her mother's hand tighten on hers. "How did he come to die?" asked Beatrice in a voice little above a whisper.

"It was in the evening, when all men were asleep, and he was returning to his lodging in Antwerp. Just outside his door two strangers came up, and they thrust their knives into him. They ran away before his men could reach him," Alberic paused. "You know how he always strode ahead."

"Did he die at once, without time—?" Matilda felt her hand hurt from the pressure of her mother's fingers.

"No, the man who brought us word and who had been just behind him coming down the street said that for a second he sprang back with a cry, 'God—' then he gulped, and he finished, 'forgive me'. Some of his men started after the two rascals, but one ran for a priest who lived in that street. He gave the Lord

Godfrey absolution, but he said no more. By the time they opened his robe—"
Matilda heard no more. Blinded with tears, she yet remembered to loose her fingers from her mother's gently. Then, unable to find any words, she leaned against the high wooden back of her mother's chair. She felt strong arms about her, but her veil had fallen over her face, and she did not trouble to lift it. Presently, she heard Alberic's voice as if he were answering a question. "The man said they were going to bury him there in the Cathedral at Antwerp."

Matilda winced. And then she lifted her head and flung back her veil.

"His father is buried at Verdun, and his son at Canossa. It is a long way," said Beatrice sadly.

"You forget that the dead are all at home, Countess."

The old Countess shook her head. "The dust is lonely."

Looking at her mother through her tears, Matilda saw that the eyes with which she was gazing into the fire were still dry. It was then that her own self-control broke, and she fled blindly.

When the first terrible convulsion of weeping and sobbing had spent itself, she lay on her bed in a stupor. Several times she heard steps come into her room and go out again. Once she felt the yellow light of a candle in her eyes. But she could neither speak nor move though it seemed as if her mind were quite awake within the shell of her body.

Once she heard her mother's voice very low, "Come, Ermengarde, there is nothing we can do for her tonight but leave her alone," and at the strange note of helplessness in her mother's voice, her heart went out to her, and she tried to rise and tell her that it was not so bad with her as that. But she could not move, and the words rattled noiselessly in her throat.

She tried to pray. Godfrey's father and son would have found him now in that country where all the ages are as one. But Godfrey, his father, who had been so gentle, and the baby who had not known sin, would be in heaven now. Tomorrow she would have Masses said. Tonight all she could do was pray to the Virgin. Godfrey, whose mother had died when he was a child, had never set much store by women. Saint Michael and Saint George and the other shining ones of the sword should be his company, but if he were lonely or frightened or the weight of deeds done or undone lay heavy on his soul, Mary would understand and would know how to give him the comfort that his wife would not have dared to offer even if she had been there.

Now the old anguish came again, but with a new bitterness. For always, she saw now, she had hoped that she and Godfrey would come to understand each other. No, with the terrible candor of the ultimate remorse, she saw now that she had hoped that Godfrey would understand her, that he would come to see eye to eye with her. She had not dreamed of changing her view, her certainty of what she thought right. She had only hoped to persuade him to see!

And now her chance was gone—she lay still and rigid in her bed while the warm pain flowed through her body like liquid fire. She tried to pray, she tried to ask the mother of all struggling women to let Godfrey know that she was sorry she had made nothing better of her part in their marriage—but the thought was too bitter even for prayer. She would forget herself, she would leave her failure where it was, she would ask Mary only to have a care for Godfrey, so confident in his own world of arms, surely so bewildered—with sudden tenderness, she wept only for the man who was dead in his prime.

Once Matilda must have fallen asleep, for she was going down a dark way alone, whether inside a building or out in the night she could not tell. At the time she did not think of where she was. It was only afterward that she wondered and could not be sure. But of one thing she was confident. She had come face to face with Godfrey. He looked at her as he would in life, not smiling, but showing that he was thoroughly aware of her presence in the look of his eyes. She had cried out, "It is you, Godfrey. Then I am dead." She had awakened then, and she had cried.

A little later she arose and took up the candle burning at her bedside. The house was quite still, and she could see nobody in her room. Noiselessly, she slipped from her bed and carefully dropped the curtains. She had no clear notion of what she was going to do. Only she knew she was stifling, and she could not bear to disturb anybody.

On a sudden thought she took the candle again and held it up so that she could see the whole chamber. On the floor at the foot of her bed the girl Maria was stretched out on a skin, fast asleep. Moving noiselessly, Matilda set the candle back on the table, and quietly opened the door.

In the passage without, the night wind was blowing cold, bringing with it the sound of the river. For a minute Matilda stood there listening to that curious effect of many voices merging into one and then disintegrating again into a multiplicity, both so quickly that the ear was at once teased and held by the mystery of identity.

Without realizing yet what she was doing, Matilda moved softly down the passage until she came to the end. Here there was a low door opening on a narrow wooden balcony above the water; its high railing she could just rest her elbows on, and by leaning out as far as possible she could see not only the flat gray pile of the houses on the opposite bank, but the restless surface of the stream itself. There was a moon tonight, and the broken path of its light flecked the waters to her feet. A little farther down, another ribbon of light, more jagged, more tenuous, ran out into the river from a lantern hung to the corner of the house, she fancied, and left burning there in forgetfulness from the evening before.

The Arno was running high and fast tonight with a low roar that wavered unsteadily in the wind. She tried to watch one line of foam running through the shadows of the water like a steel needle through a dark cloth. But always she had lost it before the darkness broke again in the second band of light. Then she watched the little waves of white tumbling over each other with such haste to dash into the darkness. Out of the darkness into the light and into the darkness again. Such a fragile thing of air and water, this foam that flashed its brilliant moment in the light and was dark even as it fell to rest.

So, oblivious of the cold and the time, she hung there, and knowing how futile it was to try to seize with the eye the mystery of that passing, she yet found it impossible to tear herself away.

Presently the spell was broken by the voice of her mother, "The dead are more than the living now. There is no reason, Matilda, why we should either of us fear to die."

Matilda turned and looked at her mother's face, so white and still in the moonlight, and slowly she shook her head.

But at that gesture the look on her mother's face sharpened. "It isn't your time yet. Life is very brief after all, and always there is so much that one wishes were different."

The next morning Matilda sat down and, taking quill in hand, she began the first letter she had written to the Pope since her return from Rome. Her hand shook as she wrote, "Matilda, Countess of Tuscany to His Holiness, Gregory, Bishop of Rome," but she took a fresh grip on her pen, and she wrote: "I have just learned that Godfrey my lord is dead, and I beseech Your Holiness of your charity to pray for the rest of his soul." She watched the period expand in the drop of water that had fallen on the sheet of parchment. Then she reached for her penknife.

When she had cleaned what she had written, she took up her quill again and considered what she should say next. But all she could think of was the water of the night before rushing with such passionate haste to the sea that would engulf it, with only the night wind to bear away the cry of its passing. So she folded her letter and sealed it.

✳ BOOK IV ✳

CANOSSA

CHAPTER I

AFTER the death of Godfrey, it seemed to Matilda that her mother took hold of life again. She began to see the bailiffs and the intendants and the various messengers from friends and vassals that came so often in the spring. She began even to send messengers and write letters again. Especially when news came from Germany, Beatrice would spend hours questioning the messengers as to the sympathies and resources of the various princes and bishops. And still more hours she would spend in her chamber with her daughter, telling her what she remembered from her own girlhood of the great German families and their traditions and ambitions. Some of her earliest years Beatrice had spent in Saxony, and over and over again she would tell the German envoys that Henry was foolish to think that the Saxons would ever consent to give up their ancient liberties. The great nobles and the bishops might walk barefoot and naked of arms as they had done last fall at Spires, but as soon as Henry had turned his back, the Saxon lands would be in flames again.

But to her daughter, Beatrice was equally emphatic that the intelligence of Henry was not to be underestimated.

"He is not a good man," said Beatrice one day, when Matilda had exclaimed at the folly of a man whose willfulness and profligacy had given such deep scandal to the whole Christian world, "but he is not just the villain of a preacher's example. He has courage to the point of recklessness, he has a very great deal of determination. I know of no man living, but the Pope, who has so much. And he is intelligent in his power of fitting means to ends. He understands the weaknesses of men and how to use them, but he does not understand the devotions or the dreams of men. That is why he thinks the Pope is an ambitious priest who wishes to put his heel on a king's neck."

Matilda shook her head miserably. She had picked up a strip of linen which Ermengarde had been embroidering in colored wools, deep rich shades of woad and vermilion and madder. For a moment she let the bright colors run through her fingers. Then she looked at the pattern with needle poised for attack. It was a scene of two knights with owl-like helmets and huge kite-shaped shields, fighting from horseback. She put it from her in disgust.

"Mother, why must men always be fighting? And why in everything they take up, must they set about it in the fighting way?"

Her mother looked at her sharply, and then she considered. She was herself putting the last stitches into a magnificent altar frontal of purple silk, and a maid kneeling before her was holding up the end of the heavy web so that her mistress' hands might not tire of its weight. "It is the way of this world, Matilda, and there is no use asking why."

Matilda laid the rejected tapestry back on the chest from which she had taken it. "But, Mother," she cried, trying to keep the fretfulness from her voice, and, she knew, failing, "think what might be done to make this world a clean and peaceful place if only Henry would behave like a Christian."

"This is this world and not the next," said Beatrice doggedly. "Sometimes, too, I think that if Adalbert of Bremen and Anno of Cologne had been less interested in watching each other and trying each to forestall the other, Henry might have started out with a higher regard for clerical motives."

"But that is why the Pope is anxious that the princes should not appoint the bishops, for they are the sort of men that they will choose every time." Matilda knew there was no reason why she should rush so passionately to the defense of the Pope from her mother of all people.

For the first time in some days Beatrice smiled. "And yet," she added judiciously, as if looking at the matter from all angles, "I don't know who would have done the work those two men did. In dark and chaotic days they kept order, and they maintained the rights of the Church and of law and the helpless in a world where might threatened to be the only power. You don't put a monk in charge of a castle that is being besieged, Matilda."

"Can you build the Kingdom of God by violence?" Never before had Matilda spoken so frankly to her mother of the thoughts that lay heavy on her heart.

But Beatrice shook her head firmly. "You must not judge one time by another. Perhaps you will be able to do the work of God by the means of God in a more quiet time, or more likely, your son—"

Matilda did not look at her mother, but she heard her catch her breath as soon as she had said the words.

To break the silence Matilda went on, "It is likely to be an unquiet life all our days. One thinks with envy of the Romans who lived in a world that was fixed and certain, where the powers did not clash—"

A child, bare and brown, in a canvas shirt stood in the doorway of the chamber, looking at them solemnly, while he turned a lump of charcoal in his hands.

"Forgive me, my lady, for letting him bother you," cried a woman appearing in the doorway, and kneeling down, half to apologize and half to take the child up in her brown serge apron.

Matilda called the child to her, and bade Maria bring her a little ivory box from the bridal chest in her chamber. While they waited, the woman hovered about, curtseying every time Matilda spoke to her or her child, but the little boy gazed at his mother's mistress with complete self-possession. When Maria returned, Matilda took from the ivory box a chain and cross of gold which had belonged to her child, and she placed it around the little fellow's neck. The woman sank to her knees in awe.

When they had gone, Beatrice rose decisively. "Come with me, Matilda, and see that Paschal candlestick I ordered. The rascal of a sculptor has sent word that he has it ready at last in time for use next year."

"You are not going all the way to his shop? It is too much for you." But however much Matilda protested, Beatrice insisted, until finally her daughter had to yield. Now Matilda felt a little ashamed. "Here I have been moping around, and she wants to take my mind off my griefs," she said to herself, "even if she overtaxes her strength."

But once they were actually on the way, Matilda had to admit that her mother had recovered her strength and her vivacity to an amazing extent, for she insisted on going into the shed where the candlestick still stood in the sea sand that covered the ground. The sculptor, an olive-skinned Greek whom Matilda remembered to have seen one morning at the palace of the Bishop of Pisa, receiving the Bishop's directions for the making of a reliquary with eyes dancing with enthusiasm, ran the edge of his canvas apron up the shaft of the candlestick and stood back for his work to be admired.

It was a beautiful thing, a tall, slender, twisted shaft of a warm peach-colored marble, inlaid with ribbons of mosaic gleaming like jewels.

"It is the top," said the sculptor, shyly stretching his hand up to the capital-like cup for the great Easter candle.

Matilda looked at it closely. Here the warm marble had been carved into clusters of laurel leaves, with an ox shouldering his way boldly out of the leaves.

"It is like the capitals of the ancient pillars in Rome," he explained proudly.

Matilda expressed her admiration. It was rough work and stiff, but it had an energy and sincerity about it that drew her heart to the young sculptor.

"Do you see it so in your mind's eye before you begin to cut it?" she asked partly out of curiosity, partly out of homage to the artist.

The dark eyes flashed, and then as quickly they grew soft and limpid.

"Ah, Madonna, not so. It is lovelier in the mind's eye. This work is—" he groped for words; and he took up a bronze chisel from a rough pine chest at his side, "what this can chip out of the stone, breaking down its hard resistance. But what I see in my mind's eye is the stone bursting into flower, as if just for a moment the wind had left blowing the leaves, and the creatures had held their breath. That is what I see in the mind's eye, my lady, but this—" He held out his hands desolately, all the pride in his work gone out of him.

Beatrice smiled grimly. "That is dreams, not stone, young man," she said, yet not unsympathetically.

But something deeper than the pride in his own work had been struck into life in the young artist, and there came a spark into his eye as he answered, "No, Madonna, men have done the dreams in stone. Come and see."

He led them across the shed and out into a walled yard, one end of which had been roughly thatched. In the back of this was what at first looked like a manger filled with rather damp-looking and sodden straw. With his bare hands the sculptor swept it off, and exposed to view a marble top, white with delicate purple and gold veinings in it. Matilda knelt down to look beneath it. What she saw made her cry out.

For it was an antique sarcophagus with a frieze of marble nymphs dancing through garlands of flowers. Her first cry was of wonder and delight in the fluid grace of movement and the exquisite proportions of those marble figures. For here the hard stone seemed to have flowered not only in grace of shape but in music and in light. There was a certain ecstasy in its beauty, a quality of abandon in its perfection and of majesty in its exhilaration that moved her heart to an almost unbearable delight.

A spasm of pity shot through Matilda's pleasure when she thought of the capital she had just seen and of the anguish of the artist who, feeling this in his heart, could only painfully hack out those stiff and jagged masses of stone which they had just seen. She looked up at the young sculptor, and at sight of the tears in his eyes, she felt the tears well into her own.

"What is your name, my friend?" she asked.

"I am Hilary the Greek."

"Hilary the Greek," she said gently, "we are all dreamers trying to carve out of stone with blunt tools and awkward hands in this late and desolate age of the world's misery."

He looked at her, only half-comprehending what she said, she suspected, but seeming to divine the fullness of sympathy that prompted the obscure words.

"Remember they were pagans, and they had not the comfort of Christ," Beatrice reminded him suddenly.

Again his eyes glowed. "Ah, but, my lady, I would have my marbles sing and dance in praise of the true God, for all these beauties are his."

"Hilary the Greek," said Matilda, rising and dusting the sand from her knees, "I'm afraid I shall not have much chance to praise God with singing and dancing, but I shall not forget you. It is a fiercer stone at Canossa, but if ever I have peace, I shall have you give thanks to God for me in stone."

Beatrice laid her hand on her daughter's arm, "Matilda, when I am dead, I should like to have you lay me in that sarcophagus and leave me to sleep here in Pisa."

"But, Mother," and then Matilda paused, overwhelmed by hearing spoken in the clear sunlight the theme of so many midnight watchings.

Beatrice seemed completely oblivious of her daughter's pain. "When I was young, Matilda, I dreamed of building again the beauty of the ancient world. Your little stoneworker is right. Christ is to be praised with all the voices of His creation. What man has done can be done again. But not in every age or every place. It has been a hard and violent world, and most of the time there was no question of joy or praise. It was fighting just to keep the law of Christ alive in the world. I remember a time of famine when I was a child. My father was away fighting in Italy for the King, and my mother was alone in her castle with us children, and there was a drought that burned every blade and stalk from the baked earth. Men went frantic, and barbarous folk from over the river began to break into our lands, and our serfs were so faint that they let themselves be slain like cattle. And still no word came from my father. And we children whimpered around my mother's knee."

They had reached home now, and Beatrice drew her breath sharply and sat down on the stone balustrade of the porch to rest. Matilda sent Ermengarde into the house for wine that she might not vex her mistress with her alarm. In spite of the ancient arcades over the streets, the spring sun was hot, and the way to the cathedral workshops longer than they had counted.

"I shall never forget," continued Beatrice, drawing her breath more slowly at last, "how my mother gathered up her jewels and sold them to merchants for grain. And when that was gone, she sold her clothes, the silks and furs, and her missal that had been her mother's before her and had come from an ancestor who had been one of Charles' bishops. Then she sold her father's sword that had a splinter of the True Cross in the hilt of it. And then when there was nothing in the great hall to sell but the chests and stools and the weapons she dared not give up, for evil men were stirring all through the land, she took the vessels from the altar, and, crying over them, for they were the greatest treasure of her lord's family and far-come from Rome and Ravenna and Aix, she gave them to the merchants, too."

Matilda pressed the cup of wine which Ermengarde had brought, to her mother's mouth.

"I told her—" began Ermengarde, indignantly, but Matilda raised her finger to her lips.

"Ours was the richest castle in all the land of Lorraine," went on Beatrice, wiping her lip, "but when my father came home, it was bare as any peasant's hovel. There are other kinds of famine, but the principle is the same."

In the middle of the night Matilda awakened with a nameless feeling of anxiety. She had been dreaming that her mother and the elder Godfrey had come and stood by her bed. She had tried to waken the younger Godfrey lying by her side, but she could not. Now that she was awake, she found herself trembling. For some minutes she lay thus. She tried to tell herself that Ermengarde was sleeping in her mother's bed, that nothing could possibly be amiss. But she could not free herself of that sudden anxiety.

There was a taper burning by the head of the bed in her mother's room, and the curtain on that side was scarfed up to the canopy, but she could not see the sleeper's face in the shadows. She came nearer. She could hear the heavy breathing of the woman on the farther side of the bed, but close to her there was silence.

She was wondering whether or not if her mother were simply asleep, she would wake her if she bent over the pillow, when she heard her mother's voice. She was quite awake in the shadow, and now that Matilda came nearer, her eyes were bright. "It is foolish of you not to be sleeping, Matilda, when you can."

Matilda felt the warm blood in her face. "I had a bad dream, and I was anxious about you." She tried to laugh as she spoke.

Her mother smiled, "One has lived in vain, Matilda, if when she reaches my age, she does not know how to die."

"You must not think of dying yet. What should I do without you?" It sounded flat and silly as she said it and in some way insincere though it came straight from her heart.

But her mother's voice was quite placid as she answered, "You will simply do what you have to do."

"What I have to do," Matilda echoed desolately.

"Only don't fret about it. Every generation has its work to do. It may not be what you want it to be, and still less is it likely to prove what you think it is. But there it is to be done. It isn't poetry or bridges or gentle manners for you. It is justice and order. It is the Church—not those beautiful basilicas in Rome or the poems of Prudentius or the speculations of Augustine—it is something much simpler and much harder, to see that Christians behave like Christians. It is what the Pope is trying to do. I am glad that you are here to hold up his hands when I cannot."

Again Matilda was worried lest her mother overtax herself. So she bent down and kissed her and went back to bed to sleep. She was still sleeping when Ermengarde came into her room the next morning, crying that she had awakened to find her mistress dead at her side.

CHAPTER II

THE funeral Mass for Beatrice, Countess of Tuscany, was sung in the Cathedral of Pisa, and her old friend and adviser, Anselm, the Bishop of Lucca, preached the funeral sermon. He took for his text, "Who can find a virtuous woman? For her price is far above rubies," and he preached with a certain limpid grace that held the crowd that had assembled to do honor to the Countess Beatrice spellbound with its felicity. Matilda remembered what Alberic had once said, that if you wished to know what man was like in his unfallen state, look at the face of Anselm of Lucca. Never had that sentence spoken half in jest and half in admiration been more justified than now. For the Cathedral of Pisa, in its present half-finished state, lacked that spacious clarity of the great Roman basilicas. Here in its ruder masses and its pendulous shadows, one was more conscious of the mystery of life than of the radiance of faith, and this solemnity of aspect was now only heightened by the black cloths with which the nave had been hung, and the high-piled bier on which the black-shrouded body of the dead woman had been laid, and the whiteness of the taper lights in the morning air. As Anselm stood in the marble pulpit to preach, the sunlight fell through the opaque bluish glass of the window over his head and enhanced with its faint luminousness the purity of his finely-carved features. There was nothing severe in that purity and nothing cold. There was rather in it something guileless and open, as if the shadow of good and evil, for all his years, had not yet fallen across it.

He spoke in a beautiful voice, clear and warm and moving without any trace of striving for effect. There was something effortless and quite selfless in his speaking as if he believed that he had but to fix his eye on his theme to do justice to it. For that, Matilda, still smarting with the rawness of grief, was grateful. He spoke with enthusiasm, too, of the great gifts of the dead woman, of her steadfastness of loyalty, of her balance of judgment, of her courage and resourcefulness, of her charity to the poor and her devotion to the Church. What he said was quite enough to make a less affectionate heart swell with pride. And yet Matilda, thinking of her mother's voice that last night, found herself less than satisfied, for it seemed to her that the final secret of her mother's power was untouched.

For the woman whom Anselm of Lucca had described was the valiant woman of the Book of Wisdom who finding herself in possession of unusual powers and resources had used them as a woman should in the service of those whom God had put in her care. And she had been charitable to the poor, and she had been devoted in her ministry to the Church of God. Once only did it seem to Matilda that the preacher came at all near to the things that had defined the individuality of Beatrice, and that was when almost without thinking, it seemed, he added that brought by the Providence of God to high place, she had used that place not for her own honor or her own aggrandizement or her own ease but for the high purposes to which she had set her hand. At that, Matilda looked sharply at the preacher, but he seemed to misunderstand her speculation as to how much he had penetrated his subject. For looking a little discomfited, he stumbled for a moment and used the wrong word and began again. But Matilda had turned away, and now she was watching the light on the pavement at her feet. Moving ever so slightly as the breeze stirred the candle flames, it flickered softly on the inlaid marbles that made up the pavement in the Roman fashion.

When the last blessing had been given and the body laid within the antique sarcophagus where it had been placed close to the high altar, Matilda for the first time felt a certain misgiving about her mother's choice. Seen in the Greek's shop, the dancing figures had seemed the fulfillment of the dreams that had been thwarted and stifled in the rough stone of the Paschal candlestick, and Matilda had entered with full sympathy into the whim of the moment, as astonishing as it was in one given so little to impulse as her mother. But here in the solemnity of the heavy-pillared cathedral, close to the almost austere loveliness of the marble ciborium over the high altar, the pagan marbles for all their perfection left the heart hungry. Far from touching the somberness of their environment with their own radiance, they seemed rather an unassimilable intrusion, an irrelevance. They seemed but to skim over the surface of her mother's personality without any suggestion of its strength or depth; in their indifference they seemed almost mocking.

Back in her mother's house Matilda sat down at the head of the table on the dais, took the first sip from the great cup of wine that was to be offered to all the principal guests, and watched the servants carry in the meats down the double line of tables that stretched the length of the hall. Then with a murmur of apology to the Bishop of Lucca and the Bishop of Pisa who sat on either side of her, and a bow to the lords who sat beyond, Matilda rose and left the hall. But meticulously she lingered for a moment in the pantry to make sure that the steward had all the wine at his command that he deemed necessary for the credit of the family. She even looked into the kitchen, almost invisible from the cloud of smoke and steam in the midst of which the half-naked cooks still knelt before their fires, basting a crackling pig or a fowl browning slowly for the replenishing of the great pewter and silver platters. Nor did she forget to unlock the spice chest and give the steward a little bowl of brown sugar for the pastries and confections at the end of the feast.

Then oblivious of his solicitous inquiries as to whether he might not send some meat to her chamber, Matilda passed into the courtyard of the house and on into a little office where her mother often interviewed the merchants and agents who came to see her on business. She was startled to find herself not alone as she had hoped to be, but looking into the astonished face of the priest Donizo. Slowly he arose from the table at which he had been busied, and running his inky fingers through his hair, he bowed.

Though he was little older than she was, he had yet been her tutor, and now Matilda remembered with a sharp pang how often her mother would come and sit with a piece of embroidery in her fingers or the frame of a tapestry before her and work while Donizo taught her daughter to read the long scroll of Virgil's great story or the haunting beat of melody in a hymn of Prudentius'.

Sunlit days on the battlements of Canossa or winter days by the fire in the great hall with the men of the household dozing along the benches—they seemed alike inexpressibly dear now that they were forever past.

It was on her lips to ask him why he was not in the hall with the rest of the family, but, looking at his white and drawn face, she knew the answer.

He seemed to guess her inquiry, however, for he pointed to the litter of papers on the table before him. "I thought you might want to look these over before you talked with the messengers."

Here was another task to detain her in the house that had begun to stifle her. She paused indecisively. They were beginning to sing in the hall. She wanted to put her hands to her ears, to shut out that sound, but she only looked at Donizo. He was a frail little man with sandy hair that had a droll way of standing up in a lock at the poll of his head, and two of his front teeth just touched his lower lip even when he shut his mouth, but at this moment, it seemed to her that he represented all the understanding and sympathy for her grief that there was in the world. Nervous under her glance, he began to shuffle the papers.

"Nothing special there?" she asked. He would know that she could not bear to read now all the messages of condolence that had poured in from city and countryside.

"Nothing that you need worry about now," he said. "There are also letters from Germany and from Rome on business, but the messengers can wait for a day or two."

For a moment she thought of asking Donizo to come with her, but then she realized that she could not ride along without paying attention to him. So without any more words, she went on to her own chamber, and there she took off the gown and the veil she had worn to church. She remembered there was a plain blue stuff gown and veil such as the wives of citizens wore daily in the city, lying in one of the chests. She had used them before when she rode out alone in the late afternoon for a little air and rest from the crowded house on the river. Now she took them and hurried into them, for the vague restlessness, the inability to face the funeral feast, which had driven her out of the hall had become almost a panic.

She made no protest when two of the grooms drinking a pitcher of funeral wine in the stables insisted on riding after her, but she forbade them to tell any of the rest of the household where she had gone.

At first when she had left behind the city gates, she rode blindly, as fast as her horse would carry her. It was a warm April day with something of fall in the mellowness of the air. So the cool of the breeze on her damp forehead was welcome, and the exhilaration of riding made her forget the clutch of pain in her breast.

But presently she noticed that the gorse and broom of the open country had yielded to bare grass, great long wind-blown swaths of coarse grass of an April greenness. Here and there a stunted tree sloping cityward with a faint net of reddish green about its gaunt limbs, or a wash of sand gleaming where the surface of the earth had worn away, told the same tale. In a moment the wind was coming in with the salt, dank smell of the water's edge when the tide is going out.

Matilda looked ahead. The road on which she had been riding had been quite overgrown in the spring rains. Beyond she could see little more than what looked like the broad wale of the wind through a field of tall wheat. Presently even that went up into the sky on a sudden heaving of the earth against the luminous gray-blue of the air. From the top, she knew, one would come out on the sight of the sea lying very blue and flat. She would just look at the sea; then she would turn back and face whatever must be faced. The softness of the sky like the softness of the air seemed to give promise of a moment's rest.

She was quite right. From the top of the little knoll, probably for all its green fuzz, a belated sand dune, she found herself looking out over a stretch of sea, smooth as a threshing floor, blue but a duller blue as if a little green had been mingled with the clear blue of the sky. She was about to ride down to the water's edge when she noticed that the beach was not empty, as she had at first thought. A little wharf of scantling looking fresh and golden in the bright sunlight had been run out from the shore into the sea. On it a number of huddled brown figures were to be seen, squat and dull in the brilliant light of the afternoon. Matilda looked back. The two grooms were still lingering some distance away.

Not since she was a child had she stopped to watch men fishing. Now she left her horse to crop the thin grass of the sand's edge, while she walked to the end of the impromptu pier. The somnolence of noon still lay on the fishermen, for they paid no attention to her. They seemed rather carved out of the wood of the piles supporting the bridge, except when now and then a man would come suddenly to life, execute a great gleaming arc with his rod and line, and land a fish, still quivering and plunging with life, on the wet boards of the pier.

It was not the men, however, but the fish that caught and held her attention. They were all of the same kind, silver in the water and the sunlight with flecks of black all over their bodies and bright red jaws where the hook had torn the wet flesh. But the most terrible thing about them was the death dance they one and all executed before they flattened dankly in the fading heap of their fellows. It was a frantic thing to the eye that knew that its impulse was the failure of breath, but it had its own sprightly rhythm, its patterns of glittering in the sunshine and thumping the boards, its crescendo and its diminuendo, all with a fullness of grace possible only to the motion that engages the whole organism of a creature. Matilda watched, fascinated and horrified, until she found herself shivering in the warm sunlight.

She mounted her horse again and turned away from the pier. At the top of the hillock from which she had first caught sight of the sea, she saw a horseman standing. For a moment her heart leaped, and then she recognized from the free carriage of the head as the stranger surveyed the scene before him, Anselm of Lucca. It was like him to follow her when she had not returned.

Now she did not know whether to be angry or to be grateful for the solicitude. For a moment she was acutely aware of the fact that she had said nothing
to him of the morning's sermon. Another man might be hurt, but she knew that
Anselm would not think of it again if she did not find the words.

As she joined him, she tried to think of what she should say, but a look at
that smiling face convinced her that there was no need. It was not that he would
understand without being told. Rather, he would not even in a moment's curiosity vex her grief. So they rode back to the nearly invisible path in silence. Here
away from the sparkle of the sea, that veil of an almost autumnal softness of air
seemed again to slip over the land. It seemed ungracious to say nothing, but her
heart was suddenly empty of meaning. She remembered irrelevantly that the
masons would have the Roman sarcophagus completely sealed with mortar now.

"That was an exceptionally fine stone coffin you found," Anselm began quietly as they rode side by side through the low swish of the grass.

"My mother liked it, and I did, too. It was only the day before that we saw it."

Presently, she added, more to keep hold of her thoughts than for any other
reason, "I was not so sure today that it quite fitted into the cathedral. Out here
those nymphs would be very charming, but there—" She said no more but looked
across to where the skyline broke with the first hint of the towers of Pisa. Here
away from the sea, the sky was softer, and she rested her dazzled eyes on its blue.

She felt Anselm's quick look on her face, and then he too turned eastward.

"It makes me think of that field of the dead outside of Arles and the story
they tell of it. You must have heard it from your stepfather?" He paused.

"No," she said idly. The sound of his voice rising softly above the passing of
the breeze was not unpleasant, and she waited.

"It is an ancient place, and in the time of which the story tells, it was the
favorite cemetery of the Romans in all that land. It must have been a lovely place,
for they laid their dead in altar tombs like this one, richly carved of many colored
marbles and semi-precious stones. There they stretched in long aisles between
stately cypress trees, that rose tall and slender in long lines down the field. You
can imagine that when Christianity began to penetrate into the ancient families
of that region, there was much grief, for there were many who said that Christians could not be buried with heathen even of their own blood. So bitter did
the controversy wax that they finally carried it to the bishop, and sorely troubled
he was, for he was a compassionate man who hated to part the dead. And yet it

seemed to him that the logic was on the side of those who said that Christian tombs could not be hallowed in a pagan cemetery. He prayed, but still he could see no way out. Then that night when he was sleeping, he dreamed that he stood in the middle of the great cemetery, and it was night. But the moon was shining down the long central aisle of cypresses as down some cathedral nave, and the tops of the tombs were white among the shadows of the trees. It seemed to him that presently he came into the center of that place, and there he saw a man in a white robe, kneeling in front of a tomb and praying. And though he could not see his face, from the light about his head and his robes, he knew it was Christ himself. Presently, Christ arose, and then the bishop saw that it was really an altar at which He had been praying. And Christ stretched out His arms, and He blessed the field of the dead."

"It is a beautiful story," said Matilda.

"And a true," added the Bishop, "in the sense that matters."

"I shall not forget," she said simply, as they rode side by side through the west gate of the city.

CHAPTER III

IT was one of those autumn days that in a certain freshness and brightness of air recall the promise of spring. It was cool, but with the coolness of wine that had stood in running water. One felt the warmth of the fire within in the very freshness of its chill. Even in the full ears of the wheat there was a sparkle to the gold vastly different from the sultry saffron tone one looked for at such a season, and above the shoulder of the hill up which the wheat field ran, the sky shone cloudless, of that deep purple blue to be found in gentians and in autumn lakes.

The wheat was being trampled in great swaths by the horsemen who kept passing back and forth outside the guard lines which the Bishop of Tribur had established around his hunting lodge, just above the bank of the river. And the cool air with its sudden breezes from the warm balsam and fir forests on the slopes still higher, brought the continual buzz and hum of a large company. Even from the other side of the river, shouts and cries floated over, and the clash of armor and the stamping of horses. As she listened in a lull of the conversation, Matilda reflected grimly that there was no need to worry as to which party was the larger, that of the Pope and princes on the other bank, or that of the King at Oppenheim half a dozen miles away.

Henry pacing restlessly the wide-timbered porch of the hunting lodge, must have drawn the same conclusion, for suddenly he dropped the pose of contemptuous indifference with which he had hitherto watched the conference and broke into a passionate protest.

"My God, man," he cried, seizing the Abbot of Cluny by the sleeve, "you can't depose a King the way you discharge a thieving village bailiff."

The bitterness of the implied accusation nettled the usually placid Hugh of Cluny. "My lord, you need hardly tell us that."

"Why do you suppose," asked Alfanus, rousing himself from his usual posture of somnolent repose, "the Abbot and the Patriarch of Aquileia and I strove so hard this morning to keep that mob over there from deposing you and electing a new King in your place?"

Henry shrugged his shoulders and sat down on the railing of the porch. "You know just as well as I do that it is no Christian devotion to the Pope"—Matilda winced at the scorn of the inflection and then saw that Henry hesitated as if he had let more slip than he had intended—"or passion for morality and piety that has brought those damned rascals together over there. Do you think that an excommunication would bother those bishops if they didn't think there were better pickings in the Pope's barnyard than in mine?"

Matilda stretched out her right hand to Henry, but before she could say anything, Altman of Passau, whose brown, wrinkled face had been growing redder and redder with impatience until now it was a russet like the late apples of an old tree outside the porch, broke in, "Speak for the sycophants who have bought their croziers from you, my lord, and—"

Henry seized the hilt of the sword that dangled from his belt, but the Archbishop of Salerno raised his hand with a dispatch astonishing for one so portly, and though he spoke with that slight drawl habitual to his speech, both the Bishop of Passau and the King turned to listen. "You know, there is no use bringing up these issues on which we all know what we think. There will be plenty of time later to discuss them. At present there isn't. All of us here are agreed on one point, and that is that we do not want to hand Germany over to anarchy if we can help it."

"Well, what else have you been doing in Rome?" It was the first time the young Bishop of Bremen, Liemar, had said anything, and the blunt vigor with which he now spoke brought back to Matilda's mind his predecessor. Alberic had once christened Adalbert Thor. Would this be Wotan who now wore the cross of Bremen on his broad, steel-mailed chest?

"That is what I have been saying from the first," broke in Ebbo of Naumburg. "I wish the Pope were here. I am sure he would see the havoc that his severity has wrought." In spite of the fact that the somewhat facile good humor of Ebbo of Naumburg had, from her first meeting with him in Germany, prejudiced her against him, Matilda found herself moved by a certain note of pathos in the low, flexible voice. For a moment Ebbo paused impressively, and though Matilda saw Altman of Passau bite his lips with indignation, nobody spoke.

"I think the biggest service that our Roman friends here could do the Church would be to return and tell His Holiness what has already happened. Those barbarous Saxons have broken every pledge they gave at Langensalz and that traitor, Otto of Nordheim, has sent out a summons to all the old rebel leaders. I think if the Pope knew that all Saxony will be aflame—"

But Altman of Passau could endure no more. "The Pope knows that Otto of Nordheim first went to the King at Saalfeld and told him that if he would do justice to certain grievances of the Saxons, he would keep the Saxon people quiet. The King re—"

"It is a lie," cried Henry, passionately. "Otto had picked up a parcel of peasant complaints about the soldiers whom I had put in the castles to hold those rebels to their promises. I suppose some of them had knocked off a few of their silly straw hats."

"My lord," exploded Altman of Passau, "peasants slain on their own lands, women outraged, men of birth—"

"Those are lies of Bucko of Halberstadt," said Liemar of Bremen scornfully.

"All Germany knows they are true," retorted Altman, shaking his fist.

Henry laughed a loud, scornful guffaw. "This is not Lent, my lord Bishop of Passau, to begin hurling all the sins of the decalogue in their most lurid colors at any poor fool who will listen."

Hugh of Cluny sprang to his feet and with uplifted hand started to the King's side, but Alfanus motioned him back to his place. There was silence. Matilda looked anxiously at the Archbishop, but he seemed to have shut his eyes again. Altman of Passau's face was now purple with indignation, and Hugh looked indecisively from his colleague to the King. Henry shrugged his shoulders and turned his head to the contemplation of the wheat.

Behind him, Matilda watched a little shiver of wind run through the gold and found herself wondering how much of the wheat would be standing if tomorrow's meeting proved as difficult as the meeting had been that morning. Now as they sat there, waiting, a party of men in shining helmets and shirts of mail rode noisily by. One of them, a tiny little fellow swaggering with a shield much too large for him called out gayly to one of the guards, "Whose stronghold is this?"

"The King's," came the answer from one of the King's guards who had joined the Bishop's.

"Which King's?" retorted the inquirer insolently. His companions roared with laughter. Matilda watched Henry's hand tighten about the hilt of his sword.

"They belong to those damned Billunger robbers," said Liemar of Bremen. He looked around, but no one spoke.

"They have stolen everything they could lay hands on from the bishopric of Bremen, and now I suppose they are looking for new worlds to steal," he went on, but still nothing was said.

The last of the company of northern horsemen was not yet out of sight, when a loud yell rose beyond the house. Matilda saw Alfanus look briefly at Hugh. Altman of Passau's face relaxed. For everyone knew that at the bridge below the hunting lodge a company of the hostile princes who had summoned all the forces of the Empire to the Diet of Tribur were waiting to welcome recruits.

The priests said nothing. It was Henry's nerve that gave way first.

"Matilda," he began sharply, and, rising, came and stood before her, "someone told me today that you had been into Lorraine this last month looking after your husband's property."

"Yes," said Matilda, wondering if she should remind Henry that she had sent him messengers to claim property that had belonged to her by marriage rights and not to the duchy that had escheated to the King. Surely the King must know that his agents had seized everything in sight without making any inquiry as to other claims.

"Of course," said Henry, thinking aloud, "I must have some good fighting men there, but some of those lands I would not mind letting a strong woman have if I could count on her."

Matilda smiled. "I have land enough, my lord. All I was concerned about was certain treasure of my husband's that had been his father's before him."

Henry watched her thoughtfully. "God, I wish I had your husband now. I would give him two duchies. He was the best soldier I had."

But Alfanus of Salerno had looked up at Henry with the same casualness with which he had shut his eyes a few minutes before. "The day is passing. To-morrow things will be out of our hands if we cannot present some plan."

"You can't depose a King," cried Henry, with a quick stride from Matilda to Alfanus.

"There is some difference of opinion about that," said the latter judicially. "The best opinion, ancient and modern, is that an unjust King has forfeited the loyalty which his subjects owe him."

"Just and unjust!" exploded Henry. "Who is to decide? Do you think these princes on the other side of the bank who are jealous of my power because they know that the more power the King has the less they can do what they want, do you think they can tell?"

"That is not fair," objected Altman of Passau angrily. "They are fighting for the ancient liberties of Germany against a tyranny that threatens to ride rough-shod over every right, human and divine, for the sake of one man's will."

"Rebel!" retorted Henry with contempt.

"Don't you think this is rather beside the question?" asked the Archbishop of Salerno. "There is one point on which there can be no doubt, and that is that Christians cannot associate with a man who is excommunicate. Any man who does have anything to do with an excommunicated person is himself liable to the same sentence. All Christendom agrees to that, my lord. There is no question of who is to judge there."

Henry's face grew scarlet. "But I was excommunicated unjustly, by—"

"Again," said the Archbishop with the same quiet insistence, "let me remind you that that is not the question now."

"But it is," Henry shouted in his indignation. "To excommunicate the King whose authority comes from God just as much as ever did the Pope's, even if—"

Alfanus raised his hand, and the King stopped. "That, again, is a much-discussed theme, the relation between the two swords, and it is not the point now at issue. The King is a Christian, subject to the law of God and of the Church like every other Christian, just as the Pope himself is. All Christendom except your flatterers will agree to that, my lord."

"I won't," said Henry.

For a moment the Archbishop waited. Matilda wondered if it were to let the clamor from the other side of the river come to Henry's ears, but the face of Alfanus was so impassive, so expressionless that any ulterior motive hardly seemed possible.

The same thought must have come to Henry, for he again faced the Archbishop with the challenge, "Do you think it is Christianity that animates those traitors over there? I tell you that they are seizing upon religion as an excuse to save their own individual power."

For the first time in the conference Alfanus smiled. "Then if it is only a pretext, why not snatch the pretext away from them? If you make your peace with the Pope, then those who are sincere will rally to your support and help you deal with those who are not."

Henry stared at the Archbishop.

"There is something to that." Liemar of Bremen shook his head.

"It is only a pretext," said Henry doggedly.

There was nothing sleepy in the look which Alfanus now gave Henry. "My lord, that is one of the penalties of faithlessness, that one ceases to trust any man. I know that some of those lords and bishops are using your present plight as a pretext, and I know that there are others who in simple faith and conscience cannot do otherwise. Only God knows what the relative proportions are, but only a man in whom all faith is dead would deny the difference between the two."

Again Henry seemed to consider. Finally, he laughed bitterly, "It would be a neat turning of the tables on the Pope if I did get rid of this excommunication. Proud as he is, I suspect there is nothing he wants less than to have me turn penitent."

Matilda had watched the face of Hugh of Cluny blench under the impact of the King's speech. Now he leaped to his feet.

"Before God, you make it hard for your friends, my lord," he cried with something like a sob in his throat.

The Archbishop of Salerno rose slowly. "My lord, why do you think we have tried to save you a chance to recover your crown? The Pope himself gave us as his final command that under no circumstances were we to allow a new king to be chosen at this meeting. His one desire is that you shall return to your Christian duty. He is waiting to give you absolution as soon as you ask for it."

For a moment Matilda wondered if she should add her witness. Even in the last letter she had received from Rome before going into Lorraine, the Pope had begged her to pray for the repentance of Henry. But as Henry wavered, she judged it better to wait.

A bitter look of self-contempt came over the face of Henry. "What can I do? Those who owe me faith have betrayed me. This last summer those two bastard sons of Gero surprised me, and if the Mulde had not risen that night and let me get off by boat, I should have been taken, and I suppose dead by now. Here these rebels gather the whole nobility of the Kingdom to insult me to my face. And my enemies—"

But Hugh had sprung to his feet and seized the King's arm. "Not enemy, ever, my lord. The Pope is your father, waiting to forgive, and we are here to help you to find your way back."

Henry looked at Liemar of Bremen and at Ebbo of Naumburg. The former gazed fixedly at the planks in the floor, without looking up. The latter raised his eyebrows and shrugged his shoulders.

"Then," said Henry, "I suppose it would be rude to keep this tender father waiting any longer."

"May I remind you, my lord," interposed Alfanus, "that to profane the sacrament of penance is something more than insolence to the priest whom one deceives?"

"Our desire to rid ourselves of this excommunication," said Henry haughtily, "is sincere enough for any penance."

Matilda saw Altman's face redden and Hugh's face shadow with anxiety, but Alfanus only said, "Then right after Mass tomorrow, my lord, I will bring you the terms of the agreement."

"Remember, I insist on my fatted calf," laughed the King as the Pope's emissaries took their leave. Again it was the Archbishop of Salerno who answered for all with a low bow.

CHAPTER IV

If the Pope felt any satisfaction in the reports of the meetings at Tribur, Matilda could not discover it from his demeanor. The submission from the King himself which Udo of Trier presented on his knees was received with grave attentiveness and the briefest and most formal of acknowledgments. Nor was there any sign of triumph in the quiet vigilance with which Gregory followed the businesslike and thoroughly objective account of Sigehard, the Patriarch of Aquileia. Gregory seemed completely absorbed in the effort to grasp fully and exactly what had happened. Indeed, it seemed to Matilda that of all the company he was the one most detached from any personal preoccupation, the most free from any distraction of emotion. Hugh of Cluny was obviously uneasy, for he never took his eyes from the Pope's face. Altman of Passau seemed on the point of interrupting several times but apparently thought better of it. Udo of Trier, obviously relieved at the completion of his part in the transactions of the day, yet followed Sigehard's narration carefully. Sigehard himself spoke with the somewhat strained care of a man who knows that any misrepresentation on his part may have disastrous consequences, and who is continually disquieted by the realization that he is not entirely sure of the full meaning of the facts that he is reporting. Only Alfanus of Salerno sat easily in his seat, his eyes half-closed as usual, and his long, plump hands resting lightly on the carved animal heads that stopped the arms of his chair.

Without any sign of emotion Gregory heard Sigehard tell how the princes of Germany decreed that unless Henry secured release from the sentence of excommunication within a year from the date of its publication, they would depose him and elect another in his place. Matilda wondered if later Sigehard would tell the Pope how Hugh and Alfanus had struggled with the enraged assembly to keep them from decreeing the immediate deposition of the King. The same question was apparently in the mind of Hugh, for though his pale face showed no sign, his thin hands clasped and unclasped within his long sleeves, the folds of his loose mantle shifting with the veiled movement. Altman of Passau's face lighted at the memory, but Sigehard kept on without any quickening or rise in his even, rather thin voice. For not the first time Matilda found herself wondering if some of what had seemed to her an almost pedantic dispassionateness in the Patriarch's manner were not rather a general lack of enthusiasm for the whole crisis. She thought she found some further evidence for this suspicion in the occasional spasm of indignation that passed over the face of Altman of Passau as some particularly dramatic passage in the happenings of those days was glossed over in Sigehard's matter-of-fact narration. Incongruously, she found herself remembering an old bailiff of her mother's who failed to make any response to her demand of supplies for a campaign on which she was then suddenly engaged. As soon as peace was made, her mother summoned him to Mantua for an accounting. To everybody's surprise, the old man explained his failure by saying that he had worked a good many years to organize the labors of that village so that they would yield what he considered adequate returns for his lord, and he could not bear now to have those plans disturbed by the disorganization that would follow the calling-away at that time of the men who would be needed to prepare and convoy the required supplies. Several times the cool, reasonable face of the old man explaining his action to Beatrice and her company, quite unperturbed by the titters and jeers of those standing by, came back to her mind as she listened to the monotonous voice of Sigehard.

But there came a moment when Matilda saw the Pope's eyes gleam with excitement. Sigehard had just repeated the invitation of the assembled nobles of Germany to the Pope to come to an assembly of all the notables of the land, to be held the next February at Augsburg. There they would take counsel together as to the problems of the German Kingdom, and they would ask the Pope to pass judgment on the justice of the claims of the opposing parties. At that point the Pope leaned forward with shining eyes fixed on the face of Sigehard. Nor was Matilda alone in her observation, for the Archbishop of Salerno opened his eyes almost wide as he looked up at his superior. But Sigehard went on calmly with the various undertakings of the princes to furnish an escort for the arrival of their invited judge and to refrain from any strife among themselves until they should have had a chance to plead their case before the throne of Peter.

"It is a complete rebuke to that outrageous Henry," exclaimed Altman of Passau when Sigehard had completed his recital and stolidly rested. "The princes of Germany have lost patience with his crimes and his equivocations and his broken promises."

"But," Hugh of Cluny interrupted eagerly, "the King has already sent Your Holiness his submission and his repudiation of the outrage of Worms. He is ready to do penance."

"Not for his sins but to have his kingdom. He knows his enemies will lose no time in deposing him if he gives them the chance," retorted Altman, the wrinkles in his brown face deepening with scorn. "They would have deposed him at Tribur if it had not been that the representatives of the Pope saved him."

Matilda saw Hugh of Cluny look anxiously at the Pope, and for a moment she was amused by the thought of how uneasy the rashness of the man of action must often make the contemplative. But the Pope only looked thoughtfully from one to the other. It was then that Alfanus of Salerno spoke for the first time since they had all sat down.

"I am sure I have seen more convincing penitents than the King, so far as his past acts in themselves are concerned. But there can be no question of the sincerity of his desire to hold on to his kingdom, a desire with which I am sure," and here for the first time the Archbishop of Salerno looked around the company with a glance curiously searching in contrast to the languor of his habitual movements, "we all of us have nothing but sympathy."

Altman of Passau snorted but apparently thought better of it, for he said nothing. Only the lines of his mouth tightened grimly.

The Pope nodded, half absentmindedly, as if his thoughts were busy elsewhere. For several minutes no one spoke, and the look of anxiety deepened on the face of Hugh and of indignation on the face of Altman. A look of stolid repose had settled over the countenance of Sigehard, and Alfanus of Salerno had resumed the contemplation of his own thoughts.

Suddenly, the Pope raised his head and with his eyes swept the attention of the company to his face. The look of absentmindedness had now left it, and it shone with enthusiasm. "This meeting at Augsburg is the answer to our prayers. God alone knows what can be accomplished when the princes of this world turn at last to His Church and setting their individual ambitions aside ask what justice and truth demand they should do. If one great kingdom alone should try to conduct all its affairs, public as well as private, in justice and peace, I think all Christendom would be moved to imitate it."

No one answered. The Archbishop of Salerno leaned over, and taking the small shovel before him stirred the graying charcoal in the copper brazier at his feet, but the feeble glow seemed to make no difference to the dank December air that filled the library. For the first time Matilda was aware of the acrid smell of old parchment and the slightly musty aroma of decaying leather. The same sense of gloom was deepened by the half light that even in the morning was all that came through the opaque greenish-yellow glass in the high windows, but it was also at the same time relieved by that sense of intimacy that comes to those who are imprisoned by the weather, as the dry rattle of the rain drops on the roof high overhead filled the silences.

Matilda had felt her heart leap at the words of the Pope, and even now it seemed to her that the radiance of his face lighted the grayness of the room and the day with a warmth against which the chill of December beat in vain. But she found little response in the faces of the men about her. True, the mobile face of Hugh of Cluny had lighted in sympathy, but now a minute later that radiance was fading in a wan dubiousness. Altman of Passau's heavy eyebrows were still raised in a look of astonishment which was already beginning to fade into a cynical smile. There was more of incredulity to the surprise on the face of Sigehard of Aquileia. Only Alfanus of Salerno seemed to keep his habitual inscrutability of mien, apparently absorbed in the contemplation of the rod of bronze in his hand.

Again it was Alfanus who broke the silence, "That is a dream dear to the heart of all of us, Your Holiness."

"A dream?" There was a sharpness of anguish in the voice of the Pope. The light on his face faded.

"You can't trust a word Henry says. Everybody in Germany now sees that," said Altman.

"But the princes of Germany?" There was a tension in the voice of the Pope as if he were hesitating about drawing the sword he would presently be forced to take.

Altman laughed bitterly. "The princes of Germany are like the King of Germany only that what is to the interest of the one is not to the interest of the other."

"But you remember," interposed Hugh, "that the princes promised the King that if he secured the Pope's pardon, they would accompany him to Italy to receive the imperial crown. Then they would all go to the south to rescue the lands of Peter from the Normans."

"Yes," said Altman, "but, my dear Abbot, there are more things in the heart of man than are dreamt of at Cluny. The worst freebooter on earth loves to gild his enterprises with some dust of piety. What could better please these Saxons than to have Henry safely engrossed in Italy instead of trying to extend his grip on their everyday affairs? What could better please the whole lot of them, Saxon, Bavarian, Lorrainer, or Swabian, than to have the run of the Norman lands with all that means for plunder?"

The Pope looked thoughtfully at Altman. "Robert Guiscard has been making overtures. He seems really anxious to be a loyal son of the Church."

"Robert Guiscard is no fool," observed the Archbishop of Salerno.

The light had quite faded from Gregory's face, leaving its weariness heavily shadowed.

The note of somber passion deepened in his voice. "The heart of man is a well of mystery, and who shall say with confidence what he will draw up when he lets down into it? Surely, the children of this world are cynical enough and faithless enough without our swelling their mistrust. That a robber prince whose hands are stained with his brother's blood should trust no man is reasonable enough, but we who are the servants of a Master who offered His life in the hope of the redemption of sinners, if we fail in trust, then is the world dark indeed."

Hugh's face flushed, and the feet of Sigehard stirred uneasily on the tessellated pavement.

"Your Holiness," said Altman of Passau, "I beseech you not to trust yourself to these men. They made noble speeches and they passed high-sounding decrees, but when the meeting actually comes to pass, they will each study how best to advance his own interests. And when Your Holiness opposes to the little human greeds of the moment the divine care of the Church for the peace of all men in the future as well as the present, then they will use every trick they have of violence and deceit. For it is not in their thought to sacrifice their interest to the good of the Church but to use the Church for the service of their purposes."

The Pope shook his head. "That is why, my lord Bishop, I cannot let pass any opportunity to rescue the Church from their clutches."

Again, silence fell upon the little company, and listening to the whispering of the rain on the roof, Matilda found herself wondering if after all they needed words. For it seemed to her that each man had spoken as one would expect him to, and the self-contained little speeches to which they had been listening this last hour had rattled against each other like dry pebbles in a pail without any visible attrition. She was wondering if men ever changed each other's minds by words when she heard the voice of the Archbishop of Salerno speaking again.

"We must not forget," he began in his way of talking things over with himself, "that for Peter it is not just one kingdom or one time but all the kingdoms of the world and all times. Such a battle is won and lost at many times and in many places. There is not only the question of the sincerity and faith of the German princes or of the German king. With the Pope in Germany running the risk of various accidents of detention or obstruction, there is Rome here to think of, the Normans, the princes of France. Then, too, there are the enemies on the frontiers of Christendom."

For the first time the Pope seemed to falter. And then suddenly Matilda saw it all clearly. These voices of caution to which they had all been listening for this last hour had stopped their ears to the memory of the great hope that had lighted the Pope's face when first he heard the invitation of the German princes. They were no longer young, these men. Nor was she in the first confident pride of youth, but the memory of that fire that had burned in her own heart not so long ago was yet warm. Why should all the rashness and boldness belong to the children of this world alone? All over the earth men risked every day their lives and their honors on hazards far less certain than this, for mere baubles.

"Your Holiness," she began, feeling all eyes turn to her with surprise, "I think no one can deny the cogency of all the arguments these reverend fathers have advanced. But we have our faith today because in the providence of God the Apostles and the saints of old took hazards greater even than these. Peter, in whose seat you sit, when he turned back from flight into safety to die on the cross, Leo when he went out to meet the Hun whom no man would trust, Gregory, whose name you have made live afresh, when he stayed at his post in the midst of famine and anarchy and kept burning those lights of faith and hope without which our Italy would have gone down into the darkness—all of these, I think, speak even louder than these voices of prudence."

The Archbishop of Salerno smiled. "I remember no beatitude, young lady, promising the earth to the rash."

"'He that shall lose his life for me,' my lord?" She tried to keep her voice level.

But the Pope smote the arm of his chair with resolution, "The courage of what the world calls a weak woman puts us to shame, my lord bishops. The Countess is right. This is a moment when not to risk everything is to betray our trust."

"My lord," began the Archbishop of Salerno, "at least you will do nothing till the German princes have sent to Rome the escort they promise."

But Matilda had risen, and now she knelt at the Pope's feet, "My lord, all my forces are at your disposal. I will summon my vassals, and I will open my treasure, and I will bid my people pay me the taxes they owe me, and I will see you safely on your way."

For a minute the Pope looked down upon her gravely. Then putting out a hand, he raised her from the floor. "In you your mother lives again."

"At least—" began Alfanus, but the Pope had risen, too, lifting his hand for silence.

"You have our answer and our commands, my lords of Passau and of Aquileia. Tell the German princes that we will be there at Augsburg at the time they have appointed, to judge between them and their King. And tell the King that he is to remain in retirement as he has promised until we come. Then he will have every opportunity to present his case to us and have his sentence lifted, if he will behave like a loyal son of the Church. And all these are to wait in peace as men should who have appealed to a judge and look to have their claims settled in justice."

As Matilda was about to leave, the Pope made a sign for her to wait. Then when all had left the room but the Abbot Hugh, Gregory sat down again and motioned to her to do likewise.

"You have given me back myself when I was almost persuaded by these timid counselors of mine," he began with a smile.

"I only urged Your Holiness to do what you wanted to do all along."

The smile rose from the lips to the eyes. "Is not that what men look to your sex for always?" Then the smile faded, and Matilda saw how a shadow of reserve came upon the tenderness of his voice, "You have heard what the lying voices of our enemies have said?"

Matilda caught her breath sharply. "Yes."

"Rumor is the most volatile of all the world's winds. You can silence those voices by going back to Canossa and leaving me to fend for myself." He looked at her speculatively.

She shook her head. "Your Holiness knows there is no dodging the world's malice. I propose to sell my life dearly."

For a moment the Pope said nothing but looked at her hard. "I am not sure that it may not, God forbid, prove dearer than you think. The offer you have made would tempt any man, but I do not want to deceive you as to its price, if our less optimistic friends should prove right. One should be rash only when he knows that he can pay the price of failure. You are young still and beautiful, and the world has many possibilities for you."

For a moment Matilda's heart rose. It was many a month now since she had thought of herself as young and beautiful, and these words spoken, as she knew, without flattery, ran through her head like the call of a trumpet.

"No, Your Holiness, there is no peace in crying for what one cannot have. And even if I could have it, I think now I know what I am. My son is dead, and with him any dream of a mighty house to rise above my grave. I have known great joy and great pain, my lord. So there is no reason why I should be afraid, or hoard myself. What God gave me, I wish to give back to Him to His use."

For a moment the Pope looked into her face, and Matilda saw that he could find no words for his feelings.

Smiling, she shook her head. "I am a sword put into your hand, Your Holiness. Draw it in your need. The splintered steel will make no complaint."

CHAPTER V

EVEN for January it was a bitterly cold day to spend on the roads of Lombardy, and more than once Matilda thought anxiously of the objections which the Pope's advisers had not ceased to urge against the journey. So far as the weather was concerned, their worst fears had been generously realized. Even where the roads through the mountains north of Rome were not blocked with snow, the wind had blown with the edge of a knife, so that sometimes, it seemed to Matilda, she rode with her eyes in a blur of blood or fire. Even now when they had safely crossed the ice-filmed Po, and were riding down a winding road through the valley, the wind howled in the leafless poplars and the frost-shattered cypresses and flapped and moaned through the brush on the roadside. Even in the bright purple-blue of the sky overhead there was something hard and staring rather than cheering, and the iron of the horses' hoofs rang harshly on the frozen ruts in the road.

But so far the Pope had borne the journey very well for a man of his years, who only a few months before had been seriously ill. Indeed, he seemed to take the hardships of the long, cold ride with far more indifference than men much younger. Most of his companions had drawn their heads into their riding hoods, like turtles into their shells, and kept their eyes set doggedly on the leaden strip of road ahead. Conversation had pretty much died down along the line of riders, and all were riding with that grim air of husbanding their resources for the mere effort of motion that is so discouraging to conversation. So though each man rode with a faint whiteness of mist about his mouth, no words came, only now and then a low whistle of weariness or a half-choked cough. But the Pope, though he had pulled his thick wool hood close about his face with the rest, yet seemed to have strength enough to look about him and to take some stock of the land through which they were passing.

With Arduino della Palude at her side, Matilda had ridden down the line of her company to see that all was well with the riders, and that the horses loaded with supplies of cordials and meat and extra arms for emergency on the journey were keeping up with the procession. She had been anxious all day, for she knew that the farther they advanced into the Lombard lands the greater was the danger of a surprise attack by some of the many turbulent bishops of the country who were impatient of the restraints of Rome and anxious to win the favor of the King. Several times she had seen a small group of riders on a hill above the road looking down at the long procession, but so far she had traveled all day quite unmolested. She reflected now with some pride as she looked down the line and caught the glint of the sun here on a helmet and there on a spear, that the baronage of her lands had answered her summons generously and promptly. Knight and bishop alike, they had ridden down from their high castles and their walled cities with their companies of men-at-arms and retainers about them, and now, even as they rode there, weary and stained with travel, they yet bore witness to the prosperity of her domains in the brightness of their arms and the warm wool and leather of their garments. She could think of none of the Lombard bishops or princes who alone would be strong enough to meddle with such a company, and she hoped that too many of them would not make common cause together. All day this had been in her thoughts, and now as the curiously hard and bleak winter brightness of the day began a little to soften in the distances beyond the narrow road, she felt at once a fresh anxiety as to what the twilight hours might bring, and that breathlessness of anticipation that comes when the burdened mind knows that its uncertainty is drawing to its period.

Her own face was rigid with the cold, and at times her breath came so sharply that it took all her pride to keep from huddling into her cloak like her neighbors. Yet she found herself a little irritated that the rill of laughter and chaffing that had run down the line earlier had now dried up. So having made as sure as she could of the discipline of her escort, she turned back and rode hard until she came abreast of the Pope.

"I suppose you will keep on to Mantua tonight even if the sun goes down before we get there?" he asked as she checked her horse at his side.

She nodded. "Then too," she hastened to explain, "there will probably be messengers waiting for us. Indeed, I am surprised that we have not met any on the road. For those I sent into Germany have had more than time enough to come back."

"To say nothing of those I had sent," he replied thoughtfully. "There may be something to that rumor the Bishop reported last night, of Henry having left Spires. Yet surely, the German bishops at least, if not the princes, could spare enough men for an escort."

"Penance is weary work"—the Archbishop of Salerno looked up suddenly from the apparent contemplation of his horse's mane—"and cautious men are probably waiting until it is quite clear that it will be necessary."

"It will be necessary," said the Pope firmly, though with a less certain look at his companion.

"After all," suggested the Abbot Desiderius, "there is less excuse for a bishop to behave as these creatures of Henry have than for a layman. They know the law, and if they flout it, with what grace shall they face their flocks?"

Alfanus of Salerno pulled off the glove of his left hand with his teeth, and rubbed the neck of his horse until the bare flesh turned blue.

"You know," he said, "you monks must not forget that it is not always so easy for a bishop to see his way. He has many things to consider. With all the souls dependent on him, and the many ways in which he must deal with the world— justice, war, finance, building, order, charity—it is not surprising that sometimes he misses in his judgment."

"I should have thought the way was fairly clear here," said Desiderius, lifting his head somewhat impatiently out of his loose cowl.

The Archbishop shook his head. "You must remember that most of the time a bishop cannot have just what he wants. He has to take what he can get. If he insists on more, he may lose all, and the punishment of such a failure for a man so entangled with the world as a bishop is swift. It is not surprising if sometimes he underestimates what human nature will bear rather than overestimates it, as you monks are sometimes accused of doing."

"If you are suggesting that the life of an abbot is a quiet one beside the life of a bishop—" began Desiderius.

Alfanus smiled, "To the most popular abbot in Christendom I fancy I might. Every time I think of that visit of yours with the Guiscards, I am reminded of that old legend of the damned monk whose manners were so obliging even in Hell that the Devil himself thrust him out for corrupting with his gentleness the savagery of eternal torment."

"Nonsense," said Desiderius. "It is simply that the popular imagination after investing the Guiscards with horns and tails proceeded to deck me out with a halo when I proved that they were human after all."

There was a laugh in the company round, a laugh in which Matilda found herself joining with a good deal of relief.

"From the letters that come to me," said Gregory when the laughter had subsided, "I am not so sure that abbots have such a quiet time as you suggest." Again there was a chuckle, which swelled into a roar, as the Pope's companions had time to remember how often the theme of abbatial letters to Rome was the encroachments of local bishops.

"That is not what I mean, Your Holiness," said Alfanus. "Rather it seems to me that the nature of an abbot's life and of his relations to society gives him a better chance to keep a delicate conscience than does a bishop's."

"God knows that is true," said the Pope wistfully.

"Oh," laughed Matilda, thinking to comfort him, "I thought it was only princes and women that knew not which way to turn in the choice of evils."

But the Pope's smile was only half-hearted, and again the company settled down to its steady plodding on in the cold. It would be less than two hours' riding to Mantua now, Matilda thought, looking about her and catching in the hooded cross of a wayside shrine on a little hill above the road a familiar landmark. Indeed, from the top of the hill, she remembered, one could see the towers of Mantua against the curtain of the hills on a clear day. The sun was sloping fast now, and the snow-dappled fields were rolling into purple shadows as the air softened before their tired eyes. Please God, they would soon be within sight of her own people on the walls of her own city.

Suddenly, without warning and as if in answer to her thoughts, there appeared on the crest of the road in front of them a single horseman poised against the sky as if looking down on them. Involuntarily, Matilda clutched the sword at her side and looked behind her for Arduino. But the little general was already putting spurs to his horse.

She looked back and for the first time she realized how the day was passing, for the figure of the horseman lay flat and black against the seemingly clear sky. Then the figure began to lose its distinctness, and she realized that he had started toward her.

The whole company seemed at once to raise their heads and to take a firmer clutch on their reins. And curiously enough, they all began to talk, while watching for the nearer approach of the horseman and from time to time scanning the lowering hilltop for sign of further companions.

"It is Virgil's land," said the Pope softly to Matilda, and for a moment she forgot her alarm.

"No," she smiled, "not like this. It is in the summer when the bees are in the thyme and clover, or in the autumn when the carts come in on groaning axles, and the girls with the grapes on their heads and the men with baskets of glistening olives, that I think of him."

"The unlabored earth, and the oarless sea, and the Child who was to bring the peace that would not pass," he mused, looking over the bleak scene before him, with the bare hills rolling away from the river valley on either side, and the blackened olives and the torn gray ropes of vine for the only accents to its grimness.

"It was easier for him than for us to dream such dreams," said Matilda, feeling her heart ache with the loveliness of the words even in the moment's anxiety. It was only a messenger who came thus alone. But the learned said that in Virgil's day men might travel the roads of Italy in peace without fear of neighbor or stranger.

"We have the promise of Christ that He will be with us all days," said Desiderius softly.

At that moment two of the men from the head of the line were making their way down the side of the road with the stranger. As he dismounted slowly and awkwardly as if he were half-frozen, Matilda saw that he was one of the men from her mother's house in Mantua.

"My lady," he began, struggling for a moment to recover his breath, "men have just come from over the mountains who say that the King has left Spires."

"Thank you," said Matilda, disappointed after her alarm. "We had heard that last night."

"But," said the man, recovering his breath with the jealousy of one who brings news, "there is more. They say he is gathering an army and that he is not waiting for the coming of the Pope but that he is coming down into Italy at once. And before I left, another man came with word from the Patarine chiefs in Milan that the usurping Bishop has gone out to meet the King, and that some of the clergy of the country about and the chief nobles of the city are making ready to receive him."

"Trust them to," said Desiderius.

The Pope considered. "That he has left Spires, I believe, but that he could get together much of an army now without any hindrance from his princes seems to me doubtful."

"I should have known that Henry would not keep his promise," said Matilda ruefully, remembering long hours of argument and of pleading in Rome.

But the Pope was not dismayed. "No, we will not turn back. We cannot break our promise to the German princes on a rumor. There may be word at Mantua as to that escort."

The messenger was very positive, however, that no word had come from the Bishop of Tribur or any of the German princes. There was much speculation as to just how much credence could be put in the rumors that had disturbed them, and in spite of the deepening of the cold with sunset, there was a noticeable acceleration in the progress of the whole line. By the time Matilda caught her first glimpse of the towers of Mantua standing like reeds in the gold and purple reflection of the sunset on the northwestern sky, the whole company was riding forward as if they expected attack at any moment.

"I will send my best man tomorrow morning to Altman of Passau," said Matilda as they rode through the half-open southern gate of the city, "and we will wait here until we hear from him." The Pope agreed.

But the morning brought fresh alarm in the shape of a messenger from Adelaide of Susa, who had ridden all night from his mistress' castle outside of Turin. Adelaide, as might be expected of the mother of the long-suffering Bertha, was in no mood to yield lightly to the caprices of her son-in-law. So her message that

Henry had sent to ask her help in crossing the Alps into Italy filled the whole company in the house at Mantua with consternation.

One only refused to be dismayed. "I have said I would be at Augsburg to meet the princes of Germany," said the Pope, "and the fact that the King will not keep his promise does not absolve me from mine."

"Impossibility absolves us all." The full lips of Alfanus of Salerno were suddenly grim.

"But Adelaide will not help Henry," said Matilda, wondering whether Bertha's patience would come to the aid of the husband who had abused her so shamefully.

The Pope considered. "Adelaide certainly has more reason to be satisfied with his rival, Rudolph of Swabia, as a son-in-law than Henry."

"I don't think Henry is going to find it so easy to gather an army and get it out of Germany as he thinks," suggested Matilda more hopefully.

But the Archbishop of Salerno shook his head. He was sitting in the chair in the great hall in which Beatrice used so often to sit.

"It isn't the question of the army or getting the army down into Italy that we should consider," he said thoughtfully. "But we all know the state of things in Lombardy, and how many of the Lombard bishops are to be counted on. Once the word goes abroad that the King is coming, half of them will go out to meet him. We all know that they would welcome any chance of support in their resistance to reform."

It was Azzo, Marquis of Este, who spoke for the company of knights and barons who had gathered about the fire to listen to the talk of their leaders, "Then, Your Holiness, we will escort you into Germany ourselves, and Heaven help any of those Lombard renegades who tries to hold us up."

A loud cheer rose from the knights about him, and from all over the hall the men-at-arms and the servants ran up to swell the enthusiasm. For the first time the Pope looked uncertain, and Matilda, whose heart had swelled with pride in the loyalty of her followers, gazed at him in wonder. But the knights had snatched up the shields and spears which had been placed against the walls and were clashing them together in triumph.

"I have always wanted a go at some of those Rhine towns," exclaimed one handsome boy, his face shining with excitement. "They say those burghers are fat as porkers with all their pelf."

There was a roar of laughter from all over the hall, and a little dwarf jester, who had come in from the kitchen, snatched up an ash-tipped copper poker from the fire and shouted above the tumult, "I am Taillefer who led William's army into England." Chanting at the top of a surprisingly bell-like tenor voice, "The Tuscan pigs went up the Rhine, up the Rhine," he started a march around the hall, into which presently all the knights and the men-at-arms and the house servants and the maids fell in, laughing and shouting. Only the Pope, the Archbishop, the Abbot, and Matilda remained seated, looking at each other in astonishment.

It was the Archbishop who recovered first and asked with a smile, "It seems to me I remember a snug little closet of your mother's in which she sometimes received visitors, my lady?" Under cover of the uproar the leaders withdrew.

As they seated themselves in the little room, the Archbishop smiled at his hostess: "Don't look so distressed, my lady Matilda. This is the pre-campaign carnival, that is all."

"I'm ashamed," she said, unable to respond to the lightness of his smiling banter.

"There is no cause," he said gravely, "that does not suffer a deep-sea change when it becomes popular."

"But I never thought to march like an invader into Germany," protested the Pope, his face suddenly looking gray with horror.

"No," Matilda reassured him, "just ourselves and a small company."

"By God, no," said a voice suddenly from the doorway. Arduino della Palude stood there, for all his diminutive stature looking suddenly very formidable. "You may want martyrdom, my lady Matilda, but you have no right to leave your lands to the devil knows what. Marching through all Lombardy and into Germany with such a small company!" And still grumbling, the little general stalked in and sat down.

"I quite agree with you," said the Archbishop. "Martyrdom is an honor no man has a right to run upon."

Matilda tried to keep the disappointment out of her voice. "Then, if you think it all so risky as that, there is nothing for us to do but to go to Canossa. From there I can send messengers over all the country."

"That," cried Arduino, "sounds to me like sense." Then warming with enthusiasm, he added, "Let Henry and all those Lombard renegades come to Canossa, and we will show them what stone and honest men can do."

"God forbid," said the Pope with the look on his face of a man who sees his enemies closing in upon all sides.

The Abbot and the Archbishop filled the next half hour with their arguments, all of the same tenor, that in the present state of the land with Henry's movements still obscure, it was madness to persist in the journey to Augsburg. But the Pope stood by the promise he had given. The nobility of Germany had asked him to come as their judge. If he failed to go, through cowardice, the guilt of the chaos of Germany and the contempt of the Church would be upon his head. As they saw their best arguments break in vain upon the rock of that conviction, the anxiety on the face of Desiderius deepened to fear, and a look of deep concern shadowed the placid features of the Archbishop of Salerno.

Five days later, Matilda was still trying vainly to persuade the Pope from his resolution, when word was brought to her that a messenger had come from Turin. Half her household was in the courtyard, but they fell back, and she saw the messenger draining a cup of wine, with one arm on the shoulder of the man next him. A dozen voices told her his news. Henry had crossed the Mont Cenis pass, and reached Adelaide of Susa's castle outside Turin.

"But everybody reports that the passes are full of snow. And the man who came through three days ago saw nothing unusual on either side of the mountains," she instantly objected.

The messenger shook his head. "The King was practically alone, the man who came into Turin that night said."

"Henry alone and putting himself into Adelaide of Susa's hands. He must have lost his wits." But the eagerness with which all about her picked up the suggestion disquieted her. Reckless, wild, Henry had always seemed to her, but not the man to lose his head.

The Pope listened gravely to the messenger's report. To Matilda's surprise, it was the fact that Henry had come alone that seemed to worry him most.

"I told him explicitly in my answer to his last letter that it was no use for him to try to persuade me to lift the ban before the meeting at Augsburg. No matter whom he sent for agent, nor what guarantees he offered, I was through with his promises, and I would not listen to anything more from him until he pleaded his case in the presence of his kingdom where all might judge of his good faith. And I will not," he added, grimly.

There was now, however, no question of his continuing the much-controverted

journey, Matilda reflected, half with disappointment, half with relief. But the relief soon vanished when she began to consider the immediate problems facing
the Pope's protector in this now certain danger. Gregory had been completely
indifferent to all considerations of personal safety—she looked at him sitting
now by the window, reading some letters in the moment's freedom that the
sudden disruption of the household had given him. Looking at his face, cool and
resolute, completely absorbed in his reading, she knew it was useless to plead the
danger to his person if Henry should succeed in raising an army.

But if—her very despair gave her an idea. She went up to him and stood
waiting.

He looked up and shook his head, "Matilda, when there is confusion in the
high places—here is a petty baron seizing merchants and exacting the half of
their goods for toll!"

"That is what I was going to say to you, my lord. If you stay here, and any
harm befalls you, the indignation of all good men will move them to revenge.
And where then will be our hope of peace?"

He smiled at the pious opportunism, but almost to her surprise, he did not
at once brush aside her plea. Looking hard at her, he seemed to consider her argument. Emboldened by his silence, she hastened to add that they all knew how
strife gave the evil the advantage they sought in vain from more ordered times.
She held her breath. But that argument seemed to move him at last as had none
of the others, and he capitulated. The next morning the whole company was on
the road to Canossa.

CHAPTER VI

BUT though she had undertaken the journey to Canossa in great anxiety,
Matilda soon found that she had little time for worry. Each day seemed to bring
its own business, so engrossing that not until evening did she pause to take stock
of her position, and then she was too tired to do more than sleepily commend
her perplexities to Infinite Wisdom and yield with relief to the exhaustion of
the flesh. Sometimes, she tried to invoke the intercession of her dead, but the

crowded days left little room for memory or grief, and though at every turn the humblest objects of the household world and the most trivial incidents of the day brought back the thought of her mother or the two Godfreys or the child, often in an unbearably poignant flash of recognition, yet always in the press of the present there was little time to seize upon the fragment and build up the living memory. Only in sleep did the past come back with matter-of-fact full-ness. More than once she woke up, wondering uneasily how she should persuade her husband to let her send the extra meat or wine that would bring cheer to some snow-fast mountain village, only to realize with sickening clearness that this particular problem would never trouble her lonely days. Or she would find herself wondering what her mother would say to some decision made in haste the day before, and then as her brain cleared of the fog of sleep, she would know in a sudden flash of wistfulness that now she must contemplate her action in its own naked fact. Sometimes in the water-gray lucidity of such moments of recov-ered consciousness, she would wonder if some day the anxieties of the present, too, would come back to her with such a warmth of things lost about them.

But for the most part she thought little of herself, and in the full tide of the day's occupation she knew these moments of twilight between sleep and waking for the sickness they were, and gave all her energy without thought to the problems of the moment. These were quite sufficient. To begin with, there was the company that had come from Mantua. They were at white heat with enthusiasm for the cause of the Pope and indignation at the perfidy of the King. Consequently, they were spoiling for action. For a day or two after their return, Arduino kept their leaders busy with plans for a defense of Canossa and the country about that would have taken all the resources of the German Kingdom to do justice to it. Indeed, the dwarf Hatto suggested that they send some of their forces to the aid of the King, for he was sure that there were not enough men in all Germany to make so elaborate a defense interesting. But, fortunately, Matilda happened to be passing through the end of the hall just in time to save Hatto from a whipping.

To pacify Arduino she suggested sending the light-hearted dwarf back to Mantua. For she knew that ever since some of the giants in the company of Godfrey the Younger had mocked the diminutive stature of Arduino by pre-tending to mistake Hatto for the Countess' general, the sensitive soldier had not been able to endure the sight of the dwarf. Her mother had solved the difficulty by keeping the clever little man with the beautiful voice and the never-failing wit at her house in Mantua, and there he had done much to beguile the loneliness of her latter days. Now Matilda blamed herself for having thoughtlessly let Hatto slip into her company in the excitement of the retreat from Mantua. And she decided to repair the mistake by sending him at once with a small party that in pursuance of Arduino's strategy were setting out that day to reinforce the garrison at Reggio.

But she had not reckoned with the high spirits and brutal humor of the mob of knights and barons who filled her hall. Immediately, they pounced on the suggestion and hailed Hatto as Arduino's deputy for the siege of Reggio. Only the intervention of Antonio, who had been watching the reckless consumption of his mistress' wines with a colder and colder eye, saved the half-drunken company from Arduino's wrath. His suggestion of excellent weather for hunting in the forests on the hills above Canossa caught the attention of the men, and Matilda hastily urged Arduino to agree.

But before the week was out, complaints of slaughtered cattle and broken fences and village women insulted began to come into Canossa, and Matilda was forced to face her problem anew. Opportunely enough, a messenger from the Bishop of Spires arrived at this time with definite confirmation of the King's departure and some details of his endeavor to gather support from the barons of the neighboring countryside. When, therefore, Arduino brought out the map of his plans for the defense of all the important points to the north of Canossa, Matilda welcomed with relief the elaborate strategy that would reinforce the garrisons of every grange and fortress along her borders. At least, the scheme would give the impatient fighting men something to do, and by the time the complaints of the burghers and villagers would demand further attention, the situation would be a little clearer, and she could judge of the prudence of sending her disorderly cohorts back to their own lands.

For the present that problem was at least on the way to being solved. But there were others no less puzzling. For while every messenger from friends in the north brought tales of fresh flights from castle and episcopal palace to the borders of Germany, not a day passed without the arrival of some German or Lombard bishop or abbot, and sometimes several, to kneel at the feet of the Pope and ask pardon for their share in the blasphemy of Worms. Many of these men came in the dress of penitents and pilgrims, almost unattended, but others brought large retinues of knights and clergy. The result was a constant rearrangement and reassignment of chambers that sorely taxed Matilda's ingenuity and the patience of the steward, whose pride in the sudden importance of the castle struggled sorely and not always victoriously with the order of his housekeeping in which he had so long taken untroubled pride.

There were other visitors, too, no less deserving of consideration, representatives of all the monastic houses in the neighborhood, who came to do homage to the Pope and to bring various offerings of treasure or supplies to his journey. Benedictines, Cluniacs, Canons Regular, Vallombrosans—white, gray, and black, they came with all sorts of presents from sheep to relics. It was a relief to Matilda when at last Alberic appeared among them with a smile of amusement at the throng about him.

"Thank God, you've come," Matilda greeted him warmly. "Now you can take over the entertainment of the regulars and relieve poor Antonio and me of that care."

"I'm not so sure of that," answered Alberic, looking around him thoughtfully. "To begin with, there are those among the ancient brethren who regard us of Cluny as little better than sons of Belial. They are morally sure that we have steel under our black habits, and they are convinced we have murder in our hearts."

Matilda laughed. "Well, whatever they think, your monks will at least give you less trouble than Arduino and I have been having with the warrior race. If it isn't all Antonio's wine, it is the peasant's cattle, and if it isn't the cattle, it is the women, until I could almost wish that Henry and his army were here."

Alberic shrugged his shoulders. "Each trade has its own griefs, I suppose. I should have been here days ago, but some of our rascals have taken to visions in the middle of the night. A sort of Ezekiel and Saint John with Henry and the Pope for their themes."

"Angels or devils?"

Alberic laughed. "They certainly are not the two I should choose for any revelation I wished to make, but," sobering, "the older I grow, the more reason I see, Matilda, to suspect that Heaven does not see eye to eye with me in all things."

"Did you bring the men along?" Matilda stared at the monks, standing behind their Prior at a respectful distance, with new curiosity.

"Good Lord, no. Until I see some sure sign of supernatural interposition, I am bound to proceed in the light of nature. One of the two was a priest. So I sent him up to a wretched little village where the pastor, an old monk of our house, is sick, and half the village is sick with him. To give him credit, he has a gift for illness, and there isn't enough of his familiar devil, drink, in the whole place to tempt him. The other, a lay brother, I sent up to the woods with a logging party. He's a lazy devil, but he'll have to sweat to keep warm up there. If the visions still survive, then I'll listen to them."

Again Matilda laughed. "I have half a mind, Alberic, to hand the knights over to you, and let Arduino look after the monks."

But Alberic shook his head ruefully. "Remember, we are commanded to avoid the occasions of sin."

There were other arrivals, less dramatic and less impressive, but in their degree, time-and-thought-consuming. There were various craftsmen, farriers and smiths and sword-cutlers and shield-makers, who had come on the chance of their services being needed. The various officials of Matilda's household swore that half of them were thieves and the other half runaway serfs, but there was at least work enough for them to do to earn their suppers and a bundle of straw on the floor of the smithy or the barns. There were peddlers and tumblers and strolling singers and old women with herbs and a collection of riffraff from the roads that made Matilda look forward to the day when she would be free again to take her realm in hand. But of all the motley company that came in those days the one that most filled Matilda's anxious heart with a sense of the irony and absurdity of life was Hilary the Greek.

Wrapped in a bright red woolen mantle on which the melted snow and sleet had caked the marble dust, he knelt before Matilda and drew from his breast a crumpled sheet of parchment.

"Madonna, I have it at last, a capital that will make the marble bloom like those pagan figures on your mother's tomb." And his voice and eyes glowing with excitement, he laid the drawing in her hand.

For a moment Matilda stared at the man. Then she looked at the drawing. There was no question of the beauty of the design. Though the figures of lamb and ox for the two medallions seemed stiff and fantastic beside the remembered grace of the antique figures of men and maidens, there was something of the breath of life in the unfolding of the acanthus leaves that shrouded them.

"Are they not finer than the capitals of the columns of Monte Cassino, my lady?" cried the man, unable to bear the delay of her praise.

"But what should I do with it?" she asked, holding the parchment at arm's length.

The man leaped to his feet in his excitement, his eyes and his white teeth gleaming in his swarthy face.

"Ah, Madonna, I will make you a chapel here at Canossa beautiful as the choir of heaven. The marble will breathe and sing, and every one who looks at those tall columns will forget he is on this dark earth, and—"

"Alberic," called Matilda, as she caught sight of the Prior at the end of the hall, "here is another visionary for you."

The monk looked at the Greek, poised seemingly on mid-air, as he waited for his lady to listen to him again. Then Alberic shook his head. "This madness is in your bailiwick and not mine. Alas, it is a madness the world is likely to deal less kindly with; so be gentle."

Matilda looked at the Prior and then at the sculptor. "Hilary the Greek, are you quite deaf and blind to what is all about you? This is war, and do you think I can spare men or silver for marble now?"

For a moment the Greek looked around him, and his face fell. Then as his eye caught sight of the gray yellow stone of the wall with here and there a streak of bright saffron wearing through the soot, his face lighted again, "Then I shall take the stone of this place, and I shall bend its stubbornness to my will, and I will make it speak as it has never spoken before. I will make columns and—"

Then the absurdity of it all came over Matilda, and she burst out laughing. "Man, you don't make war or repel war with columns or capitals. It is mangonels and ballistas and rams and bores that I shall be needing. The dark little chapel we have is all that we need to pray God and Saint Michael for help and to bury the dead."

But there was something indomitable in the Greek. "Ah, but, my lady, in war so many things are destroyed, and the heart of man still thirsts for beauty."

"God knows that is true," Matilda granted sadly. "Well, there are so many here that one mouth more or less will not matter. You may stay."

The Greek knelt down and lifting the hem of her dress kissed it. "But what shall I make for my lady?"

"Go find the sacristan and send him to me. There is some gold in the treasure chest, and you can make a new cup for the Pope's Mass. It shall be for a memory of his stay here. And look that you tell nobody, for there are so many here that it would be a miracle if there were no thieves."

But she knew that the caution was in vain, for the happy sculptor had gone off singing, "I shall make a cup for my Lord, it shall not pass."

Before she could repent of her folly, the steward was at her elbow again to tell her that the stores of wheat in the granary were getting dangerously low. And before she had finished sealing a letter for two of her servants to take to the bailiffs of the neighboring granges, a man came running in from the smithy to tell her that one of the new workmen had cut himself and would she come to look at the wound. So the long day went from dawn to dark. It seemed to her that everywhere she turned, she found nothing but rumor and confusion and uncertainty and fresh questions for her to settle.

In all the castle it seemed to her that there was but one person who day after day met the anxiety and the confusion without any sign of strain or perplexity. And that was the Pope. She had had the bed in her own chamber moved to the wall, and a larger table and many stools carried in, and a huge iron brazier set in the middle of the room. Here the Pope sat and read letters and received visitors all day, and here at the end of the day Matilda came to sit quietly by the fire and to talk over their uncertain prospects.

The Pope nodded to her as she entered, and she sat down in a low chair to wait for him to finish the letter he was dictating to the last of his secretaries for that day. Idly, Matilda noticed how white and drawn the monk's face looked in contrast to the brown vigor of the Pope's. He must be tired; yet the clear voice dictated steadily, apparently untroubled by the occasional scratching of the stylus on the tablets. Matilda looked into the fire. Yes, she would have to see that the rushes in the great hall were changed. Already its stench was as rank as it would normally be at the end of the winter. Perhaps if she had a fire laid in one of the tower rooms, the men might dry their boots and leather jackets there. Cedar boughs in the fire and a little incense on the charcoal braziers—

The voice had stopped, and she looked up eagerly. But the Pope was gazing past her into the fire as if considering what he should say next, and the secretary was looking at him with stylus poised in the air.

The Pope spoke again more slowly, "For it is fitting that there should be sympathy between your people and ours seeing that however the forms of our worship may differ, it is the same God whom we look to for help in the common burdens of our life and whom we praise as the Maker of us all." Then he looked at Matilda and smiled, "God knows, Matilda, that Anazir, King of Mauretania, might put some of our Christian princes to shame, Saracen that he is."

When that letter was finished, the Pope looked through the pile still on his table. "From the Bishops of Sens and Bourges on the Bishop of Orleans, from Adela of Flanders on the married clergy, the complaint of the Florentine merchants against the King of France, from Solomon King of Hungary, from Sancho Bishop of Huesca, from the Prince of Kiev—these will have to wait till tomorrow, Brother Paulo. God send you the rest you have earned this day."

Gregory sighed lightly with weariness as he turned his chair to the fire, and, to amuse him, Matilda told him the story of Hilary the Greek.

As she had hoped, the dark face brightened. "He is right. The ancient poet warned us lest we suffer truth to be silenced in the din of arms. No more should beauty, which God has given us for healing and for release from the prison of our griefs."

"True," said Matilda, "and yet when I have spent the day trying to assure bread and wine for our company, a cup of gold does not seem the first of our necessities."

The Pope smiled as if he understood the press of the day that now was closing so quietly with gazing into the fire. Matilda watched the white ash film along the surface of the burning embers in the brazier.

"What worries me," she said at last, "is that with all these rumors of Henry's movements we have heard nothing of that escort which the princes promised. I cannot bear now to have that meeting at Augsburg lost."

"I am anxious, too. For if this fails, I do not know when again we shall have such a chance to put so large a piece of this chaotic world of ours in order." As he spoke, something perhaps best described as a sharp stillness came over his face. Matilda thought of a little chapel she had once come across in a journey into the desolate land of the Auvergne. It was a mean little building, but it had a certain inalienable dignity of its own, for it was made entirely of the black volcanic rock of the region itself. Small as was the Pope's head, there was yet something craggy and massive about it in its own dimension.

"This is something to which we must give our lives if necessary," he said at length. "But if in the inscrutable providence of God, all our hope is brought to naught, we must not despair. For Our Lord never promised us success; only that He would be with us in all things even to the end."

"I shall try to remember that."

The grim tension broke in his face, and he said gently, "God forgive me for seeming to preach to you, my daughter. Pray rather that I may not forget it myself in the hour of trial."

Then as she caught her breath in a sudden spasm of awe and fear, he said more lightly, "Do not go out to meet trouble with your anxieties, Matilda. Perhaps tomorrow we shall have some more certain news that will end this suspense."

CHAPTER VII

As it turned out, the Pope was right. The next day, when Matilda left the chapel after morning Mass, she went to the battlements of the wall behind to look out over the surrounding country. There was no sign of life in the plain, or in the hills beyond, or the mountains above. Even the earth itself seemed to have joined the conspiracy of stolid silence, for there was none of that eloquence of the open fields and the moving hills to be discerned in its frozen gray. A little smoke rising in the thin January sun from the villages and towns on the horizon robbed the scene of the awe of complete desolation, but even the habitual magic of distance seemed to have evaporated in the flat matter-of-factness of the winter morning.

Yet she had barely reached the stables below, to check for herself a complaint of carelessness in the care of the horses, when the horns rang out, hard and bright from the watch towers. She smiled to think of the life that must have been stirring on those hidden roads even as she brooded over their apparent emptiness. There was no need to hurry, for it might be an hour yet before the stranger reached the castle. Two of the grooms who had followed her into the stable started to rush out. She remembered the complaint of Antonio that the sense of impending crisis of the last weeks was threatening to destroy the established routine of her household. With a quick order she stayed their flight, and for a moment or two looked hard at them, watching them grow more sheepish with every moment of silence. Then she turned to her errand of inspection.

The steward had cause to complain. The superintendent of the stables had been careless in his inspection. Probably there was more than a little truth to the man's claim that it had been almost impossible to get work done these last weeks by servants who had been reveling in the sudden expansion and excitement of their household. But these were no times to rely on men who were balked by impossibilities. The superintendent could be removed, and the next in authority installed. Yes, a beating or two promptly administered might save trouble, but she would hold the new head responsible for the condition of his men, and no one was to interfere with any man who might want to appeal to the head of the household for justice.

The sordid little business sickened her, and she dismissed Antonio brusquely. Even in the trivialities of the household, right jostled right in distracting confusion. She had been sorry for the dejection of the ousted servant and indignant at the ill-concealed jeering in the faces of his underlings. As she left the fetid air of the neglected stables, she heard a loud shriek from the courtyard in front. She listened. Another shriek, and then as she stepped forward, she caught the whistling of the whip and heard the voice of Arduino, "Let him have it again, and let this be a lesson to all of you damned drunkards. The next man who drinks on watch will be swung out from the tower and dropped to hell to sober up."

For a moment she hesitated. In all these years she had never been able to make any lasting impression on the brutality of Arduino. But now the peace of Christendom might be in his hands. She slipped back into the stable courtyard and chose a narrow passage behind the kitchen to get round to the yard in front of the great hall. At that moment, it seemed to her that she would condone any piece of duplicity in the world.

It was almost with relief, therefore, that she heard the horns sound again from the northern tower. It was a messenger from Bernard of Parma, one of the few Lombard vassals on whose fidelity she could count. There was no question, therefore, of the reliability of his report, curious as it was.

Matilda read it aloud to the company in the hall. "Henry gathered a great company at Pavia, but he did not take them into his confidence. He said that he would first see the Pope, and then when he had seen him, he would return to them and help them free themselves from"—she stopped and looked across to where the Pope sat at a table, dictating letters to one of the monks, who had been acting as his secretary. She had been too indignant and ashamed to read the next words, but the Pope gave no sign of feeling when she read them—"the blasphemous tyranny of this man Gregory! So he has started out for Reggio on his way south to find the Pope, taking almost nobody with him but his wife and child and the Countess Adelaide and a few of her men."

"The only thing I cannot understand is his trusting himself to Adelaide of Susa when everybody knows what she thinks of the way he has treated her daughter." The Archbishop's usually placid face was as puzzled as his words.

It was Alberic who suggested that a penitent husband might make more appeal to a woman than to a priest.

The Archbishop's face lighted with amusement, "Oh, if you say that for Bertha, it is not impossible. But Adelaide is a lady of a very different sort, as you well know."

For a moment there was silence. There were very few in the room who did not recall that it was the enterprise of Adelaide of Susa that had deprived Alberic of some of his father's best fiefs when he was still a child and his widowed mother too weak to defend them. Alberic laughed, however, at the embarrassed faces of his friends, "Far be it from me to say anything unkind of Adelaide. I have long thought I owed her a very considerable debt of freedom."

So the company in the great hall talked away the morning, but the Pope went on writing letters and conferring with the waiting messengers as if no change in his busy days were imminent.

Matilda took counsel with Arduino and the other leaders of her company. Arduino could not believe that Henry would venture to come with so few; so he sent messengers to some of the barons who were still out hunting in the hills to the south, bidding them return at once. But the consensus of opinion was that not even a desperate man could get any considerable company across the snow-choked passes, and Alfanus of Salerno was especially emphatic in his insistence that Henry would know better than to depend on raising an army out of turbulent Lombardy. All agreed with Matilda that it was wise to send messengers to the northern fortresses and to the plain cities with instructions that the moment Henry appeared in sight word should be sent to Canossa. Then finding the slow passing of the hours intolerable, she summoned the steward and began a systematic inventory of the resources of the castle.

Several times during the following days messengers came from various friends and vassals of Matilda's. Henry had been seen near Cremona. He had reached Parma. He had left Parma and was moving in the direction of Reggio. He had been seen in the plain to the west of Reggio by nightfall. From all sources it was clear that he was traveling with the slenderest of escorts. Report varied as to his company. One story was that Adelaide of Susa was traveling with him, another that she had left him at Cremona but had sent out a strong company who were now looking for him to take him to one of her hill fortresses. It was this report that first roused Matilda to the danger of some outrage that would tarnish the good fame of the King's Italian vassals. She consulted the Pope, but he declined to advise her, declaring that this was a problem that lay outside his jurisdiction. Certainly, he would not consider it any reflection on her loyalty to himself if she took the steps that an honest vassal would ordinarily take to protect the person of his liege lord. So, though it would soon be dark on the roads, she sent out half a dozen of her best men with the grave Lord of Saviola in command of them. Her instructions were explicit. In no sense were they to join the company of the King or to take orders from him. Indeed, they could hardly have any actual intercourse with an excommunicated man, but they were to protect the King's way and to restrain any outlaw or rebel who should try to molest him.

That night Matilda slept little. Henry with a small company in the plain of Lombardy was much too tempting prey for a nobility that in the best of times was more distinguished for violence than for respect for law and that had never been known to let loyalty stand in the way of ambition. As she lay awake in a corner of the maids' chamber, she thought of a dozen men, lay and clerical, who would not scruple to stop the King for their own interest. Nor would they hesitate to profess a devotion to the cause of the Pope to give some color of principle to their habitual lawlessness. It was with a sense almost of relief, therefore, that in the first whitening of the winter dawn she heard an exchange of trumpets, seemingly on the edge of night.

While one of the monks went to rouse the Pope, Matilda watched the sleepy servants light tapers and kindle the embers of last night's fire. Even when the thin yellow flames flickered across the dark, it was still night here in the cavern of the hall, and for all the crackling of the fire, it was bitter cold. She drew her heavy woolen cloak about her and bade the half-dressed maids heat some wine.

The door at the back of the hall opened.

"Your Holiness, Henry is at Bianello. His own messengers will leave at dawn to beg you to see him. These men came away the moment he arrived last night." As she spoke, she lifted one of the candlesticks from the table by the fire and held it high so that its light fell on the Pope. For a moment he did not speak but

stood there, a shaft of red, in the cold light. Only his eyes glittered as he looked
at her. Then he moved quickly and sat down by the fire. The two messengers fell
on their knees. Absentmindedly, he blessed them and then with a sharp look at
them, he motioned them away.

"My lord," Matilda began, and then realizing that she still held the candlestick, she stopped and set it down carefully on the table.

"No," said the Pope with quiet finality, "I have told the King that I will not
see him till Augsburg. That is all I have to say to him or anyone else on that subject." His voice rose slightly at the end of the sentence but closed firmly.

Matilda looked around her. She could see more clearly now in the grayness
of the room, and as far as she could make out any object in the shadows against
the walls, she saw the huddled figures of men and women, their white faces fixed
on hers with fright and expectancy. Irrelevantly, she thought of a feast day long
ago when she was a child. It was in this same hall, and they were all gathered
here, waiting for her mother to come out from her chamber. She remembered
how she stood at her nurse's side, shy in the crowd of strangers from all over her
mother's lands. And, suddenly, she had wondered if her mother felt shy, too, before all these strangers from Lombardy and Tuscany and Lorraine, and if when
she came out and faced them, she would be confused and at a loss. It was the first
time in her life that with a prescience beyond her years she had felt the burden
of power. Now she remembered the excitement with which she had waited for
her mother, and the dread that had come to her when she suddenly realized that
some day it would be she who would have to come out that door and take the
leadership of all these waiting people.

She had stood silent so long that she felt the Pope's eyes rise curiously to
her face. She looked around the huddle of light and darkness, and she heard her
own voice speaking with perfect matter-of-factness like an echo of her mother's,
"You will have plenty to do when morning comes. You had all better go back to
bed. Antonio," she turned to where she saw the grave face of the old steward in
the shadows, "send some of this warm wine to the southwest gate tower. And I
think you had better post two men on the northeast tower before the sun rises."

The two messengers still waited in the shadows beyond the table. Matilda
looked at the Pope. He sat staring into the fire, apparently absorbed in watching
the flames licking over the fresh wood and listening to the crackling and sput-
tering of the resin along the curling edge of the logs.

"How many came with the King?" she asked.

"Only a handful—half a dozen men and the two women and the child," answered one of the messengers.

"The Queen and her son?"

"We judged so, my lady Countess. She seemed exhausted, poor thing, and the child was asleep. The older woman seemed cross about something, and the King was swearing."

"But perhaps there were others coming later?" she pursued, still incredulous.

"The King swore there were no more to come. The captain was anxious to know, and I heard him ask the King more than once. The King was angry the last time, and he said, 'It shows how I've been misrepresented that you don't take a King's word.' So the captain had to be content." In the candlelight Matilda saw the man's face looking anxiously at her.

"Did the captain seem reassured? What do you think?" asked Matilda.

"I?" The shock was unfeigned. Then the man smiled cunningly, "God forbid, my lady, that I should think when my betters are disagreeing."

Matilda was startled to hear behind her the Pope's clear laugh.

"I don't know that I should call prudence one of the Christian virtues, my man, but for one subject to authority, it is one of the most useful. I am grateful to you for rousing me, Matilda, for now I can get a look at some of those letters before Brother Paulo comes with his tablets." The Pope rose from his chair.

Matilda dismissed the two men and turned to her guest.

"As soon as Mass is finished, I am going over to Bianello, my lord." She waited.

The Pope shrugged his shoulders and bowed courteously to her. But she did not stand aside.

"My lord, have you thought how desperate Henry must have been to come with so few, and to expose his wife and child in such a winter as this?" She regretted the note of challenge that had involuntarily crept into her voice.

The Pope turned and looked at her. "You know perfectly well that Henry never waited upon discretion when his own pride or self-will were at stake."

"Then I shall tell him that you will not see him?"

"He knows that already. He knew it before he left Germany."

As she looked at the Pope's face, dark and implacable, something answeringly stubborn woke within her own troubled spirit. "I must in decency go to Bianello, then."

"That is something on which I cannot advise you. You must take the responsibility yourself." And with that he went back to his chamber, leaving Matilda gazing after him. She was defiant, but she was wretched. For her heart went with him, even as she thought of the liege lord she could not receive in her own hall and of the woman carrying her child.

And the sense of having betrayed some loyalty lasted with her all the cold and windy way to the fortress in the hills above Canossa. She was chilled through by the time her escort drew up before the lower wall of Bianello so that even in the sun of high noon she shivered. And now that she was about to face his enemy, she was sick with the thought of the pain she must have given the Pope. For the knowledge that she could do no otherwise than what she had done gave her no peace. She wondered whether Henry's satisfaction in her homage would be heightened by the thought of what it must have cost her.

But she might have spared herself the wonder, for as soon as she reached the main courtyard of the fortress, Henry rushed out and cried, "We'll be ready to start in a moment."

She shook her head.

"You mean you haven't come to take me to Canossa?"

"No, the Pope says he will not see you." Her teeth were chattering with the cold and the shock of the look on Henry's face.

"Good God, Matilda! And you call yourself a sane woman to support a tyrant like that. I'll see him damned in hell and hell frozen over like these damned hills of yours, Matilda, before I'll kneel to his pride."

"My lord!"

The King laughed. "Come, Matilda, don't look so white and shocked. Wait a minute and I'll get my sword, and we'll go over and knock his silly excommunication out of his silly hand."

Her jaws were quivering so that she could only shake her head and stagger into the hall. Henry followed her, invoking every curse he could think of on those damned priests who thought they could rule the world and the fools who knuckled under to them. The tears that came to her eyes when Bertha flung her arms about her neck a moment later in the hall were not entirely tears of sympathy.

CHAPTER VIII

FOR several minutes Matilda stood with Bertha looking down at the child asleep by the fire. There had, of course, been nothing like a trundle bed to be found in the fortress of Bianello; so Bertha had half filled a low chest with pillows and laid her son there to sleep. The cloak in which he was wrapped was yet stained with the snow and sleet through which they had come, but the face of the sleeping child was fresh and rosy, and the rhythm of his breathing low and steady.

"It must have been hard to have to take him out into the winter," said Matilda compassionately, looking down into the pretty, worn face of Bertha. But even as she spoke, her thoughts were busy with the child. How incredibly warm and alive he looked sleeping there!

"Henry said it was the only chance that little Conrad would ever have to be King." As she looked down at her sleeping son, Bertha wiped away her tears, only to have them start falling again. "Not, you know, Matilda, that I should mind about that. But Henry said that when he grew up and knew, he would hate me."

"He is very sweet," said Matilda irrelevantly.

Bertha looked up at her, her blue eyes large in her pale face, and her small red mouth tightly pursed. With a start, Matilda became aware of her intent look.

"You must have been frightened crossing the mountains," she began.

Bertha shuddered, and then the dark lines about her mouth relaxed. "They wrapped us in ox skins and lowered us over some of the worst places with ropes. Once we swung out from the ice and it was all dark below. But it came to me then suddenly that if the rope broke, I had Conrad in my arms, and they couldn't take us away from each other."

"I know," said Matilda. They had sat down now close to the fire, facing the chest in which the child lay. Indeed, Bertha's hand rested on the edge.

"I knew you would come to help us, Matilda," said a bright, clear voice.

Matilda turned to face a stout woman of middle height with keen, dark eyes and a firm lower lip pressed over the thin upper lip. Even in that first moment of greeting Matilda saw that whereas the dress and mantle of Bertha were still crumpled and travel-stained as if she had allowed the wet wool to dry on her body, the robes of Adelaide of Susa were fresh and clean. Her face, too, was bright and confident, and Matilda caught the contempt in the glance she threw her daughter as she sat down between them.

"I am sorry Bertha has been sniveling again," she said with a certain sharpness in her apology.

"It has been very hard on her with the child to think of," expostulated Matilda.

Adelaide shook her head. "She shouldn't have come in the first place. I'd let Henry threaten all he liked before I took a child of mine out into such weather."

Again Bertha tried to wipe away the tears, and again they seemed to fall the faster for the effort.

Adelaide shrugged her shoulders. "I wanted her to stay at Turin with the child, but she would come on."

Bertha seemed to take sudden courage. "But you said yourself that some of the Lombard bishops might try to seize him under pretext of helping the King."

"Well," said Adelaide, "if you want to know what I think, I am not sure that that would be so much worse than the way you are likely to spoil him. It will be the old story of Agnes and the young Henry over again without Anno of Cologne to try to stop it."

The wretched Bertha was about to make some answer to her mother when there came a step behind them. Hastily she gulped down her tears and dried her eyes. And this time no more tears came.

"How afraid she is of him!" said Matilda to herself, noting with fresh pity how the delicate prettiness of Bertha had faded to a wan pathos. But the next minute she was not so sure.

For as Henry came up to the fire, Bertha jumped up and placed another cushion in the chair in which she had been herself sitting. And when Henry patted her arm as he passed her to take the chair, her face lighted up, and a stain of color ran through her pale cheeks. When Henry had seated himself, he laughed, and catching her round the waist, he drew her to his feet. There she settled down on the footstool, spreading her full robes over her feet, and looked up at Henry as if waiting for him to speak.

"She loves him," said Matilda to herself. And she thought of the bride repudiated and the wife alternately neglected and insulted. Adelaide of Susa snorted. But Henry only smiled his most charmingly and laid his hand lightly on his wife's shoulder.

"Matilda will not fail us, puss," he said, whispering aloud to her. She smiled at Matilda, and for a moment, seeing her tear-smudged face relax as she laid her head against her husband's knee, Matilda envied her.

"Cousin Matilda," Henry went on, speaking now in the clear, low-pitched voice that she never forgot even in her hardest thoughts of him, "I am not going to offer you any lands or treasure of bishoprics"—He paused for a moment, and Matilda, looking up on a sudden suspicion of the answer to the question that had puzzled her these last days, saw the full face of Adelaide stiffen in its warm flesh.

But Henry went on as if he were quite innocent of any ulterior intention, "I know that it would be no use offering you a bribe. All the world knows your devotion to the Church, a devotion which I applaud as warmly as any man."

Matilda scrutinized Henry's face closely, but she could surprise no hint of mocking in its well-poised gravity.

"What I want to appeal to is your loyalty to the peace of the Empire of which you are one of the greatest princes and to which you are bound by every tie of blood and affection. If your husband were alive, I should not be making this appeal myself." At this point he looked straight at her, and Matilda fancied she detected a flicker of anxiety in the full-lidded eyes. But still she said nothing, for it seemed to her that so far there was nothing for her to say.

"I could have come with an army," said Henry, suddenly veering as if he had caught the wind of her unspoken suspicion. "All of Lombardy ran out to meet me. But I wanted to appear before the Pope as a penitent child of the Church. So I—"

"Liar!" exclaimed Adelaide of Susa, her face now a brick-red with half-suppressed indignation.

Nothing could have been more perfect in its assumption of outraged innocence than the glance of appeal which Henry now cast first at Adelaide, then at Matilda. Bertha raised her head, and the fright came again into her blue eyes.

"Henry," said Matilda quickly, speaking more to break the tense silence than to argue, and yet even as she spoke, unable to keep the strain of contention out of her voice, "the Pope has promised that he will hear you at Augsburg."

"At Augsburg!" Henry's voice rose. "It will just graze within the year I have to save my kingdom if I wait for Augsburg. All my enemies have to do is to put obstacles in the Pope's way and the date will pass, and they can invoke the law to declare me deposed and elect that villain Rudolf. You know they wouldn't scruple to do it, Matilda."

But she shook her head, feeling suddenly calmer as his excitement grew. "If they did that, they would have the Pope to reckon with and all Christendom."

"The Pope and all Christendom!" said Henry with lively contempt. "Where is that escort that they promised to send into Italy to meet the Pope?"

Matilda felt her throat close with indignation. "You know perfectly well that when the news came that you had left Spires, everybody was afraid of trouble."

Henry made no effort to conceal the sneer with which he retorted, "What did they expect, when a meddling priest had cut the feet from under the only power that could keep order?"

"I don't hold by that Hildebrand," the voice of Adelaide of Susa seemed like her substantial person to jostle aside the participants in the conversation, "but God knows I don't blame him this time."

"Wait till you try putting your own men into those new bishoprics of yours, and he begins excommunicating you!" retorted Henry. Frightened, Bertha rose from the footstool and stood behind her husband's chair, her small fingers clutching and unclutching the high back while she looked first at Matilda and then at her mother.

"Henry," said Matilda, "you ought to know by now that in this ceaseless struggle for power there is no security for any one. The only chance for order is in the laws of God. If every one from the lowest to the highest keeps those laws, then we will have peace and trust and order, and each of us will have a chance to reach his proper stature. But—"

"Good God, Matilda, you don't think I've not heard all that before?"

She felt the blood rush into her face.

Henry was quick to see his advantage and push it. "The Pope is always doing that. I tell you, Matilda, my power comes from God, too, and I won't be told what I shall do with what belongs to me."

There was nothing to be gained from this contest of words, Matilda told herself. The child had been awakened by the sound of angry voices, and now he was howling lustily. Bertha knelt down and took him into her arms. Matilda arose and bowed to Henry.

His voice fell, as he put out a hand to detain her, "But I recognize I'm a Christian, and I must do penance to get rid of this excommunication—like any other man," he added craftily.

"But that is what it is all about, Henry," she said, striving to keep her disgust out of her voice and seeing at once from the sulky look that came over Henry's handsome face that she had failed.

"Matilda," cried Bertha, coming and kneeling down at her feet and holding the child up to her, "please see what you can do to help us."

By the time she had come through the three walls of Canossa, it was so late that the whole household had gone to bed. Apparently, the horns at the gate had roused almost nobody, and she was not surprised to learn from the steward that after restlessly watching for her all evening, the whole company had given up hope of her return for that night. As she came into the hall, she saw only the embers smoldering on the hearth, and the nearly burned-out torches guttering in their iron holders against the walls. All around her in the darkness rose the sounds of heavy breathing from the shadows piled on the long shadows of the benches. For a moment the stench of perspiration and wool and leather and rotten straw smothered her after the clear cold of the hills, and she thought almost regretfully of the chill sparkle of the winter stars in the great emptiness of the night.

Then she saw the shadows in the corner move, and caught a flash of red. Speaking very low, she bade Antonio the steward light the tapers on the table by the fire.

The Pope came into the candlelight. "You must be weary," he said gently. The tears came to her eyes, and she was thankful that it was too dark in this half-light between the candles and the fire for him to see her face.

"He has come as a penitent," she began, "to kneel at your feet and ask absolution."

"It would have been better evidence of penitence to have kept his word and stayed at Spires," was the brief answer. All the tenderness of a moment ago had faded, and now it was the clear, cool voice of conscience that spoke.

"Your Holiness," she began again, "if you could have but seen Bertha, worn and travel-stained, all her beauty gone in her grief, with her child in her arms. Sometimes it was so steep where they crossed, that the men tied them up in ox skins and let them down the ice-covered rocks with ropes. And she was so frightened that she thought any minute they might be dashed to pieces. Your heart would have bled to see her."

"It has before this," said the Pope gravely, "when Henry repudiated her before he had honored his marriage vows at all, and ever since when he has flaunted his mistresses in her face and laughed at her scruples and anxieties."

"But, my lord, she loves him in spite of it all."

Again the voice in the darkness softened. "That is the miracle of a good woman, Matilda, and no credit to the man she serves. Indeed, I don't imagine Henry would be able to understand that even if he were moved to try. I don't suppose any man ever really understands it after all," he added thoughtfully.

"I know I never could," said Matilda. "But it went to my heart to see her, and I would do almost anything to help her."

The Pope smiled. "It is like a woman, Matilda, to think so hard of the one human being whose misery she sees that she forgets all about the millions who are not there before her eyes. Of course, the Queen and her son are a pitiful sight to move the hardest heart, but how about all those other women and those other children who will have cause enough to weep and worse if Henry goes on as he has been doing? It is they who are in my eyes tonight, Matilda, when you describe this one wretched woman out of all the world's misery."

"But those others we can't see tonight, and we can't do anything for them, but this one is on our very threshold—" she stopped in despair.

"God bless you, Matilda, for your pity, but remember this—that charity is not the only pitifulness. It is a good thing and a beautiful to comfort and relieve wretchedness, but it is a better, if you can, to prevent it. That is why justice is an older command than mercy. Law is not as winsome as charity, my child, but its good is wider and more lasting."

Again he had overcome her, and she went out of the hall, choking down her sobs.

CHAPTER IX

"THREE more of the German bishops this morning and twenty knights!" exclaimed Alberic as Matilda lingered for a moment in the chapel porch after Mass. "I should say that Henry had reason enough for penitence."

"On the other hand, the man from Bianello has just brought word of several arrivals there from Lombardy and even from Germany last night."

Alberic smiled. "One of the handicaps of being ensnared in the world's net of power and the striving for power, Matilda, is that one cannot face the facts of his own life."

"What are you trying to tell me I am being stupid about?" She was very weary after an almost sleepless night, and though she held the thought at arm's length, she was sick with discouragement.

For a moment Alberic laughed at her. Then he sobered. "The children of this world spend a good deal of time dressing up their deeds in splendid motives and noble purposes, but the basic springs of action are few and relatively simple." He paused, and then as she gazed at him in perplexity, he smiled again. "Matilda, to stand out against the Pope involves some very real risks. But the Pope is bound to act in accordance with established principles which are known to everybody. Therefore that risk is capable of certain, let us say, ameliorations. For one thing, an unsuccessful sinner can always repent. And the Pope is bound to be merciful to the penitent. But to oppose the King is a different matter. The very fact of opposition is enough to justify any vengeance the King may choose to take, in his own eyes and the eyes of most of his supporters. There you face the bare logic of power."

"What are you talking about? What do you think I should do about it?" Matilda pulled her cloak tighter about her tired body, and it seemed to her that for a moment she was drawing in her defenses against the whole world.

"Those two questions are not the same," he chided her. "That is the habitual confusion of the man of action. He will never understand that the contemplative is merely trying to take a look at the facts. The man of action is so busy with what he is going to do—"

But the vague irritation which had been gnawing at Matilda's consciousness all morning flared out. "It is all right for you to talk, Alberic, of looking at the facts. You can. I have to do something about them."

For a moment he looked at her in surprise. Then he said very soberly, "God forgive me, Matilda. It is easy for me to talk." He smiled. "No matter what you do, I shall not blame you. Only infinite wisdom could condemn a choice made blindfold among these uncertainties, and—"

As always, the anger went out of her at the first gentle word. And her own injustice made her go out to meet her adversary. "I am afraid it is worse even than you say. When I think of the Pope and Henry, I am reminded of these jousts between a man with one arm tied behind his back and a man with both arms free."

Alberic grinned. "I should say rather with an extra arm or two thrown in."

"And yet strangely enough, I think Henry means what he says at any given moment," she went on thinking aloud.

"Probably more than you or I do."

"But will he stick to it?"

Alberic laughed. "That takes no voice from Heaven, Matilda. The answer is 'No.' If that is what is worrying you, the Pope is right there."

"But when Henry asks for absolution and offers to do penance, can the Pope refuse? Oh, Alberic, I can stand anything but having the Pope in the wrong." She shuddered when she remembered how these impulsive words might be misconstrued.

Alberic shook his head gravely, "Your peace is a brittle thing, Matilda, if it stands on what somebody else does, even if that somebody is Gregory."

"Oh, I don't mean that last ground on which the soul stands alone. But all between, Alberic—" She spread her hands wide in a gesture of despair.

"There is one thing you may always be sure of, Matilda. It is true that the Pope is a man wrapped up in an ideal. He would gladly sacrifice himself and you, too, to his hope of saving Christendom, but he is also an intelligent man. He won't think the world is the way he would like it to be, just because he cannot bear to have it as it is."

She thought about it for a moment. "That sounds cynical," she decided.

He laughed with a tinge of bitterness. "God knows, Matilda, it would be easier if it were." And as she stared at him, he added, "You could give up then. Don't look so scared. You can't."

She thought of what Alberic had said, often during the rest of the morning, as she received distinguished visitors in the great hall, as she went round the battlements with Arduino listening to his plans for reinforcing the guard, as she dispatched messengers to the neighboring granges asking for fresh levies of supplies to maintain the growing city within her walls, as she sat in the Pope's chamber and made one more effort to persuade him to receive Henry. She thought of it again when having failed to move him from his refusal, she went with her maids to choose fresh linen from her chests to take to the relief of Bertha and her child. Indeed, she was so preoccupied with her own thoughts that she went on mechanically taking and rejecting from the pile of linen even when the watchmen's horns from the walls blew again and again. And though she heard running feet in the courtyard outside her chamber, she bade the maids with her attend to their task and leave the idlers to gape from the walls.

It was only when one of the watchmen rushed in breathless, flinging himself headlong into a pile of freshly lavendered linen, that she realized something had happened.

For the man paid no attention to her rebuke as he picked himself up but gasped at the laughing maids, "The King, the King—"

As she ran to the first wall and climbed to the top of the tower from which the horn had sounded, she tried to think. It was outrageous of Henry—but she was frightened as well as angry. For she knew that a bold attack like this was bound to gather up a large company of the restless and the adventurous as well as of the generous.

There was no one in the tower, but one look at the road below the castle was enough. It seemed full of people. And even as she looked, there gathered on the other side of the drawbridge what at first to her startled eyes looked like a whole army. A second glance was more reassuring. For the armed knights were few, and the men-at-arms though numerous not half the company. The majority of the crowd was a mixed rabble of country folk who had joined the procession on the way, villagers from the houses below, and the inevitable riffraff of the roads. Even as she looked, she could see some of the helmeted figures trying to drive away the stragglers. But nowhere could she see the King.

When she reached the gate of the third wall, she saw the reason why. For as she appeared on the little platform over the gate, the mob fell back, and there on the farther brink of the chasm stood a single figure without helmet or sword or any sign of rank. It was the King in a straight tunic of coarse wool with his feet bare. Even as she looked upon him, he said nothing but bowed his head and struck his breast. For a full minute Matilda stood there staring at the apparition.

It was the voice of Arduino at her back that broke her astonishment. "I'll be damned if I'll let that rabble inside the walls. I've my hands full enough as it is."

"Let the bridge down," she answered.

"But those—"

"Tell the herald that none but the King and the leaders of his immediate party are to be admitted." She waited until the trumpets blew, and the voice of the herald, almost as clear and loud, had rung out his instructions. Then as the chains of the bridge rattled, she went to the stone steps behind the platform.

It was but a handful of men who stood in the gateway when she reached it. The rest milled about the end of the drawbridge, held back by the pikes of Arduino's men. She could hear their angry muttering. She looked at the King, who still stood with bowed head and his right hand on his breast. Then she called to Arduino in the middle of the bridge, "Tell any who have come with the King to stay in the village. The bailiff will shelter them, and I will send down food for them. The men from Bianello are to return to their post as soon as they have been fed. The rest are to go where they belong and stay there." There was an angry muttering in the crowd. Matilda looked at them. In the clear light of high noon they looked wretched enough, many of them. She turned to one of her men, "Tell Antonio to send out bread for these, too, before you drive them away." She had not raised her voice, but the word flew, for she had hardly turned her back to face the King, when a loud cry of cheering broke forth from the mob.

She was astonished at the change in the King's appearance. He said nothing but gazed at her piteously. And looking there at his soiled and purple feet and his bare tunic of coarse, penitential gray, she found it impossible to doubt the reality at least of the effort he was making.

"Cousin Matilda, you see me here a penitent. I beg you to tell the Pope I am here at his door." Nothing could exceed the gravity with which he spoke.

Matilda looked around the little half-circle standing at his back. The Bishop of Osnabrück, a portly person of great dignity, now invested with more than a touch of solemnity, two barons with a look of sullen resolution on their hard features, and the Countess Adelaide, grim, with a watchful eye on Henry. Behind them stood half a dozen men of obviously less consequence but all apprehensive and awe-struck in their demeanor. One, a young knight with an open, sensitive face in the clutch of his helmet, seemed on the point of weeping.

"Henry, I cannot let you come any farther until I have seen the Pope," she said desperately.

"I am willing to wait here until His Holiness will let me kneel at his feet," replied Henry, all submissiveness.

Adelaide of Susa made an impatient movement with the arm wrapped in her cloak, but apparently thought better of it, for she said nothing.

"There is a fire in the guardroom," suggested Matilda, "and I will send Antonio, my steward, to attend to your comfort. I will be back just as soon as I can."

"I prefer to wait here in the cold as a penitent should," said Henry, but his companions began at once to dissuade him.

The Pope showed no sign of surprise when Matilda told him that Henry was in the castle. Nor did he give any indication of anger or disappointment, but when Matilda, emboldened by the calmness with which he had received the news, pressed on to ask him for his pleasure, he looked at her in surprise.

"What should I want?" he asked. "I have told Henry I will not see him until Augsburg. He knew that before he left Germany."

He turned back to the papers on his table as if there were no more to be said. But as she paused in the doorway to look back at him, he added, "Remind your household that the King is excommunicate, and therefore Christians cannot associate with him." For a moment she stood there looking at him, but he did not raise his head. Only she noticed that as he began to dictate, his voice was dry and tense.

With a heavy heart and so ashamed that she looked neither to right nor left at the crowd of her supporters and guests, Matilda went through the two inner walls into the courtyard before the main gate. For a moment she paused outside the guardroom and listened. It seemed to her that it would be easier to go in, if she could hear the voices of her guests talking as men do when they wait, perhaps even laughing. But there was not a sound to be heard from behind the oaken door. Embarrassed at the thought that she might be taken to be spying, she hurried to knock. The door opened at once, and the whole company rose, as if with one movement, from the benches on which they had been sitting.

Adelaide of Susa was the only one to exclaim upon the Pope's cruelty. The rest received the news in silence. Henry, in particular, nodded as if it were quite what he had expected. But Matilda had an uncomfortable feeling that no one in the company was disposed to help her out of her probably all too obvious embarrassment.

To relieve the tension, she sat down and began to make courteous inquiries as to their comfort. Adelaide seemed about to make some demand or complaint, but Henry hastened to assure his hostess of his complete satisfaction with the comforts which she had sent to them. With a sense of relief at finding a bad fifteen minutes over, Matilda rose and excused herself. But before she could reach the door, the King had thrown himself on his knees before her.

Shocked, she backed against the wood, but Henry seized her robe. "Cousin

Matilda, I beg just one thing of you. Let me into the courtyard before the hall that I may stand there as a penitent beggar at the Pope's very gate."

"But he will not see you. It won't do any good, I assure you." She edged away from his clutch until it seemed as if the oaken door must yield to her frantic pressure.

But the King insisted. "That is not why I want to do it. I simply want by this public humiliation to demonstrate to the Pope that I am sincere in my sorrow and that before all men I acknowledge him as my spiritual father and confessor."

It seemed to Matilda that this could not be Henry speaking, but try as she would to read his face, she could find no hint or flicker of mockery in it.

"You know, Matilda, how my enemies have lied about me. If the Pope believes one-half the lies he has heard, he cannot trust the sincerity of my repentance. I want to demonstrate it in such a fashion that he cannot fail to see it," he added pathetically.

So accurately had he read her thoughts, so exactly had he answered them, that it seemed to Matilda that she could not endure the agony of her uncertainty any longer. But looking at him, she could not believe that he did not mean just what he said.

To escape and to gain time, she answered, "Tomorrow morning after Mass, then."

She did not stop for breath until she ran into Alberic in the courtyard before the hall.

"A very pretty idea," he said when she had told him of the promise she had just given.

"But it will embarrass the Pope."

"That is the beauty of it," was his grim answer.

When after supper that night, however, she told the Pope of Henry's request and of her promise, he answered simply, "It is nothing to me. You must decide such things as you think best. I have said all I am going to say to Henry until Augsburg."

He did not speak with any sign of reproof or displeasure, Matilda noted, but with a certain air of remoteness as if they had never been much more than strangers to each other. With a desolate sense of aloneness Matilda went to bed. Mechanically, she repeated the Lord's prayer, and too weary to think, she remembered all her dead in a brief prayer for mercy. It was not till the next morning that she realized that for the first time in months she had forgotten to say a prayer for the Pope's intention.

CHAPTER X

MASS had just begun when Matilda entered the chapel the next morning. But as she took her place in the chancel, she felt all eyes turn toward her. Indeed, as she looked round at the sound of a sudden disturbance in the nave, she saw that a large number of those in the body of the church had risen from their knees to see her the more clearly. She covered her face with her hands. But though she tried to loose her mind from the tether of the minute, she could not shut out from her consciousness the restlessness of the crowd in the chapel nor the sense of all the eyes watching her.

There was an image that often came to her mind when she thought of the mystery of prayer. Like most symbolic images, it was generalized in masses of light and shadow like something seen in a dream. It was of a small ship in a narrow harbor with the dead heat of the land engulfing it round and its one sail hanging limp from the stiff mast. Then suddenly came the wind out of the invisible air and filled the empty sail and blew the becalmed ship out into the unending spaces of the sea. And the wind sang in the ropes, and the white foam flew.

She thought of that picture this morning, but no wind came. Only the whisperings and the restless jostling of an excited crowd. Once she looked at the Pope when he had raised his head at the Elevation, but the complete absorption of his face, all the tension and the striving of the will lifted up in awe, only brought home to her the more movingly the desolation and emptiness of the moment. She was not sure that in such a mood of dead estrangement she should try to receive Communion at all, but if sore need were any claim upon the mercy of God, it seemed to her that she might offer that in place of the happier anticipations of devotion.

It was as the company in the chapel rose and made way for her to pass that she first realized that something had happened. It was not that she had found comfort or hope or peace. It was simply that she had ceased to thrash about in her loneliness and anxiety and confusion. For a moment she paused on the bottom step of the choir and looked at the faces turned to her. How alive they looked now in their curiosity and their anticipation of excitement! Her first revulsion of contempt yielded to a sudden sympathy with this childlike exhilaration. Smiling to those nearest the improvised aisle, she hurried out of the chapel.

She had hardly sat down in the middle of her table, when two of the men-at-arms rushed into the hall, their eyes goggling with excitement.

"The King!" cried one of them, ducking his knees to the table on the dais.

"I gave orders last night that he might come into the middle courtyard," said Matilda, looking around the half-circle of bishops and barons gathered at her board.

"He is at the inner gate—with bare feet," interrupted the second of the two men who had broken into the hall.

There was a cry from all over the room, and several of the men at the lower tables sprang up from the benches. The guests of honor were less precipitate in their response to the news, but they turned to their hostess, and several rested their hands on the table.

Matilda smiled at the gesture, and broke the piece of bread in front of her. Then slowly she lifted her cup and wet her lips. By the time she had set it down, the whole company was again settled to its breakfast, but the parallel lines of heads down the hall almost met over the narrow tables, and the buzz of conversation was choking. It was with relief that Matilda finally made an end to her pretense of eating, and rising, with a bow to her company, left the hall. The door of her chamber had not closed behind her before she heard the rush of feet to the courtyard door....

The girl Maria turned from the bed, holding the embroidered coverlet in her hands.

"All the rest of the household is in the courtyard looking at the King, Maria," said Matilda with a smile.

The girl blushed. "If you don't mind, I'll finish the bed first." Without a word Matilda lifted the other end of the coverlet. But the girl did not move in her horror. "Please, my lady. If anybody should see us."

"No danger. They're all staring at the King but you and I—and the Pope," she added. Then when the girl had smoothed out the heavy folds of the coverlet,

Matilda laughed, "Your fillet has slipped. Tie it quickly and come with me." As Maria straightened the linen band with excited fingers, Matilda tried not to think of Henry. He would beg her to intercede again, perhaps. Or, if Alberic were right, he would simply say nothing.

As they returned to the hall, Matilda noted without surprise that no effort had been made to clear the tables. A couple of the hunting dogs had leaped upon the benches and were pulling at a joint of meat. The fire was dying down in its ashes for want of fuel. Matilda heard a stir behind her and turned, thinking to find the Pope. But a lad from the kitchen in a greasy shirt was peering round the door of the Pope's chamber. The light of mischief still danced in his eyes as Matilda jerked him from the door and dragged him out of hearing distance. But it gave way to terror when he looked up into her face.

"What are you doing here?" He was a filthy little creature, but his face whitened under the grime.

"Please, don't kill me, my lady. I—I just looked at the Pope."

"What makes you think I would kill you, child?"

"The master said if I ever went into the hall, the Countess would kill me, put me on the spit and roast me like a pig."

Matilda laughed; then she sobered as the child's terror slowly yielded to wonder.

"If you'll go out into the kitchen and ask the servants there to put a pail of water over you, I'll give you a clean new shirt and a piece of ginger. And if anybody threatens to kill you, then you call out to me the next time you see me coming out of chapel. You will not forget to see that he gets the shirt and the ginger, will you, Maria?"

For a moment she looked toward the door standing ajar, and then as the child scampered off, she shrugged her shoulders. "Imagine trying to straighten out the whole world, Maria."

When she reached the courtyard between the hall and the chapel, she saw that the space before the open gate was jammed with people. The top of the wall on either side was crowded with still more, and some boys had straddled the top of the open gate. Indeed, as she looked around, she saw that the roof of the porch before the hall door was covered with scrambling, sprawling bodies, while the pigeons that usually roosted there flapped excitedly up and down the pavement below. Everywhere there was indescribable confusion, men running up and down from one vantage point to another, women shrieking and giggling as they slipped from their precarious perches or their neighbors in sudden fright clutched at them. The wind which had come down from the hills in the night tore and whipped at their clothing, but they seemed unconscious of its violence, as they turned and darted in swirls of brown and blue and green between the reddish-yellow walls.

For a moment there was even more confusion as Matilda strode into the middle of the courtyard. Then the crowd began to make way. One of the knights came to her rescue, and with his huge scarlet-robed shoulders began to clear a way, shouting threats of the wrath of the Countess as he thrust the curious aside. In a few moments the noise sank, and here and there a member of the household, catching the fixed eye of his mistress, began to slink shame-faced out of the scene. But for the most part the crowd, shoved out of its vantage point in the gateway, fell expectantly behind the Countess. Once or twice she turned upon them, but though they shrank from her glance, curiosity was clearly stronger than prudence.

Finally, she reached the gateway and looked out on the cobbled stretch between the inner wall and the circle of half walls, half towers and block-houses that girdled the lower stretch of the hill top. It was relatively clear, for Arduino and his men were, even as she looked, closing the lower gate and shouting all kinds of threats to the men-at-arms who still thronged the tops of the buildings and the walls. And there in the middle of the cleared space, facing her, stood the cause of all the excitement.

Henry was wearing the same short woolen tunic he had worn yesterday, but here in the bright light of early morning with the wind whipping its edges about his naked legs, it seemed even thinner and scantier. And his bare feet looked pinched and purple on the sunlight-spattered cobblestones. His hair, too, looked more unkempt, and his face was smudged with weeping. Nor did he raise his head when she confronted him.

So she stood looking at him for some minutes. Behind her she could hear the whispers of the more important members of her household, for excitement had sharpened their voices, and confusion had made her every sense more acute.

"So the scoundrel has owned himself beaten at last," said one surly voice with deep satisfaction.

"It is no way for a King to humiliate himself," grumbled another.

"The poor man is half frozen," whimpered a woman.

"If I were the Pope I'd let him have all the time he wants to cool off there," laughed a reckless young voice.

But an older voice broke in, "It is a good lesson for this lawless age. Too many of these young men think they can do anything they choose without fear of God or man."

"The Pope is not one to be trifled with," said another. So the voices went on. But the King seemed totally unaware of the crowd, so lightly, and often so gayly, passing judgment on him. And calling to mind his wonted arrogance of bearing, Matilda suddenly felt sorry for him.

"The spirit of penance is admirable, Henry," she said at last, while she felt the crowd at her back press forward to catch her low voice. "But the winter is too bitter, here, for carrying this sort of thing very far. You had better return to your quarters."

Henry sighed. "I am not going to leave here until the Pope allows me to throw myself at his feet and beg his forgiveness."

She looked narrowly at him. "Is that a challenge, Henry?"

The glance of sorrowful and forbearing reproach with which he replied made her feel ashamed of herself. "Is this evil time going to make even you suspicious, Matilda? It is the true sorrow of a penitent and nothing else that makes me stand here, and all I want to do to the Pope is to convince him that I am sincere, that my enemies have misrepresented me."

At her back Matilda could hear a sneer or two, but most of the murmuring was sympathetic.

When one laughing voice called out, "Wait till the cold nips his toes a little longer," there were instant cries of shame.

Matilda threw up her hands. "As you choose, Henry. If you want me, you have only to send any of the guards for me, and I will come."

Then she summoned Arduino and gave orders that all the space on both sides of the gate was to be kept clear of loiterers. Her next directions were given to the steward. The whole household was to be busied at once with their regular duties. As for the guests, she had heard that the extreme cold was driving the wolves down from the hills into the granges and villages. A hunt would not only be diverting but a contribution to her service. She noted, however, that though there was a general movement in response to her orders, there was no enthusiasm about her suggestions.

"What do you expect?" smiled Alberic. "This is the best show most of them will ever see, and you don't expect them to want to miss it, do you?"

"I must say," she retorted tartly, "that a new habit does not make a new man."

"Alas, Matilda, every monk that ever was knows that," he answered sadly. And without saying any more, he passed on into the hall.

From time to time, for the rest of the day, Matilda looked into the courtyard. Always she found someone scurrying out of sight as she appeared, and wherever she turned, in doorway or on the walls, watchers were visible. And everywhere she went, men of low rank and of high rank were whispering in two's and three's of the King's penance and wagering on whether the Pope would see the King that day.

But though twice Matilda made excuse to see the Pope and brought up the subject of Henry each time, she could get nothing but the same forbidding silence. As the day drew to its close, Henry's head seemed to sink lower on his breast, and his bare legs and arms grew almost black with the cold. No matter what orders Matilda gave, the number of watchers increased on roof and wall, and all through the castle the tension tightened until it seemed to her she could endure it no longer. But of all this, the Pope was, as far as she could see, completely oblivious. When he went for a walk, he chose the stable and workshop end of the castle, and though Matilda was constantly at his side, he kept up such a running fire of questions and comments on the things immediately under his eye, that she could find no chance to talk to him of the problems that lay heaviest on her mind. Indeed, he seemed completely unaware of the eager and awed curiosity that watched his every move and strained at his lightest word.

Only for a moment did she have respite from the anxiety gnawing into her consciousness. It was when they came into the shed behind the smithy that had been given to Hilary the Greek for a workshop. As they came into the dark little cave, he cried out in unaffected delight and ran to them with his work in his hand. As he held it up, Matilda saw that it was a golden cup of exquisitely simple design. The Pope took it into his hand and turned it around in the light of the doorway.

"I am beading the edge," explained the artist, pointing to the rough rim of the cup.

"I like it very much," said Gregory. "It is plain but good."

Hilary looked anxiously at the Pope. "But Madonna here has promised me five gems from her treasure to put a cross in the side. It will be quite rich enough then."

The Pope laughed. "Man, I meant to praise it. One sees so many things in which the maker has tried to cover up a weak or feeble idea with ornament that it is a pleasure to see something like this which can rest in its naked form."

The artist clapped his hands with delight. "Ah, that is it, Your Holiness, it is the idea that counts. This is simple because it says, 'It is the Bread within that counts and not the hands that made it.'"

"Even so," the Pope agreed. "I understand that I am to use this. If it is done in time, I promise that when I lift it up, I shall remember before God the man who was intelligent enough to understand what he was doing."

When they came out into the winter air again, the sun was setting, and Matilda shivered as she thought of the man without the gate. She must make one more effort.

"My lord Pope," she began humbly, "you know I should never presume to judge anything you did, but will not men say that this is severity rather than justice?"

"My daughter," responded the Pope soberly, "that is not my business. I shall not be judged by what men say of me, but by what I do. And what I do must have regard not to one man but to many."

So dismissed, Matilda hurried out to the darkening gate. Henry was nowhere to be seen. In the guardroom of the third wall she found him lying before the fire. At his side knelt Adelaide of Susa, chafing his feet and grumbling as she worked. The rest of his company sat in various attitudes of weariness and dejection about the room.

"It is no use, Henry," she said.

But his voice sounded almost cheerful as he answered, "Tell the Pope I will be there tomorrow."

CHAPTER XI

Matilda's first hope came on the morning of the third day. It was a dead-cold day, with no trace of the sun in the leaden sky, and a rawness in the heavy air that made the flesh ache. Henry had risen with the gray dawn and taken up his position before the gate. Hanging lankly in the unmoving air, his woolen tunic looked thinner and meaner than ever, and his long, uncombed hair and unwashed face made him look so dejected that all but the hardiest of his enemies cried out in pity. Arduino had given up as hopeless the effort to keep the court-yard clear, and Antonio threatened in vain to whip half the idle servants. As for those of higher rank present within the castle, Matilda abandoned all pretense of entertainment. Sick with contempt and helplessness, she watched them jostle their brilliantly colored mantles with the rabble between the walls, or walk the battlements, wagering with each other on the outcome of the day.

"They are no longer betting on whether the Pope will see Henry today but only on whether it will be before dinner or after," said Alberic, as Matilda crossed the inner courtyard on her way from the gate.

"They are shameless."

Alberic's full lips puckered. "They are helpless, and they might as well enjoy the spectacle."

"Of their betters eating out their hearts?" Her indignation had given way to the agony of the indecision.

"Remember, most men do not think their betters have hearts. Their callous-ness is their revenge on the world's inequality." Something gentle had come into the mocking voice, and again Matilda realized that here was more than the man she had known of old.

"Alberic, I think Henry means what he is doing." She waited for his denial.

"So do I," he answered cheerfully.

"But I don't think the Pope does." She scanned his face to separate the mockery from the sober earnest.

For a second his eyes teased her; then the mobile face darkened. "You should know by now that those are two entirely different categories, the Pope and the King. Matilda, Henry means what he is doing now with all his heart. He knows what he wants—his kingdom. He knows what he has to do to get it. He's doing it, and I must say he's doing it well."

"But penance means more than doing, surely, Prior Alberic."

"That is a different matter," said Alberic sadly. "There is where the children of this world have the advantage of the children of light—for this world."

"Then you don't believe Henry either?" Her heart sank as she remembered that she was even now on her way to appeal to the Pope's mercy afresh.

"Do you?"

She shivered. "I do, and I don't. It sounds silly."

"And yet you are on your way to plead with the Pope again for him! God knows I'm not mocking you, Matilda, but there is the heart of the situation. You know the difference between what you want to be so and what is. So does the Pope. You feel that you must tell the truth whatever the cost, even if telling the truth means that you lose what you want. Henry is free of any such scruples. That is why if I were wagering like my friends here, I would put my money on him."

"Then we are beaten."

"Yes, in that sense you are. But don't look so frightened, Matilda. You know what you have to do. That is a good deal."

"But what should I do?"

"Go on and be beaten."

At that moment Hugh of Cluny appeared in the doorway of the hall behind his brother monk and looked at Matilda. Without a word Alberic passed on.

"The Pope has been talking to me, my lady. I think he may listen to you." There was something gently flattering in the way Hugh's voice rested on the last syllable. But Matilda said nothing.

As she entered the Pope's chamber, he looked up. The heavy lines seemed to have sunk deeper into the dark face, but there was no break or sag in the firmness of his mouth or the directness of his gaze. Looking on his face, Matilda felt something of that cool resolution pass into her own consciousness.

She had intended to fling herself at his feet, but now she came over to his chair and knelt down quietly.

"Do you think I should see him, Matilda?" he asked gravely.

"Yes, Your Holiness." She waited. She could hear the heavy breathing of Brother Paulo at her back, but the Pope's face seemed unmoved.

"Why?"

It seemed as if that brief challenge suddenly focused all her thoughts, and clear out of the confusion as if from quite outside herself came her answer, "Because, my lord, he is a penitent come to ask pardon of a priest."

For some moments he looked steadily at her without saying anything. Then he spoke in his most matter-of-fact tones, "Surely you know that a priest is bound to use every reasonable precaution to make sure of his penitent's sincerity? To neglect that is to allow the sacrament to be profaned."

She looked up into his face. "I know, my lord, but what more can he do than he has done to show his sincerity?" She clasped her hands on her breast and shivered to find them cold.

"There is one thing more he can do, and that is to put his crown and scepter in my hands and resign his kingdom to wait until I shall have a chance to inquire into the justice of the things that are urged against him, at Augsburg."

"And if he does that, my lord?"

"I will see him at once." With a little nod he dismissed her. Even as she opened the door, she heard his voice resuming the dictation she had interrupted.

She faced the crowd in the hall with sudden fear. She shook her head, but they cheered. They fell back at once, however, when she started for the court-yard; and when in the courtyard she begged them not to follow her, they stayed choked together in front of the hall and porch.

Henry did not seem to hear her when she first spoke to him. Then when she had repeated the Pope's terms, he looked at her with the petulant pathos of a man who finds himself being trifled with when he is most serious.

"But, Matilda, that is what I have done in substance in leaving my kingdom and coming here. What more does he want?" Watching her face closely, he added, "Not but what I am resolved to do anything I can to give satisfaction to His Holiness." Then as she still waited uncertainly, he added in a low voice so that the crowd, hitherto held back by awe of the Countess' presence but now pressing about them, might not hear, "Go, see my friends."

Though Adelaide of Susa was the only one to call it cruelty, all the King's party agreed that to insist on this further humiliation was to bruise a broken reed. Short of that, they were all ready, lay and cleric alike, to swear that the King would keep any promises the Pope would see fit to exact. She had to be content with that.

As she started back to the second wall, the Archbishop of Salerno rode through the outer gate and stopped his horse at her side.

"Henry is still there?" he asked, as he dismounted with some difficulty.

Walking up the space between the walls, she told him what had happened.

"I think the Pope will not insist on his giving him his crown," he said thoughtfully. "Henry would break the promise at once, anyway. Moreover, in-sistence on anything like that would give color to Henry's complaint that what the Pope wants is to take all the power in the world, secular as well as spiritual."

"Will you come with me?"

"Yes, and here is Hugh coming, too. We will take him with us."

The Pope listened in silence to Matilda's report. Then he looked at the Archbishop.

But Hugh broke in before the slow-moving Alfanus could speak. "I think to insist on Henry's giving up his crown would be to run the risk of handing Germany over to anarchy."

The Pope looked at him quickly and looked away. "My lord Archbishop?"

"Hugh has perhaps put it a little strongly. But to insist on such a requirement would not gain us anything that will not be equally well served by Henry's undertaking to abstain from any display of his insignia or any exercise of authority."

"What guarantees have we that he will keep those promises?" From the coolness of his voice, thought Matilda, no one would think that Gregory had any interest in the outcome of this discussion.

Hugh's face lighted. "I will promise for the King, and so will the Bishop of Osnabrück, and the Lady Adelaide, and all the knights who are with him."

"I hope you can persuade him to keep it," said the Pope sadly. Then as his friends said nothing, he rose from his chair and looked around the little half-circle. "I will see Henry."

"Not here," he added, as Hugh made a move toward the door. "But in the hall."

Matilda hesitated. "My household is grown so unruly, my lord, that I am not sure I can keep the room clear."

The Pope unclasped his hands and lifted them slightly. "There is no need. This concerns the whole world."

By the time the dais at the back of the hall had been cleared and swept, and the chair in which Beatrice had always sat when she heard disputes and gave justice had been set in the middle, the hall was full of people. It seemed as if all the company within the fortress, from the highest to the lowest, had assembled within the four walls of the hall. The women and children of the household stood on the benches or sat on the trestle tables to look over the heads of the men-at-arms and peasants and craftsmen who in canvas tunics and leather jerkins lined the stone walls, now and then with their restless jostling making the weapons behind them ring out in a din, matched only by the jangle of their own voices. It was with the greatest difficulty that Arduino and a small guard of his men kept the space about the hearth and a lane to the door of the courtyard open.

And still lord and bishop and abbot in their mantles of scarlet and purple and black pressed on to the dais to take their places at the Pope's side as their rank gave them claim. Everywhere the air was warm and vibrating with the din of men's voices and the roar of their laughter as some momentary accident or jest moved them. High and low seemed suddenly to be released from a great anxiety, and the lofty-timbered lacings of the roof rang with the joyous tumult.

At the last moment, Matilda remembered that Henry's knees would be stiff from the cold and the hours of standing. So she bade the steward bring her a rug from the sacristy and the maids sweep the straw from the pavement of the dais. There was a hearty laugh from all sides when, with Alberic's help, she spread the sanctuary rug in front of the footstool, and the laugh rose to a roar when with her own hands she placed a second cushion on the footstool.

"Little man or not, the Lord Gregory is master of the world today," said a clear voice, as the roar broke down into a ripple of laughter. There was a loud cheer, and Matilda turned to face the open door of the Pope's chamber. The cheering redoubled until it had risen to a tempest of applause, but the Pope stood there in his red robes with a flame-colored mantle thrown back from his shoulders, looking at the crowd with inscrutable soberness. Then he raised his right hand, and slowly the cheering died away as first those nearest him and presently the whole company sank to their knees.

Only when he had seated himself, did any of the throng rise. But though everybody pressed as close to the Pope as he could, there was absolute silence, for it seemed to each of the crowd before his chair that those keen eyes were fixed on him alone. Then when he was satisfied as to the order in the great hall, he nodded to Hugh of Cluny, who stood by the door, waiting with his eyes fixed on Gregory's face. It was a slight gesture, but it seemed as if the waiting throng, silent before, now held its breath. Only the Pope seemed to be as calm as ever, his right hand clasping lightly one of the pillars of his chair.

The hand tightened its grip on the wood of the pillar, and looking up, Matilda saw that Henry had entered the hall. While his friends knelt before the dais, Henry waited with bowed head. Then as if a spring had been released, he rushed forward and flung himself on the carpet at the Pope's feet, sobbing.

Through her tears Matilda saw the look of surprise on Gregory's face. Then, before anybody could speak, he had sprung to his feet and with a cry of joy, he had raised the battered figure and clasped him to his breast. And from all over the hall rose a pandemonium of cheers and thanksgivings and blessings.

CHAPTER XII

"LET me see if we have it all here," said the Pope, taking the parchment from the hand of Alberic. Slowly, he checked the items: "Will appear before the council and answer all charges and abide by our decision...whatever the outcome will not try to take vengeance on anyone...until the conference will not wear his regalia or perform any action of authority... those who have sworn oaths to him will be free...will dismiss Robert of Babenberg and his other evil counselors... if confirmed in his kingdom, will obey the pontiff and cooperate with him in correction of abuses in the Church."

Hugh of Cluny and Matilda nodded. Alfanus of Salerno hesitated. "There was something more, wasn't there?"

"Yes," said Alberic, "if he shall be found to have sworn with false intention in any of these things, he shall be considered to have forfeited his absolution."

The Pope took the quill and wrote in the additional clause. "There is nothing more, is there?"

"No," said the Archbishop of Salerno, "except to petition Heaven for a miracle, that he may keep them."

The face of Hugh went crimson with indignation. "Your Holiness—"

"We're all tired, Hugh," said the Pope. "Matilda, will you and Hugh take these two papers out to Henry and ask him if he has any fault to find with them?"

"He had better not," said one of the cardinals who had that day just arrived from Rome, and was rather disposed, Matilda had discovered, to stand on the letter of the Tribur agreement. Indeed, he had made no secret of his belief that the Pope in consenting to see Henry at all had done a weak thing. Nor was it difficult for Matilda to guess where he laid the responsibility for the Pope's sudden weakness. More than once in the evening's work he had interposed a contemptuous reference to the well-known tendency of women to prostitute judgment to sentiment.

"Remember, my brother," said the Pope gently, "that what is to come after depends not on what is forced from the King but what of his free will he undertakes to do. Compulsion only lasts for the emergency."

But the rest Matilda lost as Hugh held the door open for her.

Henry was asleep by the fire in the guest chamber which Matilda had assigned to him, and at first sight all the rest of his company seemed to be asleep with him. But before Matilda could move to wake him, Adelaide of Susa stepped out of the shadows by the bed, and reached out her hand for the papers. Matilda hesitated.

"I will read them aloud," said Adelaide, "and then we will all know where we are."

To Matilda there was something astounding in this suspicion, but when she saw the roughness with which Adelaide shook Henry awake, she began to wonder if now that the emergency was over, the strange partisanship of Adelaide for the man who had made her daughter's life so hard were to end as suddenly as it had begun.

Henry, instantly awake, though still blinking, nodded his approval when Adelaide had finished reading the terms to him, and looking at Hugh and Matilda with a smile, said, "That I have promised, and that I will perform."

"God help you if you don't," said Adelaide, vindictively.

"Tomorrow morning the bell will ring us all to the hall," Matilda hastened to explain. "And there we will swear for you, Henry, and sign the copies of the agreements."

"I shall never forget, Matilda and Hugh, what you have done for me these days," said Henry. As he rose from his chair, the candlelight shone in his eyes, and Matilda saw that they were filled with tears.

"I wanted peace as much as you did, Henry," she answered gravely. But he only stared at her. And then as for the first time in weeks she remembered the things he had said of the Pope and of her, she felt the blood rush to her face. She was grateful for the darkness of the hall and for the silence of Hugh as she made her way back to the Pope's chamber.

The last she saw of the Pope's face that night, it looked so weary that it seemed as if all the vital, personal energy had drawn back into some center deeply hidden below the burnt-out eyes and the frozen lips. But she was so tired, herself, that she could only stagger to the maids' chamber, where she was sleeping these days. Alberic, seemingly still fresh and awake after all the triumph and anxiety of the day, held a taper at her side as she went. But though he lifted it high as she stood in front of her chamber door, she had plunged headlong against the wood before she realized that there was anything there.

The shock awakened her, and she struggled to her feet, to find a man slowly raising himself on his elbow and blinking at her. In a second, he was kneeling before her, his face white with horror. It was Hilary the Greek.

"What are you doing here?" Alberic seized him by the shoulders.

Instantly the man's face warmed and lighted. And he took from the breast of his tunic something wrapped carefully in dirty linen. In spite of her weariness, Matilda found herself smiling. For Hilary the Greek had brought the gold cup. Proudly, he lifted it into the candlelight and turned it round so that the radiance would fall on the shining cross of jewels.

The monk, still holding the candle in his hand, stared at the glittering eyes of the artist as if fascinated.

"Is it not beautiful, Alberic?" Matilda asked. It was lovelier even than she had anticipated in its graceful lines, with strength in the slightly beveled fluting of the base and in the clean curve of the bowl away from the gleaming cross.

"But man, did you not know that your mistress had been busy with far other things these days? Where have you been?"

The Greek stared at the monk with equal surprise. "Where—why in my shop, polishing my cup. When those foolish women who brought my meat tried to talk to me, I drove them out. What is it all to me if my cup is finished?"

Alberic laughed and took the chalice from the man's hand. "You are quite right. And now the Countess, who has had to listen all these days to the foolish women and still more foolish men, is very tired, and we must let her go into her chamber."

But Matilda took the cup from Alberic's hand, and holding it to her breast she said, "I will give this to the Pope tomorrow, and he will give the King his Communion from it when he takes him into the chapel."

The next day seemed to Matilda to pass in a dream. To begin with, though it was already a couple of hours past the dawn, the morning was so dark that when the company met in the great hall, it seemed as if they had come dimly together in some half-lighted cave of the night. Even the torches which at Matilda's order soon smoked down the length of the two walls, seemed with their pale red glow only to emphasize the surrounding gloom.

But there was a moment's brilliance when the seven cardinals who were to take the oath for the Pope that he would in all things act as a fair and impartial judge between Henry the King and his enemies took up their place between the fire and the dais, and with lighted candles in their hands and their scarlet cloaks falling back from their lifted right arms, swore to keep faith with Henry and to see that his enemies did him justice. Then the black-robed Hugh and several of the purple-mantled bishops and knights with gleaming swords came and stood around Adelaide of Susa and Matilda and took the oath for the King. Only Hugh because of his monastic vows did not raise his right hand, but when the others had sworn, he stepped forward and solemnly promised on the King's behalf to keep the conditions of the agreement.

The rest passed very quickly, the King kneeling and in a low voice making his public confession of broken promises and sacrilegious attack upon the authority of the Church, the Pope with lighted tapers held on either side, pronouncing the solemn words of absolution.

The Pope had taken the King by the hand to lead him into the chapel when Matilda remembered the Greek. There he was kneeling beside the door with anxious eyes fixed upon her. Briefly, she recalled to Gregory the circumstances of the gift and bade the Greek present his cup to the Pope. For a moment, the Pope gazed in astonishment at the interruption; then as he looked into the shining eyes of the artist, he smiled and blessed him. It was the first time Matilda saw the Pope smile that day and the last.

Even when the Te Deum rose on all sides from the crowded church, and Matilda kneeling in her place inside the chancel screen saw the galaxy of tapers burning on the altar swim into a mist through her tears, there was no lightening of the awed solemnity on the Pope's face. Never had she seen his dark face so still and pale, as if carved out of old ivory, as when he turned to the congregation and holding Hilary's shining cup in his hands raised the Host. And when the King, looking somewhat awed and a little frightened, knelt before him to receive Communion, though a shiver of excitement ran through the chapel, the Pope's face lost none of its look of remoteness.

It warmed a little when side by side with the King the Pope came down the center of the chapel and all the company broke into a delirium of praise and applause. Men who had not spoken to each other for years embraced with the tears running down bearded cheeks, and women fainted with the excitement. But though the Pope bowed with grave courtesy to the plaudits, the dark eyes were unchanged. Matilda remembered how once she had caught a glimpse of a sea captain's gaze in a storm at sea. Gregory's eyes had that same look of being calmly fixed on a remote point.

Again at the banquet which the Pope offered to the King that day, though he
was, throughout, the alert and gracious host, pledging Henry and acknowledging
his toasts with every appearance of cordiality, the grave stillness never left his face.
He shared his silver trencher with the King, he offered him his cup to drink from,
he selected the candied fruits from a little casket which a company of merchants
on the road had presented to him, and placed them before his guest. He listened
attentively to Henry's complaints of his enemies and of the ill fortune which had
dogged him from the days of his youth. In low tones that could hardly have carried beyond Matilda, sitting on the other side of Henry, the Pope talked to him
paternally of the duties and obligations of kings. In all these things he behaved
with a perfection of tact and courtesy that quite clearly at once abashed and delighted Henry. But it seemed to Matilda that throughout it was as if a mask had
been drawn over Gregory's face, as if its habitual honesty and candor were veiled.

It was already night when Matilda returned from escorting Henry to Bianello. She had been uneasy when she found herself alone with him without the
restraining influence of the Pope's presence. And she had tried to keep either
Hugh or Alberic at her side, but as the road narrowed, there was barely room
for two riders. Yet she need not have been disturbed, for Henry had proved his
most charming self, gay in his new-found freedom from the worry of months,
optimistic in his plans for his kingdom once his troubles were over, enthusiastic
about the loyalty of his friends, and generous in his appreciation of the Pope's
kindness. Indeed, he spoke of Gregory in such a fashion as to give Matilda a
great deal of pleasure. It was therefore with a glow of triumph and content such
as she had not known for many a day that she saw Henry ride off with his company on the last turn of the road to Bianello.

It was growing late, and Hugh and Alberic were obviously tired. Once as
they rode along in silence, she felt rather than saw Alberic's quizzical glance
upon her face, but when she turned inquiringly to him, his eyes fell, and he made
no attempt to break the silence of the winter twilight. Even Arduino, who had
at first been disposed to talk a good deal of what he would do with his men now
that things would be a little closer to normal, gradually subsided and rode along,
half-nodding on his horse. So Matilda had several hours of pleasant thought
alone with herself as she came down the darkening roads of the plain.

She was startled when they reached the village at the bottom of the hill to
catch a gleam of light from the high-piled darkness at the top. But as they rode

up to the outer wall of the fortress, and the sound of singing and the sweet shrill-ness of the flute came to her, the fire of her triumph leaped up afresh. So pleased was she that when they had to wait some minutes for the drawbridge to fall, and Arduino began to talk of hanging the drunkards who left the walls unattended with the Pope inside, she laughed and bade him think that never again would they have such good cause to feast and sing.

And though Arduino's indignation waxed hotter and hotter as they passed through the almost deserted courtyards, her own spirits rose for all her weariness. So when they reached the door of the great hall, she was frankly ready to be pleased with the revelry she expected.

Nor was she disappointed. Never since she was a child, had she seen the hall look so bright or so cheerful. A huge fire roared on the hearth, its wind-blown flames cutting the shadows with long arms of light. All down the walls torches glowed red in their iron sockets, now leaping up so that their light touched the dark angles of the timbered roof into fantastic shapes of terror, now guttering smokily against the grayish-yellow stone. Even the ancient swords and axes and shields grimly festooning the walls tossed back gay flecks of light, while up and down the long tables the pewter cups and the black leathern pitchers shone dus-kily in the light of hundreds of tallow candles.

But brightest of all were the wine-glazed eyes of the revelers, who, with heads tossed back and laughing mouths, sang at the top of their lungs, beating out the measure with their cups on the oaken tables before them. Knight and man-at-arms sat together indiscriminately with serving-man and woman lean-ing over their shoulders to miss none of the mirth. Only a few of the older lords sat with some of the clergy at the long dais table. On a sudden impulse Matilda shut the main door and started round to the back of the hall to look for a little side door where she could slip in without spoiling the fun.

There was no moon that night, but the high windows of the hall shed a dim, foggy radiance into the dark courtyard. As she passed the chapel, she looked up at it casually, and in the dim light she thought she saw a strip of shadow along the jamb of the door. At this hour it should be locked. For the first time she was a little annoyed at the lack of order she had just been enjoying. There was no one in sight. On the other side of the wall she could hear Arduino scolding, but here there was no sign of life. Quietly, she slipped into the chapel porch. The door was ajar, but when she reached to shut the door, it swung wide open, and she caught the dull reddish-gold light of the sanctuary lamp swinging slowly in the darkness overhead. It was the sight of that swinging point of light that reminded her that not since morning had she given thanks for the joy and the victory of this day. Now that her eyes were accustomed to the darkness, she saw that the light from the hall windows grayed a little the sanctuary so that behind the sanctuary lamp she could discern the marble canopy of the altar. It was a feeble thing, this ghost of light, but it dispelled her fear of the dark and the loneliness of the place, and she sank to her knees.

As she bowed her head, she was startled to hear in front of her a low sob. She caught her breath.

Then she heard a voice, half-strangled with agony, "If it be Thy will, if it be Thy will!" It was the voice of the Pope.

She tried to move, but her feet were lead. She tried to peer into the darkness, but the thin light swam from her vision. Presently, wherever she looked, the little mist of light was dancing. She tried to speak, but no sound came from her dry lips. Only the pounding of the blood in her temples, and that terrible cry over and over, like water falling drop by drop in a still place! Presently the busy mind had stretched its tentacles over the confusion. And she saw the face of the Pope as it had looked last night, and this morning, and when the King took his leave. Somehow she stumbled to her feet and groped her way out of the chapel.

Putting her hand on the door jamb, she tugged at the iron ring until the oak scraped her hand. Then for a moment she stood trembling in the porch. The singing from the hall had risen again to a low roar, but in the dim light from the windows nobody was to be seen anywhere about. Only the jagged masses of roofs, rising one above the other, with now and then the somber grace of turret or tower to break the hard shadows, met her eye, and above them the blank gray of the sky. "It will do the Pope no good for you to stand here," said one voice within her throbbing brain. But she knew she could not leave him alone there in the dark. Yet before that anguish the ordinary impulse of pity shrank back as from contemplated blasphemy.

She stood in the courtyard between the hall and the chapel, uncertain. Presently, she had lost consciousness of everything but a wordless intercession. There was no sound now from the hall, and the mist of light had faded. Only high on the dark walls the slots of yellow-white revealed where the flickering torches still picked out the windows. A slight jarring of wood behind startled her.

The next moment a swiftly moving body brushed past and stopped.

"My lord!" she cried into the darkness.

"Matilda?" There was a shock of surprise in the husky voice.

For a moment they stood there, not moving. Then the Pope spoke with something more like his wonted calm, "It is too cold for you to be out here."

"I know," she said, pulling herself together and trying to hold her teeth from chattering. "I didn't want to disturb them."

Without any more words they groped their way back to the hall door, and the Pope opened it. She shivered as she stood and looked at the desolation before her. Most of the candles on the tables had burned out. Here and there one guttered feebly in a cup of molten tallow. The walls were dark. Only the fire still burned redly and fitfully, now and then throwing out a feeble splash of light on some dark mass slumped shapelessly over the table or fallen into a heap against a bench.

For some minutes they stood in front of the fire without speaking. Presently Matilda became aware of the Pope's hand, white against his red robe, clenching and unclenching as if it were struggling with the labor of speech. She looked up at him. His face, seen now and then in the movement of the firelight, stood out from the gray air startlingly in masses of black and white. And again she had the sense of a mask held firmly over a chaos of pain.

"My lord," she cried, sinking to her knees on the stone hearth.

The fire leaped up, and she saw his face for a moment. Something very gentle and pitiful looked out of the somber eyes, but he did not move. For several minutes he stood there, looking at her very steadily.

"It is defeat," he said at last, holding up his tightly clenched hands. "It is defeat. We shall not build the City of God in our day, Matilda. We have given the King his kingdom, and he will use it to rise up against us in his arrogance."

"I think it was the only thing to do," she said slowly, not rising from her knees.

"God knows." Then as she caught her breath in a spasm of fear, he spoke half to her, half to himself, "It is hardest to have done wrong when we thought to do right." She looked up, dashing the tears from her eyes that she might see his face. She saw his hand lifted as if to rest on her head, but it did not come near her.

"Matilda," he said, speaking slowly and gravely, "Our Lord never promised that we should win even in His cause and for His sake. He only said that so long as we held fast to Him, He would not forsake us."

He looked down at her quietly for a full minute, and it seemed as if now the mask had fallen, and the naked soul of the man looked out of those cavernous eyes. "Unto the consummation of the world," he added softly. He said the words like a benediction, and involuntarily she bowed her head. When she lifted it again, she was alone, and the glowing heaps of ashes on the hearth were falling apart in showers of sparks that for a moment glowed in the empty air and were gone.

✳ BOOK V ✳

A GOLD CUP

CHAPTER I

It seemed to Matilda that of all the many journeys she had taken to Rome, this to the Lenten Synod of 1080 was the hardest. Even for early March, it was bitterly cold on the roads, and the rain fell day after day seemingly without any prospect of ever stopping. At first, Matilda and her party had hugged the fires of friendly castles and monasteries, while the rain beating on the roof churned the roads to mud. But as the days went on, more and more alarming reports began to trickle through from the north until she decided that she must not let the weather hold her back any longer.

It was easier to be rash, because she was traveling with so small a company. The restlessness in her territories, the uncertainty as to when Henry might descend into Italy, the constant pressure from the insurgent bishops of Lombardy, had all combined to make her unwilling to disturb the present disposition of her forces. Moreover, Arduino had flatly refused to leave the Mantuan lands, where trouble threatened to break out momentarily, for any dull chapter meetings in Rome. She had therefore summoned a small company of her most dependable knights, ancient vassals of her family or generous youths thirsting for high-minded adventure, and her old friend, the Prior of San Benedetto, to escort her to Rome. The indolences and the cautions and the self-interests of middle age she left for the heavy hand of Arduino to deal with, and set out, unencumbered, on what she had planned would be a record-breaking journey to the Holy City. But the remarkably inclement weather had made pulp of her plans, and now she was straining every nerve merely to arrive before any of the crucial decisions of the Synod should have been taken.

There was plenty of chance for thought and worry, however, as she rode doggedly through the pelting rain with her head bowed almost to her horse's neck. For huddled in a riding hood of thick wool with the rain stinging her face every time she tried to look about her, she found conversation quite impossible. At the same time the mud sucking in her horse's hooves and sloshing to her own knees made progress infinitesimally slow and exhausting. Only the restless mind, sharpened by its own anxiety and the seemingly universal recalcitrancy of the physical world, raced over all its preoccupations, past and present, without seeming ever quite able to come to grips with them.

It was more than three years since Canossa now, and yet she could not see that she was any nearer to the peace of which she had dreamed. She crouched lower to avoid the rain-sodden boughs that had fallen almost across her path, and in so doing she lost control of her horse. The surprised creature started nervously and stumbled in a pool in the middle of the road. For a moment both horse and rider were covered with the flying water. Then the desperate creature managed to regain its footing.

"Just a little deeper and you would not have had to decide what to do with Henry," said Alberic sympathetically, as he helped her to pull herself together again.

She tried to laugh, but the mud seeped into her eyes, and she had to wipe it out with her handkerchief. In opening her cloak, she had let the rain drizzle in, and now she was shivering. But as usual Alberic had probed to the quick of her anxieties. In a way, she was relieved. There was no use trying to dodge the issue to which all her thoughts kept incessantly returning. If there was any truth to the continuous reports that the Saxons were sending, indeed, she ruefully admitted, by this time had sent, envoys to Rome to demand some settlement of the affairs of Germany, it would be impossible to dodge the issue any longer. Even if they were not prepared to press for the recognition of Rudolf of Swabia as King for which they had been contending now these years, the disorder of Lombardy and increasingly of all Italy would force the Pope to make some decision.

It was no comfort to her now to reflect that it was largely due to her influence that the Pope had been so incredibly patient with Henry. Not that she was alone in her responsibility. Hugh and the Archbishop of Salerno and Desiderius had seconded her efforts to persuade the Pope to remain neutral in the struggle between Henry and Rudolf. And she felt certain that most of the time the Pope had been not unwilling to be persuaded. The very extremes of personal outrage to which Henry had gone, when right after the dramatic penitence of Canossa he had first lured the Pope to a conference and then tried to ambush him, had made Gregory doubly hesitant about severity. Implacable as she knew him to be when he thought some issue of principle was involved, she knew also that no conscience could be more delicate than his when there was a possibility that personal pique might influence his actions. But even more constantly than these very real motives of personal generosity, she knew that the Pope's determination to free the Church forever from its subjection to the power of the Empire made him hesitate to commit his interests of principle and ideal to the very rough and ready arbitrament of the rivalry for secular power. He did not wish to see that city of which he had dreamed made one of the contending pawns in a duel for power. That city—she shuddered. The Saxons with their peasant hordes fighting savagely for obsolete customs, with their gibes at the Pope's hesitation, "The cock must crow thrice before Peter answer," what could they know of the Pope's dream?

She shuddered and crouched closer to the warm body of her horse. The stale pungency of the mud, the acrid dankness of the wool filled her nostrils. For three years now she had made every allowance for Henry. "It isn't love of the Pope or enthusiasm for religion that is swelling the ranks of Rudolf," Henry had passionately insisted when again she went into Germany, a year ago. "It is greed for the imperial lands, it is hatred of the power of the King to crush local tyranny and enforce justice upon feudal arrogance." She had done him justice when she reported his words to the Pope, and the Pope had held his hand. But in all the three years since his submission at Canossa, Henry had given no sign of any effort to fulfill the promises he had made there.

And now—even as she struggled on to Rome through impassable roads, she knew that always the influence of Henry was gnawing away at the order and the loyalty of her own lands. For the most part, the trouble was nothing that she could put her fingers on. In Lucca it was the clergy who bought their offices and flaunted their wives in the faces of all, who rebelled against the bishop and the overlord who tried to restore order. In Mantua it was the greedy and ambitious nobility who saw in troubled times their chance to add to their lands and escape their dues. But the first would not have been so bold but for the hope that a triumphant Henry would end the reforming endeavors of a weak and subservient papacy. And the second would not have dared to risk her vengeance but for the certainty that the King of Germany would condone any breach of faith and support any rebellion that would embarrass the Pope or his friends.

There was little she could prove. In her last interview with Henry she had charged him with all this, and his only reply had been a protest of injured innocence. Even now in the cold and wet her blood boiled as she remembered how he had looked at her with tears in his eyes and had cried, "Even you, Matilda, have let your confidence be poisoned with all these lies about me. How can a good woman believe such calumny of an unfortunate man whose enemies have encompassed him to ruin him?" For a moment she had believed him, and Henry had cunningly gone on to tell her of the rapacity of the clergy who had been fighting him, and of the barbarism of the Saxons. At the time she had believed him! No wonder the nobles whose ambitions his promises flattered should not scrutinize his claims too closely.

Yet the facts stared them in the face, as they had her when she had been moved by his pathetic protests. In the teeth of his promises he had tried to seize his kingdom without waiting for the meeting he had sworn to abide by. He had laid violent hands upon the possessions of all who had sought to thwart him. Repeatedly he had put his creatures into the chairs of bishop and abbot without any regard for the rights of the Church, which he had sworn to uphold. She could not wonder that the Pope should find the cup of his faithlessness filled to overflowing.

It seemed to her now, as they slogged through the seemingly endless mud of the Campagna, that there was no bar that prudence or clemency could put in the way of the anger and indignation that filled her heart whenever she thought of Henry and the outrages that she had endured at his hand. Surely, three years was long enough—

Yet when at last she staggered into Rome nearly exhausted from the miles of rain and morass, she was shocked to hear that already the sentence of excommunication had been renewed against Henry, and the kingdom of the faithless excommunicate declared forfeit. There was a rumor, too, of a crown that the Pope had sent to Rudolf.

"It is about time," said Adelaide of Susa, who was staying at the house of the Pierleone where Matilda had stopped for fresh linen and dry clothes.

Matilda said nothing but gazed wearily into the fire. Wine within, food, dry clothes, a bath, and the warmth of the charcoal fire in the brazier had combined to revive the exhausted body, but she was sick at heart.

"But can Rudolf make peace?" she asked at length.

"Can he?" snorted Adelaide. "At least he will try, and you know how much effort Henry has made."

Idly, Matilda remembered how indignant Adelaide had been against the Pope over his delay in seeing Henry at Canossa, and how Henry had gibed at the profit she had made of his misfortunes. Rudolf, too, was her son-in-law, and, as all the world knew, an incomparably better husband. Yet Matilda found her disappointment sharpening with contempt for Adelaide.

"If Henry should make the effort, it would be successful," persisted Matilda, unable to let go of the hope that had made her bear so much these last days.

Adelaide sat down and looked curiously at her guest. "You know that in that fight on the Elster in January Rudolf beat Henry?"

"But Henry is still in the field."

"With the Pope supporting Rudolf, really supporting him now, Henry will have to yield," said Adelaide, a look of cunning making little points in her small, dark eyes.

"You know that is not what the Pope is interested in. What he wants is the independence of the Church. Do you think he will let the Church be made Rudolf's tool any more than Henry's?" As soon as she had spoken, Matilda knew that she had been foolish.

For Adelaide stared coldly at her. "If what you mean is that the Pope is interested simply in his own power, I rather think I agree with you."

Shame at her own folly in discussing the Pope's purposes where they could only be misunderstood and anger at Adelaide made her cheeks burn. She was not sorry that at that moment Alberic knocked at the door to escort her to the Lateran.

At first, the Pope was disposed to apologize for not delaying the meeting until the most important of his lay supporters should have arrived. Matilda was grieved to see him looking so uncertain and troubled, and hastened to assure him that leaving as little leeway as she had for a journey that at this time of year was bound to be uncertain, she had no right to be disappointed that she was late.

It was the Archbishop of Salerno who cut short the Pope's apologies and Matilda's embarrassment by explaining that the Saxon delegates had been so excited with their grievances and the triumph of their recent victory that it was impossible to keep them waiting any longer.

Matilda was astonished, for it was like nothing she knew of the Pope to be thus impressed by the confidence of victory. And though she had known him always patient with human weakness and anxiety, she had never known him to be compliant with the impatience of self-will. She tried to conceal her surprise, but she must have succeeded very ill, for she looked up at the Pope to find him smiling at her.

"Of course," said Desiderius, with that quick eagerness of his that at times like these made him seem so much younger than the troubled and aging Pope, or the dignified Archbishop, or even the gentle and anxious Hugh, "that was a crushing blow which Rudolf gave Henry on the Elster."

The line of the Archbishop's mouth straightened, but there was a gleam in the eyes of the Pope as he leaned forward. "I have just finished talking with Altman of Passau. He assures me that Rudolf has not a chance in the world if Henry uses even the commonest intelligence in his dealings with the nobility of Germany. And Henry is very clever, as everybody here knows, when it is a matter of getting what he wants."

"Then, Your Holiness—" cried Hugh in astonishment and stopped, unable to go any further.

Again the Pope smiled a grim and weary smile. "No, Hugh, it was not because the Saxons were flushed with victory or because I thought that they offered a better chance of imposing my will on the kingdom that I yielded to their petitions this morning."

For a moment Gregory paused; and the face of the Abbot of Cluny flushed.

"My heart bled for their tale of the desolation of Saxony and the cruel sufferings of the innocent and the helpless. But it was not what they said but what Henry's envoys said that moved me to my decision."

Desiderius and Hugh both cried involuntarily, "Henry's?" while Alfanus of Salerno looked steadily at the Pope without a word.

Gregory shook his head, and turned to Matilda, "The company in the Lateran would hardly let the delegates of Henry speak so indignant were they at the complaints of the Saxons. But they said enough to convince me that it was the same old story. Henry is offering nothing but attacks on his enemies and the same promises which he has been making for years without any effort to fulfill them."

"Rudolf is more likely to keep his promises," said Hugh sadly.

"But do you want to depose the King with all that means for the two swords?" asked Desiderius.

Matilda looked at the gentle Abbot of Monte Cassino in astonishment. This note of direct and unmitigated challenge was something new in her experience of the man.

The Pope waited for a moment. Then with great weariness he seemed to gather up his forces to reply. "Do we need to go into all that, Desiderius? You must have heard me say, as I think all of you here have heard me say time and again, that I have no desire to meddle with the things that are Caesar's. But when Caesar is a Christian, he is subject to the same laws that any other Christian must obey. To deny that is to subject all law to the whim of power."

There was silence in the library of Pope Zachary, as he concluded. Each of the men there seemed absorbed in his own thoughts. Only the Pope looked searchingly from one face to the other.

"Do you not know," he cried passionately, "that I am as grieved as any of you to give up hope of Henry? But to delay any longer would be to seem to condone his faithlessness. Men could justly say that I was not upholding principle but fencing for advantage."

"Your Holiness," began Hugh timidly, "if we can persuade the King to ask for forgiveness, will you receive him?"

Something sharp came into the tired voice of the Pope as he replied, "You know the answer to that as well as I, Hugh. The forgiveness that the Church never denies to the repentant sinner awaits the King as well as any Christian."

There was all the old enthusiasm of Hugh shining in the eyes with which he appealed to Matilda, "You will come with me into Germany to see the King, won't you, Countess?"

It had come. Matilda drew her breath as the whole company turned to her. "No," she heard her own voice speaking quite steadily, and the sound calmed her. "I can't leave my lands long enough for that. Henry has made it impossible. Besides, I don't think it would be any use." Her voice rose in a cry of pain. She did not lift her eyes again to look at Hugh. It seemed to her that the silence in the room was smothering her.

She heard the Pope say as if afar off, "There is nothing to be gained by our talking any more." She heard Hugh stop by her chair and say her name, but she did not stir. Finally, she raised her head. She could not stay here all the rest of the day. She looked at the Pope, who alone remained in the room, as if waiting for her to speak.

She stood up. "There is nothing more I can do here, and Arduino made me promise to return as soon as I could. Things are pretty unsettled," she added, rather lamely.

There was a fresh warmth of sympathy in the Pope's voice as he answered her, "Perhaps things will be quieter by June, and you can come back to see me then, when I am not so beset with all these Saxons." He smiled a little ruefully as he spoke. But she did not linger, for her heart was too full.

CHAPTER II

I⊤ was a cool day for June. The very clearness and brightness of the air seemed but to deepen the warmth of color in leaves and flowers and sky. Even in the worn marbles of the bare cloister arches, the veins of amethyst and topaz glowed duskily under the clouded surface. And in the moving leaves of the laurels and ilex, the latticed sunbeams danced over the shadows in points of light.

"On a day like this," said Matilda, looking out over the cloister garden of the Lateran, "I can never think the world as bad as it is."

For the moment none of her three companions spoke but stood silently watching the wind shimmer through the leaves and flowers of the garden. The tawny gold of the lilies, the tight-clutched flame of the roses, the violet plumes of the iris, flowed into the purple-green shadows of the shrubbery like recurring themes in a piece of music.

It was Alfanus of Salerno who finally answered, speaking in a low voice that hardly rose above the soughing of the wind, "Even in the peace of ancient days, my lady, wise men were never sure as to the mingling of this world's draught."

"I remember," said Desiderius, "the night when our new church was consecrated. I walked out into the moonlight and seeing it there as great and white as I had dreamed it, I thought for a moment that the courts of heaven could show nothing fairer." He laughed his low musical laugh, but there was a note of self-mockery in it that made all but Alfanus smile.

"I remember once, when I was a young monk and had just finished a sequence for the Easter Mass, that the Abbot promised to send to Rome to the Pope, it seemed to me that life was so pleasant that I wanted to live forever. I confided in one of my elder brethren, and he told me that such a state of mind was not Christian," the Archbishop added whimsically.

"It does not take long for us to learn better," said Hugh, with a light sigh that made all his companions look at him quickly.

"Well, certainly for these last three years," said Alfanus, "Henry has kept us from any temptation to think the Kingdom of God had come on this earth."

"Is it just Henry?" asked Hugh anxiously.

There was a tinge of malice to the Archbishop's chuckle that brought a flush to the thin face of the Abbot. And then he sobered. "You know that none of us from the Pope down thinks it is just Henry. Why else has the Pope steadfastly refused to recognize the Saxons? But you know, too, that Henry has not made the slightest effort to keep the promises he made at Canossa."

"Hugh," said Matilda gently, "you have not been in Lombardy and Tuscany these last three years and watched every kind of trouble and disorder grow and struggled to keep your own lands quiet. And all the time, you knew that Henry's silver and Henry's promises and Henry's encouragement have been at the back of almost all the trouble—"

"But I am not saying the Pope should not have renewed the excommunication," protested Hugh. "I am only afraid that the Pope may listen to the Saxons and declare the King deposed."

"I don't believe he will do it," said Desiderius.

Hugh shook his head. "As I came through the courtyard, some messengers from Germany had just arrived. That is why the Pope is keeping us waiting now."

Desiderius began to walk slowly back and forth down the pavement of the cloister. Alfanus of Salerno looked after him soberly; then bending over with surprising ease for one of his girth he seated himself on the high step leading down into the garden. Hugh went and brought a low chair with a leather seat between its crossed arms for Matilda.

"Oh, my lady Countess," cried Desiderius, stopping in his pacing, "I hear you have a wonderful man for stone and metal at Canossa. A Greek, they tell me!"

"Ah, these abbots," laughed Alfanus. "The pillars of society may be cracking, but still they are painting the walls of chapter houses and building chapels of marble and walls and—"

"Do you think," asked Desiderius gravely, "that it would help the Church to win its battle for independence if we let beauty and art and letters and learning perish?"

"He is only teasing you," interposed Matilda, watching how the moment's uneasiness faded from the bright face of Desiderius. "So far I have been able to find enough gold and silver and marble to keep my Greek happy, but there's no denying that what he yearns for is a chapel. I have told him that he must not stay with me, if he gets a chance to go to a lord who will be able to give him what he wants. God knows I wish I could." The wind shifting its direction suddenly brought the sweetness of the garden into the still air under the cloister arches. So, it seemed to her, had the words of the great building Abbot of Monte Cassino blown back to her the old dream of making the troubled world beautiful with marble.

"I suppose he would not leave you." Desiderius lifted his eyebrows with mock ruefulness. "There is where a woman can command devotion beyond what any man could."

Matilda laughed. "You're quite wrong. With an artist, perhaps, but if you think that feminine charm has any power over the hearts of knights or barons, then you should make the rounds of my vassals, straining at the leash every time a new rumor floats down out of Germany."

The Archbishop turned his broad back slowly to break into the conversation. Then in a moment he was on his feet. Matilda turned. There in the arched doorway stood the Pope.

Matilda was shocked to see how gray the brown face had grown. And how dead were the fires always smoldering in the deep eyes. She sank to her knees. When she looked up, she was relieved to see that a little light had crept back into the burnt-out face. But the voice was indescribably weary, even to the point of huskiness.

"I am sorry to have kept you waiting. But it is as well I did, for the news I have just received rather changes what I wanted to talk over with you."

He sat down, and the Archbishop of Salerno resumed his place on the step. Matilda took the chair which Hugh had again offered her, and she saw that his hands were shaking.

"It was the Saxons," the Abbot blurted out as he turned to face the Pope.

"No," said Gregory, putting his hands quietly on his knees. "It was Henry and Guibert of Ravenna—" He paused.

Matilda caught her breath.

The Pope nodded. "Whom they have set up as anti-Pope."

Hugh cried out as if he had been struck and buried his head in his hands. Desiderius leaned heavily against the carved shaft of the arch. Only the Archbishop watched the Pope with clear eyes.

"The Saxons were here yesterday," began Gregory with a look at Hugh, who did not raise his head.

"Asking that Rudolf be recognized as King?" Alone of the group, Alfanus did not seem surprised.

Hugh took his hands from his face with a gesture of quick impatience. "My Lord Pope, I shall not blame you if you grant their request now. There is nothing to be said for Henry's doing this."

The Pope's hands moved slowly over his knees. "I have been patient," he said as if to himself. "First, Henry mocked the pardon I had given him by trying to inveigle me into his power. You saved me from that ambush, Matilda."

Again the horror of that night when on the road two of her most trusted men came to her with the news of the ambush which Henry had set, came over her. At first she could not believe that the King would violate the road which he had guaranteed with his safe conduct. Even now she shuddered at the memory of the journey to Mantua when in every rock by the road she saw the helmets of Henry's lurking troops.

"I don't suppose," said the Pope, still speaking slowly, "that we can blame Henry directly for the failure of the princes' conference in Germany. It was simply that his activities against them directly and indirectly frightened them so that they dared not spare any of their troops."

"Your Holiness," exclaimed Desiderius, "God knows you have been patient."

"And this is the end," replied the Pope, the half-smothered bitterness suffusing the weary voice.

"You can grant the request of the Saxons, of course, and give the crown you have taken from Henry to Rudolf," suggested Alfanus of Salerno, watching Gregory sharply.

Again the wind veered, and the sweetness of the garden blew in Matilda's hot face. It seemed to her that she would choke with the memory of the dead hopes that cried out in the Pope's voice.

"What good would that do?" Gregory asked, looking down patiently at the Archbishop. Then without waiting for a reply, he went on to answer his own question, "If Rudolf the Swabian had any chance of pacifying all Germany and restoring order, then I should be willing to consider it."

Hugh shook his head. "To depose a legitimate King even for tyranny is to court chaos." He looked at the Pope as if he were a little frightened of what he had himself said.

But the Pope only nodded. "That is what I thought, what I still think," he added.

The Archbishop of Salerno seemed to be satisfied, for the look of tension faded from his placid features, and he folded his plump hands in his lap. Something of his habitual air of massive repose had returned as he settled more comfortably on his hard seat. "If one is going to fail, he must be more careful of the justice of his actions," he added as if to himself.

"Fail?" cried the Pope. "It isn't success or failure," bitterly, "but the desolate fact of schism. All those weak and confused souls who will be dragged down by the promises of demagogues and the lying counsels of those who have no other aim but company in their malefactions, they all lie on my conscience. Everywhere there will be disorder and uncertainty, and only the ruthless and the unscrupulous will draw any profit from fishing in those troubled waters."

Matilda put out her hand and touched the carved lion's head that stopped the crosspiece of his chair. "My lord, you have done all that man could do."

But the Pope interrupted her fiercely. "All? What is all in a thing like this when it is not a question of blame or of excuse, but of grim fact? 'Those whom thou gavest me', lo, I have lost them!"

The bitter cry rang through the arches of the cloister, and Matilda covered her face, unable any longer to bear the sight of his anguish. How long she sat thus, she had no idea. But some minutes must have passed before she heard a low voice speaking at her elbow. Even then she did not raise her head until the Pope's voice broke into her dazed consciousness. "It is for you, my child."

She took the letter, and afraid to open it, she stared at the seal. "It is the King's." She looked around the circle of faces watching her. The pale face of Hugh of Cluny flushed, and the Pope looked away as she waited for him to speak.

For some moments she stared incredulously at the sheet before her. Then she passed it to the Pope. But he declined to receive it.

"He is on his way to Rome with Guibert to be crowned Emperor, and he bids me join him." Her voice fell. The Pope looked at her quickly. "Is that all?" he asked sharply.

"If I refuse, he will put me under the ban of the Empire and give my lands to others." She looked up to find the eyes of all the company on her.

"They have started for Rome," she repeated, and she caught the note of surprise in her own voice. A light had come into the eyes of Alfanus, but she was no longer wondering what the others must be thinking. For a fierce joy had swept into the stagnation of her despair, like a wind from the sea in a rotting fen. Here was something she could do.

"My lord," she cried joyously, "I will start at once. And I will stop Henry before he gets into Tuscany. They are lawless enough, God knows, those vassals of mine, but they will not like Henry on their own lands, laying them bare with his armies like locusts."

All looked to the Pope, but for some minutes he said nothing. Then he raised his head, "God alone knows, my child, what the end will be. You have a man's courage, and you can do a man's part."

But Matilda smiled. "You should have reminded me that all that take the sword shall perish with the sword."

Then as the Pope hesitated, she said more gently, "God knows I wish I were a man for your sake, my lord. But I shall do a man's part, and the goodness of the cause will overcome the weakness of my sex."

The Pope seemed too moved to speak. Then with a new ring in his voice he said, "Your courage shames us all, Matilda."

But it was not modesty that embarrassed her. For she knew that there was nothing of heroism in this joy of the fight that had suddenly swept upon her. Here was something she could do, something tangible and definite in a world of shadows, out of which, of late, all the familiar landmarks had been fading.

CHAPTER III

THERE was no question in Matilda's mind but that Henry and Guibert intended to come to Rome to crown and be crowned, but as the summer wore on to fall, it became clear that there were too many obstacles in their way. The Saxons, as Adelaide of Susa took care to inform the Countess of Tuscany, had renewed their attacks upon Henry. And hard as it was for their leaders to persuade the ill-armed peasant hordes to carry the struggle out of their own country, they had yet succeeded in mustering enough strength to keep Henry occupied in Germany. Guibert did try to come south and enjoyed something very much like a triumphal progress through disaffected Lombardy, but it was obvious that in the absence of the King he judged it wiser not to leave his friends in northern Italy.

The result was that Matilda had the summer in which to rally her forces and consolidate the defenses of her territories. Arduino from the first had insisted that the protection of her own lands was the most effective bar she could impose to Henry's progress to Rome, and on this she spent the labors of the hot months. Weeks on end she passed in the saddle, going from village to village and town to town, from castle to castle and abbey to abbey. It was weather to appall the hardiest, with the sun blazing on the drought-baked roads day after day. The rich, reddish-brown soil of the spring rains had baked until it was the color and texture of dried mortar. The spring wheat which had sprung so verdantly from the damp, cold earth was shriveling to a sterile gold in the July fields, and the grass was burning to brown threads in the meadows. The rivers and brooks were still fairly high from the spring freshets, and there was water to be had for the animals, but the peasants were so tired and discouraged from the unavailing struggle with the earth, that they were not disposed to much effort beyond their traditional routine.

She tried to encourage the villages to fresh exertions by promising help with seeds, and bread for the dreaded winter, and she offered certain exemptions from rents and dues in return for the saving of the stock and the salvaging of vines and trees. But she was fully aware that such relief, while it drew down on her head the blessings of the peasants, did little to help her with her main problem. For, as Arduino reminded her, she was going to need more rather than less than her usual resources in the months ahead. Moreover, all her concessions found but scant response in the sentiments of her vassals and tributaries. The monastic landlords with their superior reserves and their more efficient management could easily and did reassure their serfs, but most of the knights and barons heard of her measures with frank distrust. These were, they objected, troublous times in which land must be made to yield its maximum of support. The result was an added element of suspicion and disfavor in the surliness with which they were disposed to regard an inconveniently active overlord.

The fruits of her visits were, therefore, none too satisfactory. Not that there was much of overt rebellion or even recalcitrance. The great majority of her vassals were perfectly decent men, ready to honor their obligations when little more than words or at most promises was involved. And the forms of feudal courtesy, warmed by the fact that the lord to whom they paid homage was a woman famous for her beauty and spirit, gave a very convenient modus vivendi for the brief duration of her visit. But whenever Matilda tried to press below the surface of adulation, she became aware that whatever friendliness she had found was grounded quite as much in prudence as good will. The King was very much occupied in Germany; even the remotest castle in the Appenines knew that. Guibert of Ravenna, though obviously capable of spurts of courage and even recklessness, was in a much better position to satisfy his known proclivities for display than to head any widespread rebellion. Moreover, the family of Canossa had made a very solid record for firm, not to say, at times, ruthless dealing with its vassals. Matilda might be famous for her charity and her devotion to religion, but men who had little of either were not likely to forget that she was the daughter of Boniface. Most of her vassals were therefore disposed to conciliate the power indisputably on the spot, to which they were bound by the most solemn of undertakings and by a habit of reverence.

However little she might be disposed to waste energy wondering what people were thinking about her, Matilda could not help considering these things many a day as she sat at a banquet in some mountain fastness or towered city house, where the lord of the district plied her with his richest wines and sweetmeats and spices, and, especially if he were young and fancied himself a man of social charm, with his most adroit flattery. Sometimes she was embarrassed by some particularly fulsome compliment in a house that she knew was regularly visited by the King's emissaries. But, for the most part, she accepted the very real element of good nature in her entertainment with corresponding cordiality and rejected her suspicions as ungenerous. Only when she rode for long hours at the end of such a visit, she found herself conscious of a very small residue after so much fuss. And she reminded herself that the loyalty she had heard so eloquently expressed would not prove incompatible with a very precise weighing of relative advantages when Henry should appear on the scene.

For everywhere, it seemed to her, she ran into the far-flung net of Henry's influence. Sometimes it was but a look, a gesture, not more than a word, that showed that Henry's emissaries had been at work. It was not that they had been attempting anything revolutionary. It was rather that they had very shrewdly capitalized existing discontents and ambitions and suspicions. If it was the citizens of Florence, Henry had taken pains to let them know of the concessions which he had granted to some of the Rhine cities. If it was a bishop, loath perhaps to come to grips with the problem of simony or clerical fidelity to vows of celibacy, the King had, obviously, been represented as a faithful buffer between an exacting Pope and an harassed man of affairs. If it was a knight or baron, with an eye roving beyond his own straitened borders, the King's impending visit to Italy had been shrewdly represented as an unparalleled opportunity of access to the fountainhead of power and fortune. And always the idea had been insinuated that any triumph of the Pope over the King would mean the tightening of the fetters which clerical fanaticism had imposed on lay energy. This was the most delicate of the triumphs of Henry's agents, for there was nothing in the whole thing that anybody could lay hands on. They were all, these lords of Tuscany, thoroughly respectable Christians, who were as generous as another in their gifts to religion and as careful as any sensible man of their eternal prospects, but they were not by temper or upbringing the men to neglect the opportunities of this life or to sacrifice the fruitful present for considerations which they intended to do full justice to when the time came. This attitude they abundantly justified to themselves by that final and supreme standard of the man of this world—the practical.

So the summer passed in fencing with shadows which threatened at any moment to become actualities and yet which could not be acknowledged for what they were until the time came. The days grew shorter, the brazen sky of August softened in the haze of September, and daily the autumnal mists deepened in the folds of the weary earth. With the first coming of the cold of October, Matilda found that the vague strain and anxiety of the summer had yielded to a positive irritation and impatience. It was partly, she suspected, the return of the energies which had been stifled by the heat of summer. It was partly, too, the result of the never-ceasing flood of rumor and report with which the whole country seemed inundated in those days.

Not but that the known facts in themselves were disturbing enough without any sensational embellishment. In spite of the surprising loyalty of the Roman populace, manifested in a steady indifference to Henry's blandishments, the Pope in his letters finally owned himself worried. Guibert of Ravenna gave every sign of cheerfully weathering the anathema his schism had incurred. True, in Germany Rudolf seemed to be in a fair way to making good his claims to Henry's crown. But Henry himself never ceased to bombard Matilda with a wide variety of communications, ranging from highly optimistic accounts of his affairs to lengthy summons of his "beloved cousin and vassal, Matilda," winding up now with the most exuberant promises of reward, now with the direst threats of immediate reprisals and swift ruin, if she did not hasten to comply.

It was therefore a relief to hear of the coming into Lombardy of a definite army. One fact was infinitely less disconcerting than a thousand fantasies. Here was at least something to find out about. And to this end she at first bent all her energies, thankful to have something to do at last. Not that it was difficult to uncover an abundance of data about the composition of that army or its movements. But to sift fact from fiction she soon found a task to appall the hardiest sceptic. Certain conclusions she drew more because they squared with inherent probability than because of anything that might be called evidence. The nucleus of German origin in that horde was, as she had suspected, small. But it came toward her territory rolling up accretions like a snowball. By the time she had a fair notion of the facts, the host was already on the edge of the Mantuan region.

Arduino was against any effort to turn it back. He had a professional's contempt for this impromptu aggregation of discontent, and though he was quite aware of the uncertain temper of the nobility of Tuscany, he was sure that almost any moment now word would come of some decisive victory for Rudolf. Then, he argued, would be the time for a general rally of forces and a trial of strength.

Matilda was now at Mantua in her mother's favorite house, resting in intervals of planning various types of reconnaissance. It was pleasant to be fixed in her own quarters, and she groaned at the thought of taking to the road again. But the cautious Arduino was not satisfied with his position.

"I should not mind defending Mantua, if it were necessary," he insisted, "but there is no use attempting it when a little to the south we can make an impregnable stand at Canossa."

Matilda shook her head vigorously. "No, we should leave the road to Rome open. Then, too, it's nearly the middle of October. It's no time to let any enemy burn his way through your country. Think of what is left of the wheat and the grapes and the olives."

"It's war," said Arduino with a shrug of his shoulders.

So they argued for half that afternoon. Arduino finally gave in. They would try to stop the army of Henry before it reached Mantua. But there was one condition Arduino would insist on.

Matilda was in the mood to be conciliatory now that her main point was won. So, carelessly, she agreed, only to be indignant when Arduino propounded his condition. It was that she would leave the front line to him and stay in the rear to take charge of the plans. On no other terms would he attempt to stop Henry's army with the forces he could collect in the next few days.

Presently, she had to admit the wisdom of Arduino's point. This army they were to meet was but the forerunner of others, if Henry should defeat Rudolf. If she fell at the outset, there would be no rallying force in northern Italy for the defense of Rome, to say nothing of Tuscany.

At the word "Tuscany" she smiled. "I have no reason to play the coward for Tuscany, Arduino. I am the last of my family."

But Arduino was not to be turned aside. "As long as a man is above ground, he should defend his own. Why else do you think we are put here?" he concluded piously. Again Matilda had to bow to the unavoidable.

It proved easier than she had feared to gather up a fair-sized army. To begin with, the company which Arduino had been gathering at Mantua was well-armed and led by men whose prowess was known in all the country. As that army set out from Mantua, it was a body to inspire confidence, and as she soon saw, it did inspire confidence, for the answers to the summons she had at once sent out to the knights of the neighborhood were prompt and encouraging. True, there were excuses, but the bulk of those summoned answered in person with retinues that did justice to their resources and their obligations.

It was, therefore, with a distinct renewal of hope that Matilda found herself by the middle of October in the country below the bend of the Mincio. The days were warm and glowing with sunlight, the nights, though cold, invigorating. Everywhere the olive harvest was in full swing, and all along the road Matilda and her men met the peasant girls with great trays of the purple berries on their heads. More than once, as they stopped to rest in the open fields at noon, Matilda lingered by some village olive press to watch the men and women at work, their faces shining with the labor and the hope of the harvest, like the clear liquid light that swam out from the gray stones of the press.

There was something in the slow rhythms of the oxen who turned the press and the men and women who fed it that chimed in with the warm and placid beauty of the autumn weather. And as one glowing day succeeded another, only varied by the deepening of the warm mist in the fields, it was hard to believe that such a perfection of harmony could ever cease. True, there were quarrels among the workers, there were noisy outbursts of horseplay and of singing, there were sudden crises when a huge terracotta jar brimming with the clear first runnings of the press broke, fattening the dust with its treasure, or an ox suddenly refused to move, and the stones lay heavy on each other, but these were only surface interruptions. The basic rhythms moved on untroubled, and the unbroken moment seemed already to have taken on something of the placid integrity of the everlasting.

But each day brought its crop of rumor and report of the army moving south. One anxiety seemed relieved at any rate. For all accounts agreed that the forces of Henry were coming almost due southeast; so there was no question that presently the two armies would meet. But this certainly brought its fresh concern. For as Arduino was quick to point out, the great opportunity would come when the invaders broke their ranks to cross the Mincio. If he and Matilda could reach them before the King's forces could reestablish their ranks, their task would be much simpler. For the present, so far as could be told from the reports, the two forces must be about equidistant from the river.

There came then into the perfection of the season a new tension, as the forces of Matilda redoubled their efforts to reach the river bank before their foes. At first this acceleration of effort brought its own exhilaration, and Matilda wrenched herself from the pleasant spell of the season without much effort. But when, at Arduino's insistence, they rode all day without stopping for rest, Matilda felt the old mood slipping back upon her in the weariness of the evening.

It was with considerable effort that she roused herself to greet Arduino when, after supper, he came to the door of the shed where she was to spend the night.

"We will be at the river tomorrow noon," he said.

"Then we had better get right to sleep so we can start before sunrise," she answered hopefully. But Arduino lingered.

"If they cross the river tonight—" he began.

She shook her head. "The men are too tired."

"I suppose so," he admitted reluctantly. Then he seemed to make up his mind. "Matilda, if they get across the river before we do, we had better turn back for Canossa. They are stronger than we are."

She yawned with sheer exhaustion, but she shook her head. "We must try to hold them. If we can't, well then—Canossa."

The next morning in the watery grayness before the dawn, when only the whitening of the stars gave any hope of the breaking of night, Matilda herself rode down the sleeping lines of her men to rouse them. By the time the first pre-monitory stains of color had appeared in the eastern sky, they were on their way. But they had not gone very far when the first scout returned to tell them that the night before, Henry's forces had reached the river.

Again, Arduino counseled yielding to the inevitable, but this time their company almost to a man backed Matilda in their insistence that they try to stop the enemy.

"We will be beaten," Arduino insisted.

"Even if we are," answered Matilda, "they will know that they cannot march on Rome without trouble, and our effort, however futile, will help to rouse the countryside."

So with Arduino looking very sullen, and the whole company excited over the prospect of a battle, they reached the low ridge of hills that looked across the plain to the village of Volta. There just outside the gray palings about the town, they saw what at first sight seemed little more than a swarm of bees resting in a patch of thyme or clover. It began to move, seemingly in all directions, and a wild cheer went up from Matilda's company.

"We are outnumbered," cautioned Arduino, but even as he spoke, the wild rush of shouting men had started down the slopes into the plain. For a moment, he gazed helplessly at Matilda, and then he turned and rode down into the mob, shouting directions to which no one paid any heed.

CHAPTER IV

AT first, it took all Matilda's self-control to remember her promise to Arduino. But when the wild flurry of the start was past, and the departing riders had dwindled into something like order on the lower slopes of the hill, she settled more comfortably on her horse, to watch the meeting in the plain below.

The sun had risen high in the eastern sky now. It was a beautiful sight to see the red and blue mantles of the men flying out in pennons of color from the horses' backs and the blue steel of shields and helmets gleaming like silver in the stainless October air, with here and there a poised spear or a gilded standard cutting the cobalt-blue distance like a flash of pure light. The weather was cool and clear enough to give everything about an incomparable clarity of tone and texture, yet not cool enough to chill the warm autumnal colors. The result was that though distance speedily dwarfed the mass of any object at rest or in motion, it detracted very little from either the color or the vivacity of movement of the smallest details. There was, therefore, in the scene at Matilda's feet none of that unreality that makes so easy for the observer a sense of impartial detachment. Indeed, as she looked down at the lively microcosm at her feet, Matilda felt her heart beat at once with an excitement and a delight that were almost intolerable.

The first downrush of Matilda's party had produced an instantaneous effect on the swarm in the lee of the town. And then a very curious thing happened, which Matilda was for some time at a loss to understand. For, while the greater part of the throng at once streamed out over the intervening plain, a certain black nucleus remained on the spot, apparently milling round and round with the greatest activity but with no sign of advancing. And this they continued to do until their comrades had completely separated from them and were careening across the plain at a dizzying rate of speed. For some minutes she puzzled over the mystery in silence. Then she turned to the chief of the knights who had been left on the hill to guard their lady. He was a hard-bitten old veteran, Manfred, who had been a companion of Godfrey the Elder in his unconverted, freebooting days. Now he sat on his horse, scowling at the fair scene before him with more than a suggestion of the bile of age in his thin, bronzed features.

He shrugged his shoulders at her question. Then he reconsidered. "That

German company has picked up a good deal of riffraff and green wood as they came along. They'd run like that. The veterans would take their time."

"But the cowards aren't moving," interposed a boy's voice scornfully. Matilda looked at the speaker. He was Romella, the son of Enrico of Pisa. Earlier in the morning she had heard Arduino explaining that as swordbearer to the Countess, his place was at her side. The bright face was still red with the anger and disappointment with which he had watched the rest of the company ride off.

The veteran Manfred looked at the boy, too. "There's nothing cowardly about those Germans. Don't you forget it, son."

But Romella was so excited that he set his horse to prancing. The two armies had met in the middle of the plain. Matilda saw the dust of the first clash rise in a cloud above the golden fields.

Then came a low, dry rustling like the wind through the gorse at her feet. It was not easy to see what was happening in the dust, but the general movement of the melee might be detected in the swaying backward and forward of the mass of the fighters. Though the men about her followed the wavering of the battle with expert eyes, it was clearly impossible to tell which side had the advantage. Rather, seen in the vast amphitheatre of the valley of the Mincio, the battle took on something of an organic character, until it seemed to the watcher as if some thick-bodied earth creature were writhing on the flat floor of the meadows. So the morning passed, and the sun stood hot and blazing, just below its zenith.

So dull had the indeterminate struggle become to the watchers on the hill that when one of the men-at-arms came up with a skin of wine and offered refreshment, they all turned away and took, one after the other, the proffered cup. The wine was warm and sickish, but even so it made Matilda think suddenly of the men in the dusty arena below whose thirst must be even greater. And shamed at the thought, she returned the cup and looked down into the valley again.

The scene was unchanged, but something moving on the edge of her vision made her look beyond. The black swarm on the edge of the plain was still where it had been resting all morning, but it was again showing signs of unmistakable agitation. For a moment she watched it in wonder, and then suddenly the riddle was answered, for the aimless-seeming swarming of an earlier hour had yielded to something like coherent motion.

"They are coming into the battle," she shrieked, and putting spurs to her horse, she dashed down the hillside.

She had not waited for her companions to catch up with her, but they were already on her heels. Nor had she taken any thought of what she was going to do or what chance she would have to do it. The wild dash down the hill had been her entirely automatic response to the danger threatening from the other side of the plain.

But as she rode along those miles between, she had plenty of time to think. In her first plunge she had driven her horse straight down the hill slope through furze and briars without any thought of choosing her way. But the wild cavortings of the frightened and pained animal had made her seek out the road, and though valuable minutes had been lost in the detour, yet now she was free to think. There was nothing reassuring in the result, for though the scene from the hilltop was etched into her memory by puzzlement and anxiety, yet she could not be sure of the relative distances. At first, she was inclined to think that they must be equal. But as the clash of steel and the shouts of men deepened on the heavy noontide breeze, she began to think that perhaps she had underestimated the distance between her vantage ground and the engagement. She was certain that she had done so when she began to encounter the first stragglers from the field of battle.

Some turned and fled at sight of her. Others lifting dripping hands, or reeling precariously on frightened steeds, by their silent appearance offered their own excuse for flight. To one or two whom her coming sent back along the road, she tried to shout the news she wanted given to Arduino, but it was very doubtful if the fugitives had wits enough left to understand what she was saying. There was clearly nothing for it but to press on until she found some responsible leader, whom she could warn or, at least, send to Arduino. It was then that for the first time she remembered her promise. For a moment she hesitated, but she could not see far enough along the road to be sure of what was happening, and the constantly increasing number of stragglers was beginning to assume the proportions of a rout.

She, therefore, turned to the young Romella, who had all morning watched the battle with such obvious envy of the combatants burning in his restless eyes, and bade him find Arduino, and if it were not too late, warn him of the coming of the reserves. It was not until the boy, almost delirious with joy at his sudden release, had shot off like the proverbial arrow into the crowded road that she remembered that he would undoubtedly tell Arduino of the jeopardy into which his lady had put herself by the broken promise. But the excitement of action had laid hold upon Matilda likewise, and the immediate necessity of turning the rising tide of flight put all thoughts of personal caution out of her mind.

At first, it was not hard to send the stragglers back, for the surprise of her appearance so close to the field of action had clearly checked any tendency to closer scrutiny of the small force at her back. And her own resolution to stop the rout easily communicated itself to men who felt that the eye of their lady was upon them individually and particularly, so to speak. But it was a totally different matter when the number swelled so that as she tried to stop one or two, the others were still carried on by the momentum of their flight, in most cases unaware that any challenge had been given to their retreat. And presently, that momentum itself had accelerated to such an extent that it was no longer a question of trying to turn the tide but of merely holding her own against it so as not to be sucked into the maelstrom of panic.

It was then that, waving her sword above her head and yelling to her companions to follow, she attempted the desperate expedient of a dash through her own forces in the direction of the enemy. For a moment, the maneuver seemed to succeed. The choked road broke before her, and her companions pressed hard behind. Seeing her coming, some of the less dazed of the fugitives turned, too, and presently she was at the point of a flying wedge that drove its way straight through the rout, scattering the mob that choked the way to the sides of the road. All about her the cry of "The Countess, the Countess" rose, and, caught up by the increasing volume of enthusiasm, the frightened soldiers began to turn.

For a moment it seemed to her that she was riding on air, and everything was giving way before her. Then suddenly her horse started and with a terrible cry of pain plunged to the side of the road. Matilda yielded to the sudden jerk and pulled firmly at the reins, but her right hand still held the sword in the air, and she was not quick enough in the recovery of her balance. All she could do as the horse fell was to slip her feet from the stirrups.

She awoke to find a blurred circle of white faces above her, wavering before her eyes as if seen through water. She tried to give some sign that she was all right, but it was impossible to hold anything steady enough in her consciousness. The next thing she knew was a dull ache, seemingly all over her body. Then she felt the cool air on her face, and she awoke to find herself sitting up in somebody's arms. She looked around, and this time the faces did not fade. But above and behind the circle of half-kneeling figures she could make out the terrible drive of the rout. And the din of the crying men and horses and the jangling of armor filled her ears.

In silence she struggled to her feet with the help of half a dozen arms. Clearly, nothing was broken, but her body seemed one vast bruise. Nodding reassuringly, she looked about for her horse.

"We had to kill it. The spear had been driven in too deep," explained Manfred, leading up his own horse.

When she was mounted again, Matilda waited for a moment to draw breath. Even breathing was painful, and she was so sore that the mere effort of keeping her seat brought the sweat to her brows and made her feel faint and sick. She looked about, and slowly her companions mounted, Manfred seizing by the bridle one of several steeds that came tearing along, riderless. She forced her new horse back to the road, but it was all she could do to keep her seat.

For a moment, she shut her eyes to see if she could not down the growing feeling of nausea. When she opened them again, she knew that she was being borne along by the mob, helpless. The dust and the heat of the rout, the hot, sickish smell of blood and sweat, the noise, the panic overcame her, and shutting her eyes, she clutched her horse blindly.

It was nearly night when she stumbled, numb and dazed, into an open gate and fell into strong arms. When she awoke again, it was morning, and she was lying in a great bed in a dim, whitewashed room.

As she stirred tentatively, a familiar voice spoke. It was Arduino. "How do you feel?"

For answer she sat up and lifted the curtain.

"Can you ride?"

She nodded. Then for the first time she got a good look at him. His face was the color of ashes, and his clothes were torn and stained with blood and mire.

"Arduino!" she cried, raising herself on her elbow.

"The Abbot is afraid to have us stay here," he said curtly.

Not even when they were on the road again, would he speak, and when some of their small company began to talk in low tones, he silenced them, reminding them that they would need all their strength for flight.

"But," objected Matilda, "there are various of our friends along the way here. There is no need for us to—"

Then for the first time since they had started north, Arduino lost control of himself, "Matilda, it was you who insisted on our fighting when I knew we were hopelessly outnumbered. Then you nearly got yourself killed there on that road."

She was very humble as she answered, for the sight of the man's agony of mind was almost too great to be borne. "I saw the reserves start, and I rode to warn you."

The little man swore furiously. Then as a low murmur of protest rose from the whole company, he turned with fresh anger upon Matilda. "There is only one sensible thing you can do now. The King's men are behind us. You'll find most of your friends will prefer not to risk having their roofs burned down over their heads. And if you want to fill the cup of your folly to the brim, all you have to do is deliver yourself a prisoner into Henry's hands."

"You are going to Mantua, then?" she asked coolly, striving with her own calm to check the anger she saw rising in the faces about her at the privileged insolence of Arduino.

But Arduino hardly spoke again until they reached the walls of Mantua at noon of the next day. There was a large company of their own forces waiting for them inside the city gate, and all about, on every vantage point of tower and battlement and balcony, a huge throng waited to greet them. There was a tremendous cheer for Matilda as she came in the gate, but Arduino gave one contemptuous look in the direction of his late soldiers and spat in their faces.

For a week Matilda and her men waited behind the palisades of Mantua, watching the days pass over the shimmering surfaces of the shallow waters around the city, from the high towers scanning the northern road for any sign of pursuit. Then the news began to trickle in again from peasants, and spies, and traders.

"I don't understand, said Arduino. "But from all accounts they merely burned the countryside a little and went back across the river. There is talk of something big forward in Germany, but I am not sure. Half the rogues in the town are talking of going back to their own castles for the winter, but they don't want to move until they're sure. Damned cowards and time-servers, the lot of them!"

So they waited for another week, until now a full fortnight had elapsed since the defeat at Volta. Then the rumors began to grow more precise. There had been a great battle in Germany between Henry and Rudolf. The next day a messenger came from Adelaide to say that Rudolf had been victorious. There was a look of savage glee in Arduino's eyes when Matilda at dinner that day informed all the knights and nobles at the long tables in her hall of the victory. And when they crowded round the dais to kiss her hand and congratulate her on the triumph of what they styled vaguely her cause, she was hard put to it to conceal her mingled feelings of hope and amusement.

But when Arduino, who was never distinguished for his piety, suggested a Te Deum in the cathedral of Mantua to celebrate with fitting humility the goodness of Divine Providence, some instinct of caution made her say, "Wait." She was thankful that she had been cautious when the next day brought the first report that Rudolf had indeed triumphed but had fallen at the hour of victory. A day later, a desolate note from Adelaide confirmed the tragic news, and three days after that, a special messenger arrived from Henry with an arrogant note in which the King bade his beloved cousin rejoice at this sudden dispensation of Providence which had freed him from a particularly violent and shameless foe, and the kingdom of Germany from a contumacious rebel and disturber of the peace.

It was too late to assemble her household to communicate the tragic news to them. But when the morning came, she found that it was quite unnecessary. Fully half of the most important members of her company had come to take their leave of her. It was the same old story. They were concerned at the undefended condition in which they had left their castles. And they were sure that the best way to serve the interests of their sovereign lady was to protect their lands from the attacks of her enemies. There was nothing she could urge against such reasoning, and she was forced to see them go. That evening she consented to Arduino's plan for taking refuge at Canossa, and from that as her center attempting to rally the support of her timid and self-seeking vassals.

The next morning they started for Canossa. All the way she kept thinking of what a messenger from the north had told her that morning, pausing for an hour on his way to Rome. He was a Saxon, and he had been at Rudolf's side when he fell with a thrown dart in his breast just as the tide of battle turned in his favor. He had lived long enough to hear the trumpets ring out with the proud boast of his victory, and then he had taken the waiting crown from the hands of one of his comrades, lifted it in triumph to his brow, and fallen back dead. It was a rough soldier who told the tale, but the man wept, unashamed, as he told how in the middle of the night, with torches flaring from the hands of hundreds of Saxon warriors down the somber nave of the cathedral of Merseburg, they had laid the victor to rest with his sword in his hand and his crown upon his head, in the prime of his manhood and the triumph of all his earthly ambitions.

The Saxon had dried his tears, and half to himself and half to her, he had added, "And who shall say, my lady, that it is not perhaps as well for him?" That question rang through her consciousness again and again as with her much reduced and bitterly discouraged company she made her retreat to Canossa.

CHAPTER V

FOR some weeks after her return to Canossa Matilda was quite willing to yield to Arduino's demands and stay quietly within the bounds of the fortress. She was even yet half-ill from the shock of her fall, and all the reports she could obtain from either Germany or Italy agreed that no one could tell what was going to happen next, and that very few were willing to make any definite commitments in the face of such widespread uncertainty. Everything indicated that Henry was devoting all his energy to the task of rallying his broken forces, and while there was no question that his friends' hopes had soared with the elimination of Rudolf, there was abundant evidence that the Saxons would proceed to the election of another King as soon as they could agree among themselves on the candidate most likely to appeal to the rest of Germany. At the other extreme of the Italian peninsula, Robert Guiscard was bending every effort to the assembling of as large an army as possible for his projected invasion of the Eastern Empire. The absence therefore of any immediate and direct threat to their own peace gave full scope to the conflict of interests and latent animosities in the lands between.

Here for the time being the schism in the Church and the ceaseless activity of Guibert of Ravenna were the most important political factors in the troubled picture of northern Italy. But they were by their very nature, Matilda told herself, centripetal forces, in no way giving focus to public opinion or consolidation to conflicting interests, but constantly working to divide and disintegrate. Sometimes as news came in of some particularly flagrant breach of ecclesiastical faith and order by the schismatics, of the being of an episcopal election, of the seizure by force of a vacant abbey, of the raising of the mob against a bishop who tried to enforce the canon law to which he was bound by his episcopal oath, Matilda chafed bitterly her own confinement and blamed herself for the compliance of inaction in these lawless deeds. But always Arduino insisted that to rush to the defense of one beleaguered bishop or oppressed abbey was to stake all on the stopping of one hole when all along the dikes the sea was rushing in.

Matilda was not convinced by Arduino's insistence that the defense of her own territories was the first condition of any effective support of the Pope's cause. For she knew that from the beginning Arduino had not been much interested in the problems of Church and State. To him the whole thing was but the inevitable clash of rival powers, and the part of a wise man was to make his own profit of their follies. He was, Arduino always insisted, a good Christian, who would keep his faith and do everything in his power to serve the head of the family of which he was a humbler member and to increase its honor. As for religious enthusiasm, that he regarded as a monk's business, and he would have as soon meddled with the housekeeping of the castle or sung a love song with the maids spinning in their chamber as join in the discussion of any question of theology or ecclesiastical law. They were simply not a soldier's affair, and he was a soldier, as the good God had meant him to be.

There was plenty of time for Matilda to think these things over as the autumn faded into winter. And at first she was content to do so, but as the snow deepened on the mountains and the cold winds of December and January began to beat at the narrow slots of the windows and on the tiled roofs of hall and chapel, her imagination stirred again, and she found herself looking ahead to the spring when the vernal restlessness would seize on men and the milder airs of March would release them from their bondage to castle and grange. It was at this point that she discovered more sympathy on the part of Arduino.

From the first he had discouraged her desire to make any repetition of the journeys around her dominions on which she had spent her last summer. She could not deny that in the final outcome they had done her little good. So she was more disposed to listen to Arduino's suggestions. They were few and relatively simple. The thing for her to do, he insisted, was to stay where she was in her stronghold of Canossa and spend her energy on drawing into that center all the resources she could, both material and human. From the military point of view alone, no advice could be sounder, and Matilda knew that it represented probably the most competent military opinion in Italy, at least north of the Norman Guiscards.

But for once Arduino pressed cunningly on the less obvious issues of human feeling and hope. He pointed out that in the uncertainty and confusion of men's minds that they would turn gladly to a center that offered them at least the possibility of refuge, and that in the fears that stalked Italy at every rumor from across the Alps, the mere physical fact, apparent to all men, of the impregnable strength of the fortifications at Canossa would draw the loyalty of many who had hitherto been doubtful or wavering. This point he argued with what for his somewhat grumbling taciturnity was almost eloquence. And Matilda was forced to admit that, granted her general's conception of what her basic aims should be, his strategy was irrefutable. There was, she knew, no use arguing the fundamental differences in their views; so she contented herself with praising Arduino's judgment and asserting categorically that she would under no circumstances let an army of Henry's advance on Rome without trying to stop it. Short of that, she was willing to defer to Arduino's strategy, but on that basic issue she could not be swerved from what was for her the first obligation of conscience.

So the winter passed with plenty to keep her busy in the neighborhood, and in spite of a good deal of suffering in her villages on account of the damaged crops of the previous summer, with very substantial improvement in her stores and her fortifications, to show for her work. And as the first breaking of the winter began to open the roads in late February, she had a chance to see that there was much to justify Arduino's policy. For the rumors of an impending invasion from the north multiplied with the coming of weather that would make it not impossible, and with the rumors and the inevitable terror they bred, more and more of her vassals began to send pledges of loyalty and petitions for protection to the stronghold of Canossa. The result was that by the end of March she had a very considerable force of her own knights and barons at Canossa and the four fortresses that protected it on the crests of the engirdling hills.

No one at Canossa was surprised when the news came that Henry had been seen at the head of the Brenner Pass with a large army. But the shock of the long-anticipated fact was keen, and the younger men especially, sniffing the spring breezes from the mountains, strained at the leash. However, the folly of attempting any operations until it was clear what support the King would be able to gather from the restless Lombard cities was apparent to everybody. There was, therefore, nothing to do for the present but watch the progress of Henry's army across the Lombard plain and try by means of various trusted scouts to gauge the probable response of her various cities and vassals to the nearer approach of the King's army.

At the very beginning of her survey, Arduino warned her not to expect too much. "Those you see here every day are the most brave or the most afraid. The great bulk of men are neither." It was not easy, however, to swallow the defiance of Lucca, where the lawlessness of the nobles and the corruption of the clergy had joined forces against their bishop Anselm and driven him out to take refuge in Rome. She was at first tempted to go in person to Lucca and attempt by force, if not persuasion, to subdue the rebels. But Arduino was adamant in his insistence that this was no time to distract oneself with isolated cases of rebellion.

Florence was more satisfactory. The burghers of that city were as always grudging in their promises of aid, but they had no great love of the Empire. For in times past the King had supported a notoriously simoniacal bishop in the face of much popular indignation. The present occupant of the throne in the dim-shadowed Duomo was, if no saint, at least thoroughly respected by everybody but the more lawless elements of the clergy, whom, as Matilda knew from personal experience, he had been trying to discipline. The anti-Pope was therefore certain of no welcome in Florence, and even the King's generous promise of immunities and privileges fell upon deaf ears as coming from a man who kept notoriously bad company. Moreover, the reputation of the Countess for piety, hard work, and sober living made more of an appeal than Henry's sensational record to industrious merchants and craftsmen who themselves set much store by the austerer virtues.

The news from Rome was encouraging, too, for though the agents of Henry had been busy all winter sowing discord in the jealous and turbulent ranks of the Roman nobility, yet it was clear that they were not going to be able to raise any revolt in Henry's interest. The Pope had no reason to take the enthusiastic avowals of loyalty which his fickle city made to him that spring with too much complacency, but for the present at least the loyalty of Rome was proof against the King's gold and the King's promises.

So things stood when Henry moved south to Verona early in April. Matilda's first impulse was to answer the mocking summons which she received with the news of his arrival and to throw her army across his path. In this she received warm encouragement from most of her followers, but Arduino passionately objected. Such a move would sacrifice her present strength, would court all the possibilities of defection in regions of which she was not too sure, and would in the event of her possible capture or defeat, leave the whole land between Henry and her beloved Rome without any strong figure around whom the friends of the Pope could rally. Indeed, Arduino went so far as to suggest in no ambiguous terms that even the appearance of defeat at this time might deprive her of half the company who at present seemed so enthusiastic in her cause.

There was certainly nothing diplomatic about Arduino's speech, but Anselm, who had just returned from Rome, and Alberic, who had come from San Benedetto on the chance that Matilda might be moving north, gravely seconded Arduino's objections. Matilda was in no mood to give in without a struggle, but Anselm was able to invoke the authority of the Pope in advising her to wait. So while making it clear that she was by no means convinced that her first impulse was unsound, Matilda agreed to wait a fortnight.

The end of the period she had promised to wait found the whole company within the castle walls restless and excited, ready for any adventure. It also brought the news of Henry's swift advance through Ravenna toward Tuscany. The first messengers reported that he was on the threshold of Matilda's lands. Two days later news came that he had been seen moving on Camaldoli.

Without waiting for further news, Matilda sent the most restless of her forces south to Florence. If the Florentines kept faith and shut their gates against Henry, these reinforcements would help to garrison the city in the plain. If the Florentines opened their gates to Henry, then the Countess' men were to take advantage of the probable delay and slip south to Rome. Whatever happened, Henry would have to move quickly if he expected to invest Rome before the heat of the summer came.

Again Matilda tried to persuade Arduino that now was the time to fall upon Henry's army from the rear. But he still insisted that it was too large for her forces under the best of circumstances. Moreover, he added, this time lowering his voice so that only Anselm and Alberic could overhear, the loyalty of too many of her vassals was uncertain for her to risk defeat at this time.

The justice of Arduino's scepticism seemed to be established that evening when monks from one of the neighboring houses reported that not only had the lord of Camaldoli accompanied Henry south, but several of her vassals from the neighborhood of Florence had joined Henry in investing that city. The latter news made Arduino laugh grimly. "The next time those damned burghers will be glad enough of their lady's help!"

But news soon came to Canossa that was at once reassuring to Matilda and chastening to her general. For the Florentines had not only shut their gates against the King, but, reinforced by the men their lady had sent, they were defying his siege with such spirit that Henry was forced to gather in all his Italian resources to invest the city on the river properly.

Once Matilda was sure of the fact that Henry was for the present engaged, she summoned all her company into the great hall of the castle and there asked for volunteers to accompany her to Rome. Arduino was speechless with indignation, but before he could voice his protest, she had half the throng in the hall wildly cheering for the prospect of action after all these months of inactivity. She chose her company carefully, however, taking only men whose loyalty she could depend on, and whose strength would not fail on the forced marches she contemplated. It was a small company, therefore, that, envied by all, rushed from the hall to arm and mount. The rest she confided to Arduino's charge, and with a smile that brought a look half of indignation and half of pride to his face, she bade the company look upon him as herself.

It was not until she stood in the courtyard by her horse that Arduino was able at last to challenge her. "My lady," he began, "when you meet your father and my lady Beatrice, I hope you will do me the justice to tell them that I did everything I could to save you."

For a moment she stared at him, and then she laughed gayly, "Please God, that is some time yet. Listen, Arduino, I am going straight to Pisa. There I will raise more men, who will follow me when I am gone. Then I will go down to Volterra. I will be at Rome a week ahead of Henry, for it will be some days before he admits that he cannot take Florence, and an army of that size cannot move as fast as my little company."

Arduino's grim face did not relax. "What good do you think such a handful will do the Pope?"

"Listen, Arduino." She had mounted her horse, and now she leaned over to look into his angry and worried face. "It will not be large enough to do anything to Henry's army, but it will be large enough to encourage the Romans to resist. For my being there will be a pledge of further relief—if it is needed," she added hastily.

"Before God, Matilda—" he began, but she waved her hand to him as she rode out the gate.

Riding all that night without stopping for rest, she was more than a third of the way to Luni by morning. That day she spent in an isolated hermitage of Camaldolese monks. Just before dawn of the third day she was in Luni. The remaining miles of her journey she covered in two long days of riding. Her company was exhausted, but they were safe from surprise in Pisa, and there she rested until far into the night. When she awoke, the bishop and half a dozen of the leading nobles of the city were waiting for her, and to them she unfolded her plan. She would have to leave at once, for it would be very easy to send news to Florence, but once she was a day's journey to the south, they were to summon the men of Pisa and raise the nobility of the neighborhood. It was with difficulty that she restrained them from sounding the tocsin over the sleeping city at once.

She was a day's journey out of Volterra before the first rumor reached her of Henry's preparing to lift the siege of Florence, and she was leaving Soana when a messenger arrived from Henry. He had, so ran the haughty letter to the Roman people, decided to waste no more time with the rebels of Florence but was at once taking his way to Rome. Matilda lingered long enough to estimate with the messenger's help the probable date of Henry's arrival. It could not be before the tenth of May, they both agreed, and she was sure she would arrive not later than the fifth. So she sent one of her men ahead with orders to have his news relayed as fast as possible from monastery to monastery until it reached the Pope.

The bells of all Rome were ringing as she rode over the rim of the Campagna and through the gate of Saint Valentine into the city. And the tears stood in the Pope's eyes when she knelt down before him in the courtyard of the Lateran Palace. It was the evening of the third day of May.

CHAPTER VI

It had clearly been Henry's plan to scatter his promises and his gold through the city of Rome, so that the gates would open upon his arrival in the fields of Nero to the north of the city. But the people of Rome chose for the present to be indignant at the audacity of the King in taking arms against the head of Christendom, and they treated very roughly several of Henry's agents. The very morning of the day on which Matilda arrived, they had driven one particularly daring agitator out of the city, and one of the nobles suspected of having taken Henry's gold awoke to find the timber roof of his house on fire that night.

As rumors of the approach of the King's army reached the city, there was inevitably not a little panic. So far Henry had been singularly abstemious in his treatment of the country through which he passed. True, it had been swept clean of all cattle and grain and olives and wine as if a plague of locusts had gone over it, but that was only to be expected. So far as Matilda could determine from the various appeals for aid that followed her to Rome, no attempt had been made to pillage or lay waste the country, and though there were ugly tales of outraged village girls, of peasants killed, and of granges burned, there was little reason to believe that they were anything else than what Henry would undoubtedly claim they were, isolated breaches of discipline, in many cases half accidents. They might make the Pope shake his head, but Matilda had to admit that Arduino probably had some right on his side, when he dictated a hasty letter pointing out to his mistress that one could not expect a horde of men who had been brought into a fertile country with lavish expectations of reward to behave like a monk-led pilgrimage. The citizens of Rome were not disposed, however, to take such a philosophical attitude toward atrocities which might soon be repeated at their expense.

"These rabble have no vision," complained one of the older nobles whom Matilda suspected of a good deal of sympathy with Henry. "All they think about is their own hides."

On the whole, however, the nobility of Rome rallied to the Pope with something approaching enthusiasm. Part of this, Matilda believed, was genuine piety. A good deal was even warm admiration of the courage and steadfastness of the Pope. Much more was, she suspected, a shrewd realization that the defeat of Gregory would expose them to imperial burdens that would sadly limit that freedom to do as they pleased which for centuries had been the first preoccupation of the Roman nobility. But all of these different strands of idealism and self-interest were as usual inextricably interwound, so that all one could be sure of was a general determination not to yield to Henry, and a disposition to treat very harshly all who showed any signs of doing so.

The result was that when Henry arrived in the meadows of Nero in the middle of May, the whole population was extraordinarily united in its spirit of resistance. But even so, there was something terrifying in the sight of the army closing around the north of the city, and by the time Henry's men began to raise a low mound over against the city walls, the people in the streets were showing signs of panic. It was at this point that Matilda found she could render the service she had anticipated. For, day after day, attended by a large company of knights in shining armor, she went through the streets of Rome, while the people, remembering her services in past times of crisis for the city, cheered with renewed courage.

The arrival of the men of Pisa with fresh supplies from the west gave the Roman populace another day of rejoicing, and so did the convoy of provisions which the Guiscards sent from the Norman lands. Soon after, supplies which Arduino had dispatched from Pisa by sea came to hearten the frightened people with hope of continuing aid. But quite unseen, another ally, even more powerful, was at work. The heat of the summer was falling upon the city and the low-lying land at the foot of the hills, and covering the baking ground with its heavy pall of stagnant air. For men who all their lives had sweltered in its humidity summer after summer, it was hard enough to prosecute the ordinary business of life, but for men from the mountains and the cooler valleys of the north it paralyzed all activity.

June was not far advanced when late one afternoon Matilda looked out from the garden terrace of one of the castles on the Capitoline Hill to discover that the camp in the plain at her feet was still wrapped in the noonday immobility. It was past the time for the Roman siesta, and for a moment she wondered if they were trying to lure the besieged into some attack.

But the Pope shook his head. "They are exhausted from this heat. I remember a time when I was at the court of the King in Germany, and the summer was, they said, remarkably hot. Most of the company were too prostrate to try to do anything. Henry will have to turn back."

The Pope proved quite correct in his prediction. The next day, the first signs of some extraordinary preparation in the camp were apparent to the watchers from the walls of the besieged city, and by the end of the day, the withdrawal had begun. Most of the next day Matilda spent on the streets of the city, for many of the people of Rome, made rash by the sudden removal of their fear, were for sallying out at once to harry the retreating ranks of the northern army. It took all the Pope's and her efforts for two days to hold the delirious crowd in check and let Henry and his troops escape unmolested. And even though Gregory and Matilda did succeed in convincing the leaders of the citizens that there was nothing to be gained and indeed everything to lose in provoking a fresh assault from Henry, the restless crowds in the narrow streets still talked with bitterness of the opportunity which they had missed.

When the splendid ceremonies of thanksgiving in the Lateran had been completed, Matilda was anxious to move north again to protect her lands. True, in the week since Henry had left, there had been no report but of his steady withdrawal to the north, but the anti-Pope had remained like a cloud in the fertile lands on the edge of the Campagna, burning and wasting the country and holding up the progress of traders and messengers. The Pope, therefore, insisted that Matilda should not leave the city until they had more certain prospect of a quiet return to her own territory.

At first, Matilda was impatient. The inevitable reaction to the excitement of the last weeks had set in, and where a week ago she had been grateful for the sudden deliverance from the threat of Henry's army, she now found herself in much more of a mood to sympathize with the Roman populace. After all, the King's sudden withdrawal had been due to the accident of the weather rather than to any force they had been able to bring to bear upon him. While Henry could certainly not boast of that weather-forced retreat, neither could his enemies claim more than that at a time of danger Providence had intervened in their behalf. And there would be those even among good Christians who would attribute the deliverance to Henry's own rash choice of the time to invade the humid Roman plain. The result was that while Matilda was not ungrateful for a dispensation of Providence that postponed the day of a test of strength for which she was not prepared, she was impatient to be gathering her own resources and preparing to take her part in the struggle that still seemed inevitable.

But there was nothing to be gained by risking a sudden change of direction on Henry's part. So Matilda settled down to wait as patiently as she could for more certain news. It was not easy to wait thus. At the best of times the streets of Rome were not pleasant to nostrils accustomed to the cleaner air of the mountains. Now the heat of June extracted a richer stench than ever from their filthy gutters, so that sometimes, riding over the cracked marble pavements between the palace of the Frangipani where she lodged and the Lateran, she thought wistfully of the aromatic freshness of the hemlocks on the slopes of the hills about Bianello, or the sweet smell of meadow grass when the wind came in from the plains above Mantua, or the salt tang of the west wind at Pisa. So the hot days passed.

And then came news that made Matilda clench her hands with rage and grief. She could hardly say that she was surprised when she heard that the faithless Lucchese had sent messengers out to meet Henry's army and invited him to turn aside to their city and rest. They had already driven the reforming Anselm from their walls, and in the years since, Matilda had not been able to reinstate him with any security. But there was something gratuitous in this rushing out to commit treason that struck hard at her pride and her sense of justice. It went to the heart, too, of an old hope and dream of hers. For it was just outside of Lucca that she had had her first clear vision of the white marble of an ancient world of peace, and first had dreamed of renewing it. Now it seemed to her that whatever atonement she might wring from the Lucchese in more prosperous times to come, she could never bear to set her foot again in their faithless land.

The Pope was sympathetic with her disappointment, for he recognized the outraged affection quite as well as the outraged pride in her grief. So that afternoon he suggested she ride out with him to one of the little Alban hill villages that hung in its narrow rock-top eyrie above the edge of the plain. There in the evening she might catch a breath of wind denied to the plain below, and in the night ride back to Rome they would see the theatre of their cares at least in a different light.

At first Matilda hesitated, for the distance from the walls was considerable and, most of the way, lonely. But the Pope hastened to assure her that the same messenger who had brought her the defiance of the Lucchese had also reported at the Lateran that Guibert of Ravenna was likewise on his way north. There was nothing to be feared, therefore, that would be beyond the competence of a small but completely armed escort.

"And," added the Pope with a smile, "the Pierleone have made a park of the hill so that there is nothing of the terror of the mountains about it. And the little lake is quite as winsome in the moonlight as in the sunlight."

Indeed, it proved as he had said. After the heat of the day the shadows of the ilex and cypress and cedar were pleasant for all their melancholy, and the many-hued mist of the plain turned the scene of their anxieties and labors to a far-away peace, as they looked down upon it from the hill-top. Indeed, ever since they had come out upon the ancient pilgrim way, it had seemed to Matilda as if they were riding in another world. It was still afternoon, and the olives and the poplars on either side of the marble road were white with dust, but even in the heat of a late June day something of the coolness of time lay about the ivy and weed-grown tombs and the broken shards of marble houses that stretched along the way. And as the ride progressed for the most part in silence, these remembrances of a more ancient time came to take on the aspect of strange derelicts left high on the shores of change when the tide of that world sank never to rise again. Seen now by an eye weary of the teeming streets of Rome with all the passions of the moment seething through the shell of the past, these untroubled wrecks took on the fascination at once of something inexpressibly remote and yet, in their shadowed imperviousness, of an immediacy not to be denied.

The same thought must have run through the Pope's mind, for he said presently, "I suppose these empty houses knew tragedies as bitter as any today, and of these sleeping here some must have been as anxious as we are, and now they are lying here, and it is another day, and all that grief is as if it had never been."

Matilda made no answer, and they rode the rest of the way in silence. But now when they had climbed the hill and turned their horses to browse on the thin grass between the trees, they stood looking across the plain to the marble-peaked and shadowed hills on which they had spent the last anxious weeks. For a few minutes they rode in triumphant light above the mist-filled plain, the whiteness of the marble gleaming like something unearthly in the afterglow of the sunset. Then they slowly and imperceptibly sank into the purple-blue of the dusk. But it still seemed incredible that any hate or pain could vex that city of light.

Only once again did the Pope speak of the things that must have lain heavy on his mind through that ride. They were standing on the edge of that bowl in the bottom of which the little mountain lake sparkled in the moonlight like molten silver. There was something almost terrible in its loveliness there, environed with shadows like a suddenly lighted mirror in the cave of night.

"There is another lake like this farther up in the Alban hills, only lovelier, they say, in its remoteness," said the Pope. "And there is an old legend that has come down from pagan times about it. There was a temple there with much treasure, for men in those days came from all over Italy to visit it. A single priest offered the sacrifice, and he was a slave who had fled from his master. But all the treasure and the reverence was his and his alone. Only he knew that some day another runaway would come and kill him, even as he had killed his predecessor. And he would be priest and offer the sacrifice on his grave."

Matilda waited, but he said no more. It was the first time she realized that he might have been thinking that perhaps after all he would not be victorious.

She thought of that again when she woke the next day to find another messenger from Lucca waiting. It was a shock to hear that Henry had assembled all the nobility of the city and the surrounding country and proclaimed the ban of the Empire against the traitorous Countess of Tuscany. But once the first shock was over, she found that every nerve was alive, as if she had just plunged into a mountain stream.

"We can keep in peace only what we are not afraid to lose," said the Pope thoughtfully. But when she told him that she was returning to Canossa at once to protect her heritage from the greed of her neighbors, he did not attempt to stop her.

"I shall be back with those scoundrels at my back before Henry comes again," she had boasted, to ease a little the shame of her helplessness.

And he had smiled as he blessed her.

CHAPTER VII

ALTHOUGH Matilda had made the journey from Rome to Canossa in a series of forced rides, always in terror lest Henry or one of his new allies should stop her way, yet it was a week after her arrival at Canossa before she heard anything certain of the King's movements. He was on the edge of her territory, making his way into Lombardy. For the present at least, the immediate menace of his troops was over. True, every day brought its complaints of atrocity and its pleas for aid in the repair of damages due to the passage of the invading army. But, on the whole, what had characterized his descent into Italy still held true to an amazing extent of his withdrawal. Henry had moved so fast that there had been little time for more than incidental and, even in a sense, accidental, damage to her lands.

Quite obviously, he had made no attempt to appropriate any of her or her vassals' territories or to seize any of her cities.

Matilda was under no illusion as to the significance of this apparent forbearance on Henry's part. It was his own interest that had dictated it, and not any sudden accession of humanity or tenderness for her welfare. This became all the clearer as the weeks passed, and the consequences of the meeting at Lucca began to materialize.

At first, Matilda tried to tell herself that once Henry and his army were safely across the Alps, there would be nothing more to fear for the present. But as the summer months rolled on, it became impossible even for her optimism to pretend that he had not done her serious hurt. For in putting her under the ban of the Empire he had given a pretext and a justification to any ambitious vassal, or greedy neighbor, or lawless city, that might be tempted to throw off the yoke of her authority.

"Most men," said Alberic, as they sat on the battlements one September day, "are quite immune to any infection of ideas. You may be sure that if these feudatories of yours have ever heard of the principles at issue between the King and the Pope, it has nothing to do with their present action."

The harvest was better this fall than last, and down the silver aisles of olive trees, the warm sunlight washed the full-awned wheat to gold. That would be one thing, Matilda thought, that they would not have to worry about this year.

"No," she said aloud, "I don't think I quite agree with you there. Anselm was here yesterday, and we were talking of conditions in Lucca. Now there is no question that there the root of the trouble is to be found in the clergy who have given money for their promotions and who have taken wives. A fair share of the nobility of the city are in the business, too, by sharing in the profits of the ecclesiastical traffic and by marriage. You know what happened when Anselm tried to enforce the canon law."

Alberic nodded. "I have often thought that it needed but one or two good leaders to raise the populace there as in Milan."

But Matilda shuddered. "You remember when the people of Florence began to yell that there should be no bishop and no lord and no king! It is dangerous to all order when the powers of this world begin to fall out."

Alberic smiled. "I understand that our friend Desiderius has been trying to tell Henry that."

"I think he's right. This strife which Henry is stirring up will be the ruin of Church and Empire both."

Alberic shrugged his shoulders. "That involves a certain amount of looking ahead, and Henry's world is the present. That is, I suppose, his strength."

Matilda suddenly became aware of how tightly clutched her hands were. "Never mind Henry. What I really want to talk to you about, Alberic, is this. Arduino thinks we should stay here at Canossa, and dig in, as it were, like otters or foxes in their holes."

"Arduino's advice has always seemed to me to have a good deal to be said for it. He is not very likely ever to be cheated or—"

Matilda brushed aside the light-hearted chaff. "But I am serious. It seems to me ignominious to sit here and do nothing. You need not preach to me Christian resignation. It has nothing to do with it."

"I shouldn't have thought of preaching to you Christian resignation—just now," he added gravely. "It is Christian resolution that you are thinking of rather, I take it. As a monk, well, you know, that is rather in my line."

It was not very flattering to her guest, she knew, to stare at him so, but sometimes the fantasy of Alberic passed the patience of a reasonable being.

"There are a great many things in the world that most people put up with, patiently or impatiently," went on Alberic, with a whimsical pretense of being judicious. "A monk doesn't. A great many things that other men deem necessities of existence, the monk knows he does not need or want. Many things that the children of the world—"

Matilda rose and leaned against the wall in front of them. "Frankly, I don't see what all this has to do with what I'm talking about."

"It's the central thing, Matilda. You want to do what Arduino considers rash, impossible. That is what the monk is interested in, you know. Not the conventional, the permitted, the tolerated, but—"

"I don't know about monks, Alberic, but I do know I want to do something. In fact," she tried hard to keep the little kink of defiance out of her voice, "I mean to do something." She looked steadily at him, but he made no movement to stop or to encourage her. "I don't intend to stay here and watch any chance of helping the Pope slip out of my hands. What I propose to do is to see if I cannot rally some of the more public-spirited of my vassals and get ready to make a real stand when Henry comes down to Italy next spring."

After she had finished, Alberic considered a minute or two before speaking. "I shouldn't say you were asking my advice, you know. You sound as if you had made up your mind."

She laughed. "I have, but still it would be decent of you to approve—if you can," she added.

He shook his head. "It is your own resolution and not my advice that counts in a thing like this. If you ask me if I think your plan will have much chance of succeeding, I don't think it will. But there are some things in which one must try the impossible. It doesn't matter if you fail, but it does matter if your cause goes by default."

It was her turn to smile. "I'm not a monk—yet. Have you any suggestions for making the impossible a little more possible?"

He leaned forward and spoke with rare directness. "I won't say I'm surprised at what you tell me, Matilda. I had thought of something like it myself. Suppose you let us at San Benedetto invite the lords and knights of your lands and the bishops and abbots to meet with us to consider these things? Face to face with you and with each other, not many of them will care to admit that they think you have been guilty of any breach of the peace of the Empire. As for what they will do, well, only Heaven knows that, anyway."

Some two months later, Alberic's cynical remark came back vividly to Matilda's mind. She was sitting in the chapter house at San Benedetto, in a high seat beside Alberic the Prior. The discussion of the affairs of the Marquisate of Tuscany had been going on now for some time, and men were beginning to break through the polite and cautious formulas of the first hours of the debate.

Alberic's prophesy had proved correct. More than half of her vassals and her cities and her abbeys had responded to her summons. And even of those who did not come, a fair majority had sent various excuses—illness, disturbances on their lands, the difficulty for the old of travel in this inclement weather—excuses which, as Alberic readily admitted, might have a good deal of truth in them. On the other hand, there were some who had not troubled to answer her summons. And there were a very few who said outright that they did not think they should be held to the services of a lord who was under the ban of the Empire. Only the city of Lucca had been insolent in its recalcitrance, and its insolence had taken a form which amused Alberic, the form of scruples of conscience. As good Christians, they felt that they ran serious peril of their immortal souls if they took any part in the seditious conspiracies of a prince who had been outlawed by the King. If the Countess Matilda would give evidence of a penitent heart, they would rejoice to help her win the favor of the King, but until then their well-known concern for the peace of Christendom made it impossible—and so the letter ran on in high-flown periods that left Matilda speechless and Alberic rocking with laughter.

"Trust the devil to quote Scripture," said Alberic, when he had a little recovered his composure.

"It's that Archdeacon of theirs with all that sanctimoniousness!" Matilda was still struggling vainly to control her indignation.

"Oh, no," said Alberic, "no priest can be half as pious as a layman who has just donned the habit for the occasion. That is the work of those burghers of yours, with a hint or two, of course, from the knights."

One other letter had been distinguished by some ingenuity of impertinence, but this Matilda had enjoyed more than Alberic, strangely enough. It was from Idebrandus, the son of Roland of Pisa, who in his first youth had aspired to Matilda's hand, and ever since his rejection by the Countess Beatrice had affected to take the lords of Tuscany somewhat cavalierly. Now, when he refused to be a party to the Countess' lawlessness, he took the occasion to point out that the known weakness of a woman's judgment made her rule a calamity, unless fortified by the authority of a husband. But the other recusants were either more discreet or less resourceful, for they contented themselves with very general refusals.

Matilda, thinking of these absentees, had made gracious acknowledgment of the fidelity of those who had actually come to the meeting, when she rose to plead her case before her vassals. Then without preamble she had plunged into the issue between the King and herself. "When the Pharisees sought to trap Our Lord that they might discredit him before the people, they asked him if it was lawful to give tribute to Caesar. He asked to see the coin of the tribute, and when they showed him a penny, he asked whose image and superscription it was, and they answered, 'Caesar's.' Then he said, 'Render therefore to Caesar the things that are Caesar's: and to God, the things that are God's.'" She went on to point out that here as always what had happened in Palestine was but a type of what happened all over the world in all times. The forms in which the issue arose in different times or places might be different, but at bottom it was the same question, and the decision which Our Lord made was made not for that one time alone but for the help and guidance of his followers in the ages to come.

But they had all looked so awed, and some so frightened at this beginning, that she had hastily come to grips with the present case. She began by reminding them that God had given two authorities, that of the Empire and that of the Church, and that each authority had its own proper sphere in which it operated and in which it was supreme. But of late by reason of the weakness of fallen nature and the evil of the times, the authority of Caesar had been taking possession of those things which belonged to God. Not only the King of Germany but the princes of this world in general had been using the things of God for their own ends. They had been choosing as bishops not the most religious and learned of men, but those who would best serve their own secular interests. And the result they had all seen in bishops who pursued wealth and power rather than tended their flocks as true pastors and shepherds should. Every one knew how great the evil was that had come of this subjection of the Church to the State. For most of those ills which every one, layman and priest alike, deplored in the life of the Church might be traced back to this habit of their time of using the Church which Christ had founded for the salvation of all men for the private ends of secular power. And the responsibility for all these evils lay not just upon the evildoers but upon all those who supported the perversion of God's order which had made them possible.

Again she paused, and she saw that they were all now listening with deep attention, and that the tension of awe, characteristic of those who are a little frightened by any effort to bring them too close to the things they profess to believe, had quite relaxed. Then she went on to tell them that this was the reason why the Pope was striving so manfully to free the Church from its subjection to the State. This was why he was insisting that the bishop must receive his investiture from the Church and not from the King, that he must be chosen by clergy and people and not by the prince, and that the oaths he must swear should be first to the Church and not to the State.

But here she was conscious of a certain stiffening in the necks before her and of a certain freezing in many of the faces. For here she had come to the crux of the matter, the immediate emergency that demanded some action on their part, the making of a decision that for good or for evil might affect all their fortunes. So she noted with a sinking of the heart that many of the men before her were palpably on their guard. And with this in the forefront of her consciousness, she went on to reassure them that the Pope had no thought of usurping the things that were Caesar's, that he could not even if he wished to, but that the things which belonged to God and which Caesar had appropriated, those he was determined to reclaim that the Church of God might be free for the service of God.

For a third time she paused, but there could be no doubt of the fascinated interest with which they all hung on her words. True, the suspicion was still there; fright and reserve still hardened many faces. But sympathetic or wary, every pair of eyes in the room was fixed on hers. Almost without taking breath, she swept on. Power, she pointed out, was but a trust, and all Christian princes were bound to the service of God and his Church. It was as such a trustee that she had been, to the extent of her resources, aiding the Pope in his fight for the independence of the Church. "If all of you, my friends and my loyal vassals who have so generously answered my summons today, if all of you give me your loyal support, I am sure that we will enable the Pope to win his great purpose and free the Church of God forever, both from the powers that oppress her from without and those that corrupt her from within. I am certain that this will be the result of your cooperation. But if you do not help me, I still assure you that I will do all I can to help the Pope. If all this land of Tuscany should forsake me, and I should be left standing alone, naked of any strength or help, I should with my bare hands support this cause and with the last breath of my body bear witness to my conviction of its justice."

There was applause when she finished, and for the first hours of the debate, the awe of her plea still hung over the speakers, but as the day wore on, and the memory of her eloquence faded, she saw that men began to speak more and more plainly of what was in their thoughts. Of course, they were all loyal children of the Church, but it was clear that a good many of them were not prepared to carry that loyalty to any extremes that would jeopardize their immediate interests. Tuscany was but one of the parts of Christendom, they reminded themselves again and again, and any rash action now might mean that they would have to face the might of the whole Empire arrayed against them. Indeed, it was quite evident that a good many of them much preferred to hazard the wrath of the Pope rather than the wrath of the King, for the Pope would always be merciful to repentance, but it would be harder to placate a King with nothing to stay the vengeance of his wounded pride. And there were still others who were anxious about their legal position.

"After all," said one of these last, a short man with a great head and a mop of nervous white hair, whom Matilda presently recognized as Enrico of Pisa, "it's all very well to talk about these fundamental principles about which there is so much dispute, but the plain fact is that we would be breaking every principle of feudal law in not answering the summons of our lord the King."

"The Countess of Tuscany is our lord," objected a voice from the middle of the crowd on the benches.

But Enrico was on his feet, shaking his white hair with the earnestness of his convictions, "Ah, but do not forget that the ban of the Empire has dissolved all fealties. Not but what," he added hastily, smiling up at Matilda, "I hope that ban will soon be removed and all of us restored to the loyalty we so much value and are so anxious to render."

So the debate went, some arguing vigorously on the side of the Pope and Countess, others insisting on their loyalty to the Countess as the sole point at issue, still others hinting their uneasiness at their legal position, and a few declaring outright that they thought it absurdly rash to rouse the anger of the King. As Alberic had foreseen, the majority of them were obviously wary of any commitments. They did not want to refuse to support their lord to her face, but neither did they want to risk the consequences of declaring against the King. As a result of the meeting, Matilda had the satisfaction of knowing that she had a nucleus of loyal support to be counted on in any emergency. But she was aware, also, that there was another group who would embrace the earliest opportunity to make trouble for her. Between them was the great mass of her vassals of whom all one could say was what Alberic had said, "God alone knows."

When the conference was over, Matilda turned to Alberic. He nodded briefly. Then when all the company had taken their leave, he said quietly, "At least, you know whom you can count on. As for the others, it depends on what happens in the next few months."

"Silver?" She tried to keep the bitterness out of her voice.

"And promises and prospects of profit. It's a sordid business, but it is even in such an arena that your cause is being tried."

"I will not buy anybody," said Matilda doggedly.

Alberic smiled. "Surely, you don't mean that you will refuse to give loyal vassals money to buy food for their garrisons or arms?"

It was the old quizzical Alberic who smiled at her. Then as he ticked off the items on his fingers, he went on, "Loyalty, an understanding and an acceptance of the principles involved, statesmanship, and good housekeeping—these are your counters. Henry may give you one or two more—brutality of his troops, troubles in Germany, something particularly atrocious in his behavior, but—"

She was outraged. "Alberic, I am fighting for a principle, for the greatest thing I have ever known." She paused, ashamed.

But he only said with matter-of-fact unconcern, "By spring we shall know."

CHAPTER VIII

By spring, Matilda was ready to admit, she did know. It was a night in March, and though it was not cold, the wind had risen and was howling in and out among the roofs and towers of Canossa. Sitting fully dressed by the fire in her chamber, she had tried to sleep, but the roaring of the wind against the shutters overhead had wakened her, and now she could not sleep again. She did not want to think any more about what she was going to do tonight, for she had made up her mind, and now in a few hours it would be all over with. There was nothing else to do. Of that she was thoroughly sure.

And yet as the wind filled her head so that it seemed as if all the warm drowsiness of a moment ago had been blown away, she could not help thinking of it all again. It was not for want of effort that she had come to this. Ever since the meeting at San Benedetto, she had been working desperately to raise forces to meet the threatened advance of Henry. But though a large number of her vassals were very glad to accept her gifts of silver to strengthen the fortification of their castles, they were very slow in making definite promises of levies for the army with which she hoped to stop the advance of Henry. The same was true of many even of her bishops. They applauded the piety which enabled them to augment the defenses of their cities, but they seemingly feared to withdraw any of their troops from their own restless domains. In other words, those vassals who were willing to profess allegiance preferred to employ their treasure and hers on the strengthening of their own positions rather than on the pooling of their common resources.

As Alberic never failed to point out when she expressed her disappointment at this preoccupation of her vassals with their own advantage, one could from their point of view hardly blame them. These men might not understand any of the issues involved in the strife between the powers of Church and State; they might be, as indeed so many of them were, quite unaware that there were any fundamental issues. But they knew by instinct that in any prolonged struggle between the sources of power, there was bound to result a state of anarchy. And then it would go very hard with those who were weak, and it might go very well with the unscrupulous who were prepared to take advantage of the chances of the time.

"These are facts, not ideas," Alberic had reminded her only that morning, when he had stopped at Canossa on his way to Rome. "And for facts, the children of this world have easily the advantage of the children of light." He had said it smiling, but his eyes had told her more directly than anything he could say that he comprehended the heartbreak which she had ceased to try to put into words.

Now as she looked into the fire and wondered if it would last until Maria came to knock at her door, she found herself wondering again if perhaps she would not have done better to have tried to gather up the stray men, the footloose, and the wanderers, as Arduino had counseled, and make her army of them. She was still sick at heart whenever she thought of what had happened when the news first came of Henry's crossing the Alps in early February. In spite of all her discouragement and her anxiety, she had still hoped that when the threatened return of the King was a fact, her tardy vassals would then rally. But the effect had been entirely different.

Fully half of those who had professed their devotion had replied to her summons that they dared not reduce their own defenses until they were sure that Henry was not going to molest them. Of the others, some had come at once to Canossa with their levies, and there had been a few days when her hopes had risen high. But Henry had almost immediately proceeded to invest Mantua, and she had been forced to send all the strength she could spare to help the frightened citizens of that city. As for those men who had promised to come but had not yet come, most of them returned to their own territories, sending word that they would come at once as soon as Henry's army had passed by their lands on its way to Rome. All her hope of raising an army large enough to stay Henry had vanished. And she had been forced to remain at Canossa, helplessly watching

Henry invest first one city then another, never staying long enough to make a siege effective and capture the beleaguered city, but always making preparations that reduced the inhabitants to a state of terror and brought frantic appeals to Canossa.

So Henry had made his way to Rome, and she had hoped that once the immediate menace was past, her feeble-hearted vassals would make some effort to come together and help her. But whether it was their own timidity or the persistent efforts of Henry in stirring up trouble in village and town, the great majority of them still professed themselves unable to leave their lands in such uncertain times. At the same time, as if to justify these fears, two of her strongest vassals, the lords of Brescello and Guastalla, chose this occasion to try to settle an old dispute over some church lands, and several lords of the Lucca district openly repudiated their allegiance to the Countess of Tuscany and seized some of her possessions in the neighborhood of Florence.

At her feet the fire was falling apart in a pool of embers, and the room was growing cold. She drew her cloak tight about her shoulders and reflected that she would not have much longer to wait now. For a moment as the wind rattled at the shutters above, she thought she heard the expected knock on the door, but there was no reply to her, "Come in." She trembled a little as she waited, listening to the noisy silence.

She had been expecting the Pope's appeal ever since she had heard of Henry's coming. Indeed, she had anticipated it by sending word to Rome that in all probability it would be impossible for her to bring even the help she had brought last year. It had been a bitter moment when she had had to confess defeat in such a manner, but it was nothing to the bitterness she had known two days ago when just as the full measure of her helplessness was apparent, she had received the Pope's desperate appeal for the help he must know she did not have it in her power to give. "I know, my daughter, you are hard-pressed, but I do not know where else to turn for aid to reach me in time to bolster the failing courage of these Romans. What you can give me now will be worth many times any help that may come later."

So she had taken her resolution. She listened as she heard a sudden rattle of steel above the turmoil of the wind. Then she identified it as the movement of the men who were going out to relieve the watch. It must be midnight. It was the hour when the dead are supposed to walk again this troubled earth. How many there were who might walk at Canossa tonight! Azzo, and Tedaldo, and Conrad, and those whom she had known, Boniface, and Godfrey the Elder, and Godfrey the Younger, and Beatrice. Of them all, only Beatrice would have understood and sympathized without reservation. As for the rest—

She was sure that she heard footsteps approaching her door. Not the quick light steps of Maria that she was expecting, but stealthy, lingering steps. She held her breath. The room was nearly dark now, for without the fire the single taper on the table by the bed did little to dispel the cavernous gloom. The door fitted tightly, and it was locked. But still if anybody suspected what was happening, it would be easy on a night like this to follow her and Maria to the chapel.

She had agreed with Alberic at once when he had suggested that it would be easier for him to reach Rome in safety if her household did not know what he was carrying in the bags thrown across his horse's neck. Once out of the castle the average passerby seeing how small was his escort, would assume that he was merely carrying the usual monastic tribute of books and a little fine wine to Rome. But the real reason for her caution she knew only too well. There would be time enough later for her vassals to learn that she had sent the famous treasure of Canossa to Rome to be melted down for bread and for arms and for the convincing of the dubious and the unenthusiastic. But deeper even than that, and here she listened again for those nearly inaudible footfalls, there was the pride of her house that she was offering as a sacrifice. As a sacrifice, she reflected grimly, to a cause that those who had hung those silver and gold crowns in the sanctuary of Canossa and brought those jeweled chalices from far lands to make beautiful the home altars, would very imperfectly understand or sympathize with. All but her mother. If any of her forefathers should choose this night to protest the rifling of their treasure hoard, she hoped her mother would be there, too, for she alone of all of them would deem the cause worth the immolation of pride and family faith.

The steps came nearer. She rose from her place by the dead fire, unable any longer to bear the uncertainty, and strode to her door. But even as she turned the key, she heard the steps running toward the great hall. There were two turns in that passage, and by the time she could reach the end, the spy would be lying hidden among the sleeping forms on the benches. So she opened the door with enough noise, she hoped, to discourage further reconnoitering. She had just satisfied herself that the space in front of her chamber, at least, was empty, when she caught the sound of the steps she had been waiting for. And in a moment the low voice of Maria was telling her that the castle was quiet again after the midnight changing of the guard.

There was no need for her to worry about the candle which she lighted in the sacristy of the chapel. So feeble was its light in the enveloping darkness that there was no danger of any beam reaching the thin slot of window near the roof. Maria held the leaden candlestick while Alberic took the key from Matilda's hand and knelt down beside the great iron-hasped treasure chest. The unsteady light of the candle fell on his cowled head and threw fantastic shadows against the wall, so that it looked as if some gigantic insect were clawing at the exaggerated mass of the chest.

Nervously, Matilda laughed at the absurdity of the distortion and Maria echoed her laugh in clear-voiced, girlish relief. Alberic looked up uncertainly. In a moment the key had turned with a heavy grating of the iron wards, and with both hands he was raising the heavy cover. Then he fell back.

The first thing Matilda lifted from the clutter of sheepskins in which the treasure had been wrapped was the gold cup that Hilary the Greek had made.

"It seems a pity to have it melted up when it is so new, but we need everything we have," said Matilda, giving it to Alberic. She had hardly spoken when there came a yell of anguish from the darkness of the door behind her. Before she could move, a dark figure had rushed out from the shadows and flung himself at her feet.

"Madonna, it is the cup of dreams." It was Hilary the Greek, and in the light which Maria had turned on him, his eyes shone frantically as if he had been drinking new wine.

For a moment Matilda gazed down on him, too astonished to move. Then she remembered. It must have been Hilary who had come to the door of her chamber.

"How did you know?" she asked. The man paid no heed to her question, however, but leaped to his feet and snatched the cup from the monk's hands.

"It is not gold; it is dreams," he cried passionately.

Alberic who had yielded the cup without a struggle took the hand of the frenzied artist and held it for a moment, while he spoke in very quiet tones, "Hilary, we are all of us having to give up our dreams at this time. If Henry defeats the Pope and overwhelms him, there will be little peace in this poor world, and little chance for artist or any other man to think of dreams."

But the Greek clutched the cup to his breast. "It is the most beautiful thing I have ever made. Listen, my lord Prior, and you, my lady. One dreams of how things should look, one sees them clearly, and one thinks each time that the work of his hands will at last look like what he sees so clearly in his mind's eye. But it never does, Madonna. It never does—" His voice rose in a scream.

Matilda looked at him helplessly, unable to speak for very pity and for shame of her part in his anguish. But Alberic laid his hand on the frenzied arm waving so grotesquely among the shadows on wall and floor.

"Listen to me," he said quietly. "What you have just said is true of every man born. It is the condition of this our earthly life. Only in the kingdom of heaven shall we see the dream made immediately manifest in the thing."

Something in the low voice of Alberic, in the look of his eyes, perhaps, quieted the frantic man. He looked up almost steadily at Alberic, "But you do not see. This time I had practically done it. For once the thing I had made looked like the thing I had dreamed."

"I know," said Alberic. "It is a beautiful thing, quite beautiful enough to be offered to God. Listen, man—the Pope has been dreaming a dream, too, not of a cup, but of a world, united and ordered in God's love and in obedience to his law. It is a dream of justice for all, of peace for all. It is a dream of the world made as God intended it to be made. Will you not give your cup for that?"

For a moment the artist looked at the monk. Then without a word, he handed the chalice back to Alberic and hid his face in the sleeve of his garment. With bowed head Alberic received the cup and held it in front of him as if it contained the Blessed Wine.

Presently, he raised his head and put his hand on the artist's arm, "Hilary my friend, of one thing in this starved world of ours there is no failure. You need not be afraid. Dreams, of all the commodities of man, are alone incapable of being hoarded or destroyed. God gave you the dream of this cup. He will give you one more beautiful. Of that you may be sure."

The artist's eyes were shining now. Matilda took his hand, "Hilary, if ever again I have silver or gold to keep, you may be sure you shall have the first of it for your cup."

And without any more hesitation she knelt down and began taking from the chest the treasure which her family had been accumulating at Canossa for the last century and gave it to Alberic. When she had reached the bottom, she straightened up and checked over the things which Alberic had put on the vestment chest near by: "The crown which the Empress sent to our founder, the crown which the Emperor gave to his son, the cup which the Pope gave to his wife, the chalice and paten which the Pope sent when the chapel was built, the cup which the Eastern Emperor sent to my grandfather when he had been on an embassy, the chalice which my uncle the Pope used at his coronation, the crown which my father gave my mother at her marriage—" so the long roster of fame and wealth and triumph went on.

"They are all there," she concluded. "Tell the Pope that if I had more, I would send them. And tell him that of all these treasures, the richest is the cup which Hilary the Greek made and now gives to his service."

CHAPTER IX

It was only in June that Matilda finally dared to go to Rome. Hopeless as her affairs still seemed, the very setting out was yet something in the nature of a release. For the agony of those helpless months in which she had waited at Canossa for news of the King's movements was now over. Again, the heat had driven Henry to withdraw his troops to Lombardy, and the immediate and direct threat to the peace of her realm was past. But still more important, Henry had once again invested the city of Rome with all the forces he could muster, and once again he had been forced to withdraw without accomplishing anything.

As she waited now in the Lateran Palace for the Pope to receive her, Matilda reflected that she could fairly claim some of the credit of that result. True, rumor said that Robert Guiscard the Norman had marshaled the forces with which he had returned from the East and the vassals who had come to meet him before the walls of Rome and before Tivoli, and that those displays of festive strength had made an impression on the imagination of Henry and played no small part in the forming of his decision to retreat, however much he might attribute it to the weather. But Matilda knew that neither the Normans nor the weather had played so large a part in the determination of Henry's course as the fact that the Romans had withstood all his blandishments, verbal and monetary alike, and had refused to open their gates to him. And knowing the Romans as she had known them all her life, turbulent and venal and unstable, she reflected grimly that the gold which she had scraped together so painfully had played its part in their determination. The sword she could not wield herself she had put into the Pope's hand.

It was a beautiful day without, and she walked through the open door into the loggia opening on one of the inner courts of the Lateran. It was a shabby little garden as if there had not been much of time or energy to spend on it of late, but in its ground ivies and its laurels, its roses and its iris, and its carved marble wellhead, there was something of the peace and the gentle grace of all gardens. And though the arches of the loggia in their bare stone lines, with blank slabs of unadorned stucco work between, suggested the monastery rather than the imperial palace, they lacked neither the dignity nor the restfulness of austerity.

This bare and somewhat haggard peace seemed the fitting symbol of the state of mind in which she had arrived in Rome, where the mere fact of her presence was such a triumph, and there was nothing else but helplessness and penury for her to glory in.

"His Holiness bade me welcome you," said a thin but bright voice behind her.

Matilda turned to look at an extraordinary face, regarding her with lively curiosity. Two features immediately leaped out to her surprised eye. The first was a slightly curly down of bright red beard over a delicately pink chin. The second was a pair of gleaming eyes, almost fierce in their intensity of regard.

As Matilda stared at this startling apparition in a monk's gray robe and cowl, the fierce eyes twinkled, and the stranger answered the question in her eyes, "My lady Countess, I am Bruno of Segni."

"Ah, I remember, the Pope wrote that like his namesake the Blessed Gregory you are writing a commentary on Isaias. It must be very hard to keep your mind on a piece of writing at such a time as this," she said, watching the color deepen in the thin cheeks. What bright brown hair the little man had, who looked so much like the Judas in a tapestry that hung in her mother's house at Pisa!

There was a gleam in the tense eyes, and then the monk smiled. "But this is such a time as Isaias himself wrote in. It is the same sort of day of judgment as his when men's sins have come upon their heads, and the just and the unjust alike are in danger of perishing but for the goodness of God."

"That is certainly what it does seem like, a day of judgment," she agreed. "I suppose that is why it is hard for me to imagine thinking of any other day. And yet," she added hastily, as the gleaming eyes dilated, "I suppose the present makes it easier to understand the past."

But the little man shook his head, "I am not sure that it is not rather that the days of Isaias make it easier to understand ours. For we walk blindly through today into an unknown tomorrow. But these past times are finished, and we see how the sins of men brought their inescapable punishment. But for today, we do not know what the end will be."

"Sometimes," said Matilda grimly, "I am afraid we do."

She was at once ashamed of that discouraged rejoinder, but Bruno seemed completely unaware of what she had said. "It is a very exciting time to be alive today," he said abruptly, his eyes shining. "For the hand of the Lord may be seen bringing mighty things to pass. If you had seen the hosts of Baal turn from the walls of Rome—"

But he did not finish his sentence, for a light step came behind them, and the voice of the Pope made Matilda turn. "God is indeed good, my daughter, to bring you here."

She knelt to kiss his ring, and then she looked up into his face. It was not only that he was tired, but there was a certain look of high patience in that face that spoke more movingly than any words, of pain the sting of which could not be plucked out. The tears came into her eyes, and his face for all the sharpness of its look blurred. As she struggled to her feet, he took her hand and held it until she was leaning against the stone pillar of the arch.

"God has been very good to me, Matilda, in giving me faith such as yours," he said, sitting down on a chair against the wall and motioning to Matilda to sit down again on the low stone seat that ran below the arches. "I need not tell you that Alberic brought your treasure at a time when I did not know where I could turn for silver to buy bread for my people."

"They have stood faithfully against Henry from all I hear," she said tentatively, searching his face for some hint of what was in his heart when he fronted the future which so frightened her.

He shook his head. "They will not do so indefinitely. Not, God knows, that I blame them for finding the strain of the siege and the fear of it hard to bear. But they on whom it presses hardest, the poor and the helpless women, they are the most patient, you know. It is the merchants who see their trade stopped and the nobles who must compose their jealousies and spend their treasure against the siege who wax most impatient."

"But traditionally, you remember, the ancient families of Rome have always been jealous of Emperor or King." This was but cold comfort for a generous heart straining for a deeper sympathy, and Matilda knew it. But sometimes, she thought sadly, there is more to be depended upon in the persistence of the selfish interests of men than in their more unstable loyalties.

"They are jealous of any power that imposes restraint upon their greed and turbulence," he answered. "I don't suppose you have heard of what the Council of Clergy did in May?"

Matilda shook her head.

"They voted a motion declaring that the goods of the Church ought not to be alienated for military purposes. In other words, the resources of the Church are not to be spent for the defense of the Church."

"And they were not thinking just of the levies Henry has been making upon the German bishoprics?" Matilda asked, astonished.

"These were the Roman clergy. Some of them," said the Pope judicially, "were idealists who hate to see priests in arms and the charity of the faithful spent in blood. But those who pressed their fellows to such a decision at this time were men who had listened to the agents of Henry. They have been all through Rome, telling the simple that it is only the obstinacy of the Pope who exposes them to this hazard, that if they open to the King, there will be peace."

"It is as if," said Bruno of Segni, "a robber should say to an honest man, 'Give me your treasure, and there will be no violence.'"

Matilda laughed, but the Pope shook his head gravely, and a note of bitterness, rare for him, came into his voice, "God knows I wish it were that. If I could give the nothing of personal wealth I possess, if I could give my life to Henry, I would be glad to do so. But it is as if a bandit should come to the door of some lonely grange and say to the master, 'Now, I am a lover of peace, and I do not wish any bloodshed. So give me your wife and your children and your servants to me for slaves, and I will take them and go quietly away.' That is what Henry really says, and it is that which no householder worthy of the trust God has given him could yield so long as he had even his bare hand to hold between his family and the robber."

There was an uncomfortable silence as the Pope finished; so Matilda said hastily, "But Henry has gone back to Germany for this year."

"For this year," repeated the Pope quietly, smoothing his red robe over his knee.

"The Norman Guiscard will help you next year," suggested the monk.

"Guiscard!" In her astonishment Matilda almost gasped the name of the dreaded invader against whose forces she had fought her first battle. It brought back, too, the memory of that first girlish triumph and the unshadowed pride of inexperience. She winced at the overpowering bitterness of the memory of that first careless certainty, when she had ridden into Rome with the sword of a Norman knight rubbing at her knee and the populace cheering in the summer streets.

But the Pope seemed unaware of her exclamation, for he turned to Bruno. "Guiscard has indeed professed willingness to help us, but I have a letter from Desiderius of Monte Cassino today. And he tells me that all of the Norman lands are in a turmoil. While Robert has been trying to conquer the Eastern Emperor, his vassals at home have been making good their independence and snatching all of his possessions that they can lay hands on."

Matilda smiled grimly, and a look of compassion came into the face of the speaker as he added, "You have probably heard how even his own nephew, Jordan of Capua, has gone over to Henry without waiting for his return to consult him."

Matilda looked at him quickly. "But Jordan had sworn fealty to Your Holiness."

The Pope shrugged his shoulders. "I have given up counting the number of those who have sworn fealty to Saint Peter and forgotten their word."

"The faithless in the hour of judgment—" began Bruno, but the Pope raised his hand.

"No," he said firmly. "Who knows if, but for our sins, they might not have escaped this temptation of forswearing? I should not fear to fail if I did not know that ultimately it is my own sins and my own shortcomings that are to blame."

It was then that Matilda made up her mind to speak of the fear that had been troubling her ever since the Pope first spoke of Robert Guiscard.

"My lord," she began, "have you ever thought of what might happen if Robert Guiscard and his Normans should enter Rome?"

The Pope looked at her in unaffected bewilderment. She had known it would be hard to voice her suspicion, but now she was completely at a loss. She began over again. "I mean, have you thought of what he might do?"

"Might do?" repeated the Pope. "But Robert Guiscard would come to Rome only as the sworn defender of the Church. Remember that, though he never makes a promise unless he sees some profit, Robert Guiscard has never been accused by his worst enemies of breaking his word." There was a trace of indignation in the Pope's defence of his ally.

It gave Matilda courage to defy misunderstanding. "My lord," she said, rising and standing before him with her right hand outstretched and her left tight-clutched within her mantle, "I beg you to forgive me for persisting, but everybody in the south knows that the Normans are savages, brave it is true, but cruel and without pity. Think of what would happen—"

But a dark flush burned in the shadowed cheek of the Pope, and he raised his hand to stop her. "Do you think it would fare better with Rome if Henry were suffered to sack it? You have not heard yet what Guibert who calls himself Clement is doing. If it is not the green fields burned with fire, it is cattle slain. If it is not the cattle, it is the peasants themselves, hanged for trying to protect their miserable hovels or burned with the hay in their byres."

Her heart softened at the agony with which he said this last; yet she persisted. "But they are doing the work of Antichrist who do these things, and the deed is worthy of the cause. Oh, my lord, let me see once more if I cannot rally my misguided lands to your defense."

The indignation had gone out of his voice when he answered, "My beloved daughter and my valiant soldier, you know that not a day passes without my prayer that you will save your lands. And no misfortune of my own so grieves me as the thought of the poverty and misery you bear as the price of your fidelity to me."

He paused, and the tears came into Matilda's eyes so that she could not look at him.

"You may be sure that I will spare neither myself nor anything of mine to save the least of these my people from suffering. But I cannot surrender those things which are not mine but God's to Henry or anybody else, if there is any way in which I can save them—order and peace and justice."

Then as Matilda gazed at him without saying anything, Gregory added in a lighter tone, "Not, you understand, that I think Guiscard or his Normans the savages you fear. I grant he has long been a thorn in my side with his raids into the lands of the Church, but he has sworn to forbear any more attacks on Church property and to defend the Church against her enemies. We Italians are too prone to think any people but ourselves savages, you know."

They talked for a few minutes more. The Pope was sure that the next time Henry would be determined to break into the city, and he was afraid the Romans would not hold out.

"My lord," said Matilda at last, seeing the slow afternoon shadows lengthening on the broad paved walk in the open garden, "I do not see any way in which I can possibly get help, and I am going home to get it."

The Pope smiled, and for a moment something of the playfulness of happier hours looked out of his gaunt and shadowed face. "Spoken like a Christian, my child. When we meet in that City, we shall not grieve for the times we were beaten, but we shall rejoice that we were not overcome. God bless you."

When she turned back to the door to look at him again, he was still standing with his right hand outstretched in blessing and that look of stillness making a light in his dark and troubled face. She turned back quickly that he might not see her tears.

✳ BOOK VI ✳

THE GREEN FIELDS

CHAPTER I

IT was dark when Matilda reached the village of Canossa that night. And the few inhabitants, petty officials for the most part, who had ventured out of their hovels with torches to meet her, looked pinched and frightened. It was still raining, as it had been all the way from Mantua, but she threw back her hood that they might see her face as they crowded round her at the end of the castle drawbridge. The rain beat on the thin stuff of her veil, and she shivered, but the peasants in front of her looked so wretched that she smiled at them and reached in her purse for largesse. In the torchlight she found in her hand only a few copper pennies. She gave them to the bailiff of the village.

"It is all I have," she said. Yet the cheers of the peasants echoed behind her as she rode over the drawbridge.

But the impression of overwhelming gloom and fear descended upon her again when she entered the main courtyard of the castle and found it deserted but for Antonio the steward, standing by the hall porch with a flare in his hand. Back of him, the wet stone glistened in the light, and the beams of the porch stood out in flickering contortions of mass as the flame wavered in the dank air. So portentous did the single figure appear, lighted there in the clutching dark, that she paused for a moment to look at him. Behind, she heard her companions stop abruptly.

"How are you all?" she asked, trying to recapture the thrill of homecoming that she had lost in the village below.

The old man took a step forward. "God bless your ladyship for coming back to us. The maids will go quietly to bed now of nights."

Again she tried to smile. "They seem to have gone to bed without me tonight."

Antonio bowed stiffly, the flare winnowing the dark with grotesque flashes of light as he moved. "I sent them all to their beds at sundown. It saves fuel and light, and they are not so hungry."

For a moment she was angry at this repetition of distress she could do so little to alleviate. "You're positively croaking tonight, my friend. Is that the best welcome you can give me?" And then as the old man cringed, she was ashamed and patted his thin shoulder. "I know you have done your best, and you know I am grateful."

The frightened face lighted with pleasure, and again Matilda marveled at the mystery of affection, for which a little breath can sweeten so much labor. The old man flung the door open.

The hall was dark except for a little heap of dusky red in the center. The torch in the steward's hand threw a beam of mist upon one of the great timbers of the roof leaping suddenly out of the night with mighty show of strength and purpose and as suddenly vanishing into the night a couple of arms' lengths beyond. It was cold, too, and the air was heavy with the dank, sour smell of mouldy stone. Involuntarily, Matilda shivered again.

The old man bustled over to the fire, before which knelt something, dark and shapeless on hands and knees, blowing at it. He stooped down, and immediately the shadows pulled together, and his wife Lucia was bowing to Matilda.

"I will look after the fire, Lucia. Get her ladyship some wine. You must be very tired, my lady, coming all the way from Mantua in this rain," he said between pokes at the fire.

Matilda turned to her companions. "Make yourselves at home. My lord Bishop, will you sit here?"

The dark forms scattered, but Anselm of Lucca stayed at her side. "Please sit there yourself by the fire, Matilda," he said in his easy, clear voice. "You have ridden longer and harder than any of us."

Matilda obeyed, then she turned again to the shadows. "Maria, come and sit at my feet and warm yourself. Lucia will bring us what we need." The girl hesitated; then she protested in a voice in which habitual gayety shimmered through fatigue, "But I really am not tired, your ladyship."

"Better sit down," said the Bishop. "You know how simple folk like us always suspect their neighbors who can endure more than they can, of being in league with the devil."

The whimsy of Anselm, the bright laughter of the girl, and the sudden crackling into flame of the newly kindled fire made Matilda's heart leap up. She turned to the old steward now standing attentively at her side, "It was partly that all these months of going from one frightened town to another have made me want a little rest at home, and it was partly that I was afraid that if too many of these lies that Henry's people are always spreading about my being killed or taken prisoner or deserting the Pope reached you here, you would be completely discouraged. So I decided I had better come home."

Antonio murmured his pleasure; then he hesitated. Matilda looked at him wearily, not liking to disappoint his affection again, and yet half guessing that the old man yearned to begin on the long tale of his troubles. He cleared his throat, and now, warm and a little refreshed, Matilda tried to brace herself to what she knew was coming.

But at that moment the old woman Lucia came in with a leathern pitcher of wine, and her husband busied himself with pouring it into pewter cups. It was sour and rather thin, but it warmed the stomach, and it cheered a little the tired heart. Matilda returned her empty cup to the old man.

"I can give your ladyship some porridge and dried fish and bread," said Lucia anxiously. "If we had known—"

"Of course," Matilda hastened to reassure her. "Anything that is warm and filling will do. And anyway it is Lent—"

"Tomorrow," interrupted Anselm gently, "is Easter."

Matilda looked at him in the soft glow of light that now warmed the little circle around the hearth.

"I had forgotten," she acknowledged.

The old steward wiped his eyes. "My lady, there is so little for a feast tomorrow. You see—" he hesitated.

Matilda leaned forward in the pleasant glow of the fire. "I know I have been sending here for fresh supplies all the time, and now you are short, yourselves. It was not that I had forgotten that the harvests were lean last year, but everywhere there is so much hunger. And now—" she looked up into the haggard face of the old man—"I have left my own hungry."

"No," said Antonio hastily, "we were glad to obey your ladyship's orders."

But Lucia put her round and bustling figure between her husband and his mistress, "Only my man has been so worried that there would not be enough here to see us through the spring. And those lazy sluts of girls have grumbled because they could not stuff their worthless bellies, with all the rest of the world hungry."

"I know," said her mistress hastily. "You have done very well, and I shall not forget it."

For a few minutes there was silence, and Matilda and her companions sat gazing into the miraculous glow of the fire, their tired limbs relaxing in the warmth.

"I had thought to keep Easter of this year in Rome," said Matilda presently, more to herself than to anyone else. "It is almost two years since I have been in Rome. Two years of fighting and labor, and"—she looked up and smiled at Anselm—"defeat." She opened her tight-clutched fingers and spread them out to the fire that was now blazing gayly on the hearth.

"It is not evening of the last day yet," said Anselm quietly.

"It seems almost like it, my lord Bishop," she replied. "There is not a town in all my lands in which there is not hunger from burned and stolen crops, or fighting between those who are for the Pope and those who are for the King, or prostration from siege, or terror from the fear of siege. That is a picture of a successful ruler for you!"

But Anselm only smiled. There was nothing forced about that smile. It was as if he had suddenly found himself amusing. Then as Matilda looked at him, he said, "You can hardly expect a bishop who cannot persuade his flock to let him into his city to pass judgment on anybody else as a ruler."

But she shook her head. "You know that next to not being able to help the Pope, I count Lucca my greatest failure."

Anselm was about to reply when a lifted voice behind the little circle about the fire drew the attention of all. It was Lucia with one hand on her husband's arm and the other making an elaborate pretense of screening her own mouth. "But you should tell her, man. She will want to know."

Matilda looked at the man and wife and waited. Seeing her eyes upon him, the old man came forward, "I did not mean to deceive you, my lady, but you know that messengers from Rome usually bring you grief, and I knew you were tired." He looked appealingly at his mistress.

"Bring him here at once. I quite understand," she nodded reassuringly. "But I must see him."

No one spoke until Antonio returned, bringing a slender figure wrapped in a muddy cloak. As the latter sank on one knee before her, Matilda exclaimed in astonishment, "Piero Frangipane! What has happened that you are here?" But even as she asked the question, she knew the answer. For only in the event of some ultimate disaster would the young man, who was one of the richest and bravest of the nobles of Rome, have come as a messenger.

And the look of pity with which the young man regarded her increased her terror. "What is it?" she faltered.

"The Pope is all right," said Piero. "He was able to take refuge in the fortress of Sant' Angelo."

"Then?" said Matilda, sitting down again, now that she knew the best and the worst.

"The Romans opened to Henry." The young man clenched his right arm about the hilt of his sword as he spoke.

"Bribed?" In a low, scornful voice came the single syllable.

Matilda saw the flush of shame darken in the cheek of young Frangipane, and she turned indignantly upon Arduino. But he had relapsed into the sullen silence that had of late been his habitual manner.

The young man, however, seemed determined not to dodge the shameful fact. "It was the money which the Emperor Alexius Comnenus sent from Constantinople that enabled Henry to buy his way in."

"Alexius?" Matilda gazed at Piero. For a moment it seemed as if all the powers of the world had gathered against them, and she thought of those prophecies of the coming of Antichrist that should presage the end of the world. She remembered how as a child she had been terrified by a sermon which Peter Damian had preached on that theme. Suddenly, she envied that childish terror at the thought of the destruction of a world she could not bear to have end.

"Alexius was glad, I think, to help Henry, for it would keep Guiscard at home in Italy and indirectly protect his own lands," replied the young Frangipane.

"And you surrendered to Henry without a blow?" Again Matilda turned to the point from where the voice of Arduino came contemptuously out of the half-darkness.

But she forgot the offender in the sudden passion that lighted the face of the young man, "By heaven, no. They were fighting in the streets when I left. Every inch that Clement and Henry have won outside of the Lateran is stained with the best blood in Rome. That at least we can set against the shame of our city."

It was Anselm who came to Matilda's aid, "We must not forget how many times the Romans have stood the strain of siege. Here in Lombardy we know what that means."

The young man did not even look at Anselm, but his voice was steadier as he went on, "They have made a farce of consecrating Guibert Pope, but the three bishops who made the motions are all excommunicate. And tomorrow this Judas will put a crown on the head of Henry, and of Bertha, too."

Matilda said nothing, but as she looked at the face of the young Frangipane, she thought of how the bare names of things would impress men far away, who could know nothing of how the names had been stolen. A pretender who had been consecrated in Rome, whatever mockery and sacrilege that consecration might be, would yet have for simple men the authority of that consecration, and a king, crowned by his own puppet where better men had stood, could claim the reverence of an emperor in quarters that would never have listened to him without his crown.

"This mockery," said Anselm gravely, "may teach us not to take too seriously the names and form of power."

"It is an outrage, my lord," exclaimed the young man.

"But how is the Pope, I mean how is he himself?" That had been the intolerable thing, the thought of the grief and shame with which the Pope had fled from the Lateran. It seemed to Matilda that it would have been easier to have seen and shared that defeat than to imagine it, so far away and so helpless.

"I think," said the young man with sudden surprise as if it had not occurred to him before, "that the Pope was the calmest man in all Rome. My uncles besought him to flee in the confusion. They were sure they could hold the river way for his escape, and there were enough we could count on to protect him until he reached friends. But he refused. Rome was his post, and there he would stay until the Captain of the Guard relieved him."

"It was nonsense," said Arduino.

The young man looked doubtfully at the half-seen face of his fellow soldier. "He would not be persuaded. He laughed at us and reminded us of the time that

Peter fleeing from the city to escape persecution met Christ on the way. You remember the story?"

"I have thought of it often," said Anselm. "And of Our Lord's words when Peter asked him where he was going—'I have come to be crucified again.'"

"It is growing late," said the girl Maria suddenly, looking up at her mistress. The fire had fallen, but there was still light enough for Matilda to see the anxiety in the girl's face, and the affection that thought of her mistress even in her own weariness. Matilda laid her hand tenderly on Maria's shoulder.

"Rather I think it is growing early. It is almost morning—Easter morning," she cried sharply and hid her face in her hands.

"Christ is risen," came the voice of Anselm over her head. And Matilda was filled with wonder to hear the note of joy in that tired voice. "That is the important thing to remember today."

Matilda looked up at his face, shining in the deepening cold and darkness. So the angel must have looked to those other women who went before dawn to the sealed tomb. And it seemed to her that for the first time she understood what the message of the angel must have meant to those who first heard it.

CHAPTER II

I T was not hope that came in the cold and dark of that Easter morning. Nor was it comfort. But for a moment she saw clearly again what she had lost sight of in the preoccupations of the last months. It was hard to define, a feeling rather than an idea, but it was ever present with her. Christ had risen. It was a victory, that resurrection, but it was something more. It was a revelation of an essential fact. Man was subject to pain and grief and thwarting and death, but there was in his nature something that eluded all these things, over which these tyrants of man's life had no lasting power, in which he was forever free.

So Matilda had set out again on the day after Easter. There was so much to do, and such scant hope of doing it, and even if she could accomplish the impossible, there was not much reason to think it would do any good. But she started out doggedly. There was grain at Nonantola. If she went there and gave her word that no matter what happened, she would not let the peasants hunger, she could send that grain to Canossa. Some of the Florentine merchants had silver. They might be willing to purchase freedom from certain tolls by paying a substantial sum now. The Lord of Sorbara was being besieged by some of his disorderly neighbors. She could bring some relief to his walls, and perhaps, if he were free, he would help her to relieve other towns. She tried not to think any farther than that.

One thing had happened on that journey to Nonantola that served to reaffirm the sense of peace with which she had set forth. It was a little thing, but it stayed with her all the rest of the journey and long after. In a field by the road she saw some serfs dragging a wooden plow, a man and two women and a boy. They were all bent over, dragging and pushing, in their dirty brown canvas tunics hardly to be discerned from the earth with which they were struggling. For a moment she stood to watch them, putting her horse as close to the thin balk of earth which separated the field from the road as she could.

There was nothing different in this scene from what she had observed in countless fields during her journeys of the last month, but for one thing. That caught her eye. They seemed to be having great difficulty in drawing the share through the ground. Yet as the earth rolled up on either side, it was clear that there was nothing in its texture to cause the trouble. Then she saw the man who was pulling the plow stop and run his sleeve over his short-cropped head. For a moment he staggered; then as the boy ran to him, he shook his head and took hold of the ropes again.

When he was almost opposite her, he happened to throw his head back quickly, and she saw that he was nearly blinded by the sweat pouring from his forehead. And underneath the streaks of fresh earth, his thin face was the color and texture of mortar.

"It is heavy work," she said compassionately. The man looked at her and stopped. The two women dropped the ends of the plow, and with the boy who had been helping to drag it, they stared at Matilda without speaking.

"It is not the work but the hunger, my lady," said the man quietly, rubbing his glistening brow again.

"Hunger? But the harvests were good last fall." Matilda tried to look steadily into the pinched faces.

The man shrugged his shoulders, but the older of the two women answered in a shrill voice that seemed suddenly to have gone reckless, "The King's troops, my lady, came through here, and they killed the oxen. Then the troops of the Countess took the grain, what there was left."

"But I—" she began and paused. She saw the man staring at her with sudden fear.

"And now you are plowing again?" she said to turn the man's attention from his growing suspicion.

"What else is there to do, my lady?"

"You're quite right." She turned to one of the men-at-arms behind her and bade him give the bread and the meat which he was carrying to the peasants. Arduino looked grim but said nothing.

The serf sank to his knees. "Then you really are the great Countess?"

She shook her head, "I am nearly as poor as you are."

"Are you going to fight?" asked the old woman, her beady eyes shining out of a brown, toadlike visage.

Matilda looked at her for a moment before she replied, "If I can."

"We will pray for you," said the woman with great dignity.

Matilda thought of that now as she neared Nonantola again. Two months had gone since that day, and the brown fields were green with wheat and rye. In the evening light they looked warm and prosperous where two months before they had looked so bare. It was the old magic of June, she thought wistfully, as she urged her horse forward.

In those two months she had done a good deal, but seen now in the mass, it amounted to very little, not much more, she reflected, than the spring plowing she had watched here two months before. She had stiffened resistance where she could, she had settled one or two squabbles among those of her vassals who had given some signs of being amenable to persuasion. She had relieved some terrible instances of want; she had received certain promises from individuals and cities. Perhaps when Henry came back from Rome, she would be able to offer some resistance, but of that army that might relieve Rome and drive the enemy from its walls, she saw no more chance now than she had two months or two years ago.

It was too late to try to reach Nonantola that night. So she turned her horse toward the little Vallombrosan hermitage that crowned the one high point overlooking the plain about the city.

"It will be a wretched place to spend the night," said Arduino. "But it is too late to reach the city before dark. And everybody is too tired for us to try to force the pace." She looked around the little company of soldiers and men-at-arms. A low murmur of assent ran through them, and the fatigue-dulled faces lighted with hope.

"If there isn't room for all of us, some of you men can sleep outdoors for one night," she added, sniffing the fragrance of pine and cedar drifting down from the hilltop on the still sun-warmed breeze.

The hermitage justified the worst of Arduino's fears. It was a wretched little agglomeration of tiny huts and shacks, most of them of rough-hewn logs, stopped with mud. There was only one structure of decent size, and that was no larger than any one of several spare chambers at Canossa. The walls were covered with badly fitted planks of white pine. Built-in benches along the sides at one end of the oblong room, a slightly raised seat with roughly carved arms, and a great wood crucifix above, completed the furnishings. There was no sign of any place for fire on the clay floor.

The food which the Prior and two brethren presently set on a bare trestle table for their guests was no better than the general aspect of the chapter room would lead one to expect. A thick gruel of cracked spelt, some black country rye bread, a little goats' milk cheese, and some very sour red wine filled the beech-wood bowls and cups, and that was all.

"They say these Vallombrosans are men of good birth, too," sighed Arduino, when the Prior had turned his back to get fresh supplies of hard black bread from some one standing in the doorway. "But there is no accounting for the madness of men," he added as Matilda frowned.

But rough as were the accommodations which their hosts offered them, it was clear that they were their best. And they were offered with a solicitude and a desire to give pleasure that touched Matilda. Indeed, as the simple meal progressed, she became increasingly aware of a certain anxiety, an almost excess of sympathy in the manners of their hosts that made her wonder if something were not wrong. For the Prior and the two monks were watching her lightest gesture, even look, with a constancy of solicitude that suggested the way in which kindly men try to assuage the grief of the recently bereaved. More than once she was on the point of asking the Prior if anything were wrong at Nonantola, but it seemed easier to let the meal take its course, for she was very tired.

The mystery was soon solved, however. At the conclusion of the meal the

Prior suggested that he post some of his brethren to watch so that they might all have a chance for the sleep they so much needed.

"But there is no danger here," objected Matilda. "Very few people know just where we are, and I suppose all but a few of them are sure we are at Nonantola."

The Prior shook his head. Then as a new idea seemed to strike him, he looked curiously at his guest, "But you are fleeing from the King, are you not?"

Matilda stared at him. Then the significance of the question dawned on her. "Has the King left Rome?"

"Haven't you heard?" asked the monk in amazement. "A messenger from Rome stopped here three days ago. He was on his way to Nonantola."

"What has happened?" She tried to catch her breath, to still the ridiculous beating of her heart in her throat, but in spite of her efforts her breath caught again with intolerable excitement.

For a moment, the Prior could not believe that she did not know. He was an old man with the delicacy and the vagueness of age in his ivory-colored face, but the unusual excitement of entertaining so distinguished a company and of imparting the news of the great world to those who usually played a part in it, seemed to sharpen his wits. His light blue eyes sparkled with the exhilaration of this unwonted sense of importance, and the color flushed under the finely lined skin of his cheeks.

"The man said that in April, early in April," he added, with meticulous precision, "the Pope sent for Robert Guiscard the Norman. He asked him to come to his rescue as he had promised."

"That I know," interrupted Matilda.

But the old man was not to be hurried. He had obviously an adequate appreciation of the dramatic value of his story, and he was prepared to do it justice.

"The Norman sent word to the King, who had been crowned by that apostate Guibert. He told him that if he did not leave Rome at once, he, Robert, would come and drive him out. The King had dug his trenches around the castle of Sant' Angelo, and he was ready to starve the Pope out, if he could not batter down those old Roman walls with his rams and bores. But he had not reckoned with those Normans!"

The old man chuckled at the mere thought of the discomfiture of Henry.

"So the King raised the siege and fled?" asked Matilda hopefully.

But the Prior lifted his hand, and a look of cunning came into his innocent old face as if now that he had the ear of the world, he were not going to let it go so easily as that.

"Wait," he commanded. "He is no coward, that Henry, but then you would not want to face those terrible Normans yourself, with the dreadful way he has treated the Pope on your conscience, would you?" The old man ducked his head and looked up at Matilda through his thin upper lashes. Matilda shook her head fiercely at Arduino, who seemed on the point of losing all control.

"So," said the Prior with an air of great triumph, "Henry turned and fled like the false coward he is, but first he leveled the city of Leo to the ground. And then leaving it in ruins behind him, he started north. That is why I thought you might be fleeing from him, my lady Countess."

"But the Pope?"

"The Pope, ah." The old man's head rose in pride. "Six days later Robert Guiscard marched his army up to Rome and encamped it near that ancient aqueduct. The next day he began his assault, and those false Romans who had helped the King fell away, and the Pope was released. And the next day with those tall Normans in their horned helmets as if the devil himself had been baptized and made a good Christian, with them to escort him and protect him from traitors, the Pope went back to the Lateran Palace. And there he sits on his throne this very minute," the old man concluded in triumph.

It was quite dark now. So, his hands trembling with excitement, the old man lighted a single wax taper and set it on the table in front of Matilda. His eyes were still shining, as if he yet saw on the invisible walls of his tiny chapter house the scenes which he had been describing with so much avidity. Matilda bowed her head and tried to say a prayer of thanksgiving. But though she told herself that this was a victory which the goodness of God had given, she felt no sense of triumph, for she saw the tall Normans, taller and fiercer and handsomer even than Henry's Germans, with their long fair locks and their light beards and their flashing helmets and shields and swords, riding into Rome. And she shivered.

The next day at Nonantola she found a messenger waiting for her with a letter from the Pope. It was the same story which the Prior had told her, recounted with much greater brevity and with no sense of triumph whatever. "The evildoers have been put to rout, and the just have been delivered from bondage. But this is for the moment only, and though the wicked have fled, the end is not yet." And he concluded with a plea that Matilda do all in her power, for he was not sure how long Robert Guiscard would be content to forego that expedition against the Eastern Emperor on which he had set his heart.

There was nothing in this letter to hint of any suspicion or uneasiness, but it was quite clear that the Pope did not want to be dependent on Guiscard if there were any chance of more reliable and more sympathetic help. Matilda tried to dismiss her old fears of the half-barbarous Normans and to tell herself that here was a chance such as she was not likely to have again. For the mere fact that Henry had been frightened by the threats of Robert Guiscard would do more than any persuasion of hers to rally vassals for whom success was the supreme arbiter.

She was not jealous of the Norman leader, she told herself. She only wished that love might have wielded the power now in the hands of self-interest. But here she trembled on the brink of an abyss into which she dared not look. She was glad when the Bishop and the Count of Nonantola were announced. For this business of provisions was a clear-cut, objective one that raised no vexing questions as to the nature of this world in which for a little the alien soul found itself.

CHAPTER III

EVEN before Matilda left Nonantola, rumors began to come from Rome. At first they were vague, the sort of stories that seemed born of the uneasiness of men's minds and their expectations of trouble rather than of anything tangible or certain. But as June wore into the third week, these rumors began to assume more specific form. There was terrible fighting going on in Rome, Rome was burning, the anti-Pope had come in from Tivoli to besiege the city, Robert Guiscard had fled, the Pope was sick of the pestilence, the King was coming back—at that point Matilda felt some relief, for she knew that Henry was well on his way across the Alps. Clearly, all of these rumors could not be true.

But she soon had very little time or thought for rumor, for Henry's troops, straggling back in the wake of their master, were filling her land. In the Modenese plain one large company of them under the leadership of the Marquis

Oberto had joined forces with the schismatic bishops of Reggio and Modena and invested the fortress of Sorbara. It was only one among several such episodes that were reported at Nonantola in those pleasant June days, but it frightened Matilda more than any of the others. In the first place, though it was not in itself the largest or most important of the fortresses in her domain, the situation of Sorbara relative to the cities of Modena and Reggio gave it a good deal of consequence. If Sorbara should fall into the hands of the rebels, it would be impossible to hold the already divided populations of those cities loyal. And if they fell, the whole of the surrounding plain would be lost in the very heart of her country. The second reason why her heart sank as she listened to the accounts that drifted into Nonantola day and night was that the imperial troops had proved the nucleus of an unusually and alarmingly large gathering of all the schismatics and rebels in the neighborhood.

Nonantola had been generous in sharing its stores of grain, and for a day Matilda dreamed of raising a force of loyal townsmen and going into the neighboring countryside to rally the knights and counts of her lands. But Arduino refused to consider this plan. Schismatic bishops, glad to support the anti-Pope because he meant freedom from the supervision and the challenge of the strenuous and high-principled Gregory, rebellious priests whose mistresses were put in jeopardy by the reforming zeal of the Pope, citizens and peasants who saw in the conflict of their masters a chance to better their own condition, restless and greedy knights, counts, and nobles who hoped to make their profit out of anarchy, all of these were waiting to see the Countess overwhelmed—Arduino waxed almost eloquent in his protest. And much as she might rebel, Matilda knew that he was right. She was in no position to strike effectively here at Nonantola, and to linger was still further to expose her weakness. Consequently, and here Arduino began to blend some craft with his plain soldierly protests, it was unwise to commit herself to so great a risk until she had made sure of what was really happening in Rome.

The result was that she returned to Canossa, as so often during these years, to gather her forces and rest and simply wait.

But this time, as it happened, she had not long to wait, for she was barely settled in the great, gaunt stone hall, when the horns rang from the walls, and she knew that tidings were at hand. That it might be a messenger from Rome she hoped, but so disturbed was the condition of the land, she told herself, that she could hardly expect a messenger to come straight through. The best she could hope for was that tidings might come, relayed from one loyal monastery to another. But, in all probability, she reminded herself, this floundering from rumor to rumor would go on indefinitely.

She was, therefore, completely astonished when one of the watch brought her word that two messengers from the Pope were waiting at the gate. That surprise was considerably lessened, however, when two monks shuffled into the hall, one the short, substantial model of the general proportions of a hogshead, so dear to the tellers of tales, the other taller, but slender and boyish. The monks threw back their cowls as they entered the hall, and Matilda gasped. For there before her stood the Archbishop of Salerno and the young Piero Frangipane. The boy looked solemn, but the fat monk smiled at her amazement.

"It is gracious of your ladyship to look so amusingly astonished," he said, as she knelt for his blessing. "We have had very little to amuse us of late."

"From what we have heard—" Matilda nodded to Antonio who had started for the kitchen and offered her own cushioned high seat to the Archbishop—"it has been terrible enough."

"What have you heard?" asked Alfanus, fixing his heavy-lidded eyes with disconcerting suddenness upon her face.

"Nothing certain," she responded hastily, "but in general every sort of disaster from fire to pestilence. I was inclined to believe them until they said that Henry had returned and was besieging the city again. That I knew was not so."

But though she smiled as she said this, there was no answering relaxation in either of the faces before her. Indeed, the younger man shuddered as if she had touched some nerve on the raw. The elder had looked away from her and now seemed absorbed in the contemplation of the sunbeams streaming into the dark hall from the still open doorway. Down the tables, Matilda could see maids and men pausing in their work to wait for him to speak.

"Has anything happened to the Pope?" she asked, suddenly frightened.

The younger man looked at the Archbishop.

"The Pope is all right—physically," he added. Then he caught her eyes suddenly with his own and held them. "You remember, Countess, how you feared the Guiscard?"

But the young man interrupted with flashing eyes, "It was not the Guiscard's fault, my lord Archbishop. It was those perfidious Romans—"

Alfanus listened to the young man patiently for a moment. Then with a heavy gesture he lifted his hand. "I know, Piero. I think the Guiscard meant to keep his promise to the Pope and treat the city as his own. And I think you are right that the Romans made that attack on the Normans deliberately, though there are those who think it an accident."

"They are lying, or they are mistaken," said the young man firmly. "I know that some of those younger Savelli meant to stir up trouble so as to give the King a chance to return. They know nothing of faith or prudence."

The Archbishop shook his head. "God knows I have no reason to question what you say about the Savelli, my friend."

"But what happened?" asked Matilda, trying to steady her voice and for a moment still the panic gnawing at the pit of her stomach.

The young man shook his head, and Matilda in her own anxiety found it in her heart to be sorry for the sick look about the passionate young mouth. The Archbishop plunged in, however, without any wavering of the steady eyes.

"However it happened, Countess, the Romans attacked the Normans, and the Normans, feeling contemptuous, no doubt, of these men who had no loyalty to their own lord, returned the attack. But the Roman noble, however faithless and violent he may be, is no coward. Some of the Normans fell, and the others went mad, and like barbarians they set out to avenge their fallen comrades. But it was impossible to drive the Romans out of those high canyons of streets of ours."

The young man's face lighted with anger. "It was that wretch, Cencius the Consul, who suggested it to Guiscard."

Alfanus nodded and went on calmly, "As Piero says, it was he who suggested to Guiscard that he fire the houses. You know how they are, timber galleries and balconies above the marble walls, and rugs and hangings within. It had been very dry in Rome for weeks, too, and there was a little wind that day."

Matilda shuddered, sick at the rising tide of horror.

"You can guess how it spread, the timber above burning down until the heat consumed the marble, and the flames licking up the narrow alleys until the whole quarter was level with the blackened streets before you had time to think what could be done. Nothing, of course, could be done. I rode into the city on the second day; it must have been beyond all help an hour after it started."

"But the people in those houses?" Matilda could only whisper.

The Archbishop looked at her and looked away. "The happiest roasted. The others were butchered on the pikes of the Normans. We must not forget that they are half savage, and the flames and the madness of carnage drove them beyond themselves. I did everything I could to reach the Pope on the other side of the city, but it was no use."

Matilda tried to ask how long the horror lasted, but no words came as her lips frantically mumbled the air.

"Guiscard made no effort to check the Normans. Some claim that he had said before that he would wipe out the faithless Romans and bring in decent men from the faith-keeping north to people the city. I am not sure that he could have checked his men, even if he had wanted to, until they were sick of slaughter and sated with plunder. But when everything between the Lateran and the Coliseum was gone, he did take hold. It was at the end of the third day. I do not myself know what happened, but I was told by one of the Normans, a bishop, that the Pope had thrown himself at the feet of the Guiscard and begged him to stop the massacre."

"My uncle told me that, too." The young Frangipane looked appealingly at Matilda. "He said that the Pope lay at Guiscard's feet like one dead."

Matilda covered her face with her hands. It seemed to her that she could not bear to hear any more. For some minutes nobody spoke. She heard the feet of the servants begin to move again, but it seemed as if the sound came from very far away. She had never known before how dear the beauty of Rome had been to her, but now the thought of all that splendor in ashes and slaking lime seemed a little thing. And then she knew what she hoped, that the heartbroken Pope was dead. Dead—she would never see him again, but she did not think she could bear to look upon that anguish.

It was as if the Archbishop had read her thoughts, for he went on slowly as if the curtain of silence had not fallen between them. "His Holiness did look like one dead when I talked with him two days later. His face was the color of the ashes through which I had just come. And his eyes were glazed with horror, as if he had looked upon it until he could bear no more."

Matilda tried to swallow her sobs, but she felt her shoulders shake in spite of all she could do.

"It is Henry they should blame, and not the Pope," cried Piero.

Matilda looked up and tried to fix her eyes on the red face of the young man. But the tears came between.

"For the Pope it is past all blaming and not blaming," said Alfanus. "There would be no comfort in blaming Henry, for there this thing stands."

"So Guiscard holds the city." Matilda had recovered control of her voice.

"He will not stay. And when he goes, the Pope must go with him. For as Piero says, men blame him."

"I will go to him and bring him here," Matilda cried in sudden anger at her own helplessness.

"No. You couldn't get near the city. It was only because they deemed us two silly monks that we were able to come through at all. I don't think you need to worry about the Pope's safety for the present. Guiscard will see to that, even if not in a fashion that will give any of us satisfaction. And when they must leave Rome, and I think Guiscard is anxious to be gone, there are refuges nearer to Rome than this." Again Matilda found herself marveling at the calmness with which the Archbishop looked at the facts before them.

She tried to think of what she could do, but her mind seemed to have broken from all control, racing helplessly about those blackened streets and the face that ever rose in the midst of them. She clutched her hands to her forehead.

The low voice of the Archbishop broke into the agony of futility with which she gazed at that ashen face. "There is nothing you can do for the Pope himself, Countess, but pray. There is nothing any of us can do. I had meant to tell him how sorry I was, but when I saw his face, I knew there was nothing to say or do."

Slowly she shook her head. "But the Church?" she asked.

He smiled again. "You are right. The Church goes on. And the work which the man Gregory did goes on. That is all he ever cared for, anyway. And that was all that was in his thoughts even that day when I saw him in Rome."

"Did he give you any message for me?"

"Yes. I told him that I was going to try to see his friends. And he told me to go to you first, and to tell you to keep on. He said that he was going to get together as many of the bishops and princes in the neighborhood of Rome as he could. He will send you a messenger presently. All he asks for now is that you keep on as you are. Then he said you were the only one, prince or bishop, whom I was to bother seeing. I shall go back from here at once."

"To keep on," repeated Matilda, trying to grasp the idea with a mind that sprawled and groped and seemed incapable of laying hold upon anything.

"Just that," said Alfanus, "keep on. It isn't much, but it's all that really matters." He waited until she looked up at him, and then he added more softly, "It is not as if he were really alone, Matilda."

She made no answer, but sat there as if frozen, gazing at the pavement at her feet. When at last she raised her head, she was quite alone, and the sun was filling the open doorway.

CHAPTER IV

"THE average man is not much on theory, but he has an unrivaled eye for fact," Alberic had reminded Matilda when she told him of her fears for the popular reaction to the burning of Rome. What he said was certainly borne out by what happened in the next weeks, after the news of the events in Rome began to percolate through the Tuscan lands. For awe at the power and ruthlessness of Guiscard came to reinforce doubtful loyalty and self-interested timidity, and the success of the Pope's defiance of Henry roused men who could not be touched by the principles to which he had appealed. The result was that the city of Reggio, unable to reclaim its schismatic bishop from the party besieging Sorbara, asked its lady the Countess Matilda to come and judge certain disputes between the citizens and some of the lords of the surrounding country. And the city of Modena took advantage of the occasion to send a petition for reinforcements so that when Sorbara fell into the hands of the forces of Henry it might be able to defend its liberty and its loyalty to the Countess of Tuscany.

Both at Reggio and Modena Matilda had the satisfaction of welcoming various knights and counts who seemed suddenly to have discovered that now they could do what they had wanted to do for a long time, pay homage to their liege lady and assure her of their readiness for her service. Indeed, so considerable was the resort of knights and other nobles to her court at Modena that Matilda at first thought it might be possible to collect a force large enough to engage Henry's troops before Sorbara. But this idea Arduino energetically discouraged. This loyalty was too new and unseasoned to be put to any drastic test, and in the present mood of the Tuscan nobility there was too much to lose by defeat for her to take any unnecessary chances.

Matilda, therefore, suffered Arduino to do as he liked. Delighted at having his advice taken for once without question, he immediately proceeded to gather up the repentant knights and nobles and to carry them off to Canossa. For, as he explained to Matilda, an imposing rally of the nobility of Tuscany at the stronghold of their lord was likely to impress the tardy and the recalcitrant with the wisdom of taking the wind of success in their sails while there was still time for them to claim the merit of loyalty for what at any moment might become necessity. The optimism with which Arduino leaped ahead of the slight encouragement of the moment to ultimate victory brought a ray of amusement to the sad thoughts of Matilda. And for a moment the bitterness of the sense of irony with which she had been receiving the professions of her irresolute and faithless vassals was assuaged.

She promised therefore to fall in with Arduino's plan and, as soon as her business was finished at Modena, to return to Canossa with the company of trusted supporters whom her general had left with her. This promise she made with every intention of fulfilling it, and, in the same mood of bitter acquiescence in a destiny not likely to prove to her liking, she left Modena on the following afternoon. She moved slowly so that nightfall found her at a lonely little monastery on the edge of the Modenese plain.

It was a clear evening, and the house was on a slight rise of ground. So she could see across the plain without difficulty to where the castle of Sorbara rose black and fierce and suddenly flat against the thin lime-colored afterglow of the sunset behind her. For a moment she regretted the prudence that had made her give up trying to rescue it. Then as she breathed the cool, pine-sweet breeze of the hills, she was grateful for the chance of rest. Tonight, when they had eaten the frugal supper which would be all the good Abbot could offer them, she would talk for a little while with Anselm of Lucca, and then she would sleep early. Perhaps the ache of her days would not seem so heavy in the morning.

A step behind her startled her, for the Abbot had left her alone in his tiny walled garden. She turned to find Anselm of Lucca with his finger on his lips. In silence he joined her at the edge looking out over the plain.

"The Abbot has just told me a curious thing," he began in low tones, just audible above the soughing of the wind in the trees on the slopes below where they stood. "He says that some of the brethren were over at Sorbara yesterday, and they report that the besiegers are so sure of themselves that they have grown careless. The lord of Sorbara has most of his men in there and half the knights of the countryside. So they must be running short of food."

Matilda looked at Anselm curiously. He had been present at all her talks with her general, and he had supported Arduino against most of her suggestions.

A frown now leveled the placid brows of Anselm. "He reports that the peasants have left the plain. Even the herdsmen have taken their sheep up to the higher ground. These men of Henry's made a pretty clean sweep when they came in June, and though they clung to their fields, the serfs are afraid now of what will happen when the castle falls, and the invaders take possession of the countryside."

Matilda shuddered. But Anselm was absorbed in his own thoughts and took no notice of her. In a few moments he began to think aloud again, "The monks said that the besiegers drink a good deal in the evening and are careless of their watch."

For a moment Matilda looked at him. But his clear, open face seemed unaware of her presence. She turned away from the wall and looked back at the patch of sky above the low roofs of the monastery. There was still a faint glow of the sunset visible on the thickly piled clouds, but even as she looked, the whole sky seemed to darken.

"There will be no moon tonight," she said to Anselm. "Do you think we could surprise them?"

"That is what I have been wondering."

It seemed a rash thing even to contemplate when she proposed it, but as the sky darkened before their eyes, she forgot the caution of Arduino, and the old passion for action stirred within her. It was months now that she had waited, content or trying to be content with infinitesimal signs of progress while she burned to grapple with her difficulties and to force some decision in all this despair and helplessness. For an instant, she recognized this passion for what it was, the spurt of energies long pent-up and denied. And she tried to bring the cool judgment of reason to bear upon the temptations of the moment. She even reminded herself that, after all, a victory over Henry would do much less now than she had dreamed. For there were certain things that neither triumph nor defeat would have any power over. These things had been, and no victory would have power to expunge them from the pitiless record of things done. They would fester until the very flesh itself fell away from the naked bone.

But Anselm was sure that this was a heaven-sent chance, and they had the obligation not to let it pass. And try as she might to deny it, every pulse of Matilda's being pleaded for action.

But whatever her previous hesitations, when they had decided after supper to make the attempt, it was Matilda who took the lead. For now that the decision had been made, it was her responsibility to make sure that it should not fail. Her company was small. Even with every allowance made for courage and vigilance, her forces would stand no chance in an open fight. So everything depended upon the completeness of surprise with which they should fall upon the besieging army.

During supper Matilda had studied the Abbot. He was a comparatively young man with a good deal of the soldier he had been, still about his tall, well-made figure. Matilda felt sure that there was something she knew about him besides the fact that he was Hubert, the son and heir of the Lord of Marignano. As she watched the clever, mobile face, she was fascinated by the little glimpses of high spirit and pride that glinted now and then under the surface of monastic gentleness.

When the Abbot withdrew on a whispered summons from one of his brethren, Anselm told her what it was that she had tried to recall. "He is the man who came back from his service with your husband in Lorraine to find that his brother had married the girl whom he loved. He was a proud, passionate young man, and he was beside himself with anger and grief. But when he learned that his brother had given out false reports of his death, and had sent them to the castle of the girl and had so persuaded her to listen to him, he at once set out to find his brother that he might kill him. So sure was he of the righteousness of his anger that he prayed God and Saint Hubert to help him find his brother and bring him to justice."

Anselm paused. Then he looked up at Matilda gravely. "He found his brother, lying in the path to his wife's castle where he had hoped to see him. But he was dead, for robbers had overtaken him when he was riding alone, and they had killed him for a little gold he had. Hubert carried his brother back to the castle and helped to bury him. Then he went up to Vallombrosa to the monastery there. And when he had completed his novitiate, he came and built this house here."

"I remember," said Matilda softly. "Godfrey said he was the finest soldier he had ever had in his following."

The Abbot came back into the small guest house at that moment. He was plainly puzzled as to whether or not he should share the news with his guests.

"Anything about our friends across the way?" asked Anselm.

"One of our brethren has just come in from the plain, and he reports that the besiegers have received fresh supplies from Parma, from the anti-Pope he thinks, and they were feasting noisily when he left the neighborhood. By midnight, he says, they will all be drunk and asleep."

Matilda and Anselm looked at each other. Then they told the Abbot of their plan. Whatever doubt may have lingered in Matilda's mind vanished before the enthusiasm of the Abbot. For it was clear that the heart of the soldier still beat high under the black robe of the monk.

"You have still more than four hours to midnight," he said. "Some of our brethren can show you bypaths that will bring you there in not much over four hours. So if you leave here two hours before midnight, you will have plenty of time, even counting that you will have to cover the last miles afoot."

So they made their plans. They would ride across the plain until they were about two miles away from the castle, and then they would close in upon their sleeping foes.

"What signal shall we use?" asked the Abbot, who, when laughingly reminded by Anselm of certain restrictions upon a monk's bearing of arms, announced at once that he was going as their guide.

Matilda thought. And as so often when, for a moment taken unawares, she let the gates of her mind swing open, the face of Gregory rose before her mind's eye, as she had last seen it, still and enduring, as if carved out of stone.

"It is in Peter's cause that we fight," she said. "And it is only fitting that we should call upon his name."

"If the Countess gives the signal," said the Abbot, "the sleepers will not wake, but in the stillness of the night we who are listening will hear. Then, if every one shouts the answer as he leaps upon the guards, they will wake to find our swords at their throats."

When she had finished telling the leaders of her company about the plan, Matilda bade them order complete silence among their men. For in these days it was not impossible that soldiers of Henry might be wandering in the plain or even skulking in the shadows of the hills. One cry might ruin the whole plan.

But though the first breath of cheering was choked off outside, Matilda could hear in a hundred restless motions and little sounds, of twigs crackling under impatient feet, of ill-suppressed whispering, of muffled rattling of swords and shields, of the neighing and stamping of horses, the excitement which the news of action had stirred among the men. And though the leaders talked in low tones when they came in to report on preparations or to seek further instructions, there was no mistaking the wild delight with which they made ready for the attack. Like hunting hounds who have caught the scent of their quarry, they strained at the leash until finally, herself unable to endure the tension any longer, Matilda donned helmet and shield, and, taking her sword, gave the signal for departure.

The night was as dark as it had promised to be, and it was some minutes before Matilda could make out more than the mass of the Abbot and his horse in front of her. Presently, as her eyes became accustomed to the mirk, she could discern the shapes of trees and rocks along the way, magnified by the blackness of the night until it seemed as if strange and portentous monsters were crouching all along the invisible road. The wind had risen, and though it seemed to drum upon the darkness with a thousand muffled fingers, yet there was something reassuring in the thought that in its many voices any sound of hoof or armor must be swallowed up before it could reach suspicious ears. Yet now and then as its violence hung for a moment, imminent and suspended in the shell of night, Matilda was not so sure. For then she could hear the snortings of the horses, the ferrous jangle of iron hooves on stones, the creaking and the jingle of straining armor, and below and through and around these casual intrusions, the immemorial breathings of the night. A twig snapped, and the dry click of sound shivered through the taut strings of the ear. An owl screeched, a little grass creature wheezed in its dry pipes, a sudden impulse of life slithered through the withered furze at the side of the path, and the wind rose again and filled all the resounding air.

Matilda was taken by surprise when, finally, the Abbot stopped and held her horse for her to dismount. And now they crept on with tight-clutched swords, hardly daring to breathe for fear that steel might strike steel and with its clangor wake the sleeping guard. Some of the monks went ahead with bare feet to reconnoiter, and Matilda and her comrades rested. They were so close now to the sleeping camp that they could hear the stamping of the horses tethered by the moat.

The scouts came back from the camp to report that nothing was to be heard but the snorings and the mumblings of the drunken sleepers. Even before the tents of the bishops and the marquis the guards drowsed over their empty cans. One scout more daring than the rest had taken away a pike that had fallen from the hand of a sleeper. And Matilda shivered at the chuckle that went through the circle of soldiers as the monk swung it awkwardly.

And now the little company deployed around the invisible front of the castle. The Abbot had allowed the time of fifty Aves for this maneuver, since much of the distance had to be covered barefoot with cloaks wrapped around shields and swords to guard against accidental noise. More than once in that period Matilda shuddered at the jingle of steel upon steel or the harsh crash of metal on stone, but there was no sound from the low-piled shadows ahead.

Before the time of waiting was over, Matilda found that her eyes had become so accustomed to the grayness around her that she could just make out the darker masses of the tents in front. But she could not be sure that the ground shadows were shrubbery or sleeping men. Even when the monk who had been whispering the Aves in intercession for their adventure had ceased, she waited, for the night was still unbroken, and they were too close to their goal to risk accident now.

Then she reached out her right hand until it touched the man next to her. It was Anselm, and he whispered, "I think it is safe now."

She swallowed hard, for she was worried that her voice might not carry down the waiting lines. Then she drew her breath and shouted with all her strength, "Saint Peter for us, Saint Peter." For a moment her voice alone rang through the wind and the night. Then there came an answering roar and a rush, and before she could think, she was swept into the grayness before her. And every shred of fear and misgiving was blown away in the fierce surge of the onslaught.

CHAPTER V

THE victory of Sorbara was the turning point. In itself it was no inconsiderable triumph. The Bishop of Parma, half a dozen of the ablest captains among her foes, a hundred knights, and a host of men of lesser rank made a noble company of prisoners to be ransomed, to be exchanged, or to be held at Canossa for hostage. Several hundred horses, and great quantities of armor and clothing and swords, to say nothing of personal ornaments and treasure of gold and silver, were a welcome addition to the depleted resources of the Countess. Arduino's eyes shone when Matilda summed up the material evidence of the victory for the faithful general, who on the first rumor of action at Sorbara had rushed to the rescue of his madly rash lady.

But it was much more than a singularly successful engagement. It meant that the campaign which had been almost entirely defensive until now took the offensive. Several cities that had fallen into the hands of Henry's troops made bold to rise and turn out their new masters. Several other cities under siege strengthened their defenses and seized the King's agents, who a week before had been working almost unchecked, sapping the morale of the citizenry, and hanged them from their gates, where the defiance might be at once seen and appreciated by the besieging armies. Several lords who had been entertaining friends from Henry's forces made haste to speed their untimely guests and send presents to their liege lady. And from all over her lands knights and counts who had hitherto pleaded the pressure of local conditions for their staying at home, flocked to Canossa.

But what most touched Matilda was that the peasants of the Modenese plain, who had fled in spite of every threat and promise of their bailiffs and masters, now straggled back to weed their neglected fields and drive the crows from the swelling grain. And when they caught sight of the Countess passing down the road, they held up their hoes and the flails with which they had been scaring birds, and sank to their knees and raised their hands in blessing.

But most important of all, the victory gave Matilda courage and a certain grim and joyless confidence. The exhilaration of battle had soon failed, and when she sat down the next day to write to the Pope the story of her triumph, Matilda found that the words would not come. For there seemed something indecent in writing of victory to one who had striven so greatly and been so greatly thwarted. Before the rock of that defeat, every impulse of vanity and rejoicing fell away, abashed. And Matilda was forced to be content with the bare message of loyalty with which she had dispatched Anselm of Lucca to Rome as soon as she had made sure of an adequate escort.

"Not without hope do we labor and are burdened with many cares," said

Anselm, as he took leave of her. And that lingered with her as the sum total of her feelings until the summer had worn away, and she had again set about the reconquest of her own lands.

She told herself over and over again that she was under no illusions as to an early or an easy success. But as she strove to realize the promise of July in the months that followed, the magnitude of her task grew upon her, and she began to wonder if she had not given way to illusion completely when she attempted the seemingly hopeless task at all. For it was like crossing a morass. She would find a tuft of solid earth under her feet and pause to catch her breath. Then as she looked out over the stretch ahead of her and saw the appearance of still more substantial-seeming ground, she would be encouraged and think that now the worst of her struggle was over. But when she put out her foot to take possession of it, it would quake and give way beneath her.

"It sounds cynical to say that I am surprised when a promise is kept or a bargain fulfilled, but it is the sober truth," she told Alberic one day.

"The truth is often cynical in my experience," retorted Alberic, "but almost never sober."

The mood passed, however, and she came to be thankful for whatever advance she made, as for something beyond what she might have expected. This, too, she confided to Alberic on one of her frequent stops at the monastery of San Benedetto for a night's refuge.

Alberic to her surprise shook his head. "It is a mistake to ask too little of life, for that in itself is most often a failure of faith. And the next step is pride."

This time, however, she did not humbly acquiesce. "What are you afraid I should be proud of, Alberic?"

But he was not to be turned aside. "Being proud of things is not the real danger. It is being proud of one's sole strength that is the temptation of a strong spirit like you, Matilda."

"That is a matter of intelligence and not pride, Alberic," she said. But she did not forget. Often in the weeks that followed she found herself wondering if Alberic could fairly accuse her of being proud of what she was doing. And always half-amused, half-woeful, she reassured herself. There was nothing in what she had done that day that would make any one but a fool proud.

Once, when she had been riding since morning with a small band of men, she found herself overtaken by storm and night at once, in the fields. It was too

late to try for refuge in the next village, and the nearest monastery was even farther away. There was nothing in sight but a wretched grange. So there she sent
one of her men to beg for refuge.

And there, when it had been granted, she went with her companions at her
back. Astonished to find a lady on the doorstep, the people readily opened, but
at sight of the men behind, the old woman who opened to her shrieked in terror.

"The soldiers!" she cried, struggling to shut the door.

Matilda put her foot against the jamb. "I am the Countess Matilda," she
said, "and I promise you that these men will do you no harm, and you will be
rewarded for your help tonight."

Amazed, the old woman fell back. "Does the rain fall on a Countess, too?"

And even when Matilda had seated herself by the turf fire in the kitchen,
with the chickens clucking companionably at her feet, the old woman continued
to stare at her in wonder. Her exclamation became a jest in Matilda's household,
and many a time that autumn as they rode in fog or rain, someone would raise
an unfailing laugh by repeating the cry of the old peasant.

But if at times Matilda wondered if she were making any progress, her purpose never faltered. For every report that came to her reminded her of the need
of what she was trying to do. Even before July ended, she learned that the Pope
had been forced to leave Rome in the company of Guiscard. At first there had
been just the bare fact of his going. Then had come rumor from merchants that
the Pope was the prisoner of the ruthless Norman leader. Thoroughly alarmed
now, she sent a messenger direct to Gregory with orders not to return until he
had seen the Pope, face to face.

It was characteristic of Gregory that he at once gave the messenger a report
of the state of Church affairs with a warm commendation of the courtesy of the
Norman leader and the hospitality of Gisulf and Alfanus of Salerno. There was
no word of his own health or his own grief, but from the messenger Matilda
learned that his entourage felt that it would be unsafe for him to return alone to
Rome until the bitter resentment of the people over the Norman outrage had
abated. And when Matilda pressed the messenger for some word as to the Pope's
appearance, all she could extract was his opinion that he did not look like a man
long for this world.

But from Hugh of Cluny, again on his way to Germany to try to persuade
Henry to seek the forgiveness of the Pope, Matilda learned more. Gregory was

penniless, and he and his suite were being furnished with all necessities by Desiderius and the monastery of Monte Cassino. Hugh, dropping his voice, added that though the Pope spoke of Henry with his usual vigor and the charity he had never failed to keep toward him personally, he spoke as a man who was dead to any personal grief or hope. For the cause to which he had given his life, Hugh thought, his friends could still do much, but for the man Gregory, there was nothing more to be done.

And yet the month of August had brought the finest of Gregory's encyclicals. In spite of poverty and uncertainty and heartbreak he had summoned together the loyal bishops of the land about Salerno, and there in exile he had taken counsel as to the state of Christendom. He had reaffirmed his faith in the mission of the Church and had hurled his defiance against all the powers that would seek to turn the Church aside from that mission or to enslave her to their base ends. And he had declared his determination to spend his last breath in the defense of that liberty and that independence without which the Church was but a travesty on the purpose of her Founder.

As he set these things down in a letter to be sent to all the bishops and princes of Christendom, his heart must have soared within him, for he wrote with ringing conviction. At the end, however, the thought must have come to him of all those whom he had not been able to win to these principles, and his heart must have yearned for them. For to them he now turned to assure them that in a world of darkness and confusion the Church was the mother of men, waiting for them but to come home to her that she might embrace them with her forgiveness and her tenderness. As she read that letter, Matilda could believe what the messenger of Alfanus of Salerno told her, that the Pope had written those concluding sentences with his own hand in the night, and that the parchment on which he had left them for his secretaries had been found stained with tears.

CHAPTER VI

THE fall of that year of 1084 was an anxious time for Matilda. In September she learned that Robert Guiscard had sailed away to renew the war against the

Eastern Emperor, on which his heart was really set. It was not possible for her to leave Tuscany then, for it seemed as if there were some chance at last for her to make peace with the rebellious Lucchese. But she sent word to Gisulf of Salerno, begging him to reassure her of the Pope's safety. And she sent Anselm of Lucca with a company of her trustiest knights and all the silver she could spare, to assure the Pope that she would be at his side as soon as she could bring even to a partial conclusion her work of peacemaking.

By the end of the year she was relieved of her greatest source of anxiety, the constant threat of an army from Henry. The Saxons had renewed their struggle against the King. And whatever might be the outcome, it would be some months before Henry could again reinforce the disorderly elements in Italy. So she redoubled her efforts. By the opening of the New Year, she felt herself strong enough to attempt the reduction of those strongholds that for the last three years had been rallying points of all the forces of imperial sympathy, episcopal schism, feudal rebellion, and in some cases, plain banditry. The worst of these, the stronghold of Fontara, she invested on New Year's Day. The army she drew up about the low hill was small but it contained her most reliable troops, and Arduino took the command. Half a dozen other rebel lords and as many cities were watching these proceedings, she knew, with close attention, and Matilda needed no spies to tell her that on the outcome of this siege depended the decision of the other rebels.

The Lord of Fontara was the ablest and the most fearless of all the vassals who had defied her, but he was also the most harsh and ruthless. Especially had he been cruel in his dealings with the serfs of his lands, laying waste their fields at the first report of Matilda's approach the preceding fall, and when the terrified peasants had hidden what little grain they had been able to salvage against the winter and refused to yield it to his bailiffs, he ordered that their hamlets be burned. The result, as all the horrified country about knew, was that Fontara was but indifferently supplied with food, and there was no disposition on the part of the peasants in the neighborhood to make any effort to replenish his supplies.

Matilda had planned to leave the siege in Arduino's hands and visit some of the doubtful towns while the midwinter months held them fast within their bounds and gave them plenty of leisure to consider not only the present but the future. But Bertram, Lord of Fontara, showed no disposition to stay quietly within his walls and starve. Instead, he made two desperate sorties, that narrowly failed of breaking through Matilda's lines. The result was that at the beginning of February Matilda returned to the siege and made herself as secure as she could in a half-ruined grange close by the foot of the hill.

It was not only uncomfortable but also hazardous to spend the winter months in so exposed a place. The result was that Matilda elaborated her system of obtaining news from the ends of her lands and carefully put together all reports so that she might be sure of where her less reliable vassals were, and what was the general state of affairs within the walls and palisades of her cities.

It was, as war went, a trifle that hastened the end of the siege, but it seemed to Matilda that it justified her decision to make her camp there on the field. For she had no doubt that had Arduino been alone there, with his mistress safely ensconced at Canossa, the issue would have been very different.

It began in a trivial incident of the crowded kitchen of the farmhouse. It was a bitter day, and Matilda had taken refuge by the large kitchen fire to dictate some letters to Donizo. The cooks, two countrywomen who had been overjoyed to find shelter for the winter in the Countess' camp, were busy basting the joints that were roasting in the huge maw of the chimney. For a moment Matilda let Donizo rub the unruly locks about his poll, while she watched the brown fat sizzle under the drops of liquor.

Suddenly a spider scurried across the stone hearth, a huge, winter-logged creature, that made the girl Maria hastily draw back the edge of her dress.

One of the countrywomen laughed at her little squeal of surprise, and, diving down to the hearth, pinched up the intruder between a plump thumb and forefinger and dropped it into the fire. As it sizzled for a moment, the girl frowned, and the two cooks laughed at this queasiness of their betters.

"It would be kinder," protested the girl, a little nettled, "to put it outdoors."

"And let it freeze in the snow?" scoffed the countrywoman.

The girl shivered, and a look of malice came into the beady eyes of one of the peasants. "They are kinder up at the castle, young lady," she said, leering at the pretty waiting maid. "They are thrusting the useless mouths out into the snow to die."

Matilda who had been half-listening, turned upon the woman, "What did you say?"

"Damn your impertinence," shouted Arduino, and the woman shrank back almost against the spit.

"What did you say?" repeated Matilda, suddenly feeling sick, and hating herself for it.

"Don't be a fool, Matilda; this is war—" But as his mistress rose from her chair, Arduino threw up his hands and stepped back, glaring at the woman on the hearth.

"What is it?" Matilda took the woman by the arm and pulled her to her feet.

"I meant no harm, my lady. They are putting the old and the helpless outside the castle gates up there."

"Don't be a fool, Matilda," repeated Arduino, but she was striding out the door. It was snowing, and a sudden swirl of wind blinded her for a moment. Somebody tried to pull her back, but she shook herself free, and drawing her mantle about her body, she strode to the front of the grange. Here a small crowd had gathered to watch what was happening, as on a stage, on the level piece of ground in front of the castle.

At first Matilda could make out nothing but a hideous shrieking and a tussle of figures in front of the slightly opened gates. She wondered why none of the idlers attempted to rush the gate, and then she saw that the battlements of the tower above were crowded with tiny figures.

One of the soldiers in front of her laughed, "They must think we are fools not to know that they have their rocks all ready to drop on our heads."

Then her attention was caught again by what was happening before the gate. Apparently, the besieged were trying to close it, and somebody was clinging to the edge and blocking their way. Matilda pushed through the crowd until she saw that it was a woman, struggling and clinging with her bare nails to the edge of the wood. For a moment the gate swung open again, and a soldier came round the edge and seized upon the woman, but though he succeeded in prying her fingers loose, she kicked him with such force that he fell back into the opening, and in a second she was at his throat.

There was a wild yell of applause from the watching soldiers in front of the grange. And like an echo came a burst of childish laughter from the space in front of the gateway. The soldiers laughed again.

"The boy is an idiot, but the old woman is a plucky devil of a hell cat," said one of the men.

Again the soldier tried to struggle to his feet, but the woman was on top of him. In his effort to throw her off, the soldier rolled out of the gateway, and the wooden gate clanged shut behind them. The man beat helplessly at the great planks, but his late comrades only jeered at him. And the jeering was taken up by the soldiers watching on the other side of the danger zone beneath the rock-defended wall.

Then for the first time Matilda became aware of a little huddle of figures in the snow outside the gate. There they half-knelt, half-sprawled, sobbing, yet unmoving. Even as she looked at them, the woman who had fallen from the soldier's back leaped to her feet, took one wild look at the closed gate, and with almost demoniacal energy swooped down upon the boy that had laughed. Grabbing him in her arms, she ran toward the lines of the besiegers.

To her horror Matilda saw one of her soldiers raise a spear and poise it carefully. As the woman with incredible speed cleared the bare space beneath the walls and neared the lines of the besieging army, the man loosed the weapon, and it flew toward the oncoming woman and child. Fascinated with horror, Matilda watched her duck not a second too soon, and the spear sing safely over her head. A yell of derision for the missed shot rose from the soldiers, but in a moment Matilda heard it turn to a yell of terror when she leaped out of the lines into the empty space before the castle.

As the woman staggered into her arms, Matilda heard an arrow sing over her head. Another followed, and her arm stung. Then she was dragged, still clutching the woman and her burden back to safety.

"A fine mess," said Arduino. Matilda let go of her clutch, and the woman sank to her knees in the snow and took the sodden hem of her robe in her hands. Above her, Matilda saw the mêlée of soldiers hurling themselves like something insane against the gates of the castle.

"They went crazy when they saw that arrow strike you. Now they'll kill themselves there like a pack of idiots. And look—" He pointed to the rescued boy who sat in the snow, in spite of his obvious seven or eight years, gurgling like an infant in arms.

"An idiot!" he hissed with contempt and turned from the sight.

But the woman clutched the boy to her breast, her torn gray hair falling over his head, sobbing and crying, "He is all I have in the world, all, my darling," and the idiot, though purple from the cold, crowed with delight.

With indescribable emotion, Matilda gazed at the woman who had fought so desperately for the idiot. Then half between laughter and tears, she asked, "Your grandchild?"

The old woman looked at her suspiciously. Then as if moved to candor, she answered, "No, but his family were all killed when the village was burned last fall, and my two sons were killed too, and their wives died. So I took him, and he is mine," she shrieked as Matilda moved toward her.

But a louder cry rose from the closed gate as the rocks began to fall. Matilda tried to shout to the men to come back. But her effort was useless. Even if they had heard her, they were too far gone in the madness of battle to pay any heed. Suddenly, Matilda remembered the battering-ram on which the men had been working when she had last seen them before the excitement. But first she bade the old woman take her idiot into the grange and stay there.

CHAPTER VII

THE fall of the castle of Fontara and the surrender of its faithless lord were followed, as Matilda had hoped for, by the submission of nearly all the rest of her rebellious vassals. The cities, with the moral support of schismatic bishops to sustain them and the constant agitation of Henry's agents with their promises of silver and privileges to inspire them to continued resistance, were much slower in bowing to the inevitable. But by the end of April all but Lucca had, with varying degrees of repentance and professions of obedience, renewed their allegiance to their lady. And even Lucca had settled down into a sort of passive resistance that gave no threat to the peace of the land.

Early in May, then, Matilda set out for San Benedetto to take counsel with Alberic as to the future. For the first time since the Pope had left Canossa, she might call herself in fact as well as in theory, Countess of Tuscany. There was much to sober her even in her triumph. That dream of a land at peace, with all the orders of society fulfilling their functions in happiness and plenty, was still a long way off. For everywhere she went, the evidences of the period of chaos and disaster just ending, were apparent. Not all the burned and wasted fields had been planted again, by any means. There were still miles of land where the charred stumps of olive and fruit trees rotted in the midst of a thin film of this year's weeds. There were still castles and towns half in ruins, with crazy shells of roofless walls and heaps of sodden charcoal rotting against the piled-up stones and bricks. But most haunting of all these monuments of desolation were the lonely granges, the mills with great timbers half-burned, still jutting out of their crumbling walls, the country chapels with the May sunlight streaming into the open sanctuary and the crazily twisted crucifix or the broken clay statue of the Madonna, bleaching in the rain. These clung most tenaciously to Matilda's memory, for always in their neighborhood filthy and frightened and wan serfs crept slowly out of their holes to blink idiotically at the intruder and scurry again from sight, like the foul insects that for a moment come to light when a stone is moved and then slimily ooze back into fresh darkness. But it was not only their physical aspect that festered so sorely in her memory, for always when, lured by food and warmth, they could be coaxed to speak, they had some ghastly tale of outrage to tell, of nameless atrocities borne by simple men without hope of glory or any fruit of all that pain. Only the white form seen swinging from a charred beam on a spring evening or the voice heard screaming from the winter-drenched ashes in an April night gave immortality to the anguish of the lowly and harrowed with fresh fear their helpless survivors.

Yet though the land on which she looked was still scarred in body and spirit, for the first time in years it was hers to nurse and to heal. And now those claims which in the days of fighting had had to be sacrificed to the exigencies of bare survival, pressed about her. There was so much to be done, she reflected as she rode to San Benedetto. And yet as she looked behind her and saw how far she had come from the despair of the last summer, her spirits rose again. For she had her people at her back now, and though she knew that it would not be well to tax too severely the newly found loyalty of her vassals, she had an army to her hand. So her thoughts went again back to the hope that had first nerved her to this struggle.

All through the winter, there had come letters and messages from the Pope at Salerno. They were all alike in their note of high resolution, in their constant challenge to reform and to purification of the life of the Church within, and in their call to battle against the forces without, that menaced her freedom and her integrity. Never was there any hint of weakening or compromise in the fight which the exile was still waging against the forces that had shattered his dream and broken his heart. Nor was there any note of personal complaint or regret to be read in the words or between the lines. But there was something stark and bare in the very courage and resolution of these documents that spoke more eloquently to the anxious reader than any lament. For it was as if every vestige of the personal had been burned away in the fierce and solitary contemplation of those ultimate realities to which the writer had devoted all the powers of a great nature. Sometimes Matilda found herself shuddering when she had finished the perusal of one of these letters; and for days after, the trivialities of the passing hours would wear a new solemnity as if just without the circle of her vision were a whole world of thought and feeling of which as yet she knew nothing.

Matilda was not sure that it would now make any difference to the Pope whether or not he were ever restored to Rome, but that bringing-back of the exile seemed to her the next step in her campaign. For in these last months she had learned sharply enough how potent are the forms of success and the outward symbols of its triumph. She had always known that if God gave her the means, she would spend them for the rescue of the Pope, but that rescue had so long seemed the remotest of possibilities that now she was a little frightened at its imminence. The sword which she had been forging all these months was now in her hands. She found herself feeling it and bending it to test its temper lest it crumple when she should come to use it.

She tried to explain to Alberic how she felt, expecting that as usual he would laugh at her and mock at her fears. But he shook his head gravely, and for a moment she wondered if the relentless abrasives of life were wearing away the edge of even his laughter.

"That is the trouble with a time of great uncertainty. The terror of insecurity enters into men's imaginations and makes them demand a certainty for which there is no warrant in our experience. All living is a taking of chances on the future. And when one becomes too afraid to take those chances, he is already dead. For he has refused to meet the terms of our human life," he said, not looking at her face.

She clasped her hands and unclasped them. She was not afraid of failing. Only she dreaded the harm she would do if she should fail to accomplish what she had undertaken, but she said nothing.

"For God's sake, Matilda, what have you been fighting for all these years and months?" he asked, exasperated by her nervous silence.

But it was her own words that came back to her, "I am a sword put in your hands," and the eyes of Gregory that looked upon her, not glazed with horror but bright with the vision of his city.

Then she smiled. "I only wanted to hear you tell me that I should do what I wanted to do." It was Alberic who stared at her in astonishment.

She did not wait to explain any more but rode off to Canossa to gather her army together.

Not until early in the following month did she see Alberic again.

It was a day of wind and sunshine and the sparkle of raindrops drying after the storm of the night. The olives were glistening as if they had been washed with silver, and the new grain in the fields caught the winnowing of the sunlight until it shone like a sea of molten glass. And in the poplars and the beeches by the road, the wind danced in a thousand ripples of light and shade. The very breath of the earth-warm air went through her whole being like distilled fire.

And when on the high road to Prato she met Alberic, it seemed to her that the cup of her exuberance was full, and for the first time in years she laughed with the wantonness of sheer delight.

Alberic looked at her in some astonishment. "Have you received good news, Matilda?"

She stared at him. "I am making good news, my friend. Have you seen the host at my back?"

At her bidding he looked down the road and smiled. "You have all Tuscany behind you, Matilda. Guiscard himself would turn tail if he saw you coming."

She shook her head at his mockery. "I am really quite serious. Don't you want to come to Salerno with me?"

"You are bringing the Pope back to Rome then," he said gravely.

"Yes," she sobered. And it seemed to her that the light of the morning darkened as the face of Gregory rose before her.

Then for the first time she saw the monks waiting behind Alberic. There was a slight frown on his face as he answered her unspoken query, "I have heard a rumor from some traders."

He hesitated.

"Not from Salerno?" she asked, and in the sunshine she was suddenly cold.

"They had come through Florence, and there they had seen a man who had passed Anselm of Lucca on the road. He had spoken with some of the men who were with him, but they had refused to tell him anything. Only he said they looked very sad and frightened, and the Bishop rode by himself and did not reply to his greeting."

"But where did you hear this?" asked Matilda. "Of course, nothing had come to us in the north. And we heard nothing at Pistoia, though we spent the night there."

"I was at Taona yesterday afternoon. I started before daybreak this morning. Anselm will probably be at Florence tonight."

For a moment Matilda wavered. Then she made up her mind. "It may be only a rumor, and even if a company like this is slow, I think I'd better stay with it. I am expecting some men from Lucca some time during the day, and I want to receive them myself."

Alberic agreed. Alone with his two or three monks he could reach Florence by nightfall, when Matilda and her army would still be some miles away. But as he started away, her patience failed.

"Listen, Alberic," she cried after him. "I will ride on to Fiesole as soon as the camp is made at sunset, and I will have the gates watched for you all night."

But it was nearly midnight before Matilda reached Fiesole, and the city gates were long closed. Her companions shouted and struck at the oaken gates with their pikes, but the only response they could waken from the sleeping city was a shower of stones from the tower over the gates, which lamed one of the horses and threw the others into a panic. There was nothing to do for it, then, but to wait on the edge of the hill overlooking the plain below.

Fortunately, something of the warmth of the amber sunshine of the day still lingered on the night air, and the scene at their feet was beautiful enough to beguile any watchers. For the plain of the Arno lay at their feet, with the river shining in the moonlight, and the towers and peaked roofs of the city whitening above the purple shadows of the walls and houses below. At any other time the lush gradations of darkness in the blue and lavender folds of the plain and the clear blocks of moonlight on roof and tower and water would have filled the eye of Matilda with delight. But she was worn out with the day's labors and the anxiety that had never ceased to burrow into the crevices of the busy hours since Alberic had left her.

She must have slept, for she was startled to hear the rattle of horses' hooves over pebbles, just below the promontory where they waited. Without reflection she slid her hand to the hilt of the sword at her side, and reined in her startled horse. Then she looked at her companions. Several of them were just rounding the bend in the road that led down to the plain below. She tried to pull the rein on her horse's neck, but her hands were too stiff to move. Without any apparent signal from her, the horse started to follow.

She knew what had happened as soon as she saw Alberic. His cowl had fallen back so that she could see his face even in the darkness. It was white, washed clean of any expression but the glitter which came into his eyes when he caught sight of her.

They had come to a point where the road widened at the top of its climb from the plain, and with a sort of moon-blanched clarity, Matilda saw her own company pause and the strangers ride up. Behind Alberic, Anselm came up quickly, as she reined in her horse and waited.

Alberic nodded. "He is dead, Matilda." For a moment the whole moon-washed scene swam from her eyes into darkness. She felt her horse start and caught at the fallen rein. Then her eyes cleared, and she saw with terrible lucidity the white face staring at her with cavernous eyes.

"How did it happen?" she asked, turning to Anselm.

"Hadn't we better ride into the town?" he suggested, bringing his horse to her side.

But she shook her head, and one of the men explained hastily that the gates were shut against them.

Matilda saw Anselm look at Alberic. The latter gave no sign, and the Bishop turned back to her.

"He died very quietly, Matilda, with all of us about him and with the Sacraments to comfort him. He had been failing since that illness early in the year, but we could not any of us believe that he was seriously ill, for his words were as vigorous as ever, and he never faltered in his purpose."

Anselm paused, and Matilda saw his hand go wearily to his head, but he went on in the same calm, matter-of-fact tone in which he had first spoken. "He made no complaint though he knew he was dying. He told us that we must not give up the fight for the freedom of the Church. Henry and Guibert and all those who had brought so much trouble upon us were to be forgiven as soon as they repented, but until they repented, they were to be resisted to the last."

Anselm looked at Matilda and his voice softened. "Only one cry escaped from his lips, and that was just before he died." The firm voice broke, and Matilda tried to stifle the answering sob in her own throat. "He had received the Viaticum. Then he looked at us all, and he cried out with his old passion and something of the old flash in his eyes, 'I have loved justice and hated iniquity; therefore I die in exile.'"

Something of the passion of the original voice entered unconsciously into the low voice of Anselm of Lucca, and the cry of the dying Gregory rang on the night.

Above the sound of weeping the voice of Anselm went on, "One of the bishops said something to comfort him. It was something about the impossibility of his dying in exile to whom God had given the ends of the earth for the bounds of his house, but I do not think Gregory heard. For he said no more. And early the next morning he yielded up the ghost. It was two weeks ago," he added, looking at Matilda.

Without a word, they all made the sign of the cross, and Anselm of Lucca began the prayers for the dead. As if from a great distance, Matilda heard their voices rising from the darkness, beseeching God to forgive the sins of his servant Gregory and to grant him rest. The stars were white in the sky when finally they had done.

CHAPTER VIII

WHEN Matilda awoke the next day, the noon sun was shining through the doorway opposite the bed in which she was lying. She opened her eyes for a moment, and then she shut them again, for she had been dreaming, and she was loath to let the dream go. But though it seemed only just to have faded down the corridors of her mind, she could not catch up with it again. And the warm world of dreams faded slowly into that cold wistfulness with which the spirit returns to an alien world. But even as she relinquished the pursuit, she knew what it was that she had been dreaming.

She had dreamed that she was walking down a nameless country road in that gray world which is so vast and so indeterminate in its geography. Without any surprise, she had just met her mother, and she had stopped to greet her, joyous to see her, yet not remembering, then, the reason for that warm rush of delight. But her mother was, as always, intent upon something else, and she stopped only for a moment. Then she was gone, and Matilda turned to look after her, wondering idly who it was whom she was hurrying to meet. And then she saw that someone was coming toward her mother, but his face was covered. Only from his dress and stature, and from something in the way he stood, so tall though he was short, she recognized Gregory. And her heart bounded and she tried to call to him, but at that moment she awoke.

And then the sick consciousness of the present flooded her, and she lay there with shut eyes, for another moment hiding from the bleak day she must arise and face. For some minutes she lay there, her thoughts scurrying dizzily like waterflies on the dimpling surface of a summer brook. Her army in the rain-bright sunshine, the face of Alberic, the barred city gate, the cry in the dark with the voice of a dying man breaking into the low tones of Anselm, the prayers for the dead—she lay very still, and she felt the sick misery wash over her like the rising tide on a stone half-buried in the sand. Outside her door, she could hear a chittering of birds and the rustle of ivy leaves against the timber of the balcony. It was as if somebody were slowly pouring water through sand. And her thoughts fell into a rhythm like a litany chanted, and they were the names of her dead—Godfrey the First, and Beatrice, and Godfrey the Second, and Godfrey her son, and Gregory who was Pope.

She heard a light step, and a low sound as if rain were falling in dry leaves.

The girl Maria was standing by the foot of her bed, looking at her with the tears rolling down her brown cheeks. Matilda raised herself on one elbow, and for a moment she watched her curiously.

Then she spoke to her, "There is no cause for tears, child. They who are dead are happy." But even as she spoke, she heard her voice tremble.

It seemed to her only a moment later that she was standing in the hall of the castle of Fiesole, and all the circle of men in the bright sunshine from the open door were scrambling to their feet and gazing at her with white, scared faces. She tried to smile at them, to reassure them, but it seemed to her that the muscles of her face were frozen beyond her control. Alberic brought a light Roman chair for her, and stood behind her as she sat down.

When she had risen from her bed, she had told herself that there were many things she must do, things which could not wait even if they had lost all their meaning. But now she gazed helplessly at her companions, and out of the deep well of emptiness within her breast she tried to draw up some little word to break the heavy silence. But nothing came, and she could only gaze blankly at the helpless faces before her.

It was Arduino who broke the spell. As always, he spoke quickly, awkwardly, ripping out the words with an effort that disarmed all embarrassment. "Those Lombard scoundrels will be making trouble again, Matilda. So I am going to take these fellows here back to the northern cities and see if I can hold them in line."

She tried to grasp what he had said. True, she had heard the words, but they had slipped meaninglessly through her mind like water through the round pebbles of a river bed. Arduino said it over again, shouting to make sure she heard, but she shook her head. She had heard all there was the first time, only there was nothing there. Then she understood. She understood that it was all to do over again, and now there was no reason for doing it.

She looked around the circle of white faces all gazing at her with such scared intentness. Suddenly, she was sorry for them.

"Don't look so frightened, all of you," she said slowly, as if she were speaking to a child. "There is nothing to be frightened about any more."

"You are right, Matilda," said the quiet voice of Alberic over her head. "There is nothing to be afraid of, but there is a great deal to do."

She nodded, as she would have agreed with a child prattling at her when her thoughts were elsewhere. Arduino stood, watching her with trouble slowly clouding the opacity of his eyes. And again she was sorry for him.

"Do anything you like, Arduino," she said. Some day she would go to Salerno, and she would take Hilary the Greek with her, and she would raise a tomb of shining marble to the dust in Saint Matthew's church. Not that it would do any good....

So they let her be that day. She wandered out into the courtyard of the castle where the sun lay in pools of light on the yellow cobblestones, and the sparrows picked their way through the horse dung, searching out the golden husks. A little boy with a stick on his shoulder was marching up and down, chanting some marching song to himself, and a little white dog with an absurdly agitated tail was tagging after him. She wondered what the boy was singing so lustily. Then as he neared her on his unseeing march, his voice rose triumphantly in the intoxication of his delight in himself, "The Countess is coming, the Countess is coming, the Countess is coming." He chanted it over and over again, and

Matilda laughed at the solemnity of the little white dog until the tears were running down her burning cheeks.

But the next morning when she had left the chapel after Mass, Alberic came up to her and stood looking at her. For the first time she saw how the passing of the years had lined his bright face and deepened the hollows under the quick eyes. "He must be forty now," she thought to herself. And once he had eaten his heart out for love of her upon whom he now gazed so calmly.

"What a brief thing it is, this, this life of ours, Alberic, that we should break our hearts over it!" she said, thinking of that old grief with fresh pity.

And this strange Alberic whom the years had made so old and grave answered her, "It is brief, Matilda, but it has the seeds of immortality in it."

She nodded and, made tender with pity, she asked, "What do you want me to do, Alberic?"

For a moment he made no effort to conceal his surprise. Then, as if taking the wind of her mood, he answered her, "There are some men of Florence waiting here to see you."

"What do they want?" She strove desperately to make the palsied tentacles of her mind clutch the moment.

"Probably more privileges, remissions of dues or tolls—you know what merchants usually want." The tension in his face had relaxed, and he was smiling.

"The more I give the more they ask for, these townsmen. What do you think will be the end of it?" she challenged him, half grumbling, half trying to lay hold upon the moment's need.

Alberic opened his hands in a gesture of complete helplessness. "Who knows?" And then as if he understood the magnitude of her effort, he went on with more of the calm surety habitual with him, in his voice. "The end is not in our keeping, Matilda. We can only be faithful to the trust we have."

But she shook her head, for this was a subject on which she had thought much in the brief armistices of quiet during these last troubled years. "No, Alberic, that is not enough. We may do our best, our heart's blood's best, and the event may yet prove us wrong. The mercy of God will pardon us, you say, but the thing we sought to do will be lost nevertheless." She tried to keep her voice steady, but it shook and quavered, and she stood there trembling before him.

Almost roughly, Alberic seized her arm and there came into his voice a sharpness of alarm that shocked her. "We are not God, Matilda. We can do only what we can see. We can do only what God gives us to do by the light He has given us."

He looked at her anxiously, and again she was sorry for him. His cowl had fallen back, and out from the shaven crown of his tonsure ran a finger of white in his dark hair, which she had never noticed before. So she went with him to receive the merchants in the hall of the castle.

It was even as she had thought. There were certain dues they wished to be relieved of.

"If you will grant us this freedom, my lady," said the spokesman, flinging out his arms, "we will make of this city of yours one of the world's great cities. Its wealth will make you rich and strong, and its honor will be your honor, and the honor of your heirs to the end of time." He was a thin-faced fellow with great nervous eyes, and the sweat stood out in beads on his forehead as he talked.

"To the end of time is a long time, my friend," she said gently, watching the orator flush. "And the son who should have raised up a family for me is dead."

She saw the eyes darken and the sensitive mouth tremble. "He is not one of these rich merchants," she said to herself, "but some poor factor with a gift of words, whom they have hired to put their case. And he sees his lean share vanishing."

Then she leaned forward, "Listen to me," she began. "You townsmen are always asking for privileges, and where you will end, God only knows. I am not at all sure that giving you this privilege will ever do me any good. At any rate I do not expect to live to see it. But I think it will do you good, and for that reason I am granting it to you. Be sure that you use it well."

There was a certain smug satisfaction, not to be confused with gratitude, on the faces of the sturdy citizens as they knelt down to kiss her hand, but the face that the spokesman lifted to her was so radiant with the wonder and delight of his success that her heart went out to him.

Then Alberic was speaking to her again with the same anxious concern, "There is a young man, too, who came over from Florence when he heard that these men were coming to see you."

"Alberic," she begged, "these greedy merchants and their eloquent spokesman are enough for today. If your young man were an archangel from heaven—"

The monk smiled. "He does not come from heaven, I think, but he has come from Bologna, from one of the rhetoric schools there, and he tells me that he has been waiting and praying for a chance to see you. For he thinks, poor young man, that you might understand what he has to say."

Matilda sighed. She was weary enough to plead for mercy, and for that reason, perhaps, too proud to. "What is it all about?" she asked, weakening.

"He is a prudent young man who has heard that he should not cast pearls before swine. So he has told me nothing of his business, but to judge from what he did talk to me about, he is neither a fool nor a trifler."

There was nothing of her own she wished to do, she reminded herself. Alberic took her silence for assent and turned to the door.

Matilda looked down upon the golden head that bowed above her hand, and then the young man rose and looked at her with a directness and glow that made her heart ache. There was something fawnlike in the large brown eyes that reached so appealingly for hers. Before she could think, she found herself asking the stranger his name.

Irnerius of Bologna plunged headlong into his appeal. For a moment, Matilda was astonished to hear the young rhetoric student inveighing against the turmoil and lawlessness of the age. But she was still more surprised when she realized that this young man was not repeating what he had heard from all the Jeremiahs of the day but was speaking from his own heart the conclusions of his own thought. Then she was amused that this radiant youngster with the fair hair and the quick blood that beat so redly in the thin cheek should be solemnly assuring her that the paramount need of their time was order.

"Irnerius of Bologna," she began very gently, "I know, and I think no one knows better, that our world needs order. What I want to know is how shall we win that order that we all crave?"

But if she thought that challenge would stop the flow of youthful eloquence, she was mistaken. For the boy launched on a glowing exposition of his remedy for the world's woes that first amazed and then caught the sympathy of his hearer. There was more than a touch of youthful absurdity in the conviction that all the world needed to heal its manifold griefs was a revival of the study of the Roman law. There was nothing new in the idea, either, Matilda reflected. When she was a girl she had heard the Archdeacon Hildebrand expatiate on the beauties of the Roman law to the Empress Agnes and her mother. And every thoughtful and learned man she knew had looked back enviously to those days when the law of Rome had ordered with reason and social interest the passions and the appetites of men. But this young man was not content to look back wistfully, or to yearn for a revival of that ancient order. He was sure that he could do something to bring it about, and he had a plan for doing it. It seemed grotesquely harmless enough. He would like to start lecturing on the Pandects in the city of Bologna. If he could find a patron to protect him and to support him, he was sure that he would get students. And beginning there—"My lady, it is like throwing a stone into a pool. There is no telling how far the ripples may spread!"

"It would have to be a large stone, my friend Irnerius, to wash the shores of this pool," she said when he had finished. And then as the light wavered in the brown eyes, she could not forbear adding, "God alone knows, Irnerius, whether my protection will long avail any man, and my treasury may be empty the next time you see me. But I will send the Bishop of Bologna a letter to commend you, and here," she took the brooch that held her mantle, "is a jewel that will feed you for a year. When that is spent, send to me, and I will give you more if I have it. It certainly can do the young barbarians who flock to Bologna no harm to hear that once men lived under some other law than their own greed and violence."

As the young man paused again at the hall door to turn an ecstatic smile upon her, Matilda thought with bitter humor how simple was the view of the world that saw the wealth of a countess as inexhaustible and never suspected that the great of this world could not always make good their promises of protection; almost as simple, she reflected with a tightening of the heart, as the imagination that could oppose a youthful voice chanting the praises of Justinian to the turbulence and passion of a barbarous world.

She looked at Alberic. "So it goes on."

He nodded.

"And we give tools to those who will tear down the work of our hands when we are gone, and bread to the fools who will break their hearts against the same walls on which we have shattered our lives," she added, trying with words to hold off a little the engulfing emptiness of the world.

But Alberic shook his head. "We give beyond ourselves to ends we cannot see." And then as the tears welled in her eyes, he said more gently, "You have done today's work. Weep, if it will comfort you."

CHAPTER IX

A week later, Matilda rode out of the courtyard of the bishop's palace into the streets of Florence. After days of rain the weather had turned fair, and the slender poplars that lifted their green plumes above the yellow-gray wall of the bishop's garden were all a-shimmer with the morning light. Even the trickles of last night's rain sparkled among the muddy cobblestones, and the bright blue air was full of the delicate voices of the wind. It might have been a day in April with that wonderful freshness as if the whole world had been born again over night.

For a moment Matilda looked about her with cool eyes as her escort clattered out into the open square. She saw how at every balcony heads appeared, and from the porch of Santa Reparata and the little stalls leaning against it, and from the portico before the cloth market and the shadows behind the octagonal pile of San Giovanni, men and women and children ran to stare at the Countess and her cavalcade. Even at the fountain the girls set down their copper jars and the water slopped in silver over their bare red feet. From the vine-wreathed door of the white tavern opposite, a couple of dark-faced fellows in bright tunics looked out upon the knights and men-at-arms with impassive faces. And in the gutter some half-naked boys ducked about the horses' legs while anxious little girls pulled away wholly naked babies from the iron-shod feet. For a moment the smell of horses and the clashing of steel and the laughter of men and the impatient whinnying and stamping of the horses filled the little square, and then they were off, with all the watchers cheering for the brave show and for the lady who had been so generous to the city.

"They are enthusiastic enough today," thought Matilda, quite without any cynicism but with the strange patience that had been rising in her heart this last desolate week. For she knew that she was going back to Canossa to begin all over again the work she had hoped was done. Even though less than a fortnight had elapsed since she had met Anselm of Lucca, the tidings of the end of the story at Salerno were already abroad in the land. It would be weeks, perhaps months, before they would hear the news of the election of a new pope. And no one believed that the new hand on the helm would be as firm or as strong as the one that had fallen. It was a generous tribute this to the leader who was dead, a tribute in which those who had hated him joined as dramatically as they who had loved him.

"I can think of no one whose death could make so vast an emptiness in the world," Anselm had said that night. And it seemed to her now that that was still the predominating character of the world upon which she looked this June day. Already word had come from Anselm of Lucca that his city would not admit him within its walls, and the schismatic bishops of Reggio and Parma, whom she had released after Sorbara, had been seen together on the road to Pavia. There was a whisper of wild rejoicings in Milan at a great banquet which the Lombard leaders had given to celebrate the death of their foe, and a merchant had told of how the poor sobbed in the streets when they learned that there was no one in Rome or Salerno to rebuke the arrogance of the great. Arduino had reported, too, that most of the nobility in his army had pleaded the necessity of returning to their own castles against the troublous times ahead, and that half of the forces that had come so blithely to Prato had melted away before they reached Canossa.

For a moment a deep thankfulness welled within her as she thought that this at least Gregory had been spared. He would never know how soon his work had been brought to nought. But when she tried to share this comfort with Alberic, he looked at her doubtfully.

"We have no way of knowing," he said at last, "how much the blessed keep of the cares of earth. But this we may be sure, that in the presence of God the things of this world are seen in a different light from ours. For those things dreamed of are possessed now, and that city which he strove to build he now inhabits. He has no need of our tears, Matilda."

"Yet I cannot believe," she persisted, "that he would soon forget or cease to care."

He agreed, but in a moment another facet of the problem had seized his eye, "I am sure the blessed do remember and do care, but yet in such a fashion as not to stain their peace, for fear and regret have been left behind. And there is no soreness in the memory of the things that have been, and no impatience in the hope of things to come. For all times are gathered up in the presence of God, and the beginning and the end are at one."

But now they had come through the ancient forum of the city into that quarter where the craftsmen dwelt. It was a narrow, twisting street into which they slowly rode, with high walls on either side, streaked and blackened their weatherbeaten height, and with new balconies of still raw wood projecting here and there, and broken and charred timbers jutting out from the fire-flaked wall.

"The King's army burned this section of the city four years ago, and we have only partly rebuilt it," apologized the Bishop.

But in the doorways of the blackened houses and in open booths leaning crazily against their fronts, what seemed to be the whole population of the quarter was busily at work in the bright sunshine. Here a coppersmith was beating at the red metal with a wooden mallet, and there a glassblower had taken a lump of fire from the charcoal brazier at his feet and had put his lips to the end of the tube on which he held it. As they paused for a minute, the fire glowed red and swelled into a gelatinous bubble. Next to him on a block of stone before his door sat a man, huddled over a box on which he was working with a slender steel chisel.

"This man," said the Bishop, "has been working for four years on his casket. His house was burning before his family could get him away."

"But he got it away. It was all we saved," said a blowsy woman in a soiled blue dress, leaning over the workman.

The latter looked up. He was a meager, gray fellow with pinched face and haggard eyes. And his hand shook as he held up the casket for the visitors to see.

It was a beautiful thing. Slabs of bone carved into low flat relief, with plenty of lively if crudely suggested action in the four scenes, had been fitted carefully together with bands of gilded bronze. The cover was not attached as yet, for the bronze beading around the edge was still unfinished, but the carving was complete. The maker held it up for them to see.

"It must have been a lot of work," said Matilda when she had exclaimed upon its beauty.

"One must live," the artist replied stolidly, but there was a gleam in the eyes that made her think of Hilary, doubtless still working in his shed at Canossa, regardless of whether popes died or ladies broke their hearts.

So they went through the teeming quarter with people enough at door and window to marvel at the splendor of arms and horses but with the steady tap-tap of hammers and the grating of chisels resuming behind their backs.

"It does not matter what happens," said the Bishop as they left the noisy street behind, "they are back again at their ruined doorways, rejoicing in the sun and the fair weather, to ply their crafts."

They had ridden now beyond the confines of the city into that strip of nameless land where between the wall and the river all the traffic of the city took shelter behind the dike which Matilda had built. In some places the merchants had made quays and thrown out jetties from the piled-up earth. In others the thin-bladed grass stood up waving against the brown water of the stream. But the dike still held firm, and the Bishop, who had ridden out with the party, told Matilda that the merchants had Mass said in the little chapel by the river in honor of Saint Nicholas and their lady every spring, on the anniversary of the day on which she had come to their aid.

"The little things go on when the great have stopped," she said to Alberic. But he smiled. "You can see the little ones."

A deep-bellied sea-going barge with an orange sail, curving lightly against the green slopes of San Miniato, came slowly down the river, and a swarm of tiny shallops scurried for safety from its wash. Then Matilda and her company turned away from the river and started north.

But the memory of that morning came back to her sharply a week later. It chanced that she was alone as she rode out into the plain between the hills that girdled Canossa. Alberic had gone ahead to take another road to San Benedetto and her escort had fallen behind, jogging along slowly on their tired horses. And she was alone, on her favorite horse that never seemed to grow tired.

She patted the gray-yellow mane affectionately. He was a great creature, a Swedish horse from the north, this Gray Wind of hers, with a coat neither gray nor brown, flecked with spots of old ivory only a little lighter than his mane. He was not a handsome creature, but he was swift and seemingly tireless in a large, unhurried way that gave her confidence.

She thought of the coppersmith and the glassblower and the maker of the box puttering away in the sunny streets of Florence. The tenderness of the end of the day was coming into the blue light over the ground about her, but the peasants were still at work in the green fields, bending over the thin ribbons of the wheat and the close-packed lines of onion shoots. It had been a cold and wet spring, she remembered, and doubtless with all the extra labors of the preparation of the army, they had not been able to finish their planting when they should. But they were moving slowly over the fields, hunched brown figures, that seemed to have come out of the very earth itself. Men, and women, and children of all sizes, working together there where they had doubtless been toiling since sunrise.

They had names, these humble diggers and makers of things, and their own crowded houses and wives and children. And doubtless in the long winter cold and darkness the old women would recall the faces and the familiar ways of the dead who had held their places before them. And with tenderness they would watch the brown babies rolling into childhood until they were ready to take up the too-heavy hammer and guide the weary plow. They had no hope of long remembering or any sense of power that what they had done would make a difference in the shaping of the destinies of men. Indeed, for the most part they had been dragged helpless in the wake of great events which they were powerless to influence or even probably to understand.

And yet in their unregarded generations they toiled the days out and the months and the years, underneath all the pomp and pageantry of their masters laying hold upon the rhythms of the earth which bore them. For a moment, to the sad woman contemplating them, who had seen so many hopes perish and such heroic energies fail, there seemed something invincible in their very anonymity. They spent their monotonous days without any of the friction of ambition, and they renewed their selfless energies without any of the waste of pride.

The low voice of a bell broke into her musing, and Matilda listened to its sweetness rolling away in the hills. Then the voices of its companions rose higher and sharper in their melody as if they were climbing up invisible stairs of music. It was the bells of Evensong swinging out from the towers of Canossa. And all the peasants in the fields dropped their labor and knelt down on the bare earth.

Matilda thought of her complaint and of Alberic's answer: only the little things survive—they are the things that can be seen. Yet it was to the least of His children that the Lord of the world had come, putting on their flesh and the vesture of their lives. And it was to the common things of their unremembered days that He had entrusted His most precious gifts—bread from their fields and their making, wine pressed out of the grapes they had gathered. Plowing to an unknown harvest, sowing where they should not reap, not understanding but yielding out of a patience and a persistence beyond wisdom—of the commonplaces of the lives of humble men He had fashioned this life which He had shared.... The bells had ceased, and the brown figures in the fields had risen to labor a little more until the sunset should take the light from their fields.

The whole western sky was aflame with great swaths of color, sea-purple and deep woad-blue and cinnabar-red. Against it the castle stood out flat, black, and unreal, and yet fearfully imminent. In a moment, the trumpet would sound from its walls, and she would ride up the steep path to the gate, and the whole labor and the burden would be there to be lifted again and to be carried without hope of respite. For a moment she waited, and the face of Gregory rose before her as she had seen it last with that untroubled stillness upon it. And she knew that she, too, could labor and could wait, until in the mysterious fullness of God's time, the vision of her dead master would be brought to pass.

So she rode to the foot of the castle hill, and the trumpet rang out, as she had expected.

THE END

Made in the USA
Middletown, DE
26 July 2023

35684656R00235